CAUGHT IN HIS WEB

A Hitman Romance

L.M. Whiteley

Content Warning

This book is a dark romance intended for mature audiences, with an antihero who does bad things and a heroine who falls for him anyway. It contains themes and scenes that may be distressing to some readers, including:

- Stalking

- Mention of torture

- Graphic violence

- Gun-related content

- Death, murder, and organized crime

- Threats of harm

- Dynamics of dubious consent

- Explicit sexual content, including some elements of BDSM (mostly D/s power dynamics)

Your mental health matters. Reader discretion is advised.

DEDICATION

This one goes out to all the brats who know that "make me" is really code for "show me you're someone worth submitting to."

And to my boys. The ones who made me a published author:
To James "crawl to me" Mackenzie, who taught me I could do it.
To Dimitri "I will be your monster" Morozov, who taught me to trust my instincts.
To Wesley "you can call me Sir" Granville, who taught me I can finish what I start.

PHRASES IN SPANISH AND RUSSIAN

<u>Spanish:</u>

pendejo – asshole

gringo – slang for white guy

Tío - uncle

bruja – witch

Que en paz descanse - may he rest in peace

Ah, mi hija está aquí. Gabriella, ven, siéntate a mi lado - Ah, my daughter is here. Gabriella, come sit beside me.

Ay, mi pobre hijita, creciendo sin madre. Tengo que amarla lo suficiente como para dos personas. No puedo perderla también. - Oh, my poor little daughter, growing up with no mother. I have to love her enough for two people. I can't lose her too.

Lo siento – I'm sorry

Enana - shorty, an affectionate term

¿Qué haces? Esto no es una inquisición. ¡Vas a asustar al hombre guapo! - What are you doing? This is not an inquisition. You'll scare the handsome man away!

Si se asusta tan fácilmente, es demasiado blando para mí - If he's that easily scared, he's too soft for me

A mí no me parece blando... - He doesn't look soft to me.

Cálmate - calm yourself.

¡Hijo! Madison está aquí y trajo a su novio. Iré a buscarlo, no me oye desde esa oficina - Son! Madison is here and she brought her boyfriend. I'll go look for him, he can't hear me in that office.

¡Siéntate! Te traeré tortillas - Sit, I'll bring you tortillas

Pedazo de basura - piece of trash

Tu novio es el que está celoso, enana. Llama a tu perro. - Your boyfriend is the one who's jealous, shorty. Call off your dog.

Lo estoy intentando, pero no me ayudas. Y el no es mi novio, Tío. - I'm trying, but you're not helping. And he's not my boyfriend, uncle.

Estoy lo suficientemente cerca. Ahora, apunta con tu arma hacia otro lado, lejos de ella. - I'm close enough, now point your gun away from her.

mierda de hombre - sorry excuse for a man

Me deberás un favor. - you'll owe me a favor

la verga del gringo - white guy dick

Oye, mamá, ¿podrías preparar un plato para llevar para los dos idiotas que están en la furgoneta? - Hey, mom, can you make up a plate for the two idiots in the van?

Frijoles - beans

Mano - short for hermano - a casual, affectionate term for a friend.

Ya es demasiado orgulloso. - He's already too proud.

Russian:

svo lach' - bitch

Za zdoróvye! - to health!

PROLOGUE

Wesley

I can't believe how late I am. It's as if the world has conspired against me today. An alarm that didn't go off, a missed bus, delays on the tube, a cab with a flat tyre... If they had a place for me at this facility to park my motorcycle, this wouldn't have happened. Not that it matters much now—of all the days to be late, it had to be the last. I've probably missed sending the presentation. Harold is going to have my arse.

It's odd that Brian isn't at the desk to greet me. He must be on break—though, usually the security guards operate as a pair, and they never leave the front desk unmanned. But I'm too late to puzzle it out.

Nose glued to my phone, I punch the button for the second floor and swipe over to my email as I wait for the doors to close. Have they sent it yet? There's been nothing new in my inbox all morning, which is odd. Surely they would have copied me on the email...

The lift dings, the doors part, and I step off. The carpet squelches underfoot, surprising me enough to make me look up from my phone.

"What the fuc—" The angry exclamation dies on my tongue.

Office buildings are often colored in tones that offend no one. The industrial carpet is a soft blue, the walls are off white, the office furniture is grey. Matilda, who's worked in corporate offices all her life, described it once as "interior design to calm the inmates."

The scene before me is anything but calm. Splashes of red on those previously pristine walls. Red seeping into the blue of the carpet, creating a dark purple stain that has spread all the way to the lift. A single red handprint in the middle of the grey wall separator for the two cubicles closest...

My heart leaps into my throat at the carnage, going wild when I see Matilda's body draped over her desk, eyes open and unseeing.

So. Much. Blood.

An alarm blares from my computer, snapping me out of the waking nightmare. I come to and realize that I'm frozen in place, holding the cloth I just fetched to wipe up the spilled energy drink on the carpet. As I stare down at my shoe in the red puddle, I realize exactly what triggered that spell—even though the energy drink is an unnatural bright cherry red, the sound of it underfoot and the vaguely metallic smell...

I drop the cloth, stomp on it to absorb the puddle so the carpet won't stain, and head over to my computer to check on the source of the noise.

The alarm is coming from the program linked to Eleanor's panic button. I know she and Mac—James Mackenzie, the sniper of our trio—are currently out to dinner at their favorite spot. They're alone, without backup. Mac can handle himself in most situations, but Eleanor isn't like us. She's not an assassin; she's a civilian. And after what she's just been through, the idea that she's out there with him, panicking, twists a knot in my stomach.

I've been in those cameras at the restaurant before, and once you've hacked something, getting back in is easy. As I pull up their feeds, I call up our group chat. I can see the three dots, indicating that Dimitri—our Russian man on the ground and team lead in our merry band of assassins—is already in the chat, typing out his message. But he's got big, clumsy thumbs, and I'm faster.

3 Musketeers Chat

Eleanor's panic button just went off

Dimitri

> I saw it as well. Report in, James.

> Just started the timer. If we don't hear in 5, we're mobilizing.

There are a few camera feeds, and I cycle through, searching for that familiar handsome face or long brown hair in the small crowd. I find them at a table in the corner of the building, sitting stock straight and staring at the guest on the other side of the table. I can't see who he is—his back is to me—but the twin looks of fury on Mac and Eleanor's faces give me a few guesses.

These cameras are shite. They don't zoom and have no sound capability. Luckily, Eleanor's watch has a panic button *and* a bug—though Mac and Eleanor don't know about the latter. I figure most people wouldn't like knowing they were wearing something I could turn into a surveillance device, but in my defense, I've never used it because the situation has never called for it. Until now.

"—and what happens when you want out of this partnership? You think he's gonna just let you go?" the man is saying.

My hand curls into a fist. I know that voice.

Felix. What a fucking thorn in our side. As if being complicit in Nicole's kidnapping wasn't enough, now he's cornering Mac and Eleanor.

"If you don't know who the General is, you don't know who to protect yourself against. How you gonna keep your lady safe? What's your exit strategy, ese?"

That throws me for a loop. Is he talking about the General? Our General?

"Well, I'll leave you folks to it. Enjoy your evening. And think about what I said." Felix stands and adjusts his jacket. I expect him to turn and waltz out the front of the restaurant, but he circles the table and disappears into a hallway I know leads back to the kitchens.

A few seconds later, Mac responds to the group chat.

Mac

> Felix showed at dinner. Everyone OK. Home in 15.

I look down at the black notebook open on my desk, containing the notes I've been carefully and meticulously keeping for a decade, and consider the name listed in the most recent round of hits.

Felix Cruz.

When I first got his name from the General and started digging, I believed he was just a local cleaner. Someone who made himself useful to the local criminal element—disposing of bodies, cleaning crime scenes, providing alibis, that sort of thing—but it's become clear he's much more than that. What are his aspirations? What are his motives? Does he know he's on the General's list?

I haven't taken the hit, so it's only a matter of time before the General offers it to someone else. If Felix has somehow figured out that he's become a target, does that mean he'll want to go after the General?

Could that be a good thing for me? The enemy of my enemy and all that...

I hear Dimitri's heavy boots in the hallway outside and slip my book back into its locked drawer, getting it closed just before a heavy pounding of knuckles precedes the scarred face in the doorway. Big D—a fitting nickname for the 6'8" beast of a man—looks freshly showered and royally pissed off. But between the permanent scowl, courtesy of the deep, old scar twisting across his face, and the fact that he's the biggest, broadest bloke anyone's ever seen... well, he always looks at least a little pissed off.

"The car just pulled in," he informs me in his thick accent, going to take his usual place leaning against one of the desks I have pushed against the wall. He tends to favor the one with the half-completed electrical projects—my theory is that all the blinking lights from the single board computers on the adjacent desk freak him out.

The sound of the front door echoing in the foyer a moment later proves Dimitri right. Sound carries well across polished stone, so I usually keep my door closed because it funnels right into my office. But Dimitri didn't close the door, so we can hear Mac and Eleanor pretty clearly.

"Darlin', you okay?" Mac asks, a desperate edge to his voice that makes me uncomfortable to hear.

Her answer is quiet and tight. "I'm okay. I promise." She sniffles. "I'm a little shaken up, but no one got hurt. I'm just... worried. So go talk to Wes and Dimitri and figure this out like you guys do best. I'll be here when you're done, and *we'll* talk about it, just the two of us."

"I'll find you upstairs?"

"I'm way too stressed out to sleep. I'm going to... bake something."

There's a shuffling of feet, and when Mac speaks again, voice slightly muffled, I can picture him saying the words into her hair as he presses a kiss to the top of her head. "I'm so sorry, baby."

"I know. I just..." She inhales shakily, the sound breaking in her throat. "Sometimes I wish you didn't have to be."

Suddenly, the moment feels much too private to be listening to. I glance over at Dimitri, sheepish, and he looks just as uncomfortable, eyes downcast and shifting from foot to foot.

"Eleanor—"

"I love you, James Mackenzie," she says fiercely. "Always. Forever. We can get through anything. We'll figure this out."

"It is not right," Dimitri murmurs over the sound of two sets of feet heading in opposite directions. "That she has become a target. For Felix to make her feel unsafe."

"Agreed," I reply. "And after everything that fucking *just* happened with Nicole as well." Our team of three hardened killers has two very blatant soft spots now, and I happen to genuinely care for both of them.

Mac appears in the doorway in a rumpled suit, still smelling like aftershave. His dark hair is askew, likely from running a frustrated hand through its length. The expression on his face is hard and angry, and he barely gets the door shut before launching in.

"Felix found us. Or he's been following me, maybe. That smug motherfucker sat across the table and *smirked* at me because he knew there was nothing I could do with all those witnesses and with Eleanor..." He crosses the room and collapses into the red wingback chair, pressing the heels of his hands against his eye sockets. "I... she was with me and I couldn't... I had to get her out of there."

Dimitri uncrosses his arms and leans forward with his usual stoic resolve. Big D has the most reason to want Felix dead of all of us, considering Felix's recent role in kidnapping Nicole—so I'm a bit surprised when he simply commands, "Calm yourself and tell us what happened."

After a few deep breaths and a jerk of his chin that cracks his neck, Mac leans forward in his seat. Elbows perched on knees, he recounts how Felix showed just as their dinner wrapped up, dropped the bomb about being hired to steal the Volkevich USB drive containing the fortune in bitcoin, and the even bigger bomb of his new mission to take down the General. I glance at Dimitri throughout, watching his scowl slowly deepen.

"He wants my—our, by extension—help tracking down the General. Said he was calling in my favor," Mac finishes.

"And what was your response?" I ask, tone careful.

"Obviously, I told him to fuck right off. I only made that deal with the contingency that whatever favor he wanted wouldn't put me or mine at risk. And tracking down and killing the General? That's not just a risk..."

Dimitri finishes his thought. "It is suicide. At least we know Felix remains nearby. It will make it simpler to locate him," he shrugs.

Mac's brows lift, perhaps as surprised as I am that Dimitri is being so reasonable about this.

"Odd that he'd come to us about it," I point out. "He must know he's damn near the top of our shite list. Why would he think we'd consider helping him? And why would we help him with *this* task specifically, considering our loyalties?" As far as he knows—as far as *anyone* knows—the three of us work for the General. There's no way Felix has any idea about the truth. I've never told anyone.

Once you tell someone—anyone—it's not a secret anymore. Even the most loyal friend with the best of intentions can slip up. And with a secret this dangerous to everyone I care most about, I can't let that happen.

You have to control the flow of information. And that's precisely what I'm good at.

"Well, about that... Felix said some shit I can't unhear."

Dimitri's eyes narrow. "Such as?" he prompts.

Mac blows out a breath. "What do we really know about the General? Or his motives?"

"Nothing," Dimitri answers. I remain silent.

"Doesn't that... I dunno... give you the scratch?" Mac says, running his fingers the wrong way against the stubble on his cheek. It makes a loud rasping noise.

"Not really," Dimitri says, shrugging. Totally unbothered.

That famous Russian nonchalance rubs Mac the wrong way this time. "Are you for real? You don't care at *all*? I didn't figure you for the blind loyal type. What if he's a *bad guy* who does *bad things*?"

"My loyalty is not blind," Dimitri argues. "I owe this man for a new identity and a fresh start—"

"Technically, you owe *me* for the new identity," I interject with a half-smile.

"—I have no interest in making an enemy of him."

Dimitri glances at me, and I nod my agreement. "Considering what he hires us to do, I think it's very likely the General is a bad guy who does bad things," I say, choosing my words. I prefer not to lie. Bending the truth makes me feel better, so I'm careful not to offer more details than I need to. "But he also brought us together."

I think I understand now. Felix knows the General is after him, he wants to fight back, and he wants Mac in his corner. All that talk of having an exit strategy was his way of manipulating Mac into making a fear-based decision. After all, he has Eleanor to think about now—and most hitmen don't retire peacefully.

Mac rubs the back of his neck. "Yeah, well, I'd sleep a helluva lot better if I knew I wasn't helping a new power rise in the underworld of Ulysses."

That surprises me. "A new power? In Ulysses?"

"I know we've done jobs all over, but look at the ones we've done since we settled *here*. An arms dealer. The fuckin' mayor. The leader of the most powerful *Bratva* in the state... Are we taking out the trash, or are we eliminating the competition?"

I watch the question land and roll right off Dimitri's frozen landscape of a face, but a frown forms between my brows that deepens with each question. The General wants to take over Ulysses? I didn't consider that possibility. And it makes a twisted kind of sense for a man with a veritable army of hitmen at his disposal. "So, Felix thinks the General sees him as competition?"

"Felix thinks he was set up with Kyle and the USB drive, and that the General wants him dead."

"Why does the General not just give us the hit, then?" Dimitri scoffs. "That would be much simpler."

I make a face. "Well..." I hedge.

They both fix me with twin looks of startled expectation.

My eyes dart between them for a few seconds, then I sigh. Normally, I don't share the details of all the hits we receive if I decide in advance we aren't going to take the job. But in this case, the information has just become relevant. Whether Felix is friend or foe remains to be seen, but either way he's involved. They need to know. "Technically, the General did give us his name."

Mac's eyebrows lift, and he exchanges a look with Dimitri, who demands, "Explain."

"The General always sends us names in batches. Part of my role is to parse them out. I start my research before we ever begin our surveillance—it saves time if I can eliminate someone because they don't follow the criteria we all agreed to. "

"Why didn't we know this?" Mac asks.

"You never asked?" I shrug. When he scowls in response to that terrible answer, I fall back on snark to avoid suspicion. "This is my job, right? I handle intel, logistics, and data erasure. Do I tell you how to line up a shot?"

Mac crosses his arms and grumbles, "Still feels like something you should have told us."

"I agree," Dimitri says.

"Fine. Going forward, I'll just send you both the list as I receive it, and we can make the call for each name together. Yeah?"

"Good," Mac agrees. "So, wait, you're saying Felix was one of the names? That means he's right. The General is after him."

"Why would he want Felix dead?" Dimitri presses. "He is just a cleaner, *da*?"

Mac shakes his head. "Calling Felix *just* a cleaner is like saying Michael Jordan was *just* a baller. Cleaning crime scenes pays well, but he's got powerful connections, and he's building an empire of his own. He's got his own network of spies and informants, too. Maybe the General's right to be threatened by Felix. Maybe he *is* competition."

Dimitri inclines his head thoughtfully. "In my mind, this changes very little. The General wants Felix dead, and we want to kill him."

Mac blows out a breath. "Look, I'm all for taking his ass down because fuck that guy. And I'm not saying we should work with him or trust anything he says, but he *might* have a point about the General. Not knowing who this guy is—if it even is a guy, or a woman, or a *group*—or what he's up to, or what part we're all unknowingly playing in whatever game this is..."

"This never bothered you before," Dimitri observes quietly.

"Yeah, well, not knowing doesn't work for me anymore. That's why I got out of the military, ya know?"

Dimitri shakes his head. "The General is anonymous for a reason. He does not want us to know who he is. A powerful man who can protect his identity is a terrible enemy to make."

"Maybe if we're careful—"

Dimitri cuts him off. "James, this path will only lead to having targets put onto our backs. You are... used to safety behind a long-range weapon. You had security in your position as a soldier. You could not ask questions of your superiors, perhaps, but the worst you had to fear was a dishonorable discharge.

"Being a hitman is a very different thing than being a soldier. We are the hand that holds the gun; the handler is the arm that points it. This is the only balance of power that can be allowed. I have watched many hitmen become targets themselves for asking questions."

Big D has a point, and as a former-*Bratva*-enforcer-turned-career-assassin, he's the most qualified of us to make it. Mac knows it, too. "I suppose a hitman who can't be controlled is worse than a loose cannon."

"*Da*. He is a loose cannon with perfect aim who usually knows how to disappear."

Mac blows out another frustrated breath. His eyes cut to me, and I know he's noticing how quiet I've been. "What's your read on it, Wes?"

I rest my elbows on the arms of my office chair, steeple my fingers, and tap my pointers against my top lip. My eyes dart back and forth, not seeing—calculating. "You've both got reasonable points. But the lack of information about the General seems intentional, and that implies dangerous secrets—and if I'm participating in some kind of hostile takeover, I'd quite like to know.

"It's just... I can't find the General, Mac," I say honestly, so close to the truth that it makes my pulse race. "I've tried. None of my usual methods work. I've tried accessing the code to the platform he uses to contact us, but it's completely locked down. I traced the email, and it takes me through maze after maze with nothing but dead ends. Our payments are bitcoin, scrubbed abroad and redirected back to us in a way that's totally untraceable"—as well as totally familiar—"so, whoever he is... he's protected by his anonymity and he knows it."

"See, but that just makes my point," Mac jumps in. "What's he hiding? What's he hiding so well that not even Wes can find him?"

"I must admit, I'd quite like to know," I agree.

"But how would we proceed if you are the best and even you cannot find him?" Dimitri asks.

We could do what I've been doing all along. Only this time, they can help. "We can focus on the targets. If we can figure out what all our targets have in common, we might be able to figure out the General's motive and thus who he is."

Dimitri grunts his agreement.

"You mean what they have in common other than the fact that they're scumbags?" Mac points out with a half-smile.

"Yes, other than that. Obviously he's not some sort of vigilante hero with deep pockets. His purpose is self-serving, or perhaps even personal. I think we ought to continue to take the hits, but do some digging of our own."

"This is still risky," Dimitri argues.

"But Wes is the best," Mac jumps in, shooting me a grateful smile. "And he's careful. He knows how to cover his tracks, right?"

"Kind of the job description," I say, flashing Dimitri a rueful smile. "We still have laptops and tablets and cell phones from some of those dickheads. I can start going through our old files."

"Very well, though I still think we should focus our efforts on finding Felix," Dimitri grumbles.

"I'll do both to the best of my ability, and proceed with the utmost caution," I promise, holding up two fingers. "I've already got flags for Felix in all the usual places—there's not much we can do about him until he pops up again. In the meantime, I'll get stuck in with the old targets and see if we can't uncover something about the General's motives."

"The real question is, what does he want with a shithole like Ulysses?" Mac says.

"Indeed. Follow the money. It's always the money," I remark distractedly as I pull my keyboard towards me. Once I crack open a new can of energy drink, Mac and Dimitri shuffle out of the room to let me do my thing.

Which I'll be doing out in the open from now on—an exhilarating, anxious thought. This new territory of partial truth is going to be a tricky one to navigate.

Good thing I'm the best at what I do.

1

MADISON

I may not even really exist outside of zeros-and-ones

```
NoBody: You got that package for me yet?
  mermaidav: Working on it. Tomorrow.
  NoBody: Yeah, that works. Wait, what are you
still doing online?
```

I send him the middle finger emoji.

```
  NoBody: Real nice. Aren't you going to be
late?
```

My eyes flick to the clock at the bottom right of my monitor. Shit. I'm gonna be late.

I tab over to the main window and shoot a quick goodbye to my odd little collection of internet strangers, which is answered with some genuine farewells from the newbies and some affectionate profanity from the people who've known me longer. It makes me grin as I log out of the various windows and chats I always have up, and start shutting down the programs that don't need to run while I'm gone. When one gets stuck, I jiggle the mouse and curse—unsurprisingly, no help—and it throws a spinning wheel of frustration back at me.

This damn computer. With her white housing, black monitors, and gray internal components, she's basically my Frankenstein monster I built two years ago for a fraction of what she would have cost new. She's overpowered as fuck, which is necessary for both the redundant security protocols I use and the reason I have those protocols. And while her pieced-together form has served me well, I've been pretending to ignore how slow and unreliable she's been getting for months now. It's past time for an upgrade, but my sporadic paychecks keep getting split between pesky things like food, insurance, rent, and nursing home bills.

Damn, I miss not having to worry about money.

Once upon a time, I had a cool apartment in a good neighborhood in downtown Ulysses, NJ. I could afford the best weed, I bought new tech when I felt like it, and I even had an emergency fund. Then, Abuela had her bad fall, and we decided to move her into the nursing home, and it's... *very* expensive. Well, good care is. With people who know what they're doing, who show empathy and like their jobs. After a ton of research—I toured over a dozen facilities—I found the perfect place, but it has pretty strict visiting hours...

Shit. I *am* going to be late. Abuela hates when I'm late.

I sniff the armpits of the hoodie on the back of my computer chair, shrug, and tug it on as I hurry through my bedroom door into the hallway and living area, ignoring the state of an apartment in desperate need of a clean.

Even dirty, the inside of my apartment looks like an old Mexican lady decorated it. Because she did. I took over Abuela's much cheaper lease when she moved into the nursing home, and I didn't really change much about the place. The couch is comfy, the art and pottery and little ceramic dishes everywhere are colorful, and while I haven't subscribed to the ideology of it all in a long time, all the little gold-inlaid statues of various saints and prayer candles with the Virgin Mary decals bring me comfort in their familiarity.

My cat opens one accusatory eye from his curled-up position on the couch, irritated at the interruption. My furry son is a handsome tuxedo lad named Some Bills, both because that's what he is—a fucking free-loader who can't even catch the odd fly that gets in through an open window—and because it's a great excuse to leave a social event. The looks

I get when I tell people I have to go home to take care of some bills? Priceless.

"I'll be back later. No loud parties this time," I instruct him as that eye drifts back shut.

I shove my feet into some boots, effortlessly balancing the process of pulling on my sweater and arming the security system. At the last second, I remember the cranberry orange muffin I bought for Abuela, and dart over to grab the bag off the counter.

On my way out, I check my mailbox, and I'm not quick enough ducking out the door to miss my neighbor on his way in. I almost can't contain my groan.

Ugh. This guy.

Todd is such a dude-bro. He's cute in a twentysomething/former jock/peaked in high school kind of way, but he acted like I was a joke that the universe made up specifically for him the first time we ran into each other. Maybe it was the black lipstick. Or maybe it's because I didn't trip over myself to appeal to his conventionally attractive ass. I've found that his particular flavor of *hot guy* gets really butthurt at being denied the opportunity to deny someone first.

Men are the fucking *worst*.

Dressed in sweats and clearly on his way back from the gym on this fine Sunday, he smiles to himself with a mean kind of glee as he turns to unlock the door adjacent to mine. His eyes flick down to the grease-stained paper bag in my hand, like he's got some kind of butter homing device. "I thought I smelled fast food. Should have known it was you."

Now, I love a good roast, but only when it's well done. I was the brown, chubby girl in Catholic school, and pre-teen girls are much more creative and way meaner than Todd could ever hope to be. It's frankly kind of sad for him, because I do think he's genuinely trying to get a rise out of me with these lame-ass insults.

"Todd, so good to see you—and by that I mean it's nice to see less of your face," I gesture to my own chin with the pointer finger of the hand still clutching the rolled-up top of the paper bag. "Are you trying to grow a beard, or did you lose a bet? Because that is not coming in well, my guy."

His lip curls, but he ignores the jab otherwise. "Where are you headed? I know it's not the gym—even though it really should be. You know, you'd actually be pretty hot if you started working out, and cut eating all that crap."

Unfortunately for his ego (because having a six-pack is his entire personality), being thin has just never been a priority, even if—or, perhaps, because?—society wants me to think that my value depends on how flat my stomach is. It's pure vanity anyway, since my semi-regular doctor's visits confirm that I'm healthy as a damn horse. Plus, I like how I look, just as I am.

"Are you really trying to convince me that not everyone loves a big-booty Latina?" I ask rhetorically with a sweet smile.

As intended, his eyes widen at the phrase. I may have hacked his search history, but in my defense... it was easy. He was mooching off the free Wi-Fi I set up for my elderly upstairs neighbor Mrs. Louis, so he was basically asking for it.

He snorts, trying to save face, but I take inordinate pleasure in the sudden red stain creeping up his cheeks from his thick neck.

Yeah, that's right, *pendejo*—I know your dirty little secrets.

"I'd have gone with 'fat ass'," he hisses.

"How unoriginal." I roll my eyes. "Those last two brain cells you've got are really fighting for third place, huh?"

His smile freezes into something ugly. "The fuck did you just say to me?" he asks, tone rising.

"The irony of being too stupid to understand when someone calls you stupid," I mutter loud enough for him to hear, laughing and shaking my head. Not sure why Todd starts this shit—at this point he must know that he can't finish it.

"Say it to my face," he growls.

Cautiously, my eyes flick over to him at the aggression in his tone, but though he's standing rigidly, he's not poised to make a move. So, I just shake my head and breeze past him towards the front doors.

"Eat a dick, Todd," I reply, bored with his posturing.

"I got one for you right here, bitch."

I don't have to see the gesture to know that he's gripping himself through his pants. Just before stepping outside, I get the last word. "No thanks, I'm allergic to shrimp."

He curses me out as the door swings shut, and I chuckle to myself, pleased and exhilarated. I've been sitting on that one for a while, and I'm so pumped he gave me the opportunity to use it.

I'd never let someone like *Todd* get to me—he's the kind of guy who'd call you fat in front of his friends and jerk off to your profile picture in secret. Hypocrisy chafes me worse than forgetting to wear bike shorts under a dress.

But, hey, he can hate-fuck his hand thinking about me all he wants... Still, thank God for thick walls, because I don't want to hear that shit. It's bad enough I've been seeing him more often since I took that job at SmarTech, where he works as a desk jockey in IT.

Just another reason to look forward to the big dramatic exit tomorrow.

My apartment is in a reasonably nice area of town—no one has a backyard, but you hardly ever hear gunshots. It's an old building, one like many others on the street that was turned into six units back in the 90s, and I somehow always manage to snag an up-front parking spot.

Since it's the middle of the afternoon on a Sunday, my drive across town is a breeze. Construction is minimal on weekends, potholes are easy to avoid with fewer cars on the road, and I only have to give one asshole in an SUV the finger—all in all, a fairly tame ride. *Fuck around and find out* is a creed by which I live my life, and I don't mind playing chicken with my inherited 20-year-old Corolla. Pretty sure it's running on pure Toyota magic at this point, anyway.

Sunset Hills, the facility where Abuela lives, is nestled in a stretch of recently developed farmland. There's plenty of convenient parking, lots of helpful staff, and it smells more like antiseptic than aging bodies. Afternoon on a weekend day is peak visiting hours, and there's a spectrum of noise—high-pitched childish glee and calls of "Grandpa!" at one end, and polite, strained, "So, how have you been?" at the other. Both make me feel icky, like I need to visit more.

I'm escorted to Abuela's room by Manny, one of the nurse aides on her floor. He's an imposing guy, looking more like a biker than a nurse—a few inches taller and wider than most people, and with much more hair. I've caught him staring at my ass once or twice, but I know Abuela likes him, so I've decided to just let him have it as a little treat.

Abuela's room is as bright as my apartment—shades of yellow and orange everywhere you look. The woman herself sits in a swivel lounger facing the TV. She turns her chair on its spinning axis to face me, and it's like seeing my reflection 50 years from now... if I dyed my hair back to its natural color. Vasquez women are small-boned, short, bronze-skinned, and have dark features with full lips, a round-tipped nose and an otherwise broad face with hollow cheekbones. Some of the brown in her complexion got diluted by my Caucasian bio dad, but otherwise I'm the spitting image of every Vasquez woman in my family. And I love that about my heritage.

"*Hola,* Abuela," I greet as I stand in the doorway leading from the sterile white hallway into the cozy room that smells faintly of Windex and Vicks Vapo-Rub.

"Ah!" she hisses instead of greeting me, laser-focused on my hair. "Who is this punk rocker? Not *my* granddaughter."

With a chuckle, I tuck a green lock behind my ear. "You like it?" I ask rhetorically.

"Why did you do that again, Madison?" she admonishes. "It was finally a nice, natural color!"

Only the front pieces are colorful this time, but I probably should have waited until after visiting her to go from the "nice, natural" shade called *Dragon Fire* back to my tried-and-true *Green with Envy.* Though I suppose it only would have delayed the argument...

The frail woman being swallowed up by her lounger may be slowly losing pieces of herself, but she is as vain and opinionated as she ever was. Her hands shake too badly for eyeliner now, but she still swipes on classic red lipstick every morning and religiously winds curlers in her hair every night before bed. I've wondered if she wants to look nice because she found an old dude to do it with. Apparently, STIs are a real problem in retirement homes.

"I'm just not a nice, natural girl, I guess," I shrug, entering the room and hanging my purse on the hook by the door. I leave the bag with the muffin in the mostly empty mini-fridge.

She glares at me for my flippant response.

When Abuela turns back to the TV, I exchange a look with Manny. "It's a good day," he assures me, where *good* is code for *lucid*. Then, he lifts his voice and addresses Abuela. "Isn't it, Mrs. Vasquez?"

"Why are you asking me?" she snaps. She launches into a tirade in rapid Spanish about how her new doctor doesn't know anything and how stupid they all are and how she can't believe her own granddaughter would leave her in this place.

Manny shoots me a helpless look. I'm glad he doesn't speak Spanish because I'd hate for Abuela to get a reputation as a mean old lady—I don't want it to go on her old person permanent record, or get her blacklisted from Bingo or something.

"Abuela, English," I cut in. "You're the one who taught me it's rude to speak Spanish around *gringos*—no offense," I add for Manny's benefit, though I'm not sure he'd know what to be offended about.

She makes a *hmmph* noise, her eyes following the Mexican actors as they throw themselves around the set of her favorite *telenovella*. "I can't believe they let you have that hair at your job," Abuela grumbles, still frowning. "You'll never get a promotion."

"Good thing I just quit, then." She doesn't really need to know it hasn't happened yet; she'd just try to talk me out of it.

That gets me her full attention, and she spins all the way around to face me. "What?!"

"I'm... gonna go." Awkwardly, Manny ducks his head and trots out of the room. Gotta appreciate the ones that know how to get out of the way of family drama.

"You quit that good job your *tío* got you?" she demands.

I narrow my eyes. "Is that what he said? That he got me the job?"

She sniffs. "Bettina told me."

Of course he took credit. Of course he talked about it to his *mamá*, who talked about it to Abuela. Gossip is an Olympic sport for these women. The entire congregation probably knows, so I need to choose my words.

"It..." I search for the right description. "It served a purpose. I'm not cut out for working in an office, Abuela. I don't like it."

She clutches her rosary in hands that tremble no matter which meds they put her on, and casts her eyes skyward, nearly as dramatic as the people she watches in a literal soap opera. "*Dios mio.* My granddaughter would rather live out on the streets than keep a good job because she *doesn't like being in an office,*" she says, trying to mimic my American accent. She lifts a brow, mirroring my expression. "I cleaned houses for 47 years, Madison Rosa. You think I liked it? No, I did it to put food on your table and pay for your education and those expensive computers you always wanted."

I sigh. As a Catholic, she has an advanced degree in guilt. "I know, Abuela—"

"What are you going to do if not work in an office?"

"I'm going to start looking for another gig. You know I don't like being bored."

"More computer nonsense, no doubt," she says, disdain creeping into her tone. "My neighbor Joan's daughter is a professor at the college. Francine's granddaughter is a doctor. You're smarter than both of them, and you waste your potential on these *máquinas*."

"Abuela—" I cut myself off, hearing the frustration in my tone at the tired conversation. "I don't want to fight."

"Hmmph."

I sigh. Her ire and judgment used to really bother me, but now it just rolls off my back because I understand why she lashes out. She wasn't always a mean old lady. She knows she's losing pieces of herself, and all I can do is watch her hate it and feel guilty about putting her in a home, even though we made that decision together.

It's fucking awful.

Abuela raised me when her teenage daughter was killed in a car accident and my teenage father washed his hands of the tiny brown baby that would "ruin his bright future." I became her *hijita*—her little daughter. She paid for me to go through private school—Catholic, obviously—and bought me my first computer. She was ridiculously strict and probably the reason I started rebelling to begin with, but she also made every birthday cake I've ever had, kissed all the boo-boos, came to every school recital, soothed the tears after every breakup, celebrated all my achievements and pushed me to be better.

I can't let myself get mad at her. I refuse to. Even though she doesn't really understand or accept me, she's all I've got. And she loves me in her own way.

In my arsenal, misdirection is the best weapon when dealing with Abuela in this mood. "What have you been working on here?" I tilt my head to get the full picture of the incomplete jigsaw puzzle spread over her table. So far, only the perimeter is complete, but the picture on the box has kittens in a field of daisies. Too freakin' cute.

The table is barely big enough to hold all the pieces, but I take a seat and start sorting by kitten color. "It looks new," I observe as my sleeve comes away covered in tiny cardboard shavings from the cutting machine.

"Manny brought it," she replies, her voice crackling before dissolving into a harsh cough that makes me frown. She doesn't seem too bothered by it, but I'll need to remember to ask if she got her flu shot.

"That was nice of him."

"They'll pass it around when I'm done, but it's nice that he brings it here first, I guess. He says I've never lost a piece," she adds with some pride.

When Abuela starts to struggle out of her lounger, I refocus on the puzzle because I know better than to offer her a hand to get up. The agony of each step shows on her face as she makes her way over to the table, clutching her bad hip. She settles next to me, in her usual spot facing the windows in the chair with the memory foam cushion.

With one hand, Abuela clutches her rosary to her chest and with the other, she selects a puzzle piece and finds its spot instantly. I have absolutely no idea how she does that. I still haven't even gotten one.

"*Bruja*," I mutter under my breath, accusing her of using her puzzle witch powers.

She cracks a smile, grateful that I broke the tense silence—not that she'd ever admit that. But I know that the fiery anger has melted into shame for trying to make me feel bad when I won't hit back. Besides, I'm used to being the one to offer an olive branch.

"You know I don't want to fight either, Madison. But you've always been so... contrary," she says, emphasizing the word in a way that isn't quite disdainful and certainly isn't approving. "With your crazy hair colors and nose rings and attitude about the world. Sometimes I think that's my fault."

Thoughtfully, I finger the metal in my right nostril. "*You* taught me to be strong."

"I did," she smiles, but it's kind of a sad one. "But it isn't weakness to want someone to take care of you, *m'hijita,* or share the burdens of life, like my Carlos, *que en paz descanse.*"

She thinks I need someone to take care of *me*? The irony of this woman saying that to me, after the sacrifices I've made to ensure she's happy and comfortable... *I'm* the caretaker, now; I don't want or need anyone telling me how to live my life—not even someone who means well.

And given my line of work, I can't really afford to let anyone close enough to try.

I shake my head. "I know, Abuela. But I like being alone. And I don't want to work in an office. And I like my green hair and nose ring. I just want to live on my own terms. Is that so bad?"

She sighs, and her eyes soften. "Not bad, just... difficult. Living on your own terms is a luxury few can afford," she remarks sagely. "You seem lonely sometimes, *hijita.*"

"I'm not," I say, though it doesn't feel quite like the truth.

To her, I look lonely. I went from being a weird, closed-off teenager to a weird, closed-off adult and neglected to learn how to make friends along the way. At this point, I'm not sure if it's because I'm bad at relationships or if it's self-sabotage. It's not like I don't know the rules of engagement; it's just that, well... people don't just befriend people for no reason. It's a give and take. You tell people stuff, and find common ground, and share experiences, and give pieces of yourself in exchange for pieces of them.

But I hate sharing details about myself—I can't talk about work, and I didn't have the rosy childhood that people like hearing about. Real relationships with real people are exhausting sometimes.

Internet friends are another thing completely. They can't judge you if they don't know who you really are. The anonymity is... freeing. Intimacy takes on a much different meaning when you can't see someone's facial reactions, and the manners people would expect face to face are all but meaningless. Online, I get to be who I say I am—nothing more, nothing less. As far as they're all concerned, I may not even really exist outside of zeros-and-ones.

And as far as dating?

Well... it's probably for the best that I'm not trying to date right now. I can't imagine most potential romantic partners would be cool with the straight-up illegal nature of my income and interests.

Yeah, that's why. It's *definitely* not because I'm comparing every person I meet against a certain spymaster who moderates a certain chatroom I frequent...

"I just want you to be happy. I worry about you."

"I know. You don't have to worry about me, though, okay? I'll be just fine—I'm very smart and good at things."

"Hmmph. Pride," she says archly—a warning, though her lips twitch in hidden amusement. "It's a deadly sin, Madison."

"I don't think pride's the one they're going to get me for," I mutter, loud enough for her to hear, and quiet enough for her to pretend she didn't.

After a few seconds, I reach for her hand and give it a little squeeze. She feels much more fragile than she used to, with skin like thin, warm silk and bones that might crunch under the pressure of a firm handshake.

"Te quiero," I say softly.

She nods like the queenly matriarch she is, knowing it's her due, and squeezes my hand back. *"Te quiero, hijita."* Then, she places another piece.

We chat as we puzzle. She presses for details about every single man in my life as a potential romantic partner, asks about my cat, about my online friends, and if I'm eating enough beans. In that order. My answers are almost always the same, and, as always, I avoid mentioning any of my *extracurriculars*, because it would probably kill her, and her last thought would be how disappointed she was in me.

Luckily, I know how to keep a secret.

2

WESLEY

I love a challenge.

I sit in the quiet darkness, watching, still as a spider in the middle of its web, waiting for prey. As usual, I'm holed up in the intentionally shabby Bugs-B-Gon exterminator van. The outside blends in well among the run-down streets and disrepair of Ulysses, NJ, but the inside is an FBI agent's wet dream.

The hum of power consumption surrounding me is constant enough to be classified as white noise, and the blue light of a wall of monitors set to dark mode is too faint to be perceived through extra dark window tinting. The screens don't make a sound as they cycle through the various windows I always call up—hacked traffic and nearby security cameras, weather, and satellite updates, local police scanners, my command terminal, code editor, system logs, comms control for the earpieces we all wear, and local network security monitors, to name a few.

It's cramped, so not the most comfortable place for a long-term stakeout—but I have plenty of nutritionally barren snacks, extra energy drinks, a padded chair, and a job to do. I've already disabled our target's home security and hacked into any cameras that might capture our misdeeds, as well as a few others in a several-block radius, casting their feed to keep our perimeter secure and rerouting their footage so it won't be saved.

Mac is in place, set up with his sniper rifle in a vacant home across the street. He'll keep watch over our favorite Russian through the lens of his scope. There's no safer—or deadlier—place to be. And Dimitri just slipped in through an unlocked window with a grace in total contradiction to his physical enormity. Though his prized Japanese steel is in hand, that's simply a precaution. Our target shouldn't be home.

The target in question: Javier Alfano, Ulysses drug lord, and the man single-handedly creating and feeding the fentanyl problem in our fair city. The bachelor pad where he runs his drug empire is on the outskirts of Ulysses, in an area where all attempts at gentrification have run screaming in the opposite direction. With so many neighbors, it's not the ideal place for a hit if things go south, but Alfano is about to leave the country for a month and this is the best chance we're going to get.

Normally after this many weeks of surveillance, we would have killed the dickhead by now. But we're being extra cautious because, frankly, we all need this job to go smoothly. It's the first hit we've taken since a certain *cleaner* got a little too involved in our business, and since Felix has become the proverbial needle in a haystack *and* thorn in our sides... well, we're all a little on edge.

"Fuck. I have a... situation. A cold one."

"Who?" I ask, stomach sinking. It's never a good thing to find an unexpected dead body in the home of the man you intend to kill eventually. "Alfano?"

"I believe so. His face is a mess, so we will need to use his tattoos for the ID." His thick Russian accent is slightly more garbled through the earpiece, but it's clear enough to hear his irritation.

"So much for that payout," Mac grumbles.

"James, you said there has been no movement in the house?" Dimitri asks, voice strained with effort, like he's lifting or moving something.

"I haven't seen anyone in or out, and I've been sitting here with my thumb up my ass all fuckin' day," Mac grumbles, his southern drawl somewhat acidic. To be fair, our eyes in the shadows rarely miss any important details, so it's understandable why he'd be defensive.

"What's the state of the body?" I ask.

"Room temperature, but still stiff. In his pockets"—there's a rustling noise—*"a wallet full of cash with no identification. No weapon on him."*

"Who kills someone and takes the ID out of the wallet, but not the cash?" Mac wonders aloud, echoing my thoughts.

I frown. "Wait a minute. If he's room temperature but in full rigor mortis, that means he's been dead at least half a day, but not more than two. We saw him this morning, and if Mac hasn't seen anyone go in or out, that means—"

"The killer is still in there!" Mac finishes in a hiss.

Suddenly, there's a sharp flurry of Russian curses, the sound of an impact of flesh against flesh, and a roar of pain... and then the explosion of a gunshot, audible but clearly silenced from the lack of echo in the night air.

Fuck!

"Fuck!" Dimitri yells.

"D? What the fuck was that? You good? Too many goddamn fucking curtains... What's happening?" Our levelheaded gunman's voice is rigid with concern.

I switch between camera feeds, trying to find some way to see into the house to check on Dimitri, and catch movement in the bottom corner—a man, sprinting through the back door of Alfano's place.

When I chose this spot to park the van, I noticed the other car parked in the alley next to Mac's, but took it for one of the neighbor's. It's a mid-tier sedan, too old to be police-issued and too low grade to belong to anyone connected to the flashy drug lord who likes to display his wealth with diamonds and Escalades.

But as the shooter comes bursting around the corner, I realize, "He's headed this way!"

"Grab him, Wes!"

With mere seconds to hatch my plan and no easily accessible guns within arm's reach, I grab the closest weapon—a tyre iron—and time the opening of my door perfectly. Even bracing myself, the impact of his face into the metal bar reverberates up my arms.

Clotheslined, he goes down, cracking his head hard on the pavement as he falls. Blood pours in rivers from his nose where he hit the iron, pooling under his head, but his chest is moving.

I tap the earpiece using my shoulder, knowing that unmuting myself will allow them to hear my ragged breathing and strained tone. "Got him."

"You're the man. Big D, how you doin'?"

"I have been shot," comes the grumbled reply, anger dripping from every accented syllable. There's a rustling, like he's checking for damage. *"Again."*

Leave it to Dimitri to consider a gunshot wound a mere inconvenience.

Mac makes a choked noise, and the amusement in his voice is plain, if wry. *"Need an assist?"*

Dimitri heaves a deep sigh, then admits, *"Yes,"* like the act of accepting help is what's truly painful.

"Be right there," Mac chuckles.

I set about checking the man's pockets for all the things we'd normally collect. Empty. For most people, this would be odd. In this case, it likely means he's a pro. I don't carry anything that can be used to identify me, either.

I've just popped the boot of Mac's car when he and Dimitri appear in the mouth of the alley. Mac is sagging heavily to the side, supporting Dimitri's weight as they make slow, careful movements. He leaves Dimitri against the side of the van, then continues down the alley towards me, wiping at some blood on his shirt—like that'll help. Luckily, I've perfected my blood stain removal paste made of peroxide, bicarbonate of soda and salt.

"Dead?" Mac asks, shoving at the man's shoulder with his toe. The body tilts up an inch, then settles back into place like so much, well, dead weight.

"Knocked out. Where the fuck did he come from?"

Mac throws Dimitri a look over his shoulder. "Hiding in the closet, right, D?"

Dimitri nods tightly and carefully removes the strap of a slim laptop bag from his shoulder. "Yes. He did the jump on me."

"He *got* the jump on you," Mac corrects.

Dimitri scowls at him. "That is what I said. Here. Laptop." As he leans forward to place the bag on the desk just inside the opening, pain lances his features around the eyes and mouth, causing the old, deep scar on his face to pinch. "It was well done to leave him alive," he rasps. "Now we can question him."

"That better be the royal 'we,'" I remark dryly, lifting a brow at his grimace of pain. He's normally in charge of interrogations, but something tells me he's going to have to sit this one out. "You all right, big guy?"

"Fine," he replies curtly.

"Where'd he get you? The leg?" I assume from the limp.

When he doesn't respond, I glance at Mac, who's somewhat uncharacteristically not even trying to hide his amused grin. It makes me frown—Mac's not one to revel in the discomfort of another, and being shot isn't something he'd normally take the piss out of Dimitri for.

"An attack from the rear," Mac explains, laughter dancing in his eyes.

"Ah." My own lips twitch, but I school my expression before the chuckle slips out. The only thing worse than having a laugh at Dimitri's expense is letting him see you do it. Not that it'll stop our sniper from sniping at the big Russian bear. He's reckless that way, and a bit too fond of butt jokes. "Well. Mac's about to become insufferable."

Mac laughs. "Yup," he agrees brightly, throwing Dimitri a grin. "I'm gonna be a real pain in the ass about this one."

I snort as Dimitri turns an icy glare on Mac, gingerly pushing away from the wall of the van, favoring his left leg and—I imagine—buttock. "Finish moving the body," he growls. "I am bleeding and leaving more evidence with each breath you waste on terrible jokes."

With another unbothered chuckle, Mac gestures at the shooter, and we get to work. In a coordinated movement, we hoist opposite ends of the sleeping man and carry him over to the car. He doesn't fold in easily, and when Mac slams the lid, there's a distinct crunching noise that makes both of us wince.

We head back to the van. I step inside and settle on my stool, itching to start organizing all my new acquisitions—wallet, guns, Alfano's laptop...

"Okay. I'm going to drop Sleeping Beauty at the freezer and get our ass-assin home." At Dimitri's angry, dismissive noise, Mac turns to me with a wide grin. "When I come back, we can head in to clean up. You stay here and keep an eye on the streets?"

"Will do."

"Anything comes up, you nip it in the butt."

Dimitri grinds his jaw.

"It's *bud*. Nip it in the bud," I correct, hiding a smile as I grab a spare USB-C cord from the bin to plug in Alfano's laptop.

Mac flashes that mega-watt smile. "Oh, that's right," he chuckles, as obvious as he is unrepentant about the intentional mistake.

Dimitri curses him under his breath, and I don't quite catch the whole phrase—a real tragedy, since the man is as creative as he is explicit when it comes to foreign insults—but I catch something that roughly translates to *turd from a haunted toilet.*

I watch them climb into Mac's car, then close myself back into the glowing blue lights and relative quiet of my surveillance van. My heart is still pounding hard—both from exertion and the remnants of adrenaline—and I realize my earpiece channels are still open as I hear the car doors slam, the engine start up, then the radio come on.

After a beat, there's a low grumble: *"If you start singing, I will kick you out."*

"But then who's gonna drive your bloody arse home?" Mac quips, trying to imitate my accent. *"Hey Wes, think Nicole's got a Band-Aid big enough?"*

"Dunno. But she's certainly the only one of us willing to kiss it better."

"Then I *will jump out,"* Dimitri continues, dramatic with his threats in a way I don't think he fully appreciates.

"Tuck and roll," I reply breezily.

"Yeah, and it's a full moon *tonight, so at least you'll be able to see to make your way back."*

"Mudak!" Dimitri hisses.

With a chuckle, I long-tap my earpieces to block out their bickering while I get to work. I plug in Alfano's laptop, then fire it up and groan at the dreaded update screen. Brilliant. This is going to take ages.

But at least I've got a distraction.

A notification dings, and the corner of my screen blinks, flashing green and blue from her custom avatar in the IRC—internet relay chat—I set up for my spiders. She's one of them, but she's so much more than that, too.

My spiders fall into two broad categories—people who do things for me, and informants.

The task monkeys get the chores that I could do, or could create a program to do for me, but it's easier if I pay them for their time. They review security footage when I'm up against a time crunch, manually sort through unsearchable data, or create databases from stolen records acquired elsewhere.

My informants range from enthusiastic amateur sleuths to professionals dealing in secrets that I can buy for the right price. Some of them are one-offs, when the right person was in the right place at the right time and learned something useful. Some of them have a passing interest in true crime, some fancy themselves detectives, and some have the right connections.

She is in a class of her own. I can only daydream about what I could do if I had a team of people like mermaidav at my disposal. We'd rule the world.

I know all my spiders by username, bank account info, who vouched for them, and not much else. Of course, I always perform an initial test to ensure a potential informant isn't law enforcement, but otherwise I make it a point to encourage anonymity. A business that deals in secrets wouldn't thrive if I didn't let my informants have their own. I don't ask personal questions; I don't entertain any. But after almost two years of intriguing exchanges, I have to admit that I've done a bit (a *lot*) of extracurricular digging on my favorite spider. Fat lot of good it did me.

In the past, it's taken me as long as a few hours to get someone's social security number and online passwords with nothing more than an IP address to start. But not mermaidav. Her IP is blocked, which isn't normally a problem, but I couldn't get around it—so whatever she's using is as impressive as it is illegal. Perhaps even homemade.

And damn if all that futile digging didn't just make me admire her even more. I love a challenge.

All I have to go on is that she is a woman, likely in her mid-to-late 20s based on the slang she uses, and is awake during hours that indicate we're in roughly the same time zone. And that she can get pretty much whatever I want. It's honestly mystifying. She's either the best hacker I've never heard of, or she knows people on the inside.

As I pull up her chat window, I check the time and swallow down the urge to admonish her for her ridiculous sleep schedule. It's 2 AM, which means she's probably messaging me from bed. A grin tugs at the corners of my mouth.

SpyderMan: Can't sleep?

mermaidav: You know me. I finished the short story collection you sent, too, so I'm fresh out of reading material that'll put me to sleep.

I grin.

SpyderMan: Isaac Asimov isn't for you, I take it.

mermaidav: I'm still not sure how the least boring person I know has the most boring taste in books.

SpyderMan: You say boring; I'd call it classic. Refined, even.

mermaidav: lol of course you would. Either way, the book is dry as hell.

SpyderMan: Well, it is hard sci-fi. Story-forward, character development takes a back seat…

mermaidav: That and a distinct lack of wieners. To its detriment, I'd argue.

That drags a laugh from deep in my chest, and I send her an amused reaction in the chat.

mermaidav: Nothing against sci-fi, but I prefer it in my books when the world's ending, or the aliens are invading, or the machines are rising up… and someone's getting railed. Preferably by the aliens or machines.

SpyderMan: Oh, I'm aware. Your picks for our little book club are always very… educational.

mermaidav: Yes! See? You get it. I love how nontoxic your masculinity is. Romance books are basically a how-to guide, and men are sleeping on it because they don't want to read *girl books*. I love our book club.

Really, we go back-and-forth trading recommendations, but calling it a book club amuses both of us. What she doesn't know is that I've already read every book in the digital library she shared with me. Not because I particularly care to read about women getting banged by blokes with bat wings, but because she does and I'm interested in what *she's* interested in. And, frankly, like she said, it's a bit of a cheat code into the female psyche and their sexual fantasies.

And if my research has told me anything, it's that her sexual appetites lean towards a man who knows how to take charge. And isn't that just too fucking perfect?

mermaidav: Since I didn't finish your last pick, I'll let you pick again.

SpyderMan: Very kind of you.

mermaidav: I'm a giver. Hit me with your best shot, nerd. Or I may not be so generous next time.

I chuckle, a warmth curling through my belly at both the teasing nickname and challenge.

SpyderMan: Let's try *Dune*. That's had a resurgence in popularity lately.

mermaidav: Hmm... that's the one with the giant sandworms, right?

SpyderMan: Correct

mermaidav: A giant sandworm is kind of like a wiener, I guess.

If there had been something in my mouth, I would have spat it out.

This girl. So bright. So damn funny. No one else so consistently surprises and amuses me. It makes me eager to talk to her every time—eager to try to keep up. It makes me look at things that happen in my daily life and wonder what kind of humorous spin she'd put on them if she were there.

SpyderMan: Not if it's got teeth. Christ. What sorts of dicks are you dealing with?

mermaidav: A lady never tells.

SpyderMan: Cheeky.

mermaidav: Anyway, if I can't sleep, I might as well make some $. I was about to post an offer for services, but you got anything better up for grabs, boss man?

SpyderMan: If you're going for honorifics, I much prefer "Sir."

The dots appear, letting me know she's responding. I feel myself stirring in anticipation of her quip, knowing it'll be her characteristic mixture of sass and wit. To distract myself, I toss back the rest of my energy drink and drop the empty can into the bag at my feet.

mermaidav: Careful, Sir, or I might report you for workplace harassment.

I scrub my face with a groan and inhale deeply. I could flirt aimlessly with her all night, but I've got a dead cartel dealer, and I'd quite like to know who beat us to the punch. So I switch to the encrypted text so she can use her private key to read the next message. No one should ever be listening on my own private IRC, but someone in my position can never be too careful. I drop a file into the encrypted chat.

SpyderMan: Better get straight to it, then. I could use a hand sorting and filling in some data for the big boss.

mermaidav: *Some data*, he says. Do you know how much computing power this is going to take? It's a pretty big ask, my guy.

I know it's a colloquialism, but the possessive pronoun stirs something deep and primal in me. Something that wants to hear it from her lips. Something that wants to *take* as much as it wants to be owned.

SpyderMan: It is. Are you saying you're not up to the task?

mermaidav: No, obviously I'm trying to drive up the price.

That makes me laugh again.

SpyderMan: Shouldn't be too hard for a clever girl like you

mermaidav: See, that's not fair. You know my weakness is praise. Lol. How much?

SpyderMan: $700 for what I need within the next 24 hours. Every hour after, -$100.

mermaidav: Miss me with your low-balling. I'm not getting out of bed for less than 1K.

Images flash before my eyes. My mind conjures dark sheets twisted around a soft body. I have no idea what she looks like, but my brain conjures smooth, bare legs and an oversized band shirt. Is she tall? Short? Pale? Tan? Thick, like I like? I don't care ultimately—it's her mind and personality I'm attracted to—but I'm still burning to know.

And I desperately want to ask what she wears to bed. I bet I'm right about the band shirt.

SpyderMan: Who said you had to get out of bed?

mermaidav: I can think of much more pleasurable things to do here than data mine.

My blood surges in my ears, a mixture of anticipation and sudden, intense arousal. Is she like so many women, with a bedside table in easy reach, stocked with naughty toys? Fuck, I hope so.

Don't go there, Wesley.

It's not about the money—I've got more than enough that the difference she wants is a drop in the ocean—and part of me would give her whatever she wanted or asked for. But it's about respect, and a well-established power dynamic. *I* make the rules. I don't let anyone dictate terms to me, and I know for a fact that my offer is more than fair. And for her, she needs the money, but that's not why she pushes back. She delights in getting a rise out of people—*me*—and eliciting reactions from an unaffected distance.

Such a fucking brat.

The back and forth is stirring my blood. It's a special kind of rush, and I know she gets off on it, too. My heart pounds hard in my chest, and my cock is starting to feel the results of that increased circulation. My extremities are tingling, muscles filling with an antsy need to move. I clench my hands a few times, watching the veins pop beneath the ink before I reply.

```
SpyderMan: Your prerogative, as always.
mermaidav: You are so lucky I'm bored. I hope
you realize you just created a situation in
which I have no motivation to give you anything
before my time is up. You'll have what you want
in 23 hours and 59 minutes, Sir.
```

The winking face she sends after brings a dark smile to my lips.

I'm not sure what I like better about her response—her flippancy or the transparency about it. As always, the confidence is fucking hot, and the bratty tone of her malicious compliance is right up my street.

She logs off, and I'm left ignoring the return of the empty feeling in my chest that always seems to disappear when I talk to her.

3

MADISON

❖

Good thing I'm totally comfortable with shades of morally gray.

"Yeah, of course, sir. I can have that in your inbox by EOD. Of course. Not a problem. Yes, I'll do it myself—gotta make sure it's done right, right, ya know? Heh, heh. Listen, not sure if you're back this weekend, but I've got a 10 AM tee time, and I thought we—"

I blow out a breath and check my watch as my boss—and I use that term in the loosest sense—Fred cuts himself short and lets the receiver fall from his ear. His chair creaks as he leans forward to hang it up, the movement causing a concerning amount of strain on the single button holding his suit jacket together.

He clears his throat. "That was Craig. Pinsley, obviously. He's at the Safer Cities Through Tech conference. Had to run to lunch with Congressman Adams."

I nod like I bought his attempt to save face, even though we all know what it sounds like when someone hangs up on you halfway through your sentence. But I don't care that Fred's attempt at kissing his boss's ass fell flat, just like I don't really care about the man who's been signing my checks, or the award he's receiving for a bleeding edge cybersecurity prototype AI.

Well, I kind of care about that last one, since this company's products protect me, too. And as a gal with plenty to hide, I love redundant safety measures.

"Right. I read about that in the email blast."

"Yup," he mumbles distractedly as he jiggles the mouse to wake his screen back up.

I've only been in here for 15 minutes, but when he hasn't been taking a call in the middle of our meeting, he's had one of those watery blue eyes glued to our work chat. And, I mean, I know he's got a big job at this company as the project lead for that cybersecurity prototype they're so sure is going to launch them into the Fortune 100—infuriatingly dubbed *Safe-T Keeper*—but... come on, man. It's supposed to be *my* one-on-one.

I can really feel the employee appreciation in the air.

I sigh, loud enough for him to hear, which draws his attention back to me. Instead of any sort of apologetic look or acknowledgment of his disrespect, he looks at me with censure. Like *I'm* the one being rude by expecting his full consideration in the meeting he invited me to.

No one thinks Fred Harvey is more important than Fred Harvey.

Men are the *worst*.

"Anyway... where was I?"

I glance down at my thumbnail, examining the regrowth. It's time to visit my girl, Natasha, for a new set. "You were giving me more responsibilities to reward my good work so far," I remind him with a saccharine smile. "Instead of, like, a title change or a raise."

He picks up on the sarcasm in my tone, and his eyes narrow. They flick up to my hair briefly, and as his mouth tightens around the edges, I fight the urge to smile. I was genuinely expecting a speech about my fresh dye job along the lines of, "Green hair just doesn't project the kind of professionalism we strive for here at SmarTech."

It's 50-50, really: he's either building up to it or he went full chicken-shit and had HR send me a warning so he doesn't have to handle the confrontation.

"Uh... It's only been 90 days—company policy prohibits big changes like that before that critical six-month mark, but we can revisit in a few months and make sure you're on the right trajectory. I assure you, it's not personal; it's business."

That one almost makes me snort. Sure, they can always change your job responsibilities and squeeze more out of you, but they can't adjust pay or title accordingly. Corporate America bullshit. I can't wait to leave this place in the fucking dust.

"Anyway, I hope you're excited about this opportunity. Hector has all the details, and your training starts next Monday. Other than that, we love the work you've been doing and expect to continue to see great things. You've got a ton of potential," he assures me, the praise somewhat undercut by the fact that he's already looking at the work chat again when he says it. "That was really all I had for our one-on-one. Do you have any questions for me?"

My phone pings, notifying me that my fix is live. Finally. A shiver of a thrill shoots up my spine, and I laugh to myself. This timing is perfect—I love a dramatic exit. "Well, this meeting could have been an email. Or, like, a kiss on the forehead." I consider what I'm about to say next, then add, "Maybe a fistfight."

He laughs, but it's a staccato, barking noise, like he's too confused to know what else to do. "Maddy—"

That nickname is nails on a chalkboard. "Fredward," I cut in, matching his tone.

That stops him in his tracks, and the laughter abruptly dies on his lips, shriveling his smile with it. "What? That's not... Fred isn't short for... My full name is Frederick."

"I quit, Frederick."

Nothing turns a middle-aged guy in a suit into a blustering old white man like hitting him with the unexpected resignation. Instantly, he goes from cool and in-control to thrown off and scrambling. "W-what? Are you serious?"

"You get a lot of people quitting on you as a joke?" I challenge.

"No, but you... I mean, just like that?" he sputters. "Is this because of the raise and promotion thing? 'Cause maybe I could talk to HR..."

"So, now it's a possibility before that *critical six-month mark?*" I chuckle at his wide-eyed expression. "No, thanks. I'm in a really good place about this decision—emotionally, spiritually, and as soon as I get the hell out of here, physically."

"What about your career?"

"What about it?" I ask, tilting my head. "You think I want to sit in an office and sell this company the best years of my life? Yeah, no thanks."

"Why did you take this job?" he demands, his tone effortlessly swinging back to accusatory.

I resist the urge to kick back and put my feet up on his desk, like a villain revealing my master plan. Unfortunately, I don't think my short legs would reach. Story of my life.

"I've been using this company's fine software to encrypt my data since I was 16. One of several layered solutions, obviously. But that last big update introduced a bug with some pretty serious—if esoteric—security risks. It was killing me. So, I fixed it."

"You're kidding," he says, his voice flat. "You applied for a job at SmarTech just to fix a bug? That's... ridiculous, Madison. Insane. Why didn't you call customer service?"

"You'd think that would be easier, wouldn't you?" I ask rhetorically, wagging my finger. "And in my defense, I did try. But in the three times I called, I was on hold with customer service for a combined total of nine hours, and no one could even find the problem to fix. So... I decided to take a look at your hiring page to see how easy it would be to just get in here and do it myself. Anyway, now that it's fixed, I don't really see a reason to stay."

I've already been here way longer than I wanted to be. The resume I made up just for this job only earned me a low-level desk in data entry. I toiled away there for a month and a half until I showed the right person a few tricks that convinced him I could handle more complex projects. Then, in true large-company fashion, the request for access had to make it through three redundant levels of management approval, which took another month. Then, I had to wait for IT to upgrade my machine to something more powerful, and get me all set up with account access and passcodes...

Honestly, it was a whole thing. But once I was finally in, finding the bug and implementing the fix took me about three days.

Well, two and a half days. More than enough time to scrape and copy a bunch of confidential files to my secret, smuggled-in portable drive.

"Don't be rash. There are plenty of good reasons to stay. I wasn't kidding—you've got so much potential. You could go far here," he says, like I should take it as a compliment. Like he *means* it as a compliment.

"Potential to do... what, exactly? Put more money in Craig Pinsley's pocket while he cuts everyone's bonuses?" I snort. "Pass."

When I rise, he stands, too. He towers over me, even at his painfully average height. "Madison, wait! I just told Craig I'd have him those reports you're working on by the end of the day," Fred admits.

It's the first time he's revealing his hand instead of trying to frame it like he has my best interest in mind. He wasn't even going to tell me it was *my* work he was taking credit for on the phone right in front of me.

The audacity is truly astounding. Breathtaking, almost.

To my credit, I don't scoff, or even roll my eyes. Someone nominate me for sainthood. "Good luck with that one, Fred."

"The team needs you, especially with the Safe-T Keeper product launch around the corner. We're drowning since Erica quit."

"Hmm... That's a tough one. But—hear me out—maybe you should consider hiring someone to replace her instead of pushing her work to everyone else to save on her salary. I know it's a wild concept." His jaw falls as I hit him with his own signature finger-guns. "I'll see myself out. Should I leave my badge with security?"

Looking completely shell-shocked, he falls back into his leather office chair, which rolls back a few inches from the momentum and throws him off balance. "Uh, yeah, with security."

"All right, then. It's been... um... fun?"

"What the fuck just happened?" he mutters to himself.

I almost feel sorry for Fred. He's a tool, but he's not the worst boss I've ever had. At least he wasn't sexually harassing his assistant, like the last asshole I worked for.

I'm almost at the door when I hear a faint, almost shocked, "Madison?"

I whirl at the sound of my name but find him staring at his phone in his hand. My movement catches his eye, and he glances up at me, brows raised. "Oh... never mind," he says, tucking it away, his tone oddly bright. He tries to tamp down on a smile, like he's seen something funny and he doesn't want to share the joke. It's fucking creepy.

"You take care," he says.

Right.

Knowing I was biding my time here, I didn't bother to decorate my cubicle. All I need is my sweater and my purse, and I'm on my way towards security. The guard at the desk is expecting me, and has the metal detector wand at the ready. It's all part of the sudden-departure protocol to ensure I'm not stealing company property. Because I've departed suddenly and stolen company property so many times now, I'm ready. Most of these guys are retired cops or wannabes who couldn't hack it at the academy. They mostly check to make sure you're not stealing office supplies—intellectual property is above their pay grade. They never think to check the cute pink panda on my keychain, which can actually hold 128 GB of data.

My breath catches as he glances at my keyring, but he waves me off with a scowl. When I get to my car, I nearly collapse into the driver's seat.

What a rush! I pulled it off. I never have to see or come back to this godforsaken building ever again.

SmarTech, my great white whale. I'd have loved to hack them properly, but I know my limitations. To be fair, I did want that security risk closed for my own reasons—it was a happy coincidence that I could kill two birds with one stone. Because now I've got the intel I need for my next payout from my *tío*, and some bonus data to sift through. I'll bet some of the rich, powerful corporations and CEOs who depend on SmarTech tools have some naughty, nasty secrets.

As soon as the door of my apartment shuts behind me, I'm greeted by a cat that's starving to death. He screams at me; in true cat fashion, it's somehow both urgent and aloof.

"Hey SB, how you livin'? Same, same," I tell him, working the panda USB drive off the ring, then tossing my keys into the brightly painted dish by the door.

I feed my fur-child, feed myself, and head back to my room, where my L-shaped desk occupies about half the space. I stick the ass end of the panda drive into the port and jiggle the mouse to start the download.

Since I'm still logged into my favorite IRC, I pull up the window and grin as I see my favorite nerd online—one of the moderators of one of the forums I use to fence my stolen intel. *SpyderMan.*

On the whole, I don't much like people, and I don't have a lot of respect for men—they tend to expect it without earning it, and fuck that shit. Like Fredward. And Todd. But SpyderMan isn't like that. He's the only guy I ever actually *want* to talk to. A top-tier hacker in his own right, he's smart and resourceful and funny... and I can get behind what I *suspect* he's doing with whoever he reports to.

I'm a hacker. I'm super into pattern recognition. SpyderMan's pattern has been pretty clear since the beginning. It's sporadic and—until recently—geographically widespread, but his targets are known gang leaders, corrupt low-level politicians, sexually predatory billionaires and healthcare CEOs happily taking six-figure bonuses while their companies reject claims from cancer patients and the physically disabled. Real scum of the earth.

And while it's not like every job he gives me is about some high-profile asshole, lots of them are. Some of those assholes disappeared or ended up in jail after I sold SpyderMan the secrets I've collected and hoarded through the years.

I never ask why he wants the intel because that's not really how this works—I choose to take the jobs, and the "mind your fucking business" part is implied. But I like to think he's taking out the trash. I wish I could.

I know I'm probably deluding myself. He's probably some criminal or mob boss, or working for one, using what I give him to blackmail and destroy lives—potentially even killing them. At best, I'm in the pocket of some up-and-coming FBI agent using my hard work to get ahead in his career. Luckily, my identity is buried, and I take precautions against being found by even the biggest brother: the US government.

I'm old enough to know and jaded enough to believe that nothing in our fucked-up system is black and white... and I know stealing data and selling it isn't exactly honorable. But if these people are on the evil side of the spectrum, and my actions help bring them to some kind of justice, doesn't the karma kind of cancel out?

Good thing I'm totally comfortable with shades of morally gray. And I can mind all of my own fucking business for the right price.

But it's not just the promise of bitcoin or satisfying my overzealous sense of right and wrong that brings me back to the IRC every day... because the little butterflies in my stomach dance around as I click on his name, then go into a fluttering frenzy when he messages me first.

`SpyderMan: Was just thinking about you`

```
mermaidav: Of course you were. I'm your
```
favorite distraction.
```
SpyderMan: You have no idea. Did you finish
```
your homework?

Aaand I'm already squirming in my seat as I try to shake off the sudden student-teacher roleplaying scenario short-circuiting my brain. That's got to be a record—horny in 10 words or less. I pull my lower lip between my teeth and bite down on the smile.
```
mermaidav: Moi? Hmm… Can you narrow it down?
SpyderMan: How you going with Dune?
```

I nearly roll my eyes. This man and his sci-fi. He's been trying to find something I like in his favorite genre for months now. Love the dedication, and that he's never butthurt when I tell him what I really think.
```
mermaidav: Initial thoughts… main character
is named Paul? Really? I'm supposed to take
him seriously as a fantasy hero with a generic
white guy name?
SpyderMan: Luckily my name is not Paul and I
take no offense.
```

I grin. Another to mark off the running list. From other conversations, I also know his name isn't Mark or Quentin. That only leaves, like, a million more possibilities.
```
mermaidav: I'll be honest—not sure I'm going
to finish this one either.
SpyderMan: Not even the giant sand worms
could tempt you?
mermaidav: Wiener-adjacent, I'll give you
that much, but not quite what I had in mind.
```

Excitement zings through me as I wait for his reply. He sends a laughing response, and I grin. People type "lol" with a straight face all the time, but I like to think that he really did laugh out loud. I wonder what his laugh sounds like. Is it restrained? Low and grumbly, in that way that makes me all shivery? Does he actually get tears in his eyes, or is he one of those guys who says "that's so funny" without actually laughing?

Dios, I hope not.

SpyderMan: There's just no pleasing you, is there?

I bite my lip, fingers hovering over the keys as I think of and discard a dozen provocative responses ranging from innocuous to outright horny. I settle somewhere in the middle.

mermaidav: Where's the fun in being easy to please? I like a man who's willing to work for it.

SpyderMan: I do enjoy a challenge.

mermaidav: That must be why you made such quick work of the code for patching that vulnerability. Thanks again for your help.

SpyderMan: Happy to do it. I'd say you owe me one, but I'm not even sure who owes whom anymore.

I roll my eyes. *Whom.* This Shakespearean fucker. I bet he's British. He talks like he's British. He says things like *brilliant* and *trousers* and spells gray with an "e." He called the stove a hob once—I had to look that one up.

mermaidav: Pretty sure it's like 10:1 in me owing you favors now.

Generally speaking, I don't like the feeling of being in someone's debt. And frankly, asking someone with SpyderMan's skillset to help write the fix elegant enough to patch SmarTech's vulnerability without being noticed felt a bit like asking Einstein for help with my geometry homework. But he always says yes, he's never *actually* asked for anything in return, and he gives my requests such complete, immediate focus that it makes me feel like a priority—like I'm his first priority.

It's... nice.

SpyderMan: Pretty sure you're right. But I'm saving my tickets for the big prize. Something I really want.

My heart instantly kicks me right in the sternum at what is probably innocuous, but feels like a blatant sexual innuendo because I want it to be. I consider my next message, drumming my fingers on the composite desk, but he beats me to it.

mermaidav: like...

SpyderMan: Let's start with the data sort

Oh, right. The job he gave me. The foundation of our relationship. My heart sinks, then lifts again in the span of a single beat at the thought of my payout. I sort through my open windows and drag a file into the chat box for him to decrypt.

mermaidav: I feel like I should make you wait since I've still got a few hours, but I'm feeling generous. And if you are too, I wouldn't say no to a tip.

The notification comes through from my banking app a few seconds later, and I grin as I see a hefty tip, with the note *Earned in bed*. I tell myself it's not charity that made him give in to my pricing demands, but respect for a consistent, quick turnaround. And maybe to keep me coming back for more.

Or... maybe—just maybe—he's even got a little bit of a crush on me, too...

mermaidav: Cute. Being in bed, easy money, a puzzle to solve... add in winning an argument and tacos, and you've got my top 5 favorite things.

```
SpyderMan: Not a bad top 5, though I'd have
thought being praised ranked higher on the
list.
```

I bite my lip. Okay, new fantasy unlocked—hearing a deep, British voice calling me a *good girl.*

```
mermaidav: who doesn't like praise?
```
```
SpyderMan: some prefer degradation.
```

Okay, amend that fantasy... a deep, British voice calling me a *good little whore.*

Dios, is it hot in here, or is that just me?

I consider my next message, drumming my nails against the composite desktop, but can't get it typed out fast enough before he goes inactive. He does that sometimes—disappears mid-conversation without explanation or apology. We've been talking regularly for around two years at this point, so I'm used to it, but I'm curious... as well as really fucking irrationally jealous.

Is it an interruption, like a significant other walking in? Does he have kids? Roommates? A willing harem of women in the cult he formed?

Not that it matters. The anonymity that keeps both of us safe is the very thing keeping us apart. Do I think I could trust SpyderMan with my real identity? Maybe... When you engage in illegal activity on the internet, it's hard to trust anyone enough to cross that line into the real world. The only thing that keeps me from getting caught is the fact that no one can connect my online persona to my real identity. Any person who knows becomes a risk or possibly a threat.

So, no. Meeting IRL probably isn't in the cards for us. Which sucks.

But whenever I get bummed about the fact that SpyderMan and I will probably never actually meet in person, I console myself with the fact that what we have is easy the way it is. Honestly, it's the best relationship with a man I've ever had, in spite of—because of?—the fact that I don't know anything about him. I'm equally as curious about who he really is as I am worried about doing something that puts what we have at risk. Because... what if he's actually a 13-year-old prodigy, or someone's racist old Pee Paw?

Okay, I don't really think he's either of those things... It just sucks when you kind of hate most guys, and the only guy you don't hate is the only one you can't have.

Plus, I really, really want to know what he looks like.

And maybe I want to see his wiener, too.

4

WESLEY

We just... get each other.

By the time I call it quits for the day, my eyes are nearly too bleary to drive, but I make it to the house and pull the Bugs-B-Gon van in the bay next to my bike. Usually I'd park such a distinct vehicle at one of the warehouses we own, far from the prying eyes of nosy neighbors, but after over 24 hours in that blasted surveillance van, I desperately need sleep, food, a workout, and a shower. Not necessarily in that order.

The "house" where my teammates and I have set up shop is really more of a compound. Nestled into one of the first developed areas as the city crept outward, we lucked into a property a previous owner had made of several lots combined into one. Built on 11 acres, it's got a main house with all the amenities and a few auxiliary buildings, all set back from the road behind an old wood grove for as much privacy as one could hope for on the outskirts of a city.

The iron fence that completely surrounds the property has a gate with digital codes and fingerprint access, and the feed from the security cameras streams directly to all our phones, filtered through a program that alerts us to unexpected movement. If someone tried to go over, the cameras would catch it. If someone tried to go under, the perimeter of pressure plates would notify us.

When you kill people for money, it tends to make you a target, yourself, so we all take safety seriously.

I spy Dimitri's SUV, Mac's nondescript blue sedan, and Eleanor's zippy Mini Cooper on the other end of the long garage. Nicole doesn't have a car—she's still under house arrest until we completely resolve some *issues* with the remaining members of the Volkevich *Bratva*.

Gang's all here, then.

The foyer is dark, since Dimitri has begun daily sweeps of the house, turning off lights and lowering the thermostats in every room the girls have left, muttering to himself about wasteful Americans. But I know Eleanor and Nicole like the prisms of light cast by the intricate chandelier that hangs between the staircases. It's flashy and somewhat gauche, and it makes me smile, too. So, I flick it on as I hang my jacket in the closet in the entryway.

It almost always smells good on the first floor of this house with Eleanor in residence. And though she's nowhere to be seen in the sparkling clean kitchen, there's still an incredible, savory scent wafting from the 12 neatly stacked black containers cooling on the center island. My stomach growls—how long has it been since I filled it with anything other than caffeine and B-vitamins?—but eating can wait. I'll grab a meal on my way back to my office after the debrief with my team.

I'm betting after patching Dimitri up and some sharp words, Nicole put him straight to bed to recover comfortably. I'm also betting Dimitri's awake now, and Mac is already running his mouth to an irritated but captive audience.

I cross the stone patio and knock at the door of what was once the most pointlessly well-appointed pool house. The patient is on his stomach, laid out on the massive king bed that dominates the entire right wall, with a pillow propping up his hips, and a thick layer of padding creating some additional bulk around his left arse cheek in a thoroughly comical image.

Mac is perched on the arm of the sofa, arms crossed, clearly exhausted from his night's work, with dark circles under his eyes and a slight slump to his posture. He also missed some flecks of blood on his forearms when he was cleaning up. He's lucky he didn't get pulled over on his drive back.

Predictably, though, I was right about the *running his mouth* part.

"Eh, doesn't look so bad," he's saying with a chuckle as I gently close the door behind me. "Just another scar for the collection, eh, Big D? It'll match your face. Hey, you love being literal—you ever hear that phrase *butt-ugly*?"

I snort. "He's only saying that because he's out of your arm's reach."

"You bet your ass, I am."

Dimitri sighs instead of rising to the bait, an excellent display of restraint. But he's clearly uncomfortable with more than just the puns, and he shifts on the pillow, trying to roll up to see me better, but wincing and falling back into place. "This is so undignified," he huffs.

I move around the bed so Dimitri doesn't have to strain to see me. "What *is* the recovery time for bruised pride?" I ask, getting in a subtler jab of my own.

Dimitri's jaw clenches, but he speaks with a softness he reserves for the mention of his personal nurse. "She will not let me rise except to take a piss for another several days, and then I will be using those to move around until the threat of tearing and infection is past." He gestures to a pair of crutches leaning against the far wall.

I gape. "Where the hell did those come from? They look about six inches too short for you."

He waves his hand dismissively. Yeah, I'll be rush-ordering something better after a bit of research—one of those knee scooters ought to help his mobility.

"Enough of this. Did he talk?"

Knowing the question is directed at him, Mac's smile dissolves into a grim expression and he nods. "He admitted to killing Alfano, but that's about all I got. I may have hit him a bit too hard," he admits with a chagrined wince. "A couple hours in, he passed out and I couldn't wake him back up, so I made the call."

"Brain hemorrhage," Dimitri assumes with a grave, but clinical air.

"Probably," Mac agrees.

"A simple mistake for someone unaccustomed to the work. I should have been there," Dimitri grumbles.

"Yeah, I wish you had been," Mac shoots back, though it's not defensive. He rubs the back of his neck as he shakes his head. "I don't have the stomach for that shit."

There's a reason he shoots to kill from 500 yards, just as there's a reason I primarily support from behind my screens. It's not easy to look someone in the eye as you take their life. I don't know how Dimitri does it, and I can't say I particularly care to.

Dimitri catches Mac's haunted expression and his brows snap down even lower, deepening the crease of the scar through his face. "As in anything, practice is the only way to improve—but this is my role on our team; it should not have fallen to you. Do not beat yourself off."

Mac snorts. "Beat myself *up*?"

"That is what I said."

Mac and I exchange grins—mine, pure amusement and his, tinged with relief. I know from personal experience how it feels to be absolved of blame by Dimitri's gruff practicality. I cross my arms, tapping at my bicep with a thumb. "I'll get to work on an ID, then. It would be good to know who he was working for."

"That is unnecessary. I found him."

"What? How?" Mac gapes.

Dimitri taps a tablet next to him, briefly waking the screen. "Wesley sent me the footage. I shot at the screen as he ran from the house and cross-referenced his photo using Wesley's files." There's a beat of silence, and my jaw falls slack. Dimitri stares back at me, eyes narrowing. "What?"

"I... didn't know you knew how to use the shared drive," I say, unable to keep the surprise from my voice.

He lifts a brow, unimpressed. "You gave me a password and showed me how."

"I did," I agree, feeling my head bob. "But that was ages ago, and this is the first time you've used it."

"Important information should not be treated thoughtlessly," he scoffs dismissively. "I do not like them, but I am not *allergic* to computers."

"Was that a *joke*? Did Nicole give him morphine?" Mac interjects.

"Of course she did; I was shot," Dimitri says, anger lacing his tone. "Can we get back to the job? I am trying to tell you that I found his mugshot in the Volkevich files."

That sobers us up right quick.

"Fuuuuck," Mac groans.

Silently, I agree. We offed the head of that *Bratva* a few months ago, stole the crime family's fortune and legacy and hid it away, but cleaning up the rest of the mess has proven to be a never-ending endeavor. Mac took out as many as he could with his rifle, and Dimitri single-handedly killed nearly a dozen while saving Nicole from a lunatic with an inferiority complex, but the rest scattered into the wind. We've been picking them off whenever we can find them, but it's like trying to stop up a leak in a dam—they just keep coming. They want their money, they're out for blood and the only ones left are smart and careful.

In a city the size of Ulysses, there are only so many distinct Russian crime families, so of course it was a possibility that the man who killed Alfano was from the same *Bratva* whose leader we killed. Still, coincidences are always suspicious in our line of work.

"You sure?" I ask, my stomach dropping.

"Confirm as you always do, but yes, I am certain," Dimitri sighs.

"What the fuck was a Volkevich doing in Mexican drug cartel territory?" Mac voices what we're all thinking. "You think it might have been a business relationship? *Bratvas* sell drugs sometimes, and they gotta come from somewhere, right?"

Dimitri's scowl deepens further. "They would not work together."

"A dispute, then? For territory?" I suggest.

"Possibly," Dimitri allows. "Though, disputes such as those are usually settled in the field, not resolved by assassinating the leader of the gang."

"A connection is exactly what I've been hoping for in my search for information about the General," I say thoughtfully. It still feels odd to share this information that I've been keeping so close to my chest for so long. It makes me rethink every word—trying to make sure I'm not giving away more than I mean to or should.

Mac audibly shifts in his seat. "Um... Now that you mention it, something the Russian said before he up and died on me makes a bit more sense now."

"Go on," I prompt when he hesitates. "The suspense is killing me. Less effectively than your interrogation tactics, thankfully."

He shoots me an unimpressed look at my joke. "I think the guy might have said Felix's name."

Dimitri goes rigid. "You are sure?"

Expression serious, Mac shakes his head. "He was babbling pretty incoherently in Russian at that point, and I'm not as fluent as I'd like to be. I *think* he said Felix. Are there any Russian words that sound like that?"

"Of course there are," Dimitri dismisses.

"Felix *was* working with Kyle Volkevich," I say. "You're thinking maybe he still has contact with them?"

Mac shrugs. "It's a possibility, right? I know I'm jumping to all kinds of conclusions, but what if he sent the Russian in there because he knew we were after Alfano, and he knew we'd show up? He's got ears and eyes everywhere, and he knows my face—he could pretty easily have me followed and figure out we were after Alfano."

Fuck. That complicates things. "You think he sent the Russian to kill Dimitri?"

Dimitri growls his displeasure. We all know he's itching to get his knife in there and settle that debt—this is fuel for that fire.

With a deep sigh, Mac reaches up and tugs at his hair. "That, or he was trying to scoop the hit out from under us—put our relationship with the General at risk or some shit. Force my hand into doing what he wants."

From what I understand of Felix, it's possible. He's smart and careful—he'd manipulate the situation to his advantage and keep his hands clean while doing it.

"Well, it's a possible new lead if nothing else," I say. "Add it to the growing list of things to look into. Mac, you keep an eye out for tails or more Russians when you head back to Alfano's. Dimitri, you dig deeper into the surveillance footage."

"Agreed."

"I'll get to work on Alfano's laptop and see if I can find anything about a history with the Volkevich *Bratva*."

Mac rubs his eyes harshly. "I need to shower and grab some sleep, then I'll get back over to Alfano's. Someone's going to find the body soon. Wes and I cleaned up, but I want to be sure they don't find any of your DNA we might have missed."

"Good," Dimitri nods, but there's a tightness around his eyes. For a bloke who's all about that heart-pounding action, the impotence of forced tummy time like an infant must be chafing him raw. He hates not being able to take the lead—and I'm sure that the mention of Felix's involvement has prompted a fresh wave of anger that he can't do anything but stew in until he's healed.

"Glad to see you're as unbreakable as ever. You'll be back out there with us in no time, I'm sure." I flash Dimitri a grin, and he nods back in gratitude.

"Thank you, my friend."

"Hey, I'm glad you're okay too, Big D," Mac interjects, pushing up from his seat to follow me out the door. "Look, all jokes aside, I just want to say thanks," he adds, sounding somehow both sincere and like he's ramping up to something that's going to get his arse kicked as soon as Dimitri becomes a bit more mobile.

Dimitri just scowls, rocking back on his pillow to see Mac's face, like he can sense the other shoe about to be dropped as well.

"From the *bottom* of my heart. I mean, your ass really took a pounding... you really took one for the team."

Dimitri makes a dismissive noise.

"Don't think he likes being the butt of the joke," I muse loud enough for Dimitri to hear, grinning over at Mac as we exit the pool house.

"You know, I was going to use that one, but it felt a bit too easy—like going in through the back door."

"*Kozye yaichko,*" Dimitri calls after us, though it's unclear which of us is the goat testicle this time.

Still turning over this new information, I grab my lunch, salute Mac on his way up the stairs, and head for my office. Stepping through the threshold into the nerve center of our operation is like being able to take in my first deep breath all day.

Dimitri wouldn't dare fiddle with the thermostat in here, but the room sits consistently around two degrees warmer than the rest of the house because I've filled it with enough computing power that the system can't keep up. I don't mind—I like it warm. It's never completely dark, either, due to the blinking lights of dozens of single-board computers. The scent of ozone from electricity consumption is as familiar as it is comforting.

The entire space is comforting, in fact. It's decorated all in warm tones, with a soft rug, light-blocking curtains, and a plush sofa where I sometimes catch a nap. Sleep doesn't come easily to me and I'm usually in front of the screens later than I ought to be, so there's also a top-of-the-line office chair that's perfectly formed to my body and a mini fridge kept well stocked with as much on-demand energy as a bloke could want.

I retrieve a cold can and crack it before sitting at my desk. It takes a password, a secondary password, a multifactor authentication, and a custom-built fingerprint scanner in my mouse to unlock my private screens. When I've gone through the motions, I see that there's a message from *her* in the IRC. I shouldn't—I have a million other things to do—but like an addict, I can't resist. Taking a sip, I open the window.

```
mermaidav: I have this fantasy…
```

The liquid slides down the wrong hole. I cough, wiping my lips, and place the can securely beyond the keyboard so I don't knock it with my elbow in my haste to get my message out.

```
SpyderMan: Involving a handsome spymaster,
no doubt.
```

```
mermaidav: lol how'd you know? Actually, this
time I was being a bit more philosophical. I
have this fantasy about having no responsibil-
ities. No one to answer to, no one to show up
for…
```

A fairly common fantasy these days, especially for those bearing extra responsibilities. Not for the first time, I wonder who she has in her life. And, more jealously, if there's some twat out there adding weight instead of lifting it.

If she were *mine*… I'd treasure no possession more.

Fuck. I hate this feeling. I'd give *anything* to know more about her. I've almost offered it, in fact. I've had a draft saved in my email for months now addressed to Vinnie, the guy who vouched for her months ago. It's an exorbitant seven-figure bribe in exchange for information about her identity and his silence. I've almost sent it half a dozen times.

But that's not how this works. She deserves her anonymity—it's an unequivocal promise I've made to my spiders, an implied contract with everyone who agrees to sell me secrets. One of my iron-clad rules.

Still, I can't quite bring myself to delete the draft.

SpyderMan: What would you do?

mermaidav: Don't laugh.

SpyderMan: I wouldn't dare.

mermaidav: Well, I'm 50-50 on disappearing into the woods to become a forest witch who befriends crows and inspires an equal amount of respect and fear in the locals… Or… I kind of want to have, like, a homestead. Be self-sufficient. Maybe get some chickens and goats, maybe start a cat rescue.

SpyderMan: Hmm… I doubt the woods have fiber optic internet.

mermaidav: Ha! Good call. I'd sacrifice a lot for my dreams, but I draw the line at symmetrical upload/download speeds.

Warmth blooms in my chest, spreading outward as I shake my head with a grin. We just… get each other. She gets me—everything from her humor to her need to be wired in.

SpyderMan: Precisely. I say, go for the homestead.

mermaidav: See, this is why I like you. You don't tear down my dreams. Love a man who can roll with the vibe.

SpyderMan: So what I'm hearing is, I'm the man of your dreams.

mermaidav: Lol! You're too fun to flirt with. You're going to ruin me for anyone else, you know that?

I have to swallow a sudden thickness in my throat as my blood pounds southward. I don't even know what she looks like, but she gets me going like no one I've ever known. What I wouldn't give to ruin her, because I'm fairly certain she'd ruin me right back.

SpyderMan: I'm counting on it.

mermaidav: Well... On that note, I have to go… Unless you've got something for me?

SpyderMan: Not tonight. Tomorrow maybe.

SpyderMan: If you're good

A little thrill shoots through me as I type it—a delicate dance around the boundaries of our online friendship. *Make me,* I want her to type back. Obviously, that's not the nature of our relationship, but every once in a while I catch sight of another side of her that appeals to another side of me. So I push, hoping it'll peek through.

mermaidav: If I'm good? I'm sorry, Sir, but you seem to have mistaken me for some other mermaid.

I throw my head back and laugh.

She logs off. Before I do the same so I can focus, I download our conversation and add it to the private folder buried deep in my personal drive. There, it joins every other conversation we've ever had and the bits and bobs I've saved from the jobs she's done—pieces of code that are truly artistic or have private jokes baked in. Perhaps it's a tad pathetic on my part, but when it's very late and she's not online to keep me company, sometimes I scroll through our old conversations in a poor attempt to relive the way she makes me feel.

My machine dings with the special sound I've programmed in to alert me to a very specific kind of message. An email from the General. That means the next batch of hits is in, and it's something of a relief. The time between emails was longer than usual, making me antsy. The long-cold trails of our previous hits have become a dead end, so with a fresh batch of names, the odds of learning something about the identity of our mysterious handler are much higher.

I scan the short list of names—only three this time—and forward immediately to Mac and Dimitri, as per my promise. Jeremy Umberlee, Louis Whitcomb, and Madison Cooper.

Time to start my digging. I crack my knuckles, open a fresh can of energy and a new bag of crisps, and settle into search mode.

5

WESLEY

Perhaps having someone to come home to changes one's perspective more than I realized.

Tightening the straps of my backpack, I head down the hallway towards the kitchen. Yet again, Eleanor is nowhere to be seen, but I know she's been here recently because Mac is sitting at the large glass-top table that occupies the entire right wall next to the windows, shoveling in some kind of casserole. Unfortunate that I keep missing her—it feels like it's been weeks since we've shared a bottle of champagne over a superfluously gruesome Japanese horror film.

If I'm surprised to see Dimitri up, it's only for about half a second. He's never been one to sit idly, even with a gunshot wound to nurse, though if he rips a stitch there will be hell to pay when the actual nurse finds out. At least he's using the knee scooter I ordered rush delivery, though it squeaks under the massive weight of his bulk as it moves. There also appears to be a bit of a learning curve.

Dimitri grabs both ends of the wide handlebar and attempts to maneuver around the large marble island to make room for me to get by, only to clip the wheel on the corner. He lets loose a stream of grumbling curses directed at the chair's lack of agility.

I place my backpack gently on a stool, then make a beeline for the dish on the hob that smells like cheese and happiness. My stomach growls as I load up my plate, and I make a face at the green bits poking out. "Does she have to put the broccoli *inside*?"

"You know who made that request," Mac laughs, eyes cutting towards our most health-conscious teammate.

"Fiber is good for you," Dimitri remarks distractedly, jerking the handle and then wincing when the whole thing shifts him off balance and he has to tense his muscles to keep his feet.

"I'm not daft; I know it's one of my five a day, and all that. Let's skip the lecture on how to grow up big and strong, shall we?"

Dimitri makes a humming noise and raises a brow in my direction. "I do not know how it is that you maintain your muscle mass with your abysmal diet."

"Good genes. The best, arguably." That earns me a snort from Mac. "Why does someone who isn't even going to eat it get a vote?"

"Speaking of this, where is what I requested?"

"Probably in the pot with the post-it on top that says 'Steamed Veg for Dimitri,'" I suggest, crumpling the yellow square into a small ball and tossing it his way. It doesn't have enough weight to get any real distance and falls onto the stretch of counter between us. I finish loading up my plate and slide onto one of the tall stools at the counter. Steam billows from the tidy pile, so I blow on it before taking a bite. It's still too hot to eat, but I'm too hungry to be patient.

Mac all but growls as he shovels in a mouthful. "I don't know why y'all can't just let my girl do her thing, why everyone's gotta request something special. Everything she makes is too good for you ungrateful assholes anyway."

Dimitri sniffs. "It is no slight to her ability. I prefer to make my own dietary choices."

"He just doesn't like that she makes something special for you," I point out to Dimitri, who nods knowingly.

Mac's fork clangs against his plate as he tosses it with some force, and he glares at me. "Damn straight, I don't. She's working her ass off every day, building her business and getting her name out there, then she comes home and makes us all something amazing, but it's not good enough for you, so she has to work even harder to think about your little *dietary choices* and make you something different."

Dimitri meets Mac's outburst with a cool expression, crossing his arms over his chest so biceps the size of my head pull against the fabric of his plain t-shirt. It's a pose that most would assume was deliberately meant to intimidate, but his voice is calm. "Has she complained?"

Mac's lips purse unhappily, turning down at the corners as he begrudgingly admits, "Of course fucking not. She wouldn't." He shoves another resentful bite into his mouth.

Dimitri nods in satisfaction. "Just as Nicole does not complain when you ask her to look at your moles for cancer. Because she is part of this team."

At that, Mac leans forward onto his elbows and points the tines of his fork at Dimitri. "Don't you dare tell her that. After what she's been through, I promised I'd keep her as far away from the action as possible."

Dimitri scoffs, though I can see the skin over his knuckles flash white as his hands clench into fists. He doesn't like thinking about Eleanor's brush with death because it reminds him of Nicole's.

"Your protective instincts cloud your reason. Obviously, I am not suggesting we put a gun in her hand and start her on the front line. She is far too soft and weak; and she is a terrible liar." He gestures to the kitchen around us. "Her contribution is done in here. It is important, and she takes her job seriously—that is why she makes separate meals for me and Nicole. She does not need you to fight unnecessary battles for her when she is doing her job. You make her little."

"Belittle her," I correct, scraping one of the last bites off my plate.

"That is what I said," Dimitri dismisses.

"Fine," Mac huffs, shoving another too-large bite into his mouth, then tucking it against his cheek to say, "As long as it's just the basic stuff. Last time she spent two hours making those stupid dumpling things you like, and we missed our show. And I've been out on surveillance nonstop, and it's been too fucking long since we... I'm pent up, you feel me?"

Dimitri and I exchange a look, and I roll my eyes. "Pent up already after a week and a half? Lucky sod."

Mac blows out a long breath and rubs his eyes. "Sorry, I'm just... antsy or some shit. Pissed someone got to Alfano first and worried about everything with the General. And I guess I'm missing my girl."

"It is part of the job," Dimitri replies, though there's an edge to his voice that snags my attention.

He's said those same words before—a common admonishment when we veer off topic, as we so often do—but this time his tone is almost... conciliatory. Dimitri understands the source of Mac's distraction now, and for the first time I can really remember, he's sympathetic to it instead of irritated by it.

Perhaps having someone to come home to changes one's perspective more than I realized.

Dimitri turns back to me. "You are heading out?"

Pushing my empty plate away, I sit back in my chair and lay a hand on my happy stomach. "You got the email I forwarded from the General? Figured I'd start recon on the next potential target."

"*Da*. The email was very... brief. Is that the usual missive—with minimal information like that?"

"Yep. It's only ever a list of names, a short description, and reward values."

He strokes his chin thoughtfully. "No indication of urgency? No requested date for completion?"

"Not that I've ever seen."

When Dimitri's scowl deepens, Mac glances at me, then asks, "Is that normal?"

Dimitri shrugs. "Not much about our handler is normal."

My brows shoot up—he's never voiced that particular opinion before. "Oh? How so?"

"We may choose our targets, but we are not bidding for jobs? And there is no deadline?" he snorts, like the very idea is ridiculous.

Mac scratches at the stubble on his jawline thoughtfully. "You think this means the General is new to this? We've only been working for him for what, four years now?"

"New... or unconventional, perhaps. Like no handler I have known."

"Or he just doesn't care who gets it done," I interject. "I've been reviewing our old jobs, like we talked about. Nearly every person whose name we've been sent is dead or missing-presumed-dead, even if we didn't take the job. Seems like if we don't take it, the General sends it to someone else."

Mac's eyes flash. "We're not the only hitmen on his payroll."

I nod. "A harrowing thought."

There's a beat of tense silence, then Mac hunches forward and shoves another bite into his mouth. He chews, then tucks it against his cheek to ask, "You find anything else?"

"Well, this batch is different," I say carefully. I don't like to make assumptions too early because often we only find out the sordid details once we really start digging into the person. But on the surface, these three aren't much like the lowlifes we usually get, and it's leaving a bitter taste in my mouth. "I've only just started collecting information, but it's not drug lords and black market dealers; it's... Jeremy Umberlee is a whistleblower, and Louis Whitcomb is a tech journalist."

Dimitri winces. As a Russian, he knows the token target of a dictator regime when he hears one. People who tell the truth are often silenced by those whose power is threatened by it. "And the other name? Madison Cooper?"

"As far as I can tell, she's a streamer—a content creator. At least, that's what the IRS thinks she does. I'll find out soon enough. I figured I'd start with her, since she's local. Umberlee is in Chicago, and Whitcomb is in New York."

Mac frowns. "Wait, *you're* going out? Like, *alone*? You want me to grab my stuff and come with?"

I shake my head. "If Felix is following you, it's best if I handle this alone. I'm an unknown to him. Unlike the two of you, Felix has never seen my face. Plus, we need to do things differently—Alfano's laptop was a dead end. I can't get past the bloody SmarTech encryption."

"I've heard of SmarTech," Mac nods. "Biggest tech security company in America."

"Second biggest," I correct.

"Only the second?" Mac snickers. "What, you having some performance issues, Short Round?"

I lift a brow. "Remember Rossi?"

"You mean the guy we killed almost two years ago? Yeah..."

"I've been trying to break into his secure files ever since. He used SmarTech for data encryption, too. I could keep trying to strong-arm it, but Dimitri might die of old age before I break it, even if I were to dump another million dollars into computing power. Not even the NSA would bother."

"Whoa." Mac looks at Dimitri, whose face hardly shifts, except for a slight deepening of a frown—perhaps at the mention of his mortality.

"I'd joke that we would have more luck trying to get into the Pentagon, but I'm pretty sure they subcontract their security to SmarTech, too."

"Do you think it is a coincidence that both Rossi and Alfano used SmarTech tools?" Dimitri asks thoughtfully.

I shrug. "Could be, but like Mac said, they're one of the biggest names in the game, and their tools are top-tier. I don't personally use them, but I know plenty of my spiders do." I sigh and rub my eyes. "I don't want to risk the same issue with the next person. If I have any hope of figuring out why the General wants these people dead, I need an *unlocked* computer, time to copy the data over, and potentially the cooperation of the target. I might need to consider making contact with her under an alias and speaking directly to her. Discreetly, of course," I add, when I feel the heat of Dimitri's intensity directed at me.

"Well, if you say you've got this, I'm not gonna complain about some uninterrupted time with my girl." Mac grins. The chair under him screeches against the floor as he pushes it back and stands. He approaches me, hand outstretched. "As thanks, I'll do your dishes. Gimme."

"What a prince," I drawl.

I grab my bag and head out to the garage. It's a nice day, so I decide to take my bike for the initial drive-by of the address I got from Madison Cooper's DMV file. No one can see my face through the mirrored visor on the helmet, and in some places a bike is less conspicuous than a van.

I run a gloved hand along the body of my Harley CVO Glide, rubbing at a smudge on the black powder-coated metal. If there's one thing Americans know, it's motorcycles. Horsepower in general, really. This one is particularly fun, cutting corners like butter and easy to open up for a sprint along the flat, straight roads surrounded by fields in the more rural parts of the area.

As I cruise through the streets, the wind slides over the leather of my jacket, chilling any exposed areas and ripping through my denim trousers. The roar of the engine between my legs disrupts the perfect silence of the scenery, making me feel oddly powerful and reckless and destructive. The city skyline disappears and then reappears in my rearview mirrors as I effortlessly circumnavigate the worst of the traffic to the east.

As suburbs abruptly shift to city, I notice again how much Ulysses reminds me of Manchester, with its roots in manufacturing, smoggy air, and scrappy population of people who'll do anything to get by. In my youth, I worked hard to smooth the harsh edges of my accent to satisfy the rich snobs at my private school, an effort that serves me well now, since I can't be him anymore. That boy disappeared long ago. He had to.

Madison Cooper lives in a decent neighborhood. I memorized the make, model, and license plate of her car, so I recognize it among the others parked along the curb in front of her building. I slow my bike and make a show of pretending to "accidentally" tap her bumper. I reach down to "check the damage," but really I'm discreetly placing a tracker in the underside of her wheel well.

I continue down the street and grab a spot in front of an Indian restaurant, angled away from her place so it looks like I'm waiting for a delivery or on my way in. Using my mirrors, I take note of my surroundings. Looks like the same cable company services this area that I've already made up a uniform and van decal for. There are other service vehicles parked on the street, too, so mine won't stick out. All good.

A flash of movement in the corner of my eye draws my attention. Her building's front doors open and... wait, is that her?

I turn my bike in the spot so I can see better as a short, curvy woman flounces down the steps and makes a beeline for the old Toyota parked on the curb that I just tagged.

Oh, fuuuuuck. Her driver's license photo does her absolutely no justice. She's *gorgeous*—my alt dream girl come to life, dressed head to toe in black and wearing some kind of infuriatingly flippy, flirty, *short* skirt. She's got green streaks in her hair, a nose ring and plenty of tattoos across her chest and arms that are on full display, dark even against her tan skin. The overall effect is badass as hell.

And that's saying nothing of her body, which is practically a crime. I'd write poetry to her luscious curves if I could. She's all tits, ass, tummy, and a cute round face with dark eyes and lips like pillows that would look incredible wrapped around me—puffy, swollen and red. Hips I could really grab onto. And she's a short thing, too, so she'd be easy to lift onto a desk, ass up.

I'm sure she's heavy, and damn if that doesn't add fuel to the fire. I'm strong, and that's just how I like to flex it. Hell, that's *why* I got strong—my ideal weight to lift is whatever hers is.

And the way her ass jiggles as she bounces off the sidewalk and circles her car to the driver's side... I know just how it would move as it absorbed a strong smack. I want to bite it, to leave a round mark and make her squirm as the arousal sharpens to pain and melts back into arousal. My hands tense against the handles of my bike, but it's a sorry substitute for what I really want to be squeezing.

She drives off, and I scramble to grab my phone from my pocket, cursing myself for allowing such a thorough distraction. I ensure the tracker is operational, then fire my bike back up.

Follow her, some deep and dark voice whispers.

I don't. Of course I don't. I don't need to; I'll know where she's off to soon enough.

Time to head home and regroup, since I got what I came for. I know what uniform and van decal to use, and I know I can comfortably park on her street without attracting too much notice. Now I need to go collect what I need for the proper surveillance to start.

Hours later, I watch Madison Cooper return to her apartment from the back of my van. I stare long after the doors shut, wishing I'd thought to block off the spot right out front so she'd have further to walk and I could watch her longer.

As I feel the blood rushing to my dick, I curse. I need to calm down. She's a proper stunner, but I can't fuck Madison Cooper, as much as I'd like to. She's a potential target, and the rules of being a hitman are straightforward.

1. Kill your mark

2. Don't get caught

3. Don't be stupid

Don't have sex with someone you plan to kill is well covered in that third category.

Still, I can't help but wonder what put a woman so fine on the General's radar, and whether she really deserves to be there. Excitement thrums in my veins at the prospect of placing all these bugs and cameras I've brought with me, both because it means I'll soon be in her private space and because I'll have unfettered access to her when I'm done. I can't wait to get stuck in.

What kind of dirty little secrets is she hiding?

6

MADISON

I'm not one to leave a diem un-carpe'd.

The café where I get Abuela's favorite muffins, The Beanerie, is a few blocks from my apartment. It's so cute and cozy with greenery and books lining the walls. The scent of espresso and the jazz music softly playing feel like a big hug. Sometimes I bring my laptop, order lunch, and sit in the corner to people-watch while I eat.

I can't stay today—as usual, I'm running a bit behind—so I order my latte and muffins to go, tuck the white paper bag into my purse, and sit at one of the empty tables to wait for my drink. There were a few people ahead of me in line, so while I wait, I pull up the IRC and bite down on a smile when I see who's online.

```
mermaidav: I've never thought to ask this,
but I have a very important question.
SpyderMan: Oh?
mermaidav: Think carefully about how you
answer. This could determine the course of our
friendship going forward.
SpyderMan: I don't think anything good has
ever followed those words. Out with it. You're
making me nervous.
mermaidav: How do you take your coffee?
SpyderMan: Dumped down the sink.
```

The unexpected answer makes a laugh punch out from my chest, and I glance up to see if anyone heard the unflattering noise. The man at the table next to me looks up when I glance at him, but his attention is on his own small screen.

mermaidav: What?? Not even a latte? Not even a lavender latte? I swear, it'll change your life.

SpyderMan: My energy comes fruit-flavored and canned, as God intended.

mermaidav: I'll have to look it up, but I think that might actually be the definition of blasphemy.

SpyderMan: I'm dead to you now, I suppose.

mermaidav: Oh, you're not going to get rid of me that easily. It takes a lot for me to let someone in, but once you're in, you're stuck with me for life. Can you tell I'm a Scorpio?

SpyderMan: Didn't realize you were into astrology

mermaidav: What can I say? I'm a simple gal. I like lattes, star charts and books with wieners.

SpyderMan: lol I don't think anyone would ever dare call you simple, though I'll admit I'm surprised you listen to the stars.

mermaidav: Why? Who cares if astrology is real or not? Let girls have our fun, silly things.

SpyderMan: I meant, "I'm surprised you listen to anyone, let alone the stars, you menace."

My face splits into a smile. A menace. I like that.

mermaidav: Ha. True. What's your sign?
SpyderMan: Also a Scorpio.

Oooh! Another Scorpio?! Talk about a sign from the universe. Since he's like me, I don't need to read about his traits on my favorite astrology app. He's thoughtful, possessive, secretive and emotionally deep. Still, I open the well-loved app to check our compatibility. My eyes flick across the paragraph, memorizing the words.

Scorpio-Scorpio relationships are intensely passionate and characterized by a strong psychic connection. Their bond can move mountains, but only if they can move past power struggles and challenges that arise from mutual possessiveness and desire for control.

Well, sign me the fuck up. I'm not afraid of a little hard work.

mermaidav: A Scorpion King. Love it. I'd suggest changing your handle, but I like the spy/spiderman pun too much. It always makes me picture Peter Parker in a suit, drinking a shaken and not stirred martini.

SpyderMan: A James Bond and superhero reference in the same sentence? I'm in love. Or trouble. Maybe both.

Hard same, my guy.

Wearing a big, stupid grin, I squirm around in my seat, trying to get comfortable and relieve some pressure on my knees from too-short legs dangling over the side of the booth seat.

SpyderMan: Wish I could stick around to chat, but I'm off.

mermaidav: You going to tell me to be good?

SpyderMan: Haha well, considering your reaction last time, I would, but…

mermaidav: I'd remind you that you literally can't tell me what to do.

`SpyderMan: Yeah, that's about what I'd expect from my favorite little menace.`

Not just a menace, but his *favorite* little menace? In his own words... *fuck me.* He's out for blood today. Conversations like this make it so hard to let go of this silly crush—those flashes of a more personal side that I'd really love to know better. A dominant, authoritative, playful side.

Like, *be good?* Fucking make me, SpyderMan.

Now I'm horny. In public. Too bad my orgasms are hard-won and the result of intense focus and vibrations, or I'd rub one out in the bathroom or something to take the edge off.

"I've got a lavender latte!"

Nose still buried in my phone, I stand and grab for my drink, hand knocking into someone else's and nearly spilling the to-go cup.

"I'm sorry!" I gasp out as he says at the same time, "Oh! My apologies!"

I feel his hand on my elbow, steadying me even though I don't need it, and his warmth brushes against my side. Usually, I don't love having strangers in my personal space like that, but this one's on me because I should have been paying attention. Sheepishly, I look up... and *up*—even in my 3" Mary Janes, I'm still ridiculously shorter than him—and our eyes lock.

Time itself fucking stops as I take in Mr. Tall, Pale, and Inked.

His tawny hair flops just to the side of one of his incredible gray eyes, framed with long dark lashes and heavy brows. His nose is straight, drawing my eyes to full lips that are slowly spreading into a smirk. His chin is broad, and the edges of his jaw could cut glass. Colorful tattoos wrap around both arms, wrist to bicep, and I'm willing to bet they extend up past the rolled sleeves of his button down. I can see a flash of them above the collar, around the base of his throat.

Show me yours and I'll show you mine...

My stomach does a little flip behind my navel, seeing he's giving me the same kind of thoroughly interested once-over. Just my fucking type, and attracted to me? No shit. Well, I'm not one to leave a diem un-carpe'd.

"You ordered a lavender latte, too?" I ask, a slightly incredulous smile playing at the corners of my lips.

"I like sweet things," he replies as a smile spreads across his mouth, nearly taking my fucking breath away. It's downright impish, how his lips curl like that and how his cheeks round, emphasizing the angularity of his jaw and hairline. There's also a faint outline of a dimple in one of his cheeks.

And he's British too? His voice is smoother than melted chocolate, and just as decadent.

"So... do you want this sweet thing?" I ask slowly, letting the double entendre linger in the air between us.

His answering smirk just about melts me, as does the gentle cock of his head to the side that makes his hair fall into his eye. He gestures to the latte, indicating that I should go for it.

"And he's chivalrous," I grin.

"Actually, that's not—"

"Here's your latte, sir," the barista says, sliding another cup towards my stranger.

When I lift my eyebrows, his smile turns rueful. "I admit, when I went for it, I only heard the latte part."

"A plain latte? Ugh, boring," I tease.

"Classic," he counters.

A sense of déjà vu washes over me, prickling at the back of my brain. *You call it boring; I'd call it classic.*

At the thought of SpyderMan, the smile freezes on my face. Suddenly, this exchange feels... weird. Wait, why do I feel guilty? Like just by being attracted to someone and having a playful, flirty conversation means I somehow cheated on SpyderMan or something? That's kind of messed up. It's not like I can just leave my life on hold, waiting for SpyderMan to cross the lines we've drawn in the hardware. I'd die in that chastity belt.

"Same word, different font," I insist, shaking off the unwelcome feelings and anchoring myself back in the moment—the moment where this fine-ass British man is staring at me like I'm the crumpet for his tea. "Neither one means *fun*."

"Point taken. If I promise I'm more fun than my coffee order, would you let me take you out sometime?"

My heart thumps hard in my chest. Maybe I read into things too much, but to me there's a world of difference between "would you like to go out with me" and "let me take you out." Asking permission versus stating intention. The former is sweet and gentle; the latter is confident and assertive. And even though he kind of looks like the sweet, gentle nerd with his button-down and soft-spoken demeanor, there's clearly something a bit more dominant lurking under the surface.

Sometimes, I really love the universe. Because somehow, when I'm ovulating and really horny and need it most, the universe has sent me a guy who's interested in me. A *hot* guy who looks like he knows how to fuck hard.

And *Dios*, do I need a hard fuck.

"You usually ask girls out before asking their names?" I challenge.

"Madison, right?" he says, but it's not really a question.

The sound of my name on his lips in that silky, rich accent sends a shiver down my spine. Then, what he said catches up with me, and I frown. Just as I'm about to ask how he knows my name, he looks down pointedly at the cup in my hands—the one that has MADISON written just under the rim, facing him.

I laugh. "Chivalrous *and* observant? This just keeps getting better."

"Oh my God, I feel like I'm watching a Hallmark movie," someone whispers, just loud enough for both of us to hear it. My eyes dart over, and the older woman behind the counter is clutching the bottom of her apron and staring at the two of us with a keyed-up expression and a faint smile. "Your chemistry just electrocuted me from over there."

We both huff a laugh and step to the side, creating some distance and getting out of the way of anyone else who needs to pick up their drink.

"Well," I peer down at his cup, "Peter…"

He interrupts, like he's expecting a brush-off for some unfathomable reason and wants to get ahead of it. "If you're not sure, I'll leave the ball in your court. Hand me your phone—I'll add my number. You can let me know if you want to meet."

Not just confident and dominant, but a little bit bossy? Oh, Petey boy, we're going to have fun.

Fighting every horny cell in my body, I shake my head. Maybe I'm paranoid, but I won't hand my phone or give my number to a stranger—not even one this devastating. After all, I'm sort of a criminal. What if he works with the police? I'd like to do a bit of research on this guy first.

"I'll do it." I create a new contact for him under *Flick-the-Bean Peter*, typing awkwardly with one hand. "Go ahead."

He rattles off his number, and I add it, then tuck my phone into my purse. His eyes track the movement, which feels kind of weird. "Well, I've got to get going. Lovely to meet you, Madison."

"Likewise. I'm glad you tried to steal my coffee."

He chuckles. "So am I. A bit gutted you caught me, though. A lavender latte sounds quite nice."

"Trust me, it's amazing."

"So I'm told."

7

WESLEY

In for a penny, in for a pound.

Madison doesn't leave the house very often, apart from the occasional coffee or food run—bit of a shut-in, that one, though I suppose I can't judge because I've been accused of the same—so I've been stuck in the van for days, waiting for the chance to get in her apartment.

While I waited, I got all the information I could from the usual places. I was able to find out where she was born, how she grew up, her school records, her social security number, her bank accounts, her car's VIN, her credit history, her payment history, her medical records, her weekly routine, her pizza order, her gym membership, her fucking Netflix account...

Once I started, it was hard to stop collecting the details of her life. And now I have everything, but it's nowhere near enough. I can't stop myself from trying to catch glimpses. My eyes are glued to her every time she goes anywhere. The pull to get those cameras inside her apartment has become almost a physical pain in my chest—and even that might not be enough to satisfy this hunger.

I know I shouldn't have made contact like that—before I had all the data and was ready—but I rationalized it because I needed to get a tracker in her purse, and I haven't had many opportunities. But truth be told, I didn't even try to come up with another plan. I saw her turning into that coffee shop, and I just went after her. And once I saw the way she looked at me with those sultry caramel-colored eyes and heard the purr of desire in her voice...

With a sigh, I grab the energy drink can from the holder in the center console and drain the last drops, making a face at the metallic tang that the last warm sip of something always seems to take on.

Madison's car tracker stops moving at the retirement home where I now know her grandmother lives, and I realize this is my chance. Last time, she was there for over an hour—that should be enough time to get in and do what needs to be done.

Before I leave the van, I shut down or divert any security cameras that might catch me, both on the block and within her building. I adjust the white hard hat and grab a clipboard that has the fake paperwork that I'll pretend to fill out using a pen with the cable company's logo. Because details matter.

The building itself requires two keys for entry, but an elderly tenant passing through lets me in even though she's "not supposed to" when I tell her I'm upgrading their internet. Madison's flat has a physical lock that I pick, two cameras that have easily diverted feeds just inside, and a door alarm that triggers after 30 seconds without a code. Luckily, this particular system has an override code that they use at the factories when refurbishing them for resale.

Oh, and a guard cat.

I bend down and allow the cat to sniff my fingers. Having given the proper greeting, I'm accepted easily, and I give him a scratch behind the ear. But when he tries to rub up against my trousers as I stand, I dodge out of the way. I like cats, but being covered in hair is sort of the antithesis of being sneaky.

I pause for a second to take it all in. This is her private space, and I get to poke about without her knowledge. I can see how she lives when no one is watching. Heady excitement thrums in my veins. I'm hardly ever out in the field anymore, what with Mac and Dimitri having it well in hand, so I half-forgot what an adrenaline rush it can be.

It's a tidy place, full of color and knick-knacks. I inhale deeply, smelling feminine soaps with indistinct florals, kitchen grease, cleaning supplies and weed. There's a pipe with blackened bits on her kitchen counter, which makes me smile, for some odd reason.

I move through methodically until I find what I'm looking for. Her bedroom. Well, her computer—it just happens to be in her bedroom.

The desk and desktop computer occupy almost half the space. I note with appreciation how well-managed her cables are and how recently she's cleaned her lint screens. She takes good care of her investments. The computer has a mismatched look, which I know means that she built it herself and that she only replaces components when they get too old or slow to serve her anymore. I'm impressed—this is more than I was expecting to find, since the vast majority of people buy machines pre-assembled. Madison Cooper must be good with computers.

I tap the mouse to wake up the screen and win that bet with myself that there's a password. Of course, there's a password. Well... that's what the cameras are for. If I can properly aim one at her desk, I should be able to see as she types it the next time she logs in. Once I have her phone cloned, not even dual-factor authentication will be a problem, if she has it.

The sound of my own phone buzzing in my pocket nearly startles me out of my skin. I check the ID and only just manage to catch my groan. For a sniper, his timing is terrible sometimes.

With a sigh, I place an earpiece in. "What?" I ask, hearing an edge in my voice as my heartbeat slowly readjusts to the lack of imminent danger.

"Hey buddy. How's it going?" Mac asks around a mouthful of something.

I swear that bloke is always eating. "Fine. I'm a bit busy for a chat," I say. Even though I'm alone, I keep my voice low—you never know how thin the walls are in a place like this. "I'm setting up surveillance in the target's flat."

The cameras are of my own design and well-built, if I do say so myself. They're incredibly small and contain powerful microphones as well as decently high-resolution cameras—but not capable of swiveling or zooming in, so strategic placement is necessary.

Mac whistles. *"You're inside her place right now? Why the hell did you answer the phone?"* he chuckles.

With a noise of frustration, I stretch up and deposit a camera just inside the lip of the air vent in the ceiling, facing the front door. "Despite all evidence to the contrary, you do *occasionally* have something useful or important to say."

"You flirtin' with me, Short Round?"

I snort and move to the other side of the room to place another camera on a bookshelf among the various knickknacks, facing the only external window in her apartment. This has a good sideways view of the couch and into the kitchen.

"Shall I draw you a map to the point or will you get there on your own?" I ask as I move to place the final camera in her bedroom, concealed atop a corner bookshelf and angled to capture her desk.

"Well, I called to check in. It sounds like you've got things handled, if you're bugging the place. But I also called because someone—not me—got himself locked out of the shared drive and didn't want to call you to reset his password."

Sometimes I feel like bloody IT support. I pinch the bridge of my nose. "Dimitri told me he wrote it down."

Dimitri's low voice is faint on the other end, like he's listening through Mac's phone. *"I lost the Post-it."*

"I told you not to put it on a *Post-it*," I grit out. "Make it memorable or there's no point in having one at all."

Distantly, there's some Russian muttering. *"He says he's sorry and he'll never do it again,"* Mac says. I can hear the smile.

"He did not," I snort as Dimitri scoffs, *"I did not."*

A loud banging noise out in the hallway startles me. I recognize the sound from my own entry and know it was the front door of the building. It reminds me of the ever-present risk of discovery. Time to go.

With my blood pounding in my ears, I move into the main room just in time to hear the grinding of a key in the deadbolt.

"Fuck," I curse softly.

"What happened?" All teasing is gone, and Mac is suddenly alert.

"She's coming back!" I whisper, darting forward to grab my clipboard off the entrance table.

"Hide!"

I don't bother to voice my sarcastic remark—fucking *obviously*—as I whirl around, assessing. There aren't many hiding spots for a bloke my size in a place this small. She might immediately need to use the loo, and the shower curtain is transparent, so that's out. Her kitchen is completely open. Her bed frame is open with no skirt, so she might see me... closet it is.

The deliberation feels like it takes ages, but by the time I get her closet door almost entirely closed—leaving it open a hair so I don't have to fuss with the knob in case I need to move quickly—she's just stepping inside her flat. I hear the metallic clinking of keys hitting a bowl and a few soft thuds that I imagine are her shoes getting tossed into the pile by the door.

"Hey SB, how you livin'?" she says. Her voice is muffled through the layers of wood and plaster, and nearly drowned out by the loud, rapid beating of my own heart. Adrenaline tends to sharpen the senses.

A loud, demanding trill follows her question.

"I know, I know, you can see the bottom of your bowl. Customer service is processing your complaints, and someone will be right with you," she grumbles.

I fight the grin. Damn it. She's funny. I didn't need another reason not to want to kill her.

"How's it going, Wes? You good?" Mac asks.

Instead of responding audibly, I send him a thumbs-up emoji in our group chat.

"We should not have allowed him into the field. It has been too long since he got up from his desk," Dimitri admonishes in the background.

"Yeah, Short Round. Getting caught with your pants down? Rookie mistake." Mac chuckles, clearly convinced I'm in no real danger. *"In her file she looked pretty small, though. If she finds you, I bet you could take her."*

Dimitri snorts. *"You say this because you have not seen the footage of his combat with that drug dealer last month. He threw away his weapon. He is lucky it was not his last mistake."*

"Gasp," Mac replies instead of actually gasping.

Anger boils up at their good-natured ribbing. I reckon I understand now how Dimitri feels when we're in his ear during missions, going back and forth. It's even more frustrating because I have to be quiet now and can't offer up the brilliant retort on the tip of my tongue. After all, it's only because I was on the phone with Mac that I missed the notification that her car was moving.

The only course available to me is to end the call, so that's what I do. I can get myself out of this one.

The bathroom door faces her room's door, so I know I can't sneak out when she uses the toilet. I can hear the water running too clearly for the door to be closed. I'm forced to listen as she moves through her space, grabbing a snack and talking to her cat as if he'll respond in that way pet owners always seem to. She moves into her bedroom, and I go stock-still, barely daring to breathe.

I hear a squeak of chair casters and some loud keyboard noises.

Fuck. Well and truly trapped. Good thing I don't have to piss.

Time becomes meaningless, ticking away as I stand still in the darkness. At least it smells lovely in here with all her clothes. Her scent wraps around me like an intriguing hug—comforting, yet also slightly arousing in its utter femininity—a combination of whatever soap she uses, and a faint whiff of something warm, like coffee and vanilla. I didn't get close enough before to really notice, but it's wonderful.

Minutes—hours?—later, just as I'm starting to shift my weight from foot to foot, she gets up from her desk. I perk up.

Please be going for a walk...

Her form flashes by the sliver opening I left in the doorway, but she's headed for her bed. I frown, cocking my head, then nearly suck in a breath when I realize she's removing her jumper. It lands atop a small pile of laundry in front of the closet door, quickly joined by her flirty little skirt. Watching as her perfect shape comes into view, I'm utterly frozen. Everything else falls away—the sound of my own breathing, the ache in my feet and persistent crick in the base of my neck, the dryness in the back of my mouth—until all that exists is the rush of blood to my dick and the slow reveal of more and more of her body.

And what a lush, curvy, tanned, soft body it is. Clothes do her no justice. She ought to be naked more. Inside, obviously—no one else gets to see this.

She removes her shirt and stands for a moment in what looks like a black lace bra. Fuck me, I do love a bit of lace and silk. It's like the best wrapping for the best kind of gift. She unhooks it in a practiced move and it joins her shirt on the floor, treating me to the sight of the soft lines of her nude back.

When she hooks her thumbs into either side of her panties, my heart jerks in my chest, drumming faster and harder as my desire mounts... I have to reach down to adjust my hardening cock in my trousers. The urge to take it out is almost unbelievably strong—even a few rough squeezes might soothe this unbearable, aching rigidity—but I don't dare.

She lowers the waistband of her panties, shifting her hips back and forth in the most mesmerizing sway I've ever seen. My balls tighten. Blood pounds in both my heads, and my thoughts feel thick.

Moving out of the narrow view I have, she climbs onto the squeaky mattress, and then her feet appear at the end of the bed I can see. Her feet kick apart.

I shift until I can see her torso, pressing my face as far as I can into the wall for the proper angle. Her body is tan against the white sheets. The sight of her curves sends waves of hot need through me—only made worse when she cups her breast and tweaks the tip roughly.

She skims her chest, her tummy, and as her hands move south towards her center, I bite a fist to keep from groaning. Or trying to coach her. I want so badly to tell her what to do to please me. I want to watch her fingers emerge, slick and shining with her own arousal. I want to watch how an erotic order lands—whether it makes her want to give in or fight. Both, I hope.

That's it, Madison. Touch yourself. Show me how you like it.

Breath bated, I wait for something else to happen—a moan, a whimper, a soft wet noise from an aroused body. She curls up on her side and reaches into the drawer next to her bed. And I'm suddenly very, *very* glad I've already got my fist to bite down on because there's no way I would have survived the shocked delight of seeing a bottle of lube and a vibrating mini wand in her hand in silence.

She likes toys.

Well, we have that in common, love.

Fuck.

When buzzing starts, I exhale slowly, because it feels like an electric shock to my own system. I've never wanted to see something more than I want to see what's happening between her propped legs right fucking now. Do I risk opening the door wider? Would it even provide the correct angle?

A low, throaty moan joins the sound of the buzzing, and a shiver crawls down my spine, lingering and fizzling out almost painfully at the base. As she makes more infuriatingly seductive noises, I squeeze my eyes shut. I need to get ahold of myself. Yes, she's the most spellbinding creature I've seen in a long time, but I'm a grown man in full control of his desires and faculties.

Still, every gasp sends a surge of blood to pound painfully in flesh that's already impossibly hard. Every whimper makes me grit my teeth so I don't breathe out louder than I should. Every moan makes me clench my fists to keep myself from cracking open the door further.

Would she make the same noises riding my face? The vision is so sudden and intense that I lick my lips, as if I'd find her taste there.

I don't know how long I listen, wishing I could see more, but eventually my own arousal settles into more of a crackling fire—still burning but no longer raging out of control. I wait for the crescendo, or some sign of her pleasure, but the buzzing suddenly stops and I frown in confusion.

Is she just very quiet when she comes, or...

The heavy sigh she emits sounds frustrated. "Fucking anti-anxiety meds," she grumbles as she sits up.

My lips twitch. I don't know what anti-anxiety meds have to do with this specifically, but it must be difficult for her to come—I'll need to keep that in mind. I've had quite a lot of fun with orgasm denial in the past, but when achieving orgasm is difficult, it's not something to weaponise.

Her feet disappear, her door opens, and the bathroom door closes. Faintly, I can hear the shower come on.

As quietly as possible, I crack the door. The bathroom door is still open, but her shower curtain has fogged with the heat, and she's facing away. I take my chance and slip out of the closet. Staying low, I make my way to the front door—something made substantially harder by my substantial hard-on.

"I was never here," I whisper to the cat as I pass where he's curled on the couch. He lifts his head inquisitively, and I can better see the line of black fur across his head that almost looks like a bowl haircut, making his look of wide-eyed wonder seem especially human and dopey.

Next time I'll bring him some treats.

When I get back to the van, I get the cameras online and debate doing something about my erection, but I can't quite shake the mental image of being a pervert in a white van—a peeping Tom touching himself while the object of his fixation blithely shows him more than she'd meant to.

I sit back on the rickety stool, easily recalling the hypnotic image of her full tits spilling out of her hands and the curve of her tummy as her body bowed. Every inch of her looks so soft and delicious.

It's a good thing the cameras weren't working at the time, or I'm not sure even my rock-hard will could resist the urge to see if the one in her bedroom had a better view than mine...

I shake the thought from my head and type "journal article, contains: 'anti-anxiety meds' and 'sexual side effects'" into a search.

8

MADISON

There is one person other than Abuela who I can count on.

In the morning, there's always more activity at Sunset Hills. Residents have more energy, so I see more of them up and about in the hallways. I've got my latte in one hand and a bag with two muffins in the other, so I wave my elbow at one lady who I know goes to Mass with Abuela.

When I get to her room, I find Manny helping get her situated in her lounger.

"*Hola,* Abuela," I greet.

She smiles when she sees me, the expression lighting up her face. *"Ah, mi hija está aquí. Gabriella, ven, siéntate a mi lado—"*

I exchange a look with Manny, and he makes an awkward face—both because he doesn't understand most of what she said, and because he knows what it means when she greets me as Gabriella.

"No, Abuela," I chide gently. "It's me, Madison. Your granddaughter. *Hijita,* remember?" There's a world of difference between *daughter* and *little daughter* to my Abuela, though I'm all she has left of the girl she loved who died too young. I'd never pretend to be my mother, but I guess the family resemblance is strong enough to be the source of her confusion.

Abuela nods, though it's an absent gesture, and I can see the confusion in her eyes as she turns back to face the TV. I already miss the smile. "Oh, right. *Claro.* Madison…"

"She had a hard night last night. She didn't get much sleep because of that storm," Manny explains, voice low.

I feel my lips stretch into a thin smile. I'm grateful for the explanation to latch onto, but we both know these episodes have become more frequent in the past few months. "Good to know."

"I'll leave you to it, then." Manny softly closes the door behind him.

"Gabriella, what did you do to your hair?" she chides, scowling at my head.

"I'm Madison, Abuela," I correct again, just as gently. I place the drink and bag with the treats on her table so I can smooth back the green pieces. "You like it?"

She makes a clicking noise with her tongue and turns away.

"I brought you a treat. A cranberry orange muffin, your favorite."

"I'm not hungry."

I swallow, trying again. "Do you want to do a puzzle?"

"No," she replies shortly, eyes never wavering from the screen.

"How about we go for a—"

"Shh, my programs are on," she cuts me off.

So it's going to be one of those days, then. I shut the door and grab one of the chairs from her table to drag it next to her. I swallow a sigh, raise the volume for her when she thrusts the remote at me, then I put in one of my earphones and start the first chapter of the next audiobook SpyderMan wants me to read.

During a commercial break, she exhales deeply and glances at me sideways, like she wants to say something. I pause the audiobook and take out my earbud.

"I hate it here, *mija*."

The pit deep in my stomach that started forming the day I realized she couldn't live with me anymore gets a little wider to make room for the increase in guilt.

She agreed to this, and I found the best place I could afford, I remind myself. But I can't help the grumble from slipping out. "Great. Glad I'm paying $8,000 a month for it."

"What was that?" she asks sharply.

She didn't hear me, but she heard the tone, and that's all she needs to be convinced of the disrespect. "I said I'm sorry to hear that. Is it something going on that I should—"

"I could live with you."

On days like this, I'm not sure if she remembers her fall. She was unconscious when I found her, and I'm not strong enough to lift her. It was one of the scariest, worst days of my life.

"We tried that, and it didn't work. Moving in here was your idea. Remember, Abuela?"

"No," she says, and the fact that she sounds more resigned than angry about the lapse in memory worries me more than anything else. Fiery, independent Abuela, I can handle. Confused, subdued Abuela scares me. It makes me feel like I'm losing her. "There's so much I don't remember. Like you."

My heart stutters, and I swear it's like the air's been punched out of me. She doesn't remember me?

"You say you're Madison, but Madison is a little girl... *Mi hijita...* she's... so young..."

"27 is young," I agree, attempting for levity.

She barely registers the comment, muttering to herself rapidly in a wet, musical tone like she's on the verge of tears. *"Ay mi pobre hijita, creciendo sin madre... Tengo que amarla lo suficiente como para dos personas. No puedo perderla también."*

I feel tears stinging my own eyes, and I choke them back. I always have a comeback. It's kind of my thing. The adults in my life have been telling me I had a smart mouth since I was five. But now? I've got nothing.

It's so seldom that I have nothing to say, I default to the childhood comfort—*un pastel* for a skinned knee, hot cocoa for heartache, sweets to make the bad times feel less bad. "Do you want a muffin, Abuela?"

Her dark eyes dart towards me, meeting mine. "Cranberry orange?"

"Your favorite."

She smiles, holding out her hand like a kid waiting for a treat. "*Claro.*"

We eat our muffins together in silence. When we're done, we hold hands, and she absently strokes my knuckles, lost in her own world.

I try to plan my visits so that it's time for me to go right about when it's time for Abuela's afternoon nap. Manny appears in the doorway with some pills in little white cups on a tray and a bottle of water, which he sets down on the table as I collect my things. Abuela doesn't even look at me as I give her a kiss on the cheek and say goodbye.

My heart feels made of sand as I approach my car. It's not breaking, per se—nothing about me is fragile or delicate like glass—but my emotions feel heavy and impossible to control as they sink and shift and settle into something low and dark. There's a horrible looming inevitability that I just haven't been able to make myself confront.

If I had friends, I would call one of them up at a time like this. All I want is the temporary comfort of another person who cares enough to lie to me and tell me it'll be okay.

But here I am, stuck in a hole of loneliness that I dug for myself—because I have one person in the world and... I'm losing her.

I choke back the tears and reach into my purse to grab my keys, but my fingers close around my phone instead. I have the IRC pulled up almost before I realize what I'm doing, like my brain on autopilot knows exactly what I need.

In fact, there *is* one person other than Abuela who I can count on.

```
mermaidav: it's been a hell of a day. Got
anything that'll make me feel better?
SpyderMan: Have you heard of William Windsor?
```

mermaidav: nope

SpyderMan: He was a lance corporal in the British Army from 2001 to 2009. He was demoted in 2006 for 3 months for inappropriate behavior during the queen's birthday.

I frown, confused. I meant a job—not a history lesson. I'll bear with him because it feels like he's ramping up to something, but I'm not really sure how British military stories are supposed to make me feel better.

A second later, SpyderMan drops a picture into the chat and I burst out laughing.

mermaidav: Is that a goat??

SpyderMan: It is. William Windsor, the cashmere goat.

mermaidav: He looks so distinguished in his little hat! Why was he demoted??

SpyderMan: He wouldn't stay in line and headbutted a drummer in the parade.

The laughter feels so good; I lean into it. The sound fills the car, wet with emotion, and I wipe the tears under my eyes with the edge of my sleeve.

mermaidav: Thank you. That legitimately helped.

SpyderMan: Do you want to talk about it?

Gnawing on my lip, I consider my response. It's no bitching to girlfriends over margaritas, but it still makes me feel warm. Because he asked. He cares. He's probably the only person in the world I would tell.

mermaidav: Do you ever wish you'd made different choices in life?

SpyderMan: Sometimes. Does this have anything to do with wanting to move to the forest and befriend crows to escape your responsibilities?

mermaidav: lol you remember that silly conversation?
SpyderMan: I remember every conversation.

My breath catches. That's... so unbelievably sweet, I'm not sure what
to do about it. Did he mean it to be sweet? I swallow and decide it's more
likely that he's just being kind of snarky, as per usual.

mermaidav: Things are hard right now, and
it's my own fault. I just can't help feeling
that if I'd done things differently, my life
would be a lot easier. If I did what was
expected of me, or acted how I was always told
to act, or prioritized different things... If
I was someone else.

He types and deletes his message a few times, and I watch the dots
dance across the screen with a mounting kind of nervous excitement.
Whenever he's extra careful in choosing his words, it's usually a doozy.

SpyderMan: It's possible—but that's the problem with what if's. The theoretical always
feels possible. You'll go mad torturing yourself with possibilities of things you can't
change.

I blow out a breath of disappointment. It's not exactly what I wanted
to hear, but he's right, and it's practical advice. Wishing things were
different is always a waste of time. I start typing a response, but then
another comes through from him.

SpyderMan: I wouldn't trade who you are for
any theoretical version of you. I like this
mermaid. This mermaid is clever and resourceful. She's daring and courageous. People like
you take risks and find your own way through

```
life. It's one of the things I admire most
about you.
```

My chest fills with warmth, and I wipe another tear that wells for an altogether different reason. To have someone I admire tell me that they admire me back is one thing... For it to be *this* person is another. The fizzy, floaty feeling of being seen and known and appreciated for who I am slowly melts into a dull kind of ache—because I've never wanted anything more in my whole life, and I can't have him.

Fuck. I don't want to be SpyderMan and mermaidav anymore. I want more. I want to know who he is—I want to show him who I really am. Even if he lives halfway across the world, or he's actually artificial intelligence being trained on human emotions and mediocre puns... I just want a chance to see if this is real.

Why can't we be more?

I sigh. I know exactly why—what I do is illegal, and what he does is probably dangerous. Even if he's trustworthy, there's no guarantee that there isn't someone looking over his shoulder, like the mob or Interpol. Any identifying detail puts not just me at risk, but Abuela as well. Even if I'd take that risk for myself, I won't put her life in danger.

I know it's better this way... it's just a bitter pill and I can't dwell on it, or I'll land right back in the sad place I just crawled out of.

```
mermaidav: How does it feel to be so sure of
yourself and have everything figured out?
SpyderMan: Ha. I wish. Don't let me fool you—I
have my doubts like everyone else. I often
question whether or not I'm a decent person or
doing the right thing.
mermaidav: Well, if it makes you feel better,
I've seen enough shit to know that bad people
don't really worry about whether they're doing
the right thing or being a good person.
```

SpyderMan: I thought I was meant to be making
you feel better.

mermaidav: You did. You always do. I guess
I just want to be that person for you, too.
Because that's what you do for your friends.

mermaidav: And we're friends, right?

SpyderMan: Of course. As much as anonymous
internet friends can be.

I suck in a breath. Fuck.

How does he always hit the nail on the head like that? I don't know if
the comment was meant to knock me back into place because he thought
I was getting too close, but it stings. And it should.

I like him *so* much. And I know he likes me, but this thing between us
isn't meant to cross over into the real world. And that's not enough for
me anymore.

I need more.

But what's a generally unpleasant, lonely-by-design internet lurker to
do? Most of the time I don't let it bother me that I don't have people in
my life.

I wasn't going to text that guy I met in The Beanerie. He's hotter than
August in hell, but I just couldn't see things working out between us.
He's so... *normal*.

I haven't had time to do a deep dive into him, but a preliminary
background check came back squeaky clean. Peter Smith, age 30, born
and raised in Surrey, in the US on a visa. No shady activity. Not a cop.

The only weird thing was his lack of credit history, but there are a
few reasons that could be the case—and only one of them is that credit
histories are hard to generate, so new fake identities usually don't exist
in the system. In this case, it's probably due to the fact that he's from
another country. Not every country uses credit scores.

It was enough to convince me that he's probably a regular guy. And, as a rule, I try to stay away from regular guys.

But I guess it doesn't have to be that serious. I mean, Peter is both fine as fuck *and* into me—which makes him exactly the kind of guy you get under when you want to get over someone else.

I flip over to my texting app and pull up a blank message to *Flick-the-Bean Peter,* snorting a little at the contact name.

> So have you tried a lavender latte yet, or do I need to be concerned that you set the bar a little too low when you promised to be more fun than your coffee order?

He responds quicker than I'd expect—I have a text waiting for me before I even get all the way home. No cool-guy prescribed waiting time to seem aloof here. I like it.

> I'll let you be the judge. You free for dinner tonight?

I smile down at my phone. He's decisive and makes plans. That's a heavy point in his favor. He's not even going to waste my time texting back and forth forever. Tonight is a bit short notice, but I can make it work, as long as he gives me a few hours.

I need to shave... everything.

9

MADISON

Oh, I'm definitely a troublemaker.

I can feel eyes on me as I lock up my apartment. I turn my head to confirm, catching Todd's gaze on my ass just before his face falls into an unfriendly sneer.

Great. I just showered, but now I feel like I need to again.

"What's with the clown makeup? Circus in town?" he sneers, smiling at his joke before he even finishes it.

I press my lips together, enjoying the feel of them sliding smoothly against each other from the vampy dark color I swiped on. If there's one thing about me, it's that I'm not going to leave the house without lipstick, and something tells me inked-up Peter liked my alternative look.

"Todd. Pleasure as always. I'd stay and chat, but... I don't want to." I flash him a smile, grab my keys from the door and turn to leave.

"Aw, didn't like that one? I was going to compare you to a cheap whore, but let's be real: no one would pay for that shit."

I sigh dramatically.

I look good. I know I look good. My everything shower took me two hours—I'm shaved and waxed 'stache to toe—and my hair and makeup took me just as long. Artfully overlined lips. Cat eye sharp enough to kill a man. My outfit? Flawless. This dress hugs me in all the right places but will only give him a flash of cleavage to leave him wanting more.

What can I say? Flick-the-Bean Peter is my whole damn type, and I'm trying to knock his socks and then all the rest of his clothes off.

"Like you could afford me."

"Heard you got fired, so you must be pretty desperate."

Fired? Figures Fred would spread that story. "Hmm. How's it going in the SmarTech talent toilet? Get that big promotion yet?" My smile is saccharine. I didn't need to work there long to know that no one at SmarTech respects him.

His brows snap down. "I'm putting in my time."

"If that's what you need to tell yourself."

"At least it's legal money," he hisses. "Not that *you people* know shit about that. Fucking destroying this country. Does your family mow lawns or clean houses? It's pathetic."

Bile creeps up the back of my throat. There are few things I hate more than racism disguised as patriotism. Usually Todd's insults are juvenile jabs at my appearance. I guess he decided to try a new tactic, since the fat jokes never bother me. But he's never stooped quite this low, and frankly, it makes me see red.

With a glare of my own, I step closer. I'm much shorter than him, and even though it means I have to tilt up my head, I don't care—because he flinches ever-so-faintly at my fury. "Know what *I* think is pathetic? Being so painfully mediocre that you're not even good at being a bully. Pathetic is expecting respect but giving none. Pathetic is thinking a six-pack or pale skin makes you somehow better than me. Because one day you won't have that six-pack. And with no personality to speak of or body to be proud of, you'll just be a sad old white man, wondering why nobody loves you."

His glare turns hostile. "God, you are such a fucking bitch," he seethes, hands shaking as they curl.

I glance down at his fist. If Todd ever let out that testosterone, it would probably be to hit a woman. He won't now, but I wish he'd try it because I'd make him regret it so hard he'd never even think about doing it again.

But I know how false his bravado really is. I know he's like a cornered animal, swiping out with his claws to find a soft part to hurt.

Good fucking luck. My body may be soft, but that's the only part of me that is. I'm immune to his insults for the same reason he's hurling them. I like myself; deep down he doesn't like himself. And he's a shitty person, so I genuinely don't care about his approval.

To show him how little of a threat I think he is, I turn my back on him. "Yup," I reply breezily, showing him my middle finger as the door swings behind me.

Hot frustration swirls in my gut, and I catch myself stomping down the front steps of the building before the impact starts aching in my shins. I need to cool off—I don't want to bring this energy to my date. Walking there might help. Peter picked a restaurant a few blocks from me, and it's a nice night for it. Plus, then if I down a few margaritas to settle the nerves, I won't have to worry about driving.

El Limon is a busy place on a Saturday night, and they won't seat us until we're both present, so I linger outside to shoot Peter a text. I guess I'm not fully calmed down from my encounter with Todd because I catch myself stewing that he's late.

I tap out something snippy, then check the time on my phone. Okay, I need to take several chill pills. He's only two minutes late.

Deleting the first text, I type out something much less antisocial. Before I've sent the message, I hear, "Madison!"

My head whips up, and I catch sight of him swinging his leg over his motorcycle.

Oh shit. On some level, I thought my memory had exaggerated his ridiculous handsomeness. Nope.

He's all piercing gray eyes and perfectly proportioned features, with a body boasting enough muscle that it's actually visible against the fabric of his henley and dark jeans. Those perfect lips are quirked up into a smirk that makes the butterflies in my stomach explode in a flapping cloud of glitter and color. Of course his hair is, like, artfully disheveled from the motorcycle helmet he's locking under the seat. *Of course* he rides a motorcycle.

God, even his walk is attractive. He swaggers, unhurried, and holds himself tall with calm confidence. His jacket shifts, giving me flashes of the colorful wings at the base of his throat.

This man would have presence, even without the biker boots and leather jacket that make him look like a total badass. But it's understated. He's not the kind of guy who fills a room; he's the kind who quietly owns it.

If he smells good, too, I might melt on the spot.

My head comes up and up, tilting further back to keep him in my line of sight as he approaches. I also forgot how tall he is. He must be over six feet because I'm in four-inch heels and he's still half a foot above me.

He stops just in front of me. "Hello," he says. That smirk would probably incinerate lesser panties.

Luckily, I've got my prettiest set on. I always wear pretty underwear whenever I need a confidence boost—my big-girl panties, if you will.

"Hi," I reply, bracing myself for that weird, polite, *nice to see you again* hug. I understand the importance of breaking the touch barrier on a first date, but we're still strangers and I don't much like being touched by strangers.

He doesn't make a move. That's another point for Peter. "Do you want to go in?" he gestures, like I should go ahead of him.

My smile is wry. "Depends. Were you trying to be funny, or are you just really unoriginal, taking a Mexican girl to a Mexican restaurant for a first date?" I tease, but there's an edge to my voice I didn't mean for there to be.

Okay, maybe Todd's insults affected me a little more than I thought. He put it in my head anyway. Best to get this out of the way—I won't be disrespected *or* fetishized for my culture.

But Peter isn't Todd. His eyes go wide, and faint splotches of pink sweep across his cheeks. *Dios mio...* is he blushing?

"No! No, of course not! I... erm..." he scrubs awkwardly at his jaw, oblivious to how the show of the spider tattoo on the back of his hand is completely at odds with the *aw-shucks* gesture. "It was the top-rated restaurant near here. I only thought that since you walked to the café you'd appreciate something close, but of course we can go somewhere else. Anywhere you like."

Between the blush and the earnest horror at the thought of unintentional racism, I think I might be a goner.

"I'm just kidding," I grin as his shoulders slump in relief. "I could literally always go for a taco. And it was pretty thoughtful to find a place somewhere close to where we met, but how did you know I walked?"

"I might have watched you walk away," he flirts, showing off a faint dimple in his cheek.

I smirk back, enjoying the feeling of his obvious appreciation. As I turn to head into the restaurant, I catch a whiff of his incredible scent. It's very subtle, but once I realize it's coming from him, my legs nearly buckle.

No Old Spice for Peter. He smells like hand soap and black tea, and somehow... that crisp, faintly bitter edge like ozone from too many electronics in a small space. It's strange and energetic and clean... and somehow warm and cold at the same time. It's not just a scent, it's a memory and a feeling—of being surrounded by computers, of feeling at peace, and knowing I'm about to make some lines of code my bitch.

Might as well call it Mad-nip. I'd be the only customer, but bottle that, and I'd buy 1,000. Goddamn, that shit is *fresh*.

"Careful, Peter," I say, my voice coming out a little huskier now. "You're giving away all your secrets."

"Am I?" His grin is curious now.

I toss him a look over my shoulder. "Well, now I know offering to let me go ahead of you wasn't about being polite—it was about the view."

With a deep chuckle that I feel in my core, he shakes his head and reaches in front of me to get the door for me. It brings him so close that I can feel the warmth of his body through our clothes. "I'm fairly certain that's always been the point of that particular polite gesture. But with a view like this, can you blame a bloke?"

I'm glad my back is to him and he can't see my face as I react to that—I'm trying to play it cool, here, and my dopey grin would totally give me away. But that was one of the smoothest things I've ever heard. And in that accent, no less?

Somebody sedate me.

They seat us in a cozy back corner at a four-person table so we can sit on adjacent sides with the corner between us. He pulls out my chair for me, then shucks off his leather jacket and drapes it on the back of his. Damn. I wish those long sleeves didn't cover so much.

Like he can sense my disappointment, he starts rolling them up—my own personal forearm burlesque show—and my mouth goes dry, watching more and more colorful, inked flesh being exposed. I'm still staring when he takes his seat, and he gives me a cheeky wink.

Busted.

Wishing I'd remembered to ask for a booth, I shift in my chair. When my legs don't touch the floor, I prefer to sit crisscross, and there's usually only enough room for it in a booth. Noticing my discomfort, Peter offers to ask for a different table. With a sheepish smile, I let him ask our waiter to move us.

Is this what it feels like to swoon?

Settled at a new table, we chat about the decor of the restaurant until our waiter shows up to take our order, saving the deeper topics for when we won't be interrupted. Once we've got our drinks—a beer for Peter, a marg for me—we jump into it.

"So, tell me about yourself. What do you do?" he asks.

"Little of this, little of that," I say dismissively, spinning my drink against the table—a fidget to release some anxiety. "What do you do?"

"Erm," he says, an odd smile on his lips at my refusal to answer. "I work for a cable company—installations, repairs, maintenance."

That sort of explains the physique. I've watched those guys carry spools of wire over their shoulders that I know weigh close to 100 lbs. "Sounds like you're good with your hands," I flirt.

"Very," he flirts back.

"And you like it?"

"It's a decent job—leaves me plenty of time for hobbies."

"Hiking? Baking? Candlestick making?"

He chuckles and sits back in his seat. "Tinkering with electronics, mostly. I've always been curious about how things work. When I was a boy, my father encouraged me to take things apart so I could teach myself and understand. Didn't tell my mother, though—she pitched a fit when she came home and her washing machine was in pieces on the laundry room floor."

A laugh bubbles up in my throat. "Did you put it back together at least?"

His grimace is conspiratorial, making me feel like I'm in on the joke. "In my defense, there were way more parts than I remembered taking out. I'm convinced my father slipped a few extra bolts in there when I wasn't looking, just to fuck with me."

I release the chuckle, relishing in the feeling of unexpectedly sharing a sense of humor with someone new. "So you were a bit of a troublemaker."

"Incorrigibly. Still am," he winks. Okay, *this* is what it feels like to swoon. "What about you?"

"Oh, I'm definitely a troublemaker. Some of my friends would call me more of a menace, though."

His smile is amused, but almost distracted, like I said something that reminded him of something else. "I meant, what do you do in your spare time?"

"You'll never believe this, but I actually take apart people's washing machines and don't put them back together."

His eyes flash, as if his amusement is tinged with something else. Desire, maybe? Does a bit of witty banter rile him up? I fucking hope so, because there's plenty more where that came from.

"What a coincidence," he muses. When he leans forward to grab his beer bottle, his shirt strains against his pecs, and I have to force myself not to stare. "Are you from around here?"

I snort. "Like that's even remotely as interesting as your back story—I'm not the one with the British accent, here. What's the leap from England to New Jersey all about?" I ask, genuinely curious. His background check gave me some insight, but dates and numbers only tell facts, not a story. According to immigration, he's been in the country for a few years.

After a long sip, he sets the bottle back down and regards me curiously. "That's the third personal question you've dodged," he observes.

I reach for my own drink to hide my shock. The guy from my last first date didn't ask me a single question—it made for a boring meal, but I didn't really mind since I don't usually share personal details anyway. It also led to an unsurprisingly selfish sexual encounter that left me so thoroughly unsatisfied that I remember thinking I didn't need a real man in my life as long as I had SpyderMan.

And here Peter is, not only asking questions but noticing my lack of answers? Like he genuinely cares and wants to know stuff about me? And that's *amazing*?

Jesus. The bar really is so low for men it's in hell.

"You do realize the point of a date is to get to know each other?" he continues lightly, eyebrows lifting.

Well, I've been thoroughly called out. "Sorry," I wince. "I'm rusty, I guess. It's been a long time since I've been out on a date."

"Really?"

The surprise in his tone is so genuine that it's flattering. And here I was, assuming that admitting I don't get out much makes me sound like a loser. Clearly he doesn't think I am. "Yeah... I guess I've been a little hung up on someone else."

A lot of guys would hear that and bristle at the idea of competition. Not Peter. Peter smiles gently, like he understands. "Well, I'm glad you're here with me."

I smile back, feeling warmth settle around my heart. "Me too." It's a nice moment, but it feels a little heavy, so I break it by quipping, "You know, I was a little nervous about this date, but I think you might be kind of a closet nerd, Mr. Motorcycle. I feel like you're the kind of guy who had a phase where you wore fedoras with sincerity."

He wants to laugh. So bad. I can see it in the sudden twinkle in his eye as he rubs his lower lip. Between the size, strength, and tattoos covering the back of those hands... the sight sends a sharp pang of need straight through my core. *Dios*, they'd look good around my neck.

"Well, that's where you're wrong, love. I've never done anything with sincerity."

I grin. Yup. Confirmed. Similar senses of humor. And "love"? I'm definitely a goner.

Our food comes, then, and our flirting is momentarily derailed by how amazing it all looks and smells. I load my tacos up with the spiciest sauce on the table, and Peter reaches for it to do the same.

"I would stick to the green one," I advise. At his questioning look, I smirk. "No offense, but you look like regular black pepper might take you out."

He throws his head back and laughs, and I'm treated to the sight of his throat bobbing. "I know British food isn't notorious for its use of spices—which I've always found odd, considering the fact that my forefathers colonized the world for them—"

"You said it, not me, 50 Shades of Beige," I cut in, grinning.

"—but don't worry about me, love. I'm made of sturdy stuff." He thumps his chest twice with his hand.

He makes his point by reaching for the sauces and using the little spoon to pour some of the red one directly on his finger. He sticks it in his mouth, maintaining a teasing kind of confrontational eye contact, but the cocky expression slowly melts into alarm as the heat hits his tongue and coats the inside of his mouth.

"Your ears are turning red, Peter." I wave my pointer finger in his general direction. "And I think I see a little steam coming out of them."

He makes a pained grunt and reaches for his water.

I tuck my lips against each other so I don't laugh at his pain and push his beer closer to him with my fingertips. "Drink this—water will make it worse."

The look he shoots me is full of gratitude and a refreshing lack of ego. After he quenches the fire in his mouth, we settle into the easiest back-and-forth conversation I can remember having in person… ever. We mostly end up exchanging stories from our childhoods, a perfectly safe topic. Some of his stories even remind me of things SpyderMan has told me, making me wonder if it's a universal boy experience to try to ride a bike with no hands and crash into a pond.

An hour goes by in the blink of an eye. Peter is… kind of perfect.

He's polite to waiters and strangers. He eats neatly. He listens intently when I speak and doesn't just wait for his turn to talk. He notices when I get cold from a draft and offers me his jacket. He's funny and smart. He waves off my offer to split the check. He laughs at my jokes and never gets offended by my personal brand of mocking, sarcastic flirting.

So when we step out into the night and pause on the sidewalk in a silent precursor to that moment where we both awkwardly prod to see how much further the other person wants to take this, I don't even hesitate. I don't want to just break the touch-barrier, I'm gonna barrel right through it.

I grab the back of his neck and pull him down to me. The kiss starts gentle and slow—a thank you, a question, a suggestion. His lips are soft against mine, though there's a rough patch of stubble under his bottom lip that drags sinfully against my delicate skin. He tastes a little spicy from our meal. I don't know if that's what gets me going, or if it's a reminder of just how amazing that date was, but it lights a spark in me.

I step into him, opening for the kiss and stretching my body so I can wrap my arms around his neck, and his response is instant. Fusing his mouth to mine, his body curls around me as he finds my waist and grips me hard enough to send a little zing to my pussy at the force. His body is so firm and warm through his shirt. I hug him tighter so the world doesn't slip away around me, and one of his hands comes up to cradle the back of my head, threading into my hair. I gasp into his mouth at the slight tug—the smallest show of force, driven by a desire too desperate to be polite. I suddenly want to tear his clothes off with my teeth like some kind of animal.

Someone wolf whistles, reminding us we're out in public. We pull apart, but we're still both so locked in that neither of us bothers to look for the catcaller.

"Whoa," I breathe, panting a little.

His eyes are wide, too. In the dim light of the streetlamps, his pupils have almost taken over the green-gray of his irises. "Whoa," he agrees.

Swallowing, he releases my hips. I unwind my arms from around his body, shivering a little when the slow drop from my tiptoes drags our bodies against each other for a few painfully short inches.

"I'll walk you back. I'll be a perfect gentleman," he swears.

I grin. "*Dios,* I hope that's not true," I say, sliding my hand up his chest because I just can't seem to help myself.

"How close do you live?" he rasps.

The urgency in his demand makes my nipples prickle. *So close. A bed is only a few blocks away if we can make it that far. Though if we can't, I won't be too mad. I've never fucked in an alley...*

I'm so turned on and ready to go, I can barely believe it when what comes out of my mouth is, "Too close for a first date."

It's not that I'm a prude—fucking obviously—or that I think dating ought to be some kind of game where the woman withholds sex. Honestly, I'm not sure what's holding me back—maybe that he's almost *too* perfect. Maybe that I actually want to know him better and I'm afraid that having sex might change that somehow...

This is new territory. I wasn't expecting to *like* him so much.

I start to pull away. He groans in sexual frustration, covering my hand with his much larger, warmer one and stilling my retreat. "Fuck. I..." he runs his free hand through his hair, disheveling it. "Christ, all I want to do is try to convince you to change your mind, but that makes me feel like a tosser. All right. You said no. I can respect that. Just..."

I don't even have time to be completely fucking charmed by that because, in a blink, he sweeps me back into his arms. This time, he holds my face. I love how delicate it makes me feel, and how warm his palm is against my skin. It's like being cradled, especially when the side of his thumb caresses softly over my cheekbone. He holds me still and brushes his lips so gently across mine that I try to lean in. I moan softly when I can't.

He pulls back, staring down at me intensely. My need is a hollow ache, and he's *right here* offering to fill it. What kind of stupid idiot turns down an offer like that? I'm kicking myself.

"Text me?" I ask, sounding just as bereft and eager as I feel.

He laughs. "I'll text you."

10

WESLEY

I'm... compromised.

I follow her home because I'll be damned if I let her make the five-block walk alone. Unguarded. Looking like that? Fuck no.

After I confirm that she's safely inside her building, I trot back to where I parked my bike. The ride to the van—parked a few miles away in an abandoned strip mall across from a garage—is short, but Madison has already changed into pajamas by the time I get my screens up. As I settle in, I turn over the events of the evening with a half-smile I can't seem to wipe away. And the night isn't over yet.

I had to be very careful when I slipped the sedative into her drink. I'm partial to a bit of sleight of hand, but if anyone had caught me, it would not have ended well. Difficult to explain. But I managed, and the carefully calibrated dose should be just enough to lull her into a very peaceful sleep in about an hour. She'll be deeply under when I break in to clone her phone and sneak onto her computer. And then, once I have what I need, I'll take it back to the house and sift through Madison Cooper's private life and discuss with my team whether or not we're taking the hit...

Dread and disappointment curl together and sit heavily in the center of my chest—which, obviously, is the wrong fucking response. She's a *target*. Always has been. But deep down I think I knew from the moment I saw her that Madison was going to be a big problem for me. Our date only confirmed it.

Physically, she's exactly what I like in a woman. But she's not just beautiful; she's also confident and funny and witty. She's quick, she doesn't back down, she knows what she wants, and if you step out of line, she'll knock you right back into the place where *she* decides you go. She made me work for it; she made me *want to* work for it. Flirting with her felt so much like verbally sparring with my mermaid, I didn't want the date to end.

And that kiss? I was half hard on the street as she sauntered away. Still am.

I lean back in my seat and shut my eyes, squeezing my thigh as the familiar fantasy crops up. In my mind, it's always mermaidav—whoever she is. The one woman I can't have. She kneels before me, half under my desk, face partly obscured by some randomly generated hair. Sometimes it's blonde, or red, or something more eye-catching and unnatural, like purple.

This time, mermaidav is wearing Madison's face. This time in the fantasy, her hair is thick and dark with green streaks as I wind it around my hand. I've barely been able to get the sounds of her sweet moans out of my mind—and now that I know how she feels in my arms, how her soft curves press into me, how she tastes...

I'm not just hungry; I'm *starving* for her—*all* of her, not this facsimile assembled through distance.

I want to know all the things you can only know from being close enough to touch. I want to know what her hair smells like, if she gets cold easily, if she hums to herself or sings in the shower, and if her hands are calloused. I want to watch her eyes light up as she laughs, or her pupils dilate with anticipation as she watches me approach. I want to know how fast she reads. I want to know if she's ticklish and what her weight feels like on my lap. I want to know how she tastes everywhere.

Fuck. I don't want to fuck my hand anymore. I'm sick of it. I want to wrap my fingers around something larger, press into something softer.

I want to feel her pulse flutter under my fingertips as she responds to the sensations I inflict. I want to feel her throat move against my palm, and the vibrations from her voice box as she begs for relief from my cock. I want both of us to watch as I slide so slowly into her body that it does nothing to satisfy the restless, hot need welling between her legs—because I value *accuracy*, and begging for my cock isn't the same as begging to be fucked...

The cock that's currently pounding with its own heartbeat, the sensitive tip punching rhythmically at the back of my fly. Fuck, at this rate I'm going to have a zipper imprint on my dick. I move in my seat, shifting the length in my trousers.

Get a hold of yourself, man.

As hot-blooded as I currently feel, I know she was just as revved up when we parted ways. I could see it in the flush in her cheeks, and the way her eyes clouded with desire. I can't help wondering with equal parts hope and dread: will she take her vibrator for another spin before turning in for the night?

Unfortunately, she doesn't get into bed and treat me to a show—though I probably wouldn't have seen much of it anyway with the camera angled how it is. She gets high and zones out in front of a horror movie, mindlessly scrolling on her phone until she succumbs to the sedative and falls asleep on her couch around 10 PM. After the feed picks up her soft snores among the suspenseful music and intermittent movie soundtrack screams, I move.

Turning off all the security cameras on the block takes no time at all. Shutting off the streetlamps for cover is a bit harder, but I manage it in a matter of a few minutes and keystrokes. No cable tech uniform and hard hat tonight; instead, I pull on a black jumper to more easily blend into the night and shove a balaclava in my back pocket just in case.

Picking the lock to the main door of her building is the most challenging, but my skills are improving.

I let the breezeway door close as softly as possible behind me. The muffled echo of my footsteps is the only sound in the dark hallway. Holding my breath, I reach for the knob of apartment 102, fully expecting to meet resistance.

It's open.

My brows snap down. She fell asleep without locking the door. Well, I'm not fucking leaving her in an open flat all night—I'll just have to hope she won't remember leaving it unlocked when she wakes in the morning.

As I crack the door open, the horror movie music plays to a crescendo. How fitting.

When the noise and motion don't seem to disturb her, I step inside. The sedative I chose is very effective, but you never know how someone will react to it. It seems to have totally knocked her out.

I stare down at her. She looks so damn soft. Soft hair, soft skin, soft body...

She's curled on her side on the couch, breathing evenly. Her head is on the arm closest to me, and her hair spills around her, wild and careless. Her legs and stomach are dark silhouettes underneath the blanket, but their rounded shape is unmistakable. In this position, her breasts press together from gravity and the weight of her arm, giving her cleavage a deep line that I wish like hell I could explore. The flimsy strap of her tank top has slipped halfway down her bicep and the neckline is dangerously low, giving me a glimpse of the edge of a dark nipple.

My heart pounds harder in my chest, the noise drowning out all rational thought as I sink to my haunches and bring our faces near enough that we're breathing the same air.

Some of her hair has fallen across her face, so I reach up and gently brush back the strands, tucking them back behind her ear so I can see her better. I liked the look she wore to dinner, but without makeup she looks more innocent. Peaceful.

The feathering of dark lashes against her skin gives her sleeping face a delicate look, and her smooth cheeks are a touch flushed, perhaps from sleep or the warmth of the room. The slight part of her lips is such a tempting invitation, I can't look away. Driven by urges I can't name or explain, I lift my index finger and touch the middle of her bottom lip, pulling it down just a fraction. Seeing the depression of my finger in the pillowy, soft skin makes me bite back a groan.

The memory of these lips against mine plays on a loop as I trace their fullness lightly. Desire flares, pounding a steady, mounting rhythm in my blood. Perhaps... just another taste...

She inhales sharply, and I startle, shifting back. It's just a small snore, and her eyes remain firmly shut, but it's enough to remind me of the stakes and snap me out of whatever trance I seem to be in. I rise, and pull the blanket up higher over her sleeping form, hiding her partial nudity like I should have done from the first.

What the hell am I doing? Other than being an absolute pervert on a sleeping woman.

I wish I could chalk it up to being rusty—it's been too long since I stepped out from behind my screens—but the truth is much more uncomfortable than that, I fear. Because where shame ought to twist and eat away deep in my stomach, there's only a cool, steely kind of vindication because what I'm doing is wrong, but it *feels* right.

Shit. I'm too close to this, too attracted to her. I'm not being rational. If we decide to take the hit, I'm not going to be able to go through with it. I'm... compromised. Perhaps I should bring Mac in to take over.

At the thought, anger rises in my chest—I don't want him anywhere near her.

Yeah, I'm definitely compromised. I don't understand this power she has over me, and it's starting to make me feel insane. I'm meant to be calm, rational, controlled. The job demands it; my role demands it. But

I've blown way past irrational, verging on obsessed. It's my own fault for letting myself get so close.

Once I have her information, I can return to my office to sort it out. Physical distance should help with the emotional distance I clearly need.

Her phone is sitting on the coffee table, so I grab it and type in the passcode I've seen her use through the cameras. Moving silently, I bring it with me into her bedroom, cloning it to my own as I go. Her computer's RGB fan casts light into the room, so when I wake the screen it's not a sudden shift from darkness to blue light.

I enter her password, confirm her identity using her cell phone, and tap around curiously through her home bar. I recognize most of the icons and feel my brow lift, seeing some of the same programs I use for writing and testing code. Madison Cooper knows what she's doing, and she's no slouch with technology. As if she needed to be more perfect.

Odd that she didn't mention it at dinner, though I suppose I had to drag personal details out of her—

I freeze, recognizing the last tab in her open browser. It's an IRC. I click on it, maximizing the window in the screen and bringing up her last conversation. A cold sweat breaks out on my forehead.

It's *my* IRC. And that's... that's *my* handle... and her handle is...

I scramble away from the screen like I've been burned, nearly toppling her office chair.

No.

No!

Madison Cooper is mermaidav.

Shit.

Shit.

The General wants her dead. *I'm* meant to kill her.

I'm not compromised. I'm screwed.

My heart beats wildly. My mind races, thoughts swirling too fast to catch and hold on to any single one. Rapid-fire bursts of alarm, dread, fear, excitement, longing, relief, vindication, and fury get all mixed up.

No wonder everything about her felt just a little bit familiar. I should have known. Well, I should have *guessed*. What are the odds I'd have such an intense connection with two people the same way? That two different women would have the same sense of humor and use the same colloquialisms?

I suppose I didn't want to see it. I didn't want it to be true. I didn't want to think that *my* mermaidav is someone I've been sent to kill...

Well, obviously I'm not fucking doing *that*. That same protective instinct I was just questioning flares. Anyone who touches a single green hair on her lovely head dies.

But the General has eluded me for *years*.

What the *fuck* am I going to do?

I need a plan.

As much as I want to stay—to wake her, to hold her to me, to hover protectively—I need to leave. Madison is going to wake up eventually, and she can't find me here. And I know that if I let myself stop for even a second to look at her again, I'll never leave.

So I don't let myself pause long enough to do anything other than place her phone back where it was and reverse pick the lock on my way out, just to ensure she's safe. I barely maintain the presence of mind to check the time before I make the call. Not quite 11 PM. Dimitri will be in bed, but Mac should still be awake.

He answers on the first ring. "Yo."

"We have a big problem."

11

WESLEY

A perfectly reasonable reason to do some creepy ass stalker shit

"Madison Cooper is one of my spiders."

The time hovers close to midnight, but the silence in the office following my news is wakeful and tense. Fully dressed but looking a bit tired, Dimitri processes the information with a scowl, parked on his kneel-chair against the edge of the desk. Mac is more disheveled—he obviously threw on whatever he could find, because his rumpled tee shirt is backwards and inside out. He scrubs his face and straightens in the faded red wingback chair he always sits in.

"Whoa, really? And you didn't know before you started watching her?" Mac's tone is full of disbelief.

"Yes, I also assumed you knew the identities of all your informants," Dimitri adds.

"You losing your edge or something, Short Round?"

I lift a brow. Personally, it thrills me she was so good at evading discovery, and my team knows better than to question my abilities. Still, I'm a man with an ego, same as they are. "She's the only one I could never find."

Mac whistles. "She must be good, then."

"She's my *best* spider," I correct, feeling oddly proud on her behalf.

"You don't want to kill her," Dimitri assumes.

"We *won't* be killing her," I correct again, trying to control my tone so it doesn't sound combative. I succeed—barely. "No one will."

Dimitri's scowl is deeply etched on his face after all these years. He cocks his head, lost in thought. "If the General wants her dead and we do not take the hit, he will send her name to another," he points out.

"I know." I nod and take a deep breath, sitting back in my chair. My resolve is made of steel, but my stomach flops over anxiously. Every second I wait is another that she's unprotected. "I won't risk another hitman coming after her—I won't allow that kind of danger to her life, or anyone important to her. I want to tell the General we'll take the hit. It'll buy us some time."

At that, Dimitri's scowl deepens. "Hmm. I suppose a skilled informant is an asset worth protecting. Though, the repercussions will be challenging to manage. Will you—"

But the expression on Mac's face shifts slightly, and he cuts in, "Wait a minute, D. I don't think she's *just* an asset. Wes... do you *like* her?"

"What is this, primary school?" I return, raising a brow at him.

"You do!" Mac realizes, eyes rounding as a grin settles onto his lips. He looks to Dimitri, wanting to share in this newfound excitement and enthusiasm, but finds only the usual emotional wall. Rolling his eyes at Dimitri's impassive face, Mac digs in his pocket for his phone. "What was her name again? Madison something?"

"Cooper," Dimitri helps.

I grit my teeth. "What are you going to do, look her up?"

"I'm gonna friend her on Facebook," Mac shoots back, rolling his eyes. "Of fuckin' course I'm looking her up. I gotta see the girl who finally caught your eye. I bet you like 'em wild, huh? Or are you more of a lady-in-the-streets kind of *bloke*—"

"You like her?" Dimitri repeats the question, but in a far more accusatory way that implies my decision-making abilities are compromised.

He doesn't know the half.

"Yes," I admit, grimacing when the word falls so woefully short of describing my feelings.

The part of me that's primitive and instinctual wants to take her—to claim her as loudly as I can so everyone knows. But old habits die hard, and there's a much louder part of me that guards the truth—even about this, even to them. It's a deep, dark fear I can't rationalize away: that bad things happen when people know the truth.

"She's much more than just a spider to me, if I'm honest," I say, and even that truth still feels like a compromise. "But even if that weren't true, she'd never pass our test. She sells information to me and, I assume, others—but she's not hurting the innocent. She's not a bad person who deserves her fate at the end of your knife. She's..."

My mermaid. My Madison, now.

Sure, I just learned her name, but you don't need to know someone's name to know who they really are. I know her heart. I know her *soul*. And I don't care if she's good or bad—it doesn't matter to me. She's *mine*. And if I'm honest, I've been hers ever since that first message.

Already several steps ahead, our fearless leader spears me with a meaningful, almost understanding look. "She will never be safe," he points out, refusing to let me ignore the very thing I've been trying to. "Even if you fake her death, she will live the rest of her life with a target on her back. And if he finds out we defied him, so will we."

I heave a sigh and lean forward onto my elbows, rubbing my face harshly. It's time for another piece of the truth.

Because he's right. There's no trying to reason with a man like the General—to convince him not to kill her. It's not as if we can pay him off, and I doubt he can be threatened effectively. If he lives, he won't be satisfied until she's dead.

It was never the plan to let him live.

I grind my jaw. "As far as I'm concerned, the General just signed his own death warrant."

Mac reels back, blinking in surprise at the vehemence in my voice. A muscle in Dimitri's jaw ticks, but he doesn't look shocked. The words sit heavily in the air. From their perspective, it's a declaration of war against the man who brought us together. A man who, for all intents and purposes, has never done Mac or Dimitri any personal wrong.

"Look, this isn't your fight—either of you," I say, giving them each a serious look in turn. Do I want their help? Of course. But I can't ask it. Not after everything I've done and kept from them. "You don't have to—"

"Oh, fuck off with that selfless bullshit," Mac cuts me off, slashing his hand through the air. "Like I'd let you do this on your own. I was all for collecting intel and being careful, since we don't know jack shit about the General, but frankly the wait-and-see approach gives me the scratch anyway. I'm all in and ready to take this fucker down. What about you, Big D?"

Dimitri casts his eyes skyward and mutters something in Russian, too low for either of us to hear—I catch *stupid decision* and *all be killed*. He sighs. "The General will become a problem eventually, I suppose. As he claims more power, he will go after anyone who threatens that power. Your spider is likely the first of many innocent targets, and I will not work for a dictator. Still, making a move on someone protected by anonymity is incredibly dangerous..." He scrubs at his scar, up through his short hair.

"I know you have other people to think about," I start. Everyone in the house knows that he and Nicole are trying for a baby. "I wouldn't blame you—"

Dimitri makes an irritated, dismissive sound. "That is not what I meant. I am with you. Of course I am with you, my brothers," he adds, emphasizing his loyalty. "I was considering the danger so we could plan for how to proceed. I do not intend to die or to allow either of you to die."

Pride and gratitude for my team—my family—swells in my chest, though it twists around the guilt. The ever-present guilt. "Magnanimous of you," I return wryly.

He waves me off, though whether it's because of the sentiment or the fact that he doesn't know that particular English word, I can't say. He taps his bicep with his thumb, thinking. "Do you have any idea why the General wants her dead?"

I shake my head. Motive is key when trying to find a killer, so that'll be my first step. "I'm assuming this has something to do with her work as an informant."

"Does he know of your spider network?"

I blanch. I never considered the possibility that the General *knows* that he sent me the name of one of my own informants. "I don't know. I've never mentioned it to him, but I have no way of knowing how far his reach is."

"*Da.* He could be anyone, anywhere. We must know who is she to him. What if she works for him? What if she sees or speaks with him every day—with or without knowing? She might accidentally give something away."

"He might have put sleepers in her life," Mac adds—another possibility I hadn't considered.

"He might be monitoring her online activity," I add, thoughtfully tapping the top of my desk. "Since we don't know who he is, I need to be as cautious as possible. Best to move quickly and do it in person. I'll let her know what I can about the situation, then we can start assembling a list of anyone she sold intel to or about. With any luck, we'll find him among those names."

"You believe she will be willing to assist us with this?"

"I'll figure out some way to persuade her," I say, though internally I lack some of the conviction I project.

I have *no idea* what I'm going to say to her.

How would she react—how would *anyone* react—to finding out the man she's dating has actually been sent to kill her? Luckily, she trusts me—SpyderMan, anyway. Once I explain everything, I'm confident that she'll cooperate, but I know her well enough to know that getting to that point will require finesse.

Excitement thrums in my veins at the idea of working to find the General together. Working with her, side by side—a personal fantasy of mine.

"What will you do to ensure the General does not learn of our plan?" Dimitri presses.

"I'll accept the job to buy some time, but I can't appear to be flagrantly ignoring a kill order, and if he finds out I'm looking for him, we're all at risk. The safest course will be to fake her death—at least until we can find him and he's not a threat anymore. We'll have to lie low."

"Will you bring her to one of the safe houses?"

I consider it. "There's that house in Edison, with the basement already set up as a clean room. We can sort through her list, check out anyone involved in her jobs one by one."

"Nah, bring her here," Mac suggests, grinning.

"James," Dimitri says in a warning tone. "This is serious."

"I'm being serious," Mac scoffs. "We're in a fucking fortress, and this office is basically a clean room. You know this is the safest place—the General can't touch us in here."

"We know nothing of this woman, except for that Wesley—" his eyes cut to me and his lips quiver just a little, "*likes* her. They have history, *da*, but he has only been watching her for a week. She is still an unknown. It would not be wise to expose ourselves that way."

"I'm with Dimitri, actually. Not because I don't trust her," I add, giving him a look of reproach. After his shenanigans with Nicole, it's a bit high and mighty of him to decide Madison doesn't get the same benefit of the doubt. "But I need to handle this delicately. She's an informant, so she's likely secretive by nature. Since she already knows me, I believe she'll be more comfortable with just me."

Dimitri nods approvingly, accepting my rationale, and Mac huffs a breath of disappointment. "You callin' me indelicate?"

"A bull in a china shop comes to mind," I quip.

"You are as subtle as one of those horns used by ships in bad weather," Dimitri adds.

"Foghorn," I offer.

"That is what I said."

I smirk at Dimitri as Mac rolls his eyes. He doesn't argue when he knows he's lost—one of his more admirable traits. "Can we get back to the important part, here?"

"I concur," Dimitri nods.

"—which is that Wes is down bad for this girl," Mac finishes, making Dimitri scowl at him like he's been tricked into agreeing to something he never would have. "You got cameras in her house?"

"You know I do—you were on the phone with me while I was placing them. What of it?"

He stretches out, putting both hands behind his head in a deceptively casual posture. "Nothing. It's just funny, is all."

I shake my head. Dare I ask? He'll tell me either way.

"I mean, everyone was giving me such shit for being all obsessed with Eleanor, but that's one line even *I* didn't cross," he grins. "How're you gonna explain that one to her?"

"I put them in when she was a job," I argue.

"And you left them in because..." he prompts.

Fuck. I roll my eyes at him. I could argue that I only just found out, but I did have time to take them down before I left. The thought never even crossed my mind. Even now, my body tightens, rebelling against the idea of losing my eyes on her.

"Because she's in danger. Someone wants her dead—"

"Ah yes, the *someone wants her dead* excuse. A perfectly reasonable reason to do some creepy-ass stalker shit. We know it well." Mac turns to Dimitri who—un-fucking-believably—nods his agreement. "Of course you gotta watch her. What if someone attacks? Has nothing to do with the fact that she looks like that." He holds up his phone proudly, having navigated to the shared files while we were talking.

I tear my eyes away from the picture on his screen, barely holding back a displeased grumble. I don't like seeing her on his phone—I need to delete her photo from that file.

"And of course you must take her somewhere safe where you can be alone and have her to yourself," Dimitri adds, rolling with the vibe with an odd twinkle in his eye. It's not a smile, but his amusement is clear.

I cross my own arms, fighting a smirk. "I'm the only goddamn professional among us. If I were taking a page from your book, I'd have just brought her here without asking or telling anyone in advance," I nod at Mac, who grins back unapologetically, "or acted like I had the situation sorted and turned up here with her in the boot of my car," I finish, raising a brow at Dimitri.

"Hey, don't knock it, Short Round. You haven't told her anything yet, and you admitted you don't know how she'll react—you might need to keep your options open. Plus, I hear a ride in the trunk of a car really riles 'em up," Mac adds, getting in a jab at both of us.

Instead of rising to the bait, Dimitri actually smirks. "Some call it foreplay. But perhaps it is more Wesley's style to take all her clothes and make her crawl up the stairs."

Mac inhales so sharply he starts choking, coughing on nothing more than air and saliva. He sits forward, thumping his chest. "You heard that?" he asks, voice strangled.

"The entrance to this house is made of stone and glass, and you believed your voice would not carry?" Dimitri asks, lifting a brow.

"You never said anything before..." Mac sucks in a breath through his teeth and grimaces. "Maybe don't tell Eleanor."

Dimitri scoffs. "I would never disrespect her like that. The blame is yours for taking something that should be private and turning it into a game on the staircase in the middle of the house."

All contrition gone, Mac tucks his hands back behind his head again with a low chuckle. "Good times."

Dimitri rolls his eyes. "Since we seem to be finished with this for now and Wesley has his plan, I am leaving. Unless there is some way for James and I to contribute?"

"No one needs stabbing or shooting just now, but I'll let you know the moment that changes," I say, a snarky promise. "And Madison and I should be able to handle reviewing her list on our own, but I expect we'll need you two when we start narrowing down suspects."

Mac throws Dimitri a look over his shoulder. "Hear that? We're off the hook for computery stuff. I like this chick already."

Dimitri makes a thoughtful noise. "Then I recommend you send the General our bid for her job and get some sleep in your own bed. You look very tired."

"Thanks for that." I roll my eyes as he grabs the handles of his scooter and maneuvers it to leave—he's really gotten the hang of that thing.

Mac stands, slapping his thighs with both hands. "Well, I can't wait to meet her," he says, all traces of mockery gone from his smile now. "Anyone who can get you worked up like that? Must be pretty extraordinary."

"I think there was a compliment in there," I observe, raising a brow.

"For her, not you," Mac assures me, matching my dry tone.

He's nearly at the door when I realize I need him to know—need to speak the words out loud instead of keeping it bottled up with everything else. "Mac?"

He pauses.

"She's the person I didn't realize I was waiting for."

Instead of responding, he cracks another grin and taps the door frame a few times, nodding his head. The sound of him whistling something happy and tuneless lingers in the hall as he heads in the direction of the woman who made him feel the same way.

I open up my email, scroll through until I find the last one from the General, and reply with a bid for the hit on Madison.

Then, unable to stand it a second longer, I log into the camera feeds on my phone and drink in the sight of her on the couch. She shifted positions—the blanket has slipped and her top is even more askew, revealing more lovely, tempting caramel skin. What I wouldn't give to be back in there with her... I'm aching with the need.

Is this what Mac felt like, watching Eleanor? I remember thinking he was daft—that no woman could so instantly and completely demand his attention or inspire his obsession.

Hand me a stone and chuck me in a glass house, because I get it.

Well, sort of. My attraction to Madison was instantaneous, but my connection with her online persona has been two years in the making—an excruciatingly slow burn. Now that the fire has taken, it's spreading fast. Too fast. I'll never be able to put it out... and I don't want to. I want to make it burn higher and hotter until it consumes us both.

I still feel half-insane with all these emotions swirling around, but amid all the totally justified anger and upset, there is a curious relief.

Because I found her. Because the woman I felt so drawn to is the same woman I've been falling for all this time. Because now that I know who and where she is, I can finally be more than SpyderMan to her.

I suppose there's an upside to finding out your best friend and possibly soul mate is on the hit list of a secretive megalomaniac—it brought us together. And frankly, I can't believe my brilliant luck. She's more beautiful than I dared imagine, and based on that date and that kiss, our chemistry is going to be explosive. I can't wait to have her under me.

All that remains now is to tell her the truth. Not my strongest suit.

I need to be careful with not just *how* I proceed, but also with what I reveal. She's careful and smart, and she knows her work is dangerous. I'm concerned that if I reveal the full extent of the truth—that she's become a target, that I've been sent to kill her—she'll simply disappear. She has the skills to go off grid.

I can't lose her; not when I've just found her.

12

MADISON

I'm a bit impulsive when I'm mad.

"No, that's the wrong color, *m'hijita*. It doesn't fit, see?" Abuela says sharply, taking the puzzle piece from me with a chiding cluck of her tongue. "Where is your head today?"

In a Mexican restaurant. Well, more specifically, on the sidewalk just in front of a Mexican restaurant—replaying that moment and wishing it had ended differently.

"*Lo siento, Abuela,*" I reply dutifully, refocusing on the color sorting task she parsed out.

Compulsively, I check my texts for the thousandth time to see if Peter has sent me anything. He hasn't. I deflate back into my chair. Is this normal? I suppose it's been less than 48 hours since we talked, but all I want to do is talk to him again. If I had girlfriends, I would go to them to ask how long you're supposed to wait after a date to text someone.

Am I supposed to text him, or am I supposed to wait for him to text me?

Ugh this is why I hate dating. I'm not used to self-doubt, and I hate it. The what if's are exhausting.

What if he didn't like me that much? What if I offended him and he was too polite to tell me? I do that sometimes. I know I'm not the easiest person to be around.

Or... What if he got hit by a bus?

Logically, I know the most likely scenario is that he's just waiting to reach out to me, as per the normal, regular, socially acceptable customs.

I hate the socially acceptable customs. I just want to know if he likes me as much as I like him.

I want to skip right to the sex so I can find out firsthand if his wiener is boyfriend material, but I also want to explore this connection with him before we do that. When you're a depression/anxiety girlie and it's hard to cross the finish line, it turns something that should be fun into a bit of an ego minefield.

Or do I rip the Band-Aid off? Get the first time over with so I can write him off if he's selfish, or he's got a tiny pecker?

Yeah... I could feel it against my stomach, poking me when I pressed into him. And it was... *sizeable*. Definitely not tiny.

Aaaand now I'm right back to overeager, wanting to text him real bad. But I don't have friends to ask this shit. I've only got Abuela. I glance up, finding her muttering to herself in Spanish, cursing how many shades of green there are.

Yeah, I can't tell Abuela about someone I'm seeing before I know if I like him—she'd have the wedding planned before our third date. So there's only one option left...

"You know I hate it when you're on your phone," she instantly scolds.

"I'm just messaging Tío. He told me he had another job for me," I lie. Since it's maybe the only excuse that gets her off my back and doesn't prompt a follow-up, she hmmphs and nods, allowing the phone usage in her presence.

```
mermaidav: You're a guy, right?
SpyderMan: Part spider, part man.
```

I tamp down on a giggle, eyes flicking up guiltily to Abuela, and my mind swings back to Peter. I swear I can hear him saying that in his sarcastic tone. Wait... That's kind of a funny coincidence—the superhero Spiderman's secret identity is Peter Parker.

mermaidav: A one-stop-shop for advice on dating and catching flies? Sold.

SpyderMan: Wait. You want dating advice?

mermaidav: Don't look at me like that

SpyderMan: lol you heard me spit out my drink from all the way over there, eh? I'll admit I'm surprised—both that you'd come to me and that you're dating. For as long as I've known you, you've always claimed to "hate people"

Yeah, he's got me there.

It's an odd sensation to feel like someone you've never seen "sees" you. It's weird how you can *know* a person without knowing them. Because even though we've talked almost every day for two years, there are so many things we don't know about each other—things you don't share when you're trying to protect an identity. It's created a strange, imbalanced situation of knowing *who* someone is without the context to understand how they got to be that way.

I know what kind of music he listens to when he codes, but I don't know where he was born. I know the definitive ranking of his favorite desserts, but I don't know if he has siblings. I know how he feels about right and wrong, but not what he looks like.

And he apparently knows that dating—opening up, considering letting someone else in—is out of character for me. And he's right.

In some ways, he knows me better than anyone else—even Abuela. I've always felt free to speak my mind and be myself with him in a way I never could with Abuela, strict and judgmental as she can be. I've told him so many deeply personal things, and he's never judged me.

Maybe he is the right person to talk to about this after all.

mermaidav: I'm not dating; it was one date. It was a good date. But to your point, I'm

rusty—I'm not sure what to do next or what the
rules are in this situation.

SpyderMan: Wait, you're doubting yourself?
You?? One moment, let me check the forecast…
yes, it does appear that Hell has frozen over.
How odd.

A smile tugs at my lips. Sometimes even a bad bitch needs a reminder of who she is.

mermaidav: You've clearly never met someone
so fine they made feminism leave your body.
The things I'd let this man do to me would get
me kicked out of a women's studies class.

SpyderMan: I take it you liked him, then?

Biting into my lower lip, I barely manage to contain the grin.

mermaidav: yeah. A lot.

SpyderMan: Wow. A lot? You know this after
one date?

mermaidav: Was the part about feminism leaving my body somehow unclear? You want me to be
a bit more descriptive? lol

SpyderMan: No. You just don't normally act
like a little girl with a crush.

I feel my brows shoot towards my hairline. Excuse the fuck outta me? It's hard to interpret tone online, but that almost sounded disapproving.

Wait a minute, is SpyderMan jealous?

The thought sends a thrill through me that makes me shake my head at myself. Yeah, I'm not dealing with that. I don't want him to be jealous—or, rather, I don't want to want him to be jealous. I'm trying to get over him.

This was a mistake. I'll browse dating subreddits for advice before I entangle myself back in my SpyderMan feelings.

mermaidav: Forget it.

SpyderMan: All I'm saying is, you're usually so rational and circumspect. I expected you to be a bit more wary of new people.

mermaidav: I shouldn't have said anything. Let's drop it.

SpyderMan: Who is this bloke, really?

mermaidav: Hold please, I'm looking for my glasses…

SpyderMan: ?

mermaidav: So I can see if I give a fuck about what you think… Oh, yeah, no I definitely don't.

SpyderMan: Fuck. That's not what I meant. I just want you to be careful. To be safe

I'm so over this conversation. While he types out his next message—sure to be another hard backpedal—I log off without saying goodbye.

Who the fuck does he think he is? Is he threatened that there's someone real in my life that caught my interest? What, he just wants me to stay hung up on him?

Okay, that doesn't really fit with what I know about him. But, then again, we've never really talked about any of this stuff… For all I know, he's married with 2.5 kids and a dog!

Was it so much to hope that my only friend would be happy for me? Was it so much to hope that my emotions about it wouldn't be this ridiculously complex?

We can't be together. It's a line we've both drawn. It's dumb to dwell on it or be upset, because we both know it's for the best. And yet, there's a small part of me that *thrills* in his jealousy. Part of me wishes he would push back harder.

And that's exactly the problem.

A voice in the back of my head warns me that texting Peter just because I'm pissed off at SpyderMan is exactly the kind of childish behavior he was just accusing me of—and I fucking hate proving a man right—but I swipe to my texts and start tapping out a message anyway.

Yes, I'm making the first move after a date. Gender conventions be damned.

And I'm a bit impulsive when I'm mad.

> I can't stop thinking about that kiss.

Just like last time, his response is so quick it's like he had his phone in his hand when he got mine.

> Me either. When are you going to let me take you out again?

The urge to type back "right now" is strong, but I don't need to consult anyone to know just how desperate that sounds. I mean, I *am* desperate, but I don't want to sound like I am... Time to dial it back.

> Tomorrow?

> It's a date.

13

WESLEY

Mine. Fuck off.

> You should come over. I'd offer to cook you dinner, but I wouldn't want to give you food poisoning. I'm sure we can find other things to do to occupy our time.

I'm back in Madison's apartment, but the text from her has stopped me dead in my tracks because I'm so fucking jealous that I can barely see straight. It was bad enough when she immediately texted "Peter" after our stupid-all-my-fucking-fault altercation, but now she's being outright flirtatious and I can't stand it. She's inviting him over. She's planning a sex date.

Even though he's me, I don't want her sleeping with Peter. I don't want her falling for the person I'm pretending to be. Well, I suppose I was being *myself* on our date, or... as much as I could be... But in her head, he's not *me*. He's not SpyderMan. He's not Wesley—though she doesn't know that either...

Fuck me, this is confusing. As well as really god-damned ridiculous. I know my jealousy is absurd, but I can't help it. It really felt like she was talking to me about another man. The person she's excited to go out with again feels like *someone else*. I hate that she's excited about someone else.

But I just learned—well, re-learned—a valuable lesson about Madison. I can't push too hard or I'll activate brat mode and she'll do the opposite of what I say simply because I had the audacity to try to tell her what to do. It's infuriating, and I love it, but being on the receiving end does require some patience.

And I am patient. Well, about most things. Getting my hands on Madison seems to be the exception.

I'm taking you out. I've already planned it, so don't say no.

It takes her a moment to respond.

Did anyone ever tell you how hot it is when you take charge like that? Because it is. Ridiculously.

I'll be thinking about you all night.

I groan and stare down at the camera in my hand. After Mac's taunting, I thought more about it and decided to take them out. It feels different now to watch her without her knowledge—not wrong; too damn right. But the invasion of privacy somehow seems more sinister, given how badly I crave her and the history we have that she isn't aware of.

My plan was to leave a bug or two, because I can justify that for her safety—cameras aren't strictly necessary. Plus, I'm nearby. I'm watching through the windows of my van and on the tapped cameras on the street. No one goes in or out of this building without me knowing.

But after that naughty little text? Will she be thinking about me later... in bed? With that vibrator in her top drawer?

The tracking app dings, so I know she's on her way back from her visit with her grandmother. Time to go. Abandoning all deliberation, I carefully place the camera back, ensuring the angle will see the entire room. On my way out, I give her cat a scratch behind the ear that he leans into with a heavy purr, and grab the prop clipboard for my cable tech disguise.

As I open the door, I hear, "Caution! Wide load!" and a human-approximation of a lorry's beeping sound.

With a curious frown, I step into the hallway. There's a bloke waiting—her neighbor, I think... Terry? Tom?—eyes fixed on Madison's door, leaning casually against his own and wearing a cruel smirk. He's got a small pile of mail tucked under his arm, like he's just returned from his box.

When he sees me, his brows shoot up and his arms slacken, falling to his sides. "Oh, uh... my bad, man."

"What?" I frown, confused.

"I thought you were... Never mind. You're, uh..." his eyes trail down over the uniform and clipboard. "The cable guy?"

Realization dawns, sending ice through my veins. He thought I was Madison. Was he... comparing her to the size of a lorry? Must have been. So, he was waiting here for her, just to be an arse and say something mean. And judging from the practiced delivery and smarmy grin, he's done this before.

From what I've seen in their limited hallway interactions from the hacked security cameras, Madison doesn't like him very much. The insults he slings at her are enough to tempt me to violence. Luckily for him, she doesn't seem to need me to intervene—she holds her own. It filled me with pride watching her destroy him so effortlessly before our date. And that was even before I realized she was my mermaid. I hate a bully as much as anyone else, but I'd have been content to sit back and let her handle it.

But then this dickhead went and waited in his fucking doorway to insult *my* lovely girl.

Anger rises in my throat; I'm practically choked by it. My fingers grip the edges of my clipboard so hard it nearly snaps in my grip as I glare. I say nothing for a few seconds, and the silence hangs between us. His awkwardness turns to nervousness, which crystallizes into a prideful kind of shame that has him rubbing the back of his neck and looking away.

"Yeah, so... I'm thinking of switching services—"

"I'm not the cable guy," I say, stone-faced. It sounds like a threat. It *is* a threat.

He falls back a half-step. "Oh, you're, uh... *with* Madison?" he asks incredulously, eyes scanning my biceps and tattoos.

Her name on his lips sends me spiraling.

Mine. Fuck off.

The urge to punch him in those stupid fucking perfect American teeth is almost too strong to control. He's a handsome enough prick, I'll give him that, but I'd like his face a lot more if it was pulp under my boot.

"And what if I am?" I challenge. "It's *Todd*, right?"

His eyes widen at my low, combative tone. For a second, I watch the emotions play out as he cycles through fear, anger, curiosity and lands right back on apprehension. Smarter than he looks, then. He straightens against the closed door of his apartment, mail nearly slipping from beneath his arm. I don't normally let my size speak for me, but I'm not a small man. I've got about three inches and 40 pounds of muscle on this dickhead—obviously he's only tough enough to go after people smaller than him. Like Madison.

And that makes the anger burn even hotter.

"Whoa, hey man. I got no beef with you."

I just stare, letting him see the sharp edges honed by a life of violence that I normally keep hidden. The instant he realizes I'm an actual threat, his eyes dart to the side, like he's gauging the likelihood that he can grab for the doorknob and slip inside before I reach him. "Did she say something to you? It's... It's just a fucking joke, okay? We joke around. Jesus Christ. She gives it right back, too—she tell you that? The mouth on her—"

That's what does it.

I step into the hallway, tucking the curious cat back into the room behind me and letting the door close. In a flash, I've got my forearm pressed against his Adam's apple, and his head hits the wood behind him with a hollow thunk. He makes a choked noise, scrabbling against my grip. Arms and legs flailing, he tries to push back, but I press harder, easily countering his jerky movements. He's strong with adrenaline, but I'm stronger and I have more training. Plus, it's hard to fight someone off when you're panicking and asphyxiating.

I need to be quick so my message lands before he passes out.

"If you ever speak disrespectfully to Madison again, I'll kill you. In fact, you're never to speak to her again. Full stop. She never has to see you again. She never has to deal with your sorry bullying arse ever a-fucking-gain. If she enters the hallway, you leave it. If she leaves her flat, you stay inside yours until she's out that door. Do you understand? Nod your head."

I'll take the trembling, jolting movement of his neck and the accompanying gagging sound as a yes.

When I step back, he falls forward, fearfully clutching his throat with both hands as he coughs. He nearly slips on an envelope in an effort to flatten himself against the door and get as far from me as possible. As he's fighting to refill his lungs, I get into his personal space one more time.

"I'll be watching," I murmur, low enough that he has to strain to hear it.

But he did hear it. The look of red-faced terror he shoots me is enough to convince me of that. He ducks into his flat, and I hear a firm deadbolt click that brings a dark smile to my lips.

Forcing myself to make unhurried, casual movements, I pause to double check the name on his mailbox and make my way out. Once I'm back in the quiet stillness of the van, anger slowly melts away, leaving room once again for logic and sense. I groan and scrub my face.

Fuck. What the hell did I just do? I acted like a damn territorial caveman. I made myself memorable to someone who knows Madison in person.

The desire to break his face only grows stronger when I think about how she has to live next to that creep. Good thing I have some time before I'm due for my "date" with Madison. Plenty of time to figure out how to deal with Todd. I'm not so gauche as to murder him just for speaking unkindly—though I could, and I want to—because there are so many more creative ways to destroy someone's life than just taking it. Plus, dealing with a body is such a fucking hassle.

In the meantime, I just have to hope he doesn't say anything to her before I can.

She believes she's seeing Peter tomorrow, but she's going to get SpyderMan.

I don't have my speech planned out quite yet. There are a lot of moving parts. And how honest should I even be? The whole story is so unbelievable she might think me insane.

Hiya, you'll never believe this, but I'm SpyderMan. Yes, that SpyderMan. I've been watching your every move for weeks because I'm actually a hitman, and I've been sent to kill you. Oh, don't worry—I'd never hurt you. I'm pretty sure I love you, and also I'd very much like to spend the next 72 hours with my face buried in your cunt. Then we're going to kill the man who wants you dead. We just need to find him first, and I need your help.

The raw material is there. The execution just needs refining.

A lot of refining.

14

WESLEY

Fuck the plan.

Madison gapes, eyes wide as she takes in the cavernous space. All around us, machines blink and whir, singing their siren calls to entice people to spend their coins—or credits now, I suppose, since payments have gone digital. "How is there no one here?" she says softly, like she doesn't want to be too loud and get us caught in case we're not actually allowed.

It only took $10,000 to rent out the entirety of Wally's Wacky Arcade for the night. I didn't want any prying eyes—no one in the crowd is a potential threat when there's no crowd to speak of. I looped the cameras, and paid off all staff to be somewhere else. It's just the two of us.

The caveman in me thrills in having her like this—no one else gets to see the tiny fucking skirt she chose in order to drive *me* crazy, or the tight, deeply cut jumper giving me more than a flash of mouthwatering cleavage, or the tights with a few wide holes that make me imagine ripping another one somewhere for convenient access...

Mine.

"I know the owner." Not strictly a lie—we met recently when I handed him a giant wad of cash.

"And he helps you with your game?" she jokes, grinning at her own pun.

"Only when my reputation for being fun is at stake."

She laughs. "It's a little post-apocalyptic," she remarks, glancing around at the colorful lights, sending warring rounds of music into the air around us. Usually the chatter and laughter of other patrons would drown it out and it wouldn't seem as discordant. "It's creepy as fuck."

Doubt starts worming in—did I miscalculate?—but then I see the smile on her lips. "I love it," she breathes. "And I love arcade games. How did you know?"

Because I've saved every conversation we've ever had, and on August 12th at 8:07 PM, you said that you weren't really into RPG computer games because you grew up on old school arcade games.

"I had a feeling you were the competitive sort."

She sends me a sly look, tossing her hair over her shoulder. "Is that, like, the polite, British way of calling me argumentative?"

"Well, I did hear from a very reliable source that you've been called a troublemaker. A menace, even, if I recall correctly."

Her grin widens, still impish but even more pleased. "Damn right. My *tío* used to take me to a place like this when I was little and I wouldn't let him take me home until my name was every top score in Pac-Man. So it's *on*—and don't think I'll pretend not to know how to play something and let you rub all up behind me to 'teach' me," she chides, dashing those hopes. She must see it on my face because she winks, "If you want to do that, you'll have to earn it."

I take a step towards her, gratified when she remains in that spot, head tilting up to watch me come. Because I can't help myself, I reach out and tuck a wayward lock of hair behind her ear, letting my hand fall to cup her jaw. I watch my thumb stroke softly at the very edge of her mouth. "And how do I earn it? Shall I win you a teddy bear?"

She swallows heavily, eyes clouding with desire as they scan my face. When she speaks, I can feel her lips moving against the side of my finger. "A teddy bear wouldn't hurt." Before I can react, she turns her face to the side and closes her mouth around the tip of my thumb. She swirls her tongue around it, eliciting a choked noise from deep in my chest. With a sultry grin, she releases me. "But I meant that you're going to have to show me something really special."

Oh, fuck me. Blood pounds in my temples and shoots down to my extremities. I let my thumb slide down so that my hand is cupping the front of her neck. Her intake of breath is sharp, and her pulse throbs against the pad of my finger, fast and hard. Excited by how close we are, or by where my hand is? Both? I'd take both.

"Gladly," I murmur, cocking a smile as I levy another challenge into what is already a charged exchange. "Try to keep up, hmm?"

Eyes locked on me, she bites her full lower lip and I groan aloud, wishing like hell she'd do it to me. With a coy grin, like she knows exactly what she's doing to me and getting the exact effect she wants, she dips a finger into the waistband of my trousers, just behind my belt buckle, and tugs my hips closer. "Don't even think about claiming you let me win when I beat your ass."

All the blood in my body shoots down to my dick. I'm half-tempted to say fuck it and drag her into the manager's office where there's surely a couch or desk I can bend her over...

No. Stick to the plan, Wesley. Not only is her face lit up with child-like excitement and joy, but there was meant to be a very specific order to the night. Play some games and feed her the best sushi in the city—her favorite food—to put her in a very good mood, then break the news about her life being in danger and all that...

And that's not to mention the fact that when I finally have her, it won't be as Peter fucking Smith. It'll be *my* name she's screaming.

Still, I can't let her get away with this kind of teasing, or I'll be half-hard all night—like any brat, she occasionally needs a reminder that her actions have repercussions. If I have to suffer through an aroused state, so does she.

I tighten my grip slightly, making her eyes widen in surprise that quickly melts into heat. Oh, fuck yes. She likes it a bit rough. And the tattoo on the back of my hand makes a fine necklace for her lovely neck.

"I don't plan to ever go easy on you," I murmur, lowering my head until our lips are almost brushing. I can feel her warm breath on my mouth—can practically taste it, "That's what safe words are for."

A small shiver wracks her body, and she licks her lips, touching mine ever so slightly with the very tip of her tongue. "Good," she declares. She pulls back on my wrist, and I begrudgingly let her go, hand clenching around nothing. Dancing away and pivoting, she tosses me a look over her shoulder. "You coming?"

"Only if the night goes really, *really* well," I mutter without thinking.

She throws her head back and laughs, sauntering away towards the row of Skee-Ball games, and I adjust my hard cock before I follow. Taking position next to her, I swipe the card the manager gave me on both machines and the balls release towards us. We both grab one, and I toss it gently to get the weight of it.

"Ready?" she challenges.

I nod. She throws first, tossing with an underhand motion, and launches hers too hard. It misses the small hole marked *Jackpot!* at the top right, bouncing off the edge and landing at the bottom in the return that gives no tickets.

"You're supposed to aim for literally any of the other ones up there, I believe."

She huffs and rolls her eyes. "All right, nerd. You'd better not be all talk after that..."

The taunt dies on her lips as I overhand throw the ball straight through the *Jackpot!*

She's gaping when I turn for her reaction. Seeing my smug expression, her eyes narrow and she crosses her arms. "Oh, I see how it is," she declares. "You're a cheater."

"Am I?" I return, grinning even wider.

"I don't know how you do things across the pond, but you're not supposed to throw the balls like that—you're supposed to roll it along the ramp so it hits the bump and flies up."

"Hmm." I reach down and take the long string of tickets, folding them and pretending to count my winnings. "Look at that. Turns out it's all the same to the machine."

Her lips twitch, and she looks very much like she's trying not to give in to what I'm sure feels like a childish impulse to chide me for my behavior.

"You *are* competitive," I observe with a laugh at her obvious frustration.

She lays a hand on her chest primly. "I am a rule follower at heart—"

"I very much doubt that," I snort.

"—unless I think that rule is stupid," she amends. Leaning down, she grabs one of the balls and shoots me a sly look.

Unexpectedly, she jumps up onto the ramp, trots over to the board and deposits the ball directly into the Jackpot hole. The smirk she sends me over her shoulder sends a zing of energy and excitement through me. With a hearty laugh, I bend down and toss her the next ball that rolls out so she can drop another into the Jackpot.

And with that, our truce is formed.

It's actually more fun finding ways to game the machines and cheat our way to jackpots than it would have been to have a legitimate competition. Any task that involves aim is no match for our teamwork. We toss aside the mallet in Whack-a-Mole and use our hands. We shake the coin pusher until it drops half its quarters. We count the seconds in the Stop The Light game, playfully but seriously arguing over the timing until we get it perfectly. By the end of the hour, we're both riding high on the slightly illicit feeling of cheating our way to the prize section.

She hops up on the counter next to the cash register and leans back on her hands, kicking her feet and scanning the wall of brightly colored stuffed animals hanging from hooks. "I want..." Her eyes dart across them, settling on one with a smile. She shifts forward and points. "The pink and purple dragon."

I let myself behind the counter through the swinging door and dutifully start feeding the tickets into the return counter. We have so many I can barely hold them in one hand. After I satisfy the price, I pull down the stuffed animal and hand it to her with a flourish.

With a wide smile, she takes it in both hands, sitting it on her lap and admiring its fuzzy purple face. "I love him," she declares, tapping the hard plastic nose. Looking up, she nods at the irregularly folded handful I'm holding. "And we still have a lot of tickets."

"Pick something else. Looks like they keep the expensive stuff in the case," I observe, looking down through the glass. "Want a neon pink hoverboard? Ages 12 and up."

She snorts. "So it can break as soon as I step one foot on it? Pass."

"A USB-powered desk aquarium?" I suggest, doing a double take as I read off the box. What in the world?

We both cringe. "Yeah, because I want a tank of water sitting next to my computer. Oh, hey, a mystery box!"

I laugh. "It's 60,000 tickets, and it just has question marks on the label. Do we risk it? We cheated hard for these," I wave the tickets.

She laughs. "True. Hmm... How about..." she peers down into the glass, tapping her finger above something. "That? Do we have enough tickets?"

No. But I'm not leaving this booth again—we're done playing silly games. She's the perfect height on the counter like that, and I need my hands on her.

I tug at the handle, but the case is locked. Figures. Even $10K doesn't get you access to the best prizes. "Do you have a pin in your hair?"

With a cynical look, she fishes one out, causing the pieces it held back to tumble around her face. The urge to tuck them back is so hard to fight, my hand nearly cramps with it. But I just crouch down, bend the pin into a straight pick, and insert one end into the lock.

"No way that's going to work," she challenges, leaning forward to watch with rapt attention all the same.

I wiggle the end through until I feel the tumblers move, then bend the other end inside so the loop will act as leverage for a handle. When it clicks and turns, I send her a triumphant look and a wink. "Eventually you'll learn to stop doubting me."

She laughs again. "Well, excuse me. I didn't realize I was in the presence of hot British Houdini. Do you do this often? Should I check my pockets?"

I puff up—I love how freely she tells me she thinks I'm hot, even when it's paired with a teasing nickname. "I promise this is the first time I've ever broken into an arcade prize case with a bobby pin."

"That was suspiciously precise," she deadpans. "What'd you use last time—a nail file?"

I chuckle, absurdly pleased that she picked up on the intentional specificity. Obviously, I couldn't claim I've never broken into anything.

Sliding the door aside, I reach in and retrieve the necklace she chose. It has a wide black cord with a silver heart-shaped lock hanging at the bottom. The sign on the box proudly states that it's "Sterling Silver Plated," which means it'll probably turn her skin green after a few wears.

She reaches for it, but I shake my head. "I'm going to put it on you," I say softly, decisively. I won't be argued with about this.

Her breath hitches. Her eyes dip to the necklace, then return to meet mine, shining with something hot and eager. She nods and spins to the side, lifting her bent leg onto the glass and grabbing her hair out of the way.

Zeroed in on the long, elegant line of her neck that she just exposed, I step forward and reach around her. My fingers brush against her warm, soft skin, making her shiver slightly. After I do up the clasp, I run the backs of my knuckles against the line of her spine. I can see over her shoulder as her chest heaves, her breath speeding as excitement swells in her veins.

She turns, and it's all I can do not to groan aloud. It's probably meant for a child because it's less a necklace on her and more a choker... and it's so fucking perfect, I can hardly stand it.

She's been so close all evening—close enough to touch—but I haven't let myself. I know one touch and I'll be lost. All plans will be abandoned.

"How does it look?" she asks in a husky tone, letting her hair drop. She cocks her head and tilts her chin up to me. A clear invitation.

Fuck the plan—I'm dying to touch her. One kiss. I *need* a taste. Just one kiss won't throw me too far off course.

I step between her legs, and rumble with pleasure as the height of the counter aligns her core to mine. She gasps softly at the sudden intrusion into her personal space, but adjusts her thighs open even wider to make room for me.

I reach up and tap the face of the heart-shaped lock. "This, I could take or leave—it looks far too cheap to be worn by a creature so magnificent. Though, I do like the look of you in a collar," I add with a smirk.

"So I'm a creature, eh?" she lifts a brow, a smile playing at the corners of her lips.

"I saw how you cheated at Skee-Ball. You're a menace to society," I murmur, leaning down.

When I hook a finger under the collar and tug her closer, her eyes go wide and her smile tilts into one of surprise and raw arousal. She grabs my arms, squeezing as far around my biceps as she can with her small hands. I duck my head and snake my other arm around her to plant my palm against her lower back and slide her as close as physically possible to me. My bulge fits perfectly in the V of her legs, under the soft roll of her stomach, and the heat coming off her is searing.

I flex my arm, pulling her forward at the same time I drop my head to meet her. Our lips crash together, igniting sparks in the atmosphere around us that sparkle at the edges of my vision. Her lips are soft, warm, smooth, and a little wet. She opens for me instantly, accepting the invasion of my tongue with a welcoming bite to the tip. Sweet and sour—her taste and her personality.

The world narrows to the touch of our lips and the feel of her soft body in my arms. When she moans into my mouth, the sound moves through me. I nearly come in my trousers. Days of riding the waves of arousal without relief are working against me now—chipping away at the tight control I normally have on my own body.

As she switches her hold and grabs at my shirt, I wind my hand into her hair and angle her head back, putting her off balance and making her depend on me to stay upright. It deepens the kiss, forcing her to let me in even further.

Time becomes meaningless, and we lose ourselves in each other. When her legs tighten, digging into my sides, and she rubs herself against the front of me, I have to pull away because I might actually come—my pulse is too strong, my blood too hot, and that familiar tingling pressure has started deep in my balls.

Both heaving breaths into the space between us, we stare at each other for a moment, and I feel the echoes of all those strong emotions from our first kiss. Arousal, of course, but also an amazed sort of excitement so unexpected and bone-deep it was practically intimidating.

But unlike that whirlwind kiss shared by strangers, this one feels different. To me at least. I know who she is now. The amazing chemistry that baffles her feels right to me—an almost inevitable conclusion. But she has no idea why our connection is so intense, and she's grappling to make sense of it.

"I've wanted this for so long," I groan, dropping my lips onto the spot where her neck and shoulder meet.

I feel her smile. "Like four days?" she teases.

To hide my misstep, I drag my teeth against her skin, and she shudders. The tiny moan that slips out goes straight to my painfully hard cock.

Okay, new plan. One kiss... and one touch.

I just need to know how badly she wants this—to feel that hot, wet heat for myself.

I pull back far enough to snake a hand down between our bodies. Her skirt moves aside easily, and I trail my fingers over her thighs, noting the odd texture of her tights. Then, suddenly, my fingers meet warm, ridiculously soft skin, and I inhale sharply at the unexpected delight.

"These tights have a few... strategic holes," she says, giving her lower lip a bite. There's a thrill in her tone and eyes.

Desire pounds even harder deep in my chest, and satisfaction roars in my ears. She wants this—planned for it, even before the night began. "And did you *strategically* wear them for me?" I demand, my voice a hard rasp.

As I find the damp fabric of her panties with the very tips of my fingers, she whimpers, and the sound zings through me, thumping painfully in my too-swollen cock. Swallowing hard, she nods up at me in answer to my question.

Okay. New, *new* plan. One kiss, one touch, and one taste. After all, my hands are dirty after handling so many arcade games. It would be unconscionable of me to put them near her sensitive, delicate skin. My mouth, on the other hand...

Gently releasing her, I sink to my knees. She watches me with a curious frown—like she's unsure whether I mean to actually do what I'm clearly getting in place to do. Apprehension edges into her expression, but when I look back up after pressing a soft, inquiring kiss onto her inner thigh, she softens, relaxes into my hold, and gives me a small nod.

She leans back on her hands to make room for my head and to maintain her view of me kneeling at her altar. Heart pounding in anticipation,

I flip her skirt up over her cute tummy and suck in a breath at the large hole ripped through the crotch, revealing almost the entirety of the black lacy panties that only just cover her.

"Fuck, Madison. So goddamn perfect," I breathe, transfixed by the eroticism of what I'm seeing. The juxtaposition of the ruined material—an easily shredded barrier barely keeping me from what I'm aching for—does something to me. It makes me want to tear and take and own.

The noise that escapes her lips is pleased, but demanding, and she squirms a little under the intense focus of my stare. "Peter," she whispers—a plea.

The sound of the wrong name on her lips does something to me. Feeling positively feral, I grab her thighs with both hands, widening her legs, and use my thumb to move her panties aside. I'm greeted by the prettiest bald pussy I've ever seen—soft, shaved skin that looks like sin and smells like heaven.

She whimpers in anticipation. For my part, I'm salivating and so eager to taste her I can barely stand it. Her legs are as wide open as I can get them, spreading her for me perfectly and teasing me with a glimpse of a swollen clit peeking out through her lips. When my mouth finally makes contact with it, she jerks in my grip. Her stomach tenses, and she releases a shout that melts into a long moan.

At the first taste, I know it's going to become something I crave—it's addictive and heady. It unlocks something in me that's more... animalistic. I'm normally a neat person, but I feel myself getting sloppy now. I lick and suck and drool. As my tongue slides over her warm, taut clit, I feel her body move and react to it. Eventually, the noises coming from her change, deepening, growing louder, and accompanied by a bucking of her hips which forces her center against my mouth harder.

"Oh fuck," she groans. "Right there. Fuck. That's so good."

Fuck me, I love some erotic direction. In fact, the break in her voice as she mindlessly chases her pleasure is the hottest thing I've ever fucking heard, and it consumes so many of my senses that I feel like I'm drowning in her. And it's exactly where I want to be.

When I feel her hand weave through my hair and hold my head exactly where she wants it, I lose it—knowing I'm pleasing her, knowing she wants it just as badly, hearing her breathy moans and feeling her quivering under my tongue...

Out of nowhere, the mounting pressure in my body crests and releases, tightening and shooting outwards. It's sudden, sharp, and intense. I make a strangled sound, pulling away as my entire body clenches. My vision blurs, pleasure rockets up my spine, and something warm and wet coats the sensitive tip of my cock.

She stiffens, releasing my head as her thighs tense like they're trying to close. "Peter?" The soft arousal is gone from her tone.

Well. That was *unexpected*. Damn. How embarrassing. "Fuck," I curse, seeing the wet spot darkening near my zipper. "I... erm..."

"Did you just..."

"Yeah."

Her brows shoot up, but there's no derision in her expression—just curiosity and a hint of amusement. She scoots back and closes her legs like she's closing the chapter on this, and I rise to my feet. She hasn't said anything, but humiliation swirls at the thought of coming without even a single touch like a horny teenager. I want to kick myself.

"Are you okay?" she asks carefully, tip-toeing around my ego. "You seem upset."

"Because I'm a wanker and I've completely ruined the moment," I admit, rolling my eyes at myself. "Coming in my trousers like a lad."

"Like a lad," she repeats, laughing in a lighthearted way. "You must really like eating pussy, huh?"

"In general? Sure. But yours? Well, let's just say *that's* never happened before," I say, letting my eyes drop to her lips.

"No?" Pride leaks into the single word, and I allow myself to hope that she doesn't think I'm some kind of embarrassment.

"No. It was... the sounds you were making and the way you taste... Goddamn, Madison. You are so incredible."

She shakes her hair back over her shoulders and leans towards me. "Well, I don't think you're a wanker or that the moment is ruined at all—because I gotta admit, that's pretty flattering," she murmurs, smiling into the words and tilting up her face towards mine like she's asking for another kiss.

My heart lurches. She's *flattered*? Fuck, that's an even better reaction than I dared to hope for. Utterly helpless against that look, I brush my lips against hers. I want another proper taste, but she pulls back.

"Honestly, this was so fucking hot, but it's probably not going to happen for me. Not your fault," she adds with a slightly guilty expression that I want desperately to kiss away. "I love that you wanted to. That you tried. No one's ever..."

In an instant, all lingering uncertainty dissolves, replaced by a tingly warmth. We're both a little embarrassed, but for opposite reasons.

"Next time, I'll make sure to control myself." She deserves to have a man on his knees for her, trying in earnest to give her as much pleasure as she wants—but from now on, that man will only ever be *me*.

She grins and admonishes, "Yeah, what the hell, man. Warn a girl next time. I thought British people were supposed to be polite. Shouldn't you have been all, 'tally ho, pip pip, good heavens, I'm arriving!' or something?"

My laughter shakes both of us. "Pip pip? Well. My sincerest apologies, luv," I say, attempting to make the endearment sound more heavily accented than usual.

She clears her throat and sits up, righting her skirt. "I'd offer to help you *clean up*," she says, eyes flashing with double meaning, "but we should probably get going if we're going to make our reservation, right?"

I check my watch and curse. I glance around, finding a door with appropriate markings. "I'll be right back," I promise.

I've only been in the bathroom for a minute when I hear her voice, muffled through the door. She's speaking to someone, her tone climbing and sounding more urgent as the conversation progresses. I'm reaching for the handle to find out what's going on when there's a knock.

"Peter?"

I open the door, still clutching a handful of wet paper towels.

Her eyes are wide. Frightened. "I'm so, so sorry, but I just got a call from my *abuela's* nursing home and I have to go."

Alarm wraps around my vocal cords, and a fierce kind of protectiveness surges in my stomach. I don't know where the danger is, but I desperately want to shield her from it. "Is everything all right? Do you need me to drive you?"

"I think she's okay, but I... she needs me. I have to go. I'm so sorry!"

With that, she throws herself at me, wrapping her arms around my neck and smashing her lips onto mine. The taste is too brief, leaving me gasping and craning my head down for more when she pulls away.

"Best date ever! Ever, ever, ever," she adds, spinning and scurrying away. "I'll text you! Sorry again!"

Well... fuck. Alone with cum slowly drying inside my trousers was not how I saw the night ending.

15

MADISON

Lick-the-Bean Peter

> Is your grandmother all right? I wanted to text you last night because I was worried, but I didn't want to bother you.

I almost texted him last night too, while I was waiting anxiously for an EKG analysis. All the doctor said on the phone was that Abuela had been sent to the hospital wing, complaining of chest pain. Several hours of tests later... turns out bad gas can feel a lot like a heart attack.

Scanning Peter's kind message again, I shove down the irritation and resistance to sharing personal information—that's what dating is, after all—and type something so honest it feels vulnerable, because I don't want him to think that I ran out on our date for something unimportant. And I never explained to Peter how important Abuela is to me.

> There was a medical emergency. She's okay now. Sorry again for leaving, but she's my only family.

> Don't apologize. I'm glad you got it sorted.

When I check my face, I realize the grin is huge and dopey. *Dios,* is this what infatuation feels like? How is he so fucking perfect?

> Thanks for asking about her. And for caring.

Briefly, I hesitate before typing out my next message. I want to choose the right words.

I can't wait to see him again. It's like a physical pull—a need so strong it's all I can think about. Between somehow engineering the best date—a private arcade? All the games, none of the screaming children? Are you *kidding* me?—another mind-bending and completely scorching kiss, and then dropping to his knees and eating me out in the middle of it all, I'm definitely a goner for this guy.

All morning I've been grinning like a fool whenever I remember that moment of confusion when I felt him convulsing between my legs. I'm so tickled that he enjoyed eating my pussy so much that *he* came, I don't even care that I didn't. And the wincing humiliation on his face when he admitted it just about made me swoon—not because he was embarrassed that he came in his pants, but because he was embarrassed that *he* came when he was trying to make *me* come. That tells me he's no selfish lover; Peter is the kind of guy who genuinely cares if you get off.

> Okay, not apologizing, but I'd like to make it up to you.

Heart racing, I press send, and my stomach flops over.

Cálmate, Madison. You're not being hunted for sport.

But this is scary! Liking someone is scary. The possibility that this could *work* is scary.

Caring about what someone thinks sucks balls.

I always find a reason to write someone off. Most people don't like me after they really get to know me, and that's fine—I'm a prickly bitch—so I prefer to be able to examine someone from arm's length and find the flaws that reassure me it'll never work. The rejection hurts less that way. It takes all the pressure off if I know we're doomed from the start and just having fun until things fizzle out.

It's not like that this time. I'm not dreading looking at my phone when he texts; my heart races when I see his name on my screen. I'm not looking for excuses to bail on a date; I'm planning how to ask him on another. I'm not anticipating lulls in the conversation; I'm trying to save and remember things so I can tell him stories to make him laugh.

It's... uncomfortable. In a thoroughly exciting way, yes, but it's making me second-guess myself because he's still a stranger and I don't know exactly where I stand. I know he wants me—that's fairly fucking obvious—but does he *like* me? I think he does, but there's still that little voice of doubt that tries to convince me that running off in the middle of an amazing date that he went to such lengths to plan for me is sure to piss him off.

I heft the paper bag of groceries under my arm and lock the car before I head inside.

My phone buzzes, and my heart plummets into my stomach with nerves, but it's not Peter. It's one of the IRCs I'm on—not SpyderMan's. I haven't even talked to him since we got into that little spat. It's been days, which is weird for us, now that I think about it. But I guess I've been riding the high of the excitement with Peter and I haven't given SpyderMan much thought.

Guilt is just a twinge, because it's drowned out by relief. Maybe it'll be easier to get over SpyderMan than I thought.

NoBody: We need to talk. In person. Text me when you get this.

I roll my eyes. For a tough guy with questionable morals, he's pretty dramatic. He probably has another job for me or is having a hard time with the data I sent him. Not really my problem, and I don't feel like doing him any favors at the moment. Luckily, I have enough in the bank that I can squeak by for a few months until I get bored. So, I ignore the message and silence the IRC.

I'm trying to get the key into the lock on my front door without looking when the wind blows my hair over my shoulder into my face. I glance over at the front entrance, then roll my eyes preemptively.

It's Todd, looking more irate than usual and—I note with a cheerful kind of curiosity—like someone kicked his ass. He's got a giant purple bruise stretching across the front of his neck, and he seems sort of... beaten. Like, he usually holds his head high and postures when he walks, but now he's slouching and subdued, almost as if he took a blow to the ego as well as the throat.

Dios, I hope that's what happened. Just because I would never do it myself doesn't stop me from wishing someone else would. It'd be a long time coming for someone who doesn't think before he speaks but likes to run his mouth.

"You know, they really recommend you start slow with the auto-erotic asphyxiation," I muse, lips twitching as I try to straight-face this one. "It's dangerous. You could hurt yourself."

He limps slowly past me, giving me the stink eye. I can't see why he'd be limping from here, so it feels... performative. Especially after he says in a hoarse voice, "You'll be hearing from my lawyer."

I narrow my eyes at him. "You mean your dad?"

"Yeah," he shoots back, oblivious to the implied insult. Of course, his dad is a lawyer.

I chuckle, unperturbed but curious. "Why, is he hot? You looking for a new stepmom? Careful, young man, or I'll send you to bed without supper." I wag my finger.

He scoffs, infusing the sound with as much disgust as he's physically able, then wincing and grabbing his Adam's apple like it hurt. "You think you can hide behind your big, scary boyfriend? He can't just go around *assaulting* people for no fucking reason. I hope he's got deep pockets, because they think my larynx is going to need surgery."

"My what?" I repeat, stuck a few sentences behind.

"Don't play dumb, you fucking bitch. It's all on video," he hisses, pointing to the security cameras in the corners of the hallway's ceiling.

"Management doesn't pay for those to work, Todd," I inform him with a small laugh. "It's security theater, meant to deter people just by having them there, like that *Guard on Duty* sign—have you ever seen a security guard here?"

He blanches and turns his accusatory stare to the cameras. "W-well... Uh... I've got a witness, too. Proof."

"Of," I prompt, waving my hand in a *get to it* motion.

"Your boyfriend, threatening and attacking me."

I open my mouth, then snap it shut. Clearly, Todd suffered some brain damage and is confused. It's really not nice to kick someone when they're down. "Right. Well, good luck with the lawsuit. I'll be sure to tell my *boyfriend* to watch who he throat-punches next time. I don't think your brain can really afford to be cut off from oxygen again." I turn the key and slip inside.

"We're gonna have his ass deported," Todd growls after me.

"You do that," I chuckle, making a mental note to check the camera feeds I just told him didn't work. Well, I was tricky with my words—I didn't say they don't work; I implied it by saying that our building doesn't pay for them.

Management may not care about the cameras, but after Mrs. Louis upstairs got mugged on her way in one day, and burst into tears at her mailbox telling me that the leasing company essentially told her to buck up, I do. I couldn't stand the look on her face—like she was afraid to leave the house. Even after I explained that I've been personally paying for and monitoring them ever since, she still insists on using an old-school camera with an actual dinosaur VHS tape recorder to capture the street view "just in case." I humored her.

What can I say? I'm a prickly bitch, but I do have a heart. And she takes care of my cat for me on the rare occasions when I go away.

If someone assaulted Todd… I kinda want to see that. Then pop some popcorn, pull it up on my TV and watch it over and over. Maybe in slow-mo with a theatric sports-announcer type voiceover.

I put away my groceries, feed Some Bills, and head into my bedroom. Wearing an anticipatory smile, I sit at my computer and pull up the historical feed from the hallway camera. The service I use saves 30 days of footage before it overwrites itself, so I should be able to find the scene I want—but I'm not sitting here and manually running through it. I write a quick program to scan for Todd's face, then isolate and highlight all of his comings and goings for the last few days. Once the program is done, I've got a few condensed minutes of the most boring short film ever: *There and Back Again and Again, Todd's Hallway Journeys*. But it's missing something.

I sit back and scowl. Why does it jump from him being fine to him leaving his apartment with that huge bruise? Where's the in-between? He didn't just imply it happened in the hallway, he straight up said it did—this camera should have the perfect view. It's the one he *pointed* at.

First, I check my code. Nope, it's fine.

Then, assuming the program just missed the event because Todd's face was turned away or something, I pull the footage from the time between his last healthy appearance and his first injured one, and watch it frame for frame on 10x fast forward.

Huh. Nothing.

Now I'm intrigued. I slow it down, assuming human error this time.

That's when I see it—a timestamp jump. This footage is missing an hour. I never would have noticed speeding through it. With a frown, I check my calendar and see that it was a visiting day with Abuela. I wasn't here.

A chill sweeps up my spine, and goosebumps rise to the surface of my skin, lifting the dark hairs on my forearms as I connect the dots. Time is missing from security cameras in my apartment building when I wasn't home, and Todd assumed the guy who beat him up was someone I knew... Was someone in my apartment? Nothing is missing or moved, so it almost feels silly to think it, but now I can't help but wonder.

My heartbeat thuds steadily and loudly in my ears as I check all my internal security from that time. Since I wasn't home and Some Bills was sleeping, it's hard to tell if the cameras are looped. But the security system... Someone disarmed it using a system override code *I* didn't even know at a timestamp that couldn't have been me...

Someone was in my apartment. But who? Who would have...

Wait a fucking minute.

We're gonna have his ass deported.

In the heat of the moment, I'd kind of thought Todd was being racist, seeing another brown person and assuming we were dating—but what if... what if he meant deported to *England*? There's one obvious recent addition to my life who fits that description. But then there's the fact that whoever broke in was good enough to bypass my security and erase themselves from the cameras. It's not exactly a common skill set to have... to get past my security, you'd have to be someone like SpyderMan... And... I've always kind of thought SpyderMan was British!

Okay, settle down, Mads. That's not jumping to conclusions; that's pole-vaulting to them.

I need proof. I need... to see the person that broke in. My cameras clearly can't be trusted, but I happen to know the only person with a record that can't be tampered with.

Mrs. Louis is retired, so she's usually home. When I tell her what I'm looking for, she welcomes me into her apartment, immediately getting busy sorting through the stack of unlabeled tapes vaguely organized by date. She chatters happily at me about her grandkids while I pretend like my hands aren't itching to take over. It takes probably three times as long as it should, but eventually she finds the tape from the day I want, pops it into her actual, real-life, somehow-still-operational VCR, and presses play with an actual button that makes a clicking sound and gets stuck, catching on years of grime.

The image is fuzzy, so I instinctively squint, like squinting is going to do anything to help with the flicker lines and rolling shutter banding. My breath is fucking bated as the timestamp I need approaches. It's the middle of a workday, so there's not much activity happening on the street. Eventually, a Caucasian, fit, tall man approaches the building. He definitely doesn't live here. He's wearing some kind of uniform, holding a clipboard, and he carries himself like he belongs, but...

When he looks up at the camera, adrenaline-spiked blood surges through my veins, bringing heat to my cheeks as the rest of my body tingles, volleying back and forth between cold shivers and spreading warmth.

"Pause it!"

It's him. It's Peter. My hot British Houdini. He even works for that cable company.

"Can I borrow this?" I ask, sounding breathless.

"Of course, dearie. Anything you need," she promises sweetly. "Did you get what you wanted?"

"I'm not sure," I mumble, then catch her quizzical look. "I mean, yes. Thank you. That's all I need. I'll bring this back soon."

As I descend the stairs with the tape clutched to my chest, I worry at my bottom lip and turn over the facts. Peter was here. No one else went in or out of the building in that time frame, and it's not like one of my neighbors has the know-how to loop cameras and disarm my security. It *had* to be him.

Peter broke into my place.

So the question is... why? Why would he be in my apartment?

Of course, my mind immediately goes to my computer—the most valuable and incriminating thing I own, with all its secrets buried deep within the drive. If anyone else ever got access to those secrets, I'd be beyond screwed. It's enough to put me away for life, or land me on the shit list of dozens of powerful, dangerous people. But I always lock it, and it would take a statistically improbable amount of luck or 100 years with a password cracking program to get in, so I'm not super worried on that front.

I can't rule out the possibility that he's after my secrets, but what if he's just... *stalking* me? Did he break in for a creepy reason—like to roll around in my bed or steal my panties? Did he beat up Todd on my behalf? Is that scary or unbelievably hot?

Peter has had plenty of chances to hurt me; that's clearly not what this is about. And my gut is saying, you can't fake the kind of chemistry we have. Talking to him has always been easy—too easy, really—and so many things about him feel so unsettlingly familiar.

But is Peter my SpyderMan? Now that I put them in the same thought like that, the name seems much less like a weird fluke and more like a joke I was too oblivious to get.

It would be the most incredible coincidence of my life if the guy I'm dating happens to be the online contact I've been in love with for two years, but... no more of a coincidence than Peter and SpyderMan being two *different* people with the exact same skill set, and sense of humor, and background.

My hands are practically shaking as I get my door unlocked. I haven't felt this alive in a long time. Nothing gets me fired up more than having a puzzle to solve—and if this one means finding out who my internet crush is, I'm not wasting a second to get started.

Well, okay, first, I'm going to upgrade my damn security.

My phone buzzes, and my stomach flips over so hard at the sight of his name I nearly drop it.

Lick-the-Bean Peter

> You invited me over last time, and I'd love to take you up on that. I'll bring dinner, if you'd like.

His texts are the perfect mix of dominance and courtesy. He never dumps the decision-making on me, and he always makes me feel like he wants to see me. I close my eyes and hug my phone to my chest, wishing it would fill up the cracks that just formed, shattering my momentary excitement.

If I'd gotten this message a few hours ago, I would have been so stoked. I'd be trying to come up with something flirty to say back and planning an outfit to make him drool. Now, I'm sitting here, wondering if I should have been more suspicious—that he's always been a little too good to be true.

Time to find out.

I start typing out my response. He can come over, and once we're alone, I'll confront him and make him tell me what the fuck is going on.

Or... wait, is that stupid? SpyderMan is a stranger on the internet, and it's possible that he's stalking me. This is how slasher movies start. He's had plenty of chances to hurt me and didn't, yes, but I should treat him like he's dangerous. An unknown. Even though it feels like I've known him all my life.

Taking a step back from our history and unusual connection, what would I say to a friend—if I had one—if she told me that a stranger from the internet found out where she lived, integrated into her life with a false identity, asked to come over to her house alone, and that this guy has been buying secrets and is maybe involved in the murder or disappearance of a dozen or so people...

Yeah, I'd tell her to fucking sprint in the opposite direction. This isn't *a* red flag; it's a military parade in China.

A normal girl doesn't just invite a guy like that into her apartment. She gets a restraining order. But I'm not a normal girl. And I've got questions that only he can answer.

Another shiver runs down my spine, but this one brings a smile to my lips. Deep down, I'm more than a little thrilled by the possibility that

Peter is SpyderMan. I *want* it to be him, and I know that makes me super weird. I should be pissed, or feel betrayed or violated—and to be fair, I *am* annoyed—but I'm also weirdly excited.

Like, yes. Be obsessed with me. Find me. Break in. Just don't be surprised if I match that energy right the fuck back.

Game on, SpyderMan.

16

WESLEY

I'm solution oriented.

Her message gets another chuckle from me as I check the time. Wouldn't want to be late.

I get ready in my rented room at the Ulysses Grand, where I've been storing some equipment and changes of clothes—we all try not to return to the mansion too often when we're on a job. As I shower, shave and change into something clean, I try to remind myself this isn't a date. Yes, I'm excited to see her, but I'm showering because I want to be clean, not because I'm expecting anything physical to happen. I'm shaving to be presentable, not so I don't give her stubble burn on her lips or inner thighs. It's pure coincidence that my shirt shows off my tattoos and hours of lifting at the gym.

And I definitely don't stop at a flower shop on my way over to buy her a bouquet because I want in her pants. I do it because... well, I'm definitely breaking the news tonight, and part of me hopes it will soften the blow—show her I mean no harm.

I know I have to do it, even if I'm still not certain of what I'll say, and I'm not certain how she'll react. For me, uncertainty always feeds fear. Fear of shocking her. Of scaring her. Of losing her.

When I knock on her apartment door, I remind myself that telling her is the right thing to do and the only way to progress to the next phase—in which we start tracking down the General. My hope is that I can leverage the trust I've spent the last two years building with her. And if not... well... I have a few contingencies. I'm a hacker—I always have contingencies.

And then she opens the door and all thoughts disappear, swept away in a sudden tidal wave of awe and arousal. I briefly lose my grip on the flowers, and the bouquet hits the ground with a soft shushing noise of plastic and petals against carpet.

She is so damn beautiful. Dark hair tumbles over her shoulders and down her back, and the green forelocks curl artfully, framing her round face. Her features are low contrast—dark eyes and lashes half-lowered seductively, deep red lips tipped up at the corners. She's in some kind of wrap dress with a tie at the waist that's cut low enough to show off the deep line of cleavage and a hint of black lace. Her waist nips in before a dramatic flare of hips that I can't wait to get my hands on again, especially now that I know how perfectly we fit together.

But perhaps best of all is that horrid heart-shaped lock dangling in the hollow of her throat like a fucking collar of ownership. She's wearing it. She's wearing the necklace. Satisfaction beats alongside victory in my chest, drumming out all rational thought.

The soft "wow" that escapes my lungs makes her grin.

"Ditto," she murmurs, and my chest swells as I realize she's giving me the same kind of thorough once-over. She swallows, drawing my eyes to the motion of her throat, and it makes my entire body tighten. Then her eyes drop to the flowers, and she quirks a brow. "Were those for me?"

Sheepishly, I stoop to collect the bundle. "I'll just grab my jaw while I'm down here," I mutter, making her hum an amused sound.

When I straighten and hold out the gift, her eyes light up. "Sunflowers! My favorite! How did you know?"

Because on March 23rd at 4:39 PM, we were talking about art, and you said that van Gogh's sunflower paintings had made such an impact on you they were your favorite flower.

"They're my favorite, too," I say. It's not strictly an answer to the question, but it's not a lie. They have been ever since that conversation.

My answer seems to surprise her, because her eyes are wide as her hand closes around the stems. "Thank you," she beams, accepting them and standing aside to let me in. "Shoes off, please—and feel free to take off your coat and stay a while, too. Any trouble finding the place?"

"Not at all."

"Ever been to this part of Ulysses before?" she asks as I slide off my boots, glancing around. She's cleaned up a bit since the last time I was in here. The faint scent of bleach and lemon stings my nose, and there are fewer items piled on every flat surface. I wonder if she cleaned for me, like she wanted to impress me. The thought is deeply satisfying, though I didn't care a whit about the clutter.

"Can't say I have," I hedge.

As I place my bike helmet on a couch cushion and shrug off my leather jacket to drape it over the arm, I can feel her watching me. I turn and she's not quick enough to avert her eyes, so I know she was stuck on the sight of my tattoos. "It's a nice place," I say with a smirk.

"Thanks." Her smile is odd, not reaching her eyes. I wonder if she thinks it's strange that a bloke would compliment her flat—I'm just trying to act like I haven't been here before. "I'm going to put these in water."

She spins and starts moving towards the kitchen, and I'm suddenly mesmerized by the hypnotic sway of her hips and swish of her skirt. Her ass jiggles more than I remember, making me wonder if she isn't throwing some extra bounce into her step just for me. I watch until she's out of my line of sight, then turn my attention to the cat curled up at the other end of the couch. I lean down to give him a scratch under his chin. "Hey buddy," I greet him too softly for her to hear the familiarity in my tone over the noise of the sink.

"I thought we'd stay in tonight," Madison says, her voice somewhat drowned out by the sound of the running water.

"Sounds good. You don't really plan to make dinner, though, do you?" I call over my shoulder.

"Why, not a fan of dick?"

I laugh. "Not when it's spotted."

I give her cat another long ear scratch, and he leans in with a heavy purr. We're both so caught up that I don't immediately realize that the sink has been turned off. I sense Madison's presence behind me before I hear her.

"No, spotted wasn't the kind of dick I was hoping for tonight."

"What a shame—"

I spin, choking on the quip as her dress slides off her shoulders and pools at her feet, revealing lingerie. The only parts of her body I can't see are hidden behind lace and clever weaving of straps, and the effect is rather devastating to the rational part of my brain. Suddenly, all I can think of is peeling back the lace and sucking on the soft skin there, or using one of the straps around her hip as leverage to jerk her against me. Blood rushes through me, going hot then cold, and my cock stiffens with desperate interest.

The coy expression reveals her intention. Something about the light in that spot is perfect, making me wonder if she chose it intentionally. It bathes her hair and body in a golden glow, highlighting the delicate features of her face, spilling down onto the tops of her breasts that swell over the lace bra, and giving her dark hair almost a halo.

"I... what?" I hear, though I'm not aware of consciously making the sounds.

"I want to skip to dessert," she purrs, and I think she's repeating herself, but I don't remember.

When it takes my brain another second to catch up, her lips twitch.

"I need..." I gulp, eyes scanning her perfect body too rapidly. I can't find a place to settle—I want to look everywhere and see everything at once, but it's physically impossible. "There's... erm... there was something..."

Fuck me, she's rendered me into a babbling moron. I palm my face and drag down. I'll admit my plan was patchwork at best, but there were no provisions for being seduced before I could even get started.

"Fuck, Madison. You look so... *good*..." I groan as the word lands, falling horrifically short, and every other word I've ever known leaves my brain. "I swear I'm usually much more eloquent."

"Mmm," she hums, and it could be an agreement. She takes a small step closer to me. "Maybe you should try doing something different with your mouth. I have some ideas if you're open to suggestions."

The blood rushes to my cock again, swelling as excitement fills me with an antsy need to move. To grab her. To close the distance between us and take what I want. And for her part, she looks very much like she wants that, too.

Wearing a grin, I mirror her movement, taking a step of my own with a much larger stride. I think I quite like being seduced. "I do need to speak with you about something," I say, but the conviction in my tone has evaporated, and now I sound hungry.

"A matter of life or death?" she asks, brows quirking up and sensing imminent victory.

It's a joke, but it makes me swallow thickly. I nearly wince, and disappointment feels like a noose around my neck. I can't let her have sex with me as Peter. When the truth comes out, she'll never forgive me for the ruse.

But, dear God, she looks like sin.

Perhaps... just a taste...

I cross the room in three large strides before she can even react and make a move to try to meet me in the middle. As my hands fill with silky skin that gives so perfectly in my grip, rational thoughts feel too distant to be important. My muscles tense and tighten, and I curl around her, angling her head back and slanting my mouth over hers. Her taste drives me wild—the way she wriggles against my body, covered by only scraps of easily shredded lace and satin, drives me wilder.

The need to be closer feels like it's tearing me apart, but I have to angle my head down so far that it makes my body bow around hers and gives me a crick in my neck. I don't want an atom of space between us; I want every square inch of her perfect, soft skin pressed into mine.

"You're so short," I growl against her lips, making her smile and giggle against mine.

"Maybe you're just freakishly tall," she counters, pulling back to smirk up at me through her lashes.

Brat.

I reach down, grab the backs of her thighs and lift her around my hips. She shrieks and grabs me around the neck with an airy laugh and half-hearted babbling of protest about being *heavy* as I walk her back a few steps to place her ass on the counter that separates the kitchen from the living space. Once again, we're perfectly aligned, and we both groan when I push my hips forward into her softness.

"There," I whisper, sliding my hands up the sides of her legs, flattening my palms against her hips and weaving my fingers under the straps of her panties.

"What a problem solver," she chuckles, releasing her death grip from around my neck and resting her hands on my shoulders.

"I'm solution oriented," I agree. "Which is why *I* am going to finish what I started the other night, and *you* are going to teach me how to do exactly what you like so I never leave you unsatisfied again."

Her breath whooshes out, heat shining in her eyes. She swallows, almost a gulp, and seems suddenly... tense. I hesitate. Is she having second thoughts, or is this part of the game she likes to play? Giving in, then shying away—like a dance she choreographs to keep me wanting more.

She tosses her hair over her shoulder. "Okay. Just... let me take care of some bills first."

I groan and drop my head into the crook of her shoulder. Her warm vanilla scent floods my nose, and I want to drink her in. Want and heat are surging through my body—as fun as the push-pull of our banter is, I'm done. I need her. Now.

"Gas and electric can wait, Madison." I try to hide the exasperation, but it leaks through.

She smirks, the ease returning to her body language as she strokes along the cut of the muscles in my shoulders and grips around the back of my neck. "Yeah, but my furry chaperone kills the mood. I should put him in the bathroom so he's out of the way."

There's a beat, then I throw my head back and laugh. "Your cat is called 'Some Bills'?"

Her smirk widens, and she nods.

"Bloody brilliant."

"I am," she agrees.

I grip her hips harder, watching as the rough action makes her brows quirk up in the middle with desire. "The cat can watch. I'm done waiting."

"Then let's move into the bedroom. As fun as it was sitting on the counter last time, we'd both be more comfortable in the bed."

"Lead the way."

Releasing her, I step back and offer her my hand so she can hop down safely. Once flat on her feet, she crooks her finger at me and turns to lead me to her room. I make a strangled sound at the new perspective she offers and shoot after her, nearly tripping in my haste. The roundness of her ass is perfectly framed by the straps of her panties, looking oh-so soft and biteable.

I already know I'll be replaying this footage from the cameras.

I let her lead me into her room, where she's already prepared the space with soft lighting. In contrast to the messy state of it last time, she made up her bed with all the blankets and pillows. She wanted this. She expected this to happen.

"Get on the bed," I instruct softly, nodding down at it. "I'm going to make you feel good, love," I clarify, hoping to draw a line.

Internally, I chant my promise to myself. *We won't be having sex. We won't. Not as Peter. Not before I tell her the truth.*

Fuck. I hope my resolve is as strong once I have her writhing underneath me, tits heaving as she gasps for air and hips undulating as she gets lost in the search for her pleasure.

Instead of doing what I tell her—because of course she doesn't—she steps into me and gives me a light shove that lands me on my arse on the mattress. My arm whips out, banding around her waist and dragging her onto my lap as I go down. There's more urgency in our kiss now, more desperation as we lick and suck and bite. My hands rove over her body, and I try to pull her more firmly down on my lap, but she hovers on her knees, refusing to grind that little pussy down on me like we clearly both want.

Fuck. Why is she fighting me, even now? Surely the plan is to give in at some point?

She did seem nervous earlier, which strikes me as quite at odds with the seductress who bared herself wearing only lingerie. But bravado is easy to fake when you've been doing it your whole life, and I have no problem reminding her just how sexy I think she is.

"Madison," I say, the intentional use of her name meant to anchor her to me. I cup her cheek to make her look at me. "I love the weight of you on me. I love how you feel in my arms, how soft your skin is," I add, skating my hand along her upper arm and pressing a kiss against the prickle of goosebumps on her shoulder. "I'm obsessed with every curve and inch of you, love."

Her eyes flash with brief uncertainty, but she quickly hides it behind a Cheshire Cat smile. Biting her lip, she shifts to the side and reaches into the top drawer of her nightstand. I nearly go rigid, knowing precisely what's inside, but I keep my attention on biting and sucking the soft skin of her neck.

When she rights herself, there are a pair of fuzzy pink handcuffs dangling from her pointer finger. I feel my brows shoot into my hairline. "Indulge me?" she asks.

Oh, *fuck yes*. All the blood in my entire body shoots immediately to my cock as visions of having her at my total mercy fill my head. Helpless against me by her own choice, I'll lick her until she's screaming my name and won't stop until she begs me to. "It would be my absolute pleasure," I agree, reaching for them.

"No," she says, shying back when I would take them. "I want *you* to wear them."

Perhaps a by-product of the lack of blood, my brain short-circuits. "Erm…"

"Please?" she says, blinking up at me with an entreating expression. "It would be so hot. You said you wanted me to tell you what I want? Well… um, I want to… sit on your face while you're restrained."

As per usual, Madison doesn't mince words. But her hesitation makes her seem nervous about her request. Perhaps she's ashamed of this desire. Perhaps it's hard for her to ask for what she really wants. Perhaps it puts her at ease to be in control the first time—makes it easier for her to come. If that's the goal, I'm all for helping out.

"Normally I prefer to be the one putting the handcuffs on, but there's a first time for everything. If this makes you more comfortable."

She smiles. "It does. Lie back," she urges, clearing her throat.

Once I'm in place, she snaps the cuff around my wrist, snakes the chain through the spindles in her headboard, and puts on the other. Dutifully, I lay still, feeling the jolt of the metal as the cuff closes.

Her smile is more excited now. More at ease. She straddles my legs and settles herself on top of my lap, and I strain against the handcuffs, dying to reach for her. I want more—more of her weight on me, more of her body on me, more of her taste, more of her scent—but like a muppet, I decided to play along. Since when do *I* give up control?

Since Madison Cooper batted those lashes at me, that's fucking when. I'm utterly helpless against that look—

"That's better," she says in a husky voice, wiggling her hips and dragging a stifled moan from deep in my chest. My cock is responding to the sensation of her heat nestled against me, stiffening painfully under her and straining against the fabric holding it prisoner.

Wait, why am I still wearing my trousers? I didn't even think... we moved so fast... Why didn't she say anything?

She inhales, making her breasts swell in their lace confines, and when she dips down to murmur in my ear, it's all I can do not to test the integrity of the chain holding the cuffs together.

"Now that we're both comfortable..."

In a fluid motion, she sits up, points a gun—where the fuck did she get that?!—at my chest and cocks it. My whole body tenses and goes cold, and my arousal sharpens impossibly as a dark, satisfied look overtakes her expression.

"Why don't you tell me who you really are, *Peter Smith?* Or should I say SpyderMan?"

17

MADISON

I knew it would be like this when we finally met.

He groans, and it melts into a low chuckle that vibrates through my whole body, starting in my core since I'm currently wide open and sitting on him. My insides clench at the sensation, and the heat between my legs that started when we kissed feels even hotter than before.

"Oh, *brava,* Madison. I'd applaud you, but my hands are a bit tied at the moment."

Fuck, I wish I didn't want to laugh at that.

"How did you figure it out?" he asks. If possible, he sounds even more turned on than he did a minute ago.

I knew it. I *knew* it. It's him. He's SpyderMan. After all this time. I can't believe we're *finally* face to face.

My pulse rockets, making my cheeks flush and my whole body tingle with excitement. A sudden swooping drop in my stomach coupled with a hard double-beat of my heart makes my hand shake a little—I hide it by pretending to adjust my grip on the gun.

Okay, be cool, Mads. I cooked this plan up when there was still a decent chance Peter was just some random stalker and I needed to assess the stranger danger. Now that I know he's the guy I've been flirting with online for two years... I'm not really sure where to go from here.

Part of me wants to stow the gun because I know my SpyderMan would never hurt me. But he's clearly not here to buy me tacos and win me stuffed animals—if he had been, he would have just told me who he was. He's been playing me since the moment we met in that café. Maybe even before. And if I know him, SpyderMan has some sort of agenda.

I need to take several chill pills and figure out what it is.

He gives his cuffs a tug, and the metallic rattle echoes deep in my core. An image flashes—of our positions being reversed. Of being under him. Restrained. At his mercy. Open, waiting, willing, *desperate...*

Snap the fuck out of it, Madison.

"I'll ask the questions," I fire back, pressing the tip of my SIG Sauer 9 mm pistol against his chest. He tenses under me. "Is your name really Peter, or should I just keep calling you SpyderMan?"

"I thought we settled on 'Sir.'"

The word sends a completely uncontrollable shiver down my spine. He practically purred it. It sounds so right on his lips, like he's totally used to the title—then I remember the conversation we had a couple weeks back where he said that.

"Funny," I drawl.

"Who's joking?"

With a scowl, I adjust my finger on the trigger to remind him that I'm holding it—and to remind myself that I'm supposed to be projecting an image of control over the situation. He looks way too fucking at ease for someone on the wrong end of the barrel of a gun. It's making *me* uneasy. "Are you seriously not going to tell me your name?"

"Maybe once you've earned it," he says lightly, but his eyes crinkle at the corners. "Until then, you can call me anything you like, love."

I frown. Once I've *earned* it? A wave of hot, indignant anger washes over me, even as the erotic image shifts from being cuffed under him to being on my knees in front of him. Of him threading those long fingers into my hair and tugging at the base of my scalp so my head falls back and my mouth falls open...

"All right then, *pendejo*—"

He chuckles, undercutting the impact of my insult. "Asshole is a bit harsh, considering our history, don't you think?"

I cock my head. "Well, SpyderMan is kind of a mouthful, and you've done nothing to *earn* the title of Sir, as far as I'm concerned."

"I think you'll find me to be a bit more than a mouthful," he promises, eyes dropping to my lips.

I lick them just to put on a show. "You haven't earned that, either," I purr.

"Fuck," he curses softly, grinning to himself and shaking his head. He pulls against his restraints like he wants to reach for me, triceps bulging against his sleeves and making the ink on his arms dance. "You really are everything I was hoping you'd be, Madison. More than."

A swell of confidence at the praise warms me as the edge of obsession and hunger in his voice sends a shivery thrill up my spine. I lean forward and watch his eyes follow the way my breasts swell over the top of the bra, shining with raw desire. It's not a push-up, more a bralette—scraps of lace and satin held together with elastic, not underwire—but it covers very little. And it's safe to say he appreciates that.

"I'd love to say the same, but you won't tell me who you really are." I sit back and press the gun harder against his sternum.

The sound of denim catching against lace is a roughly erotic scratch as he shifts underneath me, rocking his hips in a small circle. I gasp as he positions his thick, pulsing length perfectly between my lips and rocks his hips so it slides through my slit. My eyes almost flutter shut as the sensation sends a wave of heat prickling under my skin. Then I rear back and gape down at the wet spot on the front of his jeans. I'm not sure who caused it. Probably a group effort.

"Are you... getting harder?"

His grin shifts into one of true amusement. "What can I say? Nearly everything you do turns me on, but this violent side is hot as fuck."

"You're kind of a freak, huh?"

"You like it because so are you."

Fuck me. I do and I am.

Like he knows what I'm thinking, he does it again, and I have to swallow the groan. "I had no idea how you'd react to the truth, but being handcuffed to your bed and threatened with a gun is *so* much better than anything I imagined," he says.

I choose to ignore how that makes the ache deep inside of me worse, because if I let myself focus on how badly I want to unzip his pants and peel back the waistband of his boxer briefs... well, I won't get my questions answered if my mouth is too full to ask them.

"You're remarkably chill for a guy being held at gunpoint," I observe, lifting a brow.

"You won't kill me," he returns evenly.

"You're right. I won't. But shooting someone in the dick doesn't usually kill them."

His laugh is self-deprecating. "I think that particular part of my anatomy is safe—perhaps the only part of me that is, considering how badly you seem to want it."

I roll my eyes, but he's not fucking wrong. Time to get back on track. "We'll see about that—kind of depends on how satisfying your answers are. Now, how long have you known who I was?"

"Not long," he replies, his expression falling into something more serious, like he wants me to know he's not joking. "I only learned your true identity after our first date. And... it was a complete surprise, if I'm honest."

That would mean that we've been in the same city all this time and neither of us realized. Is that even possible? I desperately want to take him at his word because... well, I want to. But can he be trusted? If you had asked me last week, I wouldn't have hesitated before saying yes. Now, though?

He found me first, but he didn't say anything until now—until I confronted him with it and forced his hand. That's suspicious as fuck.

"How did you find me?" I ask, scowling. "Is there a vulnerability I need to patch in my security protocol?"

The corners of his mouth lift again. "No," he says, sounding delighted by the topic shift. "Your protocol is quite impressive—even I couldn't get around it."

Pride floods my face with warmth, but I don't want to give him the satisfaction of knowing how pleased that makes me. His ego seems big enough. "Then how? You expect me to believe you just happened to walk into the same coffee shop as me after all this time?"

"No..." The shake of his head is somewhat sadder this time, and he heaves a huge breath that rocks both of us. "Your name appeared on a list, Madison. A hit list."

The silence that follows that declaration is thick enough to cut, and I go completely still. My mind races as I analyze this information. It could be true—my information brokering could have pissed off the wrong person. My identity is well buried, but I can't rule out that possibility.

But even if it's true, it's still just a piece. It's not the whole story.

"Okay, but that doesn't really explain everything, like how you know about this hit list, or why you're here..." I watch him work a swallow, and I feel a kernel of sudden realization pop in my chest. "Unless... Is it because it's *your* hit list?"

His eyes blaze, and he stares up at me with such raw admiration I can feel it in my soul. "God, the way your mind works... You already know the answer, Madison. Keep going. Put it all together for me."

Excitement swells in my veins at the challenge. "So you're an assassin," I murmur, feeling strange saying the word out loud. He nods, urging me to keep going. "And you were supposed to kill me. Then you realized who I was and decided to... date me instead? Is that about the gist of it?"

He grins. "Got it in one." His eyes drift down my body slowly enough to draw a path of goosebumps. He licks his lips, shifting his hips under me again.

I make a humming sound of amusement. "Well, it's a nice story, I guess."

"What, you don't believe me?" he asks, unsurprised.

"You'll have to forgive my skepticism," I drawl. "But even you have to admit that it's pretty inconceivable. And it would be kind of fucking dumb to take you at your word, considering how many of your words have been big ole lies."

"If you're open to the truth, I can give you proof."

I tilt my head, examining him. I'm no expert or anything, but I like to think I can tell when someone is obviously lying. I know some of the common tells, which he's not exhibiting. He's meeting my eye, speaking calmly, and his story is consistent—if improbable.

I'd like to get to the bottom of this, and I suppose that means believing his answers at some point... as long as the proof is compelling. And I'm still in control—I've still got the upper hand. He's cuffed, and I'm the one with the gun. Sure, it's not loaded, but he doesn't know that.

"All right," I decide. "I'll look at your proof."

Relief washes over his features, and it reassures me. After how calm he was with a gun in his face, this is the right kind of response, at least. "It's on my phone, which is in my pocket."

Instantly suspicious again, I glance up at his hands in the cuffs. "Fine, but I'm not giving it to you. I'll drive."

"Fair enough."

I shift back far enough on his lap that I can reach the top of his pocket in his jeans. I curl my fingers inside, and his stomach tenses.

"The pocket of my jacket," he clarifies with a grin so amused that it reveals his dimple.

I heave a sigh, roll my eyes and dismount, hip creaking in protest as I climb off his lap. I find his phone in his jacket draped over the arm of my couch, weighing down the leather on one side, and stare down at the screen as I walk back into the bedroom. It doesn't wake with motion, and I scowl. I'd kind of been hoping to find out what his lock screen was. Is he a blue background kind of guy? I bet it's a photo of, like, a galaxy taken by the Hubble telescope or something. That seems sufficiently nerdy.

"What's your passco—"

I stop dead, seeing him sitting on the edge of my bed with a cocky grin, handcuffs dangling from his left arm—one cuff hanging open uselessly.

I gasp. What the fuck? How did he...? This giant piece of shit! Was he out of the cuffs the *whole time*? I *know* I locked them—I heard the click!

That's what I get for buying my interrogation tools from The Pleasure Chest.

"All these toy restraints have a release lever in case you lose the key," he explains in a low voice, eyes drifting down my body as he divests himself of the other cuff and lays the pair neatly next to him on the bed. His expression turns predatory as he stands, filling the room with his presence.

The power dynamic between us shifts, and my heart leaps into my throat—I have officially lost control of the situation. He's free. He's on his feet. And he's all the fuck riled up.

I feel myself physically gulp. All at once, the sheer stupidity of what I've just done comes crashing around my head. I handcuffed an *assassin* to my bed. I threatened him, tormented and teased him. And he just told me that my name is on his kill list. Fuck!

I glance down at the gun in my hand. The gun that's only as good as my ability to bluff because it doesn't have any bullets.

He follows my line of sight. "You know, you really shouldn't point a gun at someone unless you intend to use it, love," he tsks, voice lowering dangerously. "And you can't use it if it's not loaded."

Double fuck!

With a little squawk of fear, I chuck his phone at him, turn on my heel and sprint for the door. I thought I'd buy myself time—that he'd go after his device—but it clatters on the ground and with a curse, he gives chase. His heavy footfalls thump after me as I stretch my hand towards the exit, blood pounding in my ears.

I have just enough of a head start... I can make it...

Just as my hand closes around the knob, the letters inked onto the back of his knuckles appear in my line of sight, slamming the door closed again as his body knocks into mine with the force of his momentum. A grunt of pain kicks out of me, taking all the air in my lungs with it. Fuck, he's fast.

"Where do you think you're going?" he snarls. He's so close I can feel every hard, hot inch of him pressed against my back, boxing me in. I can feel his breath against my ear and shoulder. I can smell that soapy, minty, bitter musk of him. My left wrist—the one holding the gun—is in his hand, and my right arm is stuck between my body and the wood of the door.

"I'm trying to get the fuck away from you! Obviously!" I hiss back, matching his energy. I squirm against him, making a noise of frustration when he's as unmovable as a goddamn brick wall.

"And your plan was to dash out into the hallway, mostly naked? You think I'd let anyone out there *see* that?"

The bite in his voice isn't anger, I realize. It's pure, raw jealousy. He's not mad I held him at gunpoint; he's coveting the sight of my nudity. He doesn't want to hurt me... he just *wants* me. The thought literally steals my breath.

He reaches for the gun in my hand, plucks it from my grip and places it on the arm of the couch. "Now... where were we?"

He shifts his hips against mine, pressing all that rock-hardness into the softest part of me; I whimper as he grinds himself so close to and yet so far from my hot, swollen core. My whole body lights up at the friction, like someone lit a sparkler under my skin.

"You were trying to convince me that you're *not* a threat," I retort.

"I'm not," he fires back. "I'm here to protect you."

"What, like a bodyguard?" I snort, then wiggle my ass against him to make a point. "Well, your methods are a bit literal for my taste, but effective, I suppose. My body feels *very* guarded right now."

With a chuckle, his head drops, and I feel a light brush of his lips against my temple. "Just one of the *many* things I plan to do to your body." He leans down to breathe the next words right by my ear, lifting the small hairs and making me shiver. Especially when I feel the weight of his hand at the base of my neck, like he's holding me in place so I listen.

"I'm going to claim and worship every inch of you until you're dripping and writhing. I'm going to make you come until you beg me to stop. By the time I'm done, there won't be any question of who you belong to."

His words are like a punch to my uterus, and I make a sound I don't recognize, sharp and full of longing. The inherent power dynamic in this position and the way he's so easily subduing me is doing something to my body. I'm lost to anything but the overstimulated, prickly feeling of arousal so intense it hurts.

I feel his dick moving against my ass, like it's suddenly got a mind of its own. Our delicate flesh pounds a concert of our mutual need. And fuck do I need more.

"Big words from a guy who hasn't even made me come once," I rasp, hoping to taunt him into putting his money where his dirty, dirty mouth is.

He spins me, jerking my body, and I try to resist, but my limbs feel boneless. He grabs my free hand—the one that had just started reaching for a better hold on him—and it joins the other arm stretched over my head. I thought people were kidding when they said a guy could hold both their wrists in one hand, but that's exactly what he does. He pins both against the unyielding, cold door.

Then, I feel his fingers curl around the front of my neck, holding me still with my head tilted up. We're so close now that our rapid breathing becomes an exchange of air.

"Is that what you want? Tell me—use your words." I can hear the amusement and longing in his voice.

"Yes," I demand, surprised that it doesn't sound strained or muffled. He's not applying pressure to my windpipe, just right over my pulse points, slowing the blood flow to my brain.

"Ask nicely."

I tug against him, testing his hold. "Just kiss me already, nerd."

He squeezes, and my vision explodes in tiny white pinprick lights, making me whimper. He tuts. "Nicer than that. Try again."

"Kiss me, SpyderMan."

His smile is all darkness as he shakes his head slowly. "One more try. You know what I want to hear."

I do. I know exactly what he wants to hear. "Sir," I whisper, unwilling to broadcast my own submission any louder.

There's a second where I'm not sure if I'm imagining his mouth on mine or if it's actually happening. Then I feel the vibration of his moan. His lips are hard, like the rest of him, demanding that I give in, demanding that I open for him. When I do, his tongue sweeps inside, and I can taste so many things at once—the salty sourness of his saliva, the faintly minty taste of his tongue. His stubble rasps against the sensitive skin around my mouth.

I drown in the sensation and taste and smell, burning with the need to be closer. His hand sweeps down the lengthened side of my body, stopping at the lace cups of my bra to slide his fingers underneath.

When he breaks the kiss, I whine at the loss. I don't care why he's stopping; I just know that I want him to keep going. I jerk my hips, tilting my pelvis towards him, and make a needy noise.

His smile is knowing, triumphant, and oh, so dark. He pulls up the center of the bralette until both my breasts tumble out, the air cool on the overheated, delicate skin of my nipples. He pauses a moment to stare in a way that makes me squirm, then his eyes flick back up at me.

Hooking his finger into the middle of the bralette, he tugs it all the way up to my lips. "Open." My jaw automatically drops for him, and he pushes the material past my teeth. "Hold this. If you let go, I'll stop."

I bite down when I feel the fabric against my tongue. Now, I'm holding my bra out of his way so he can grab one of my breasts—big as his hands are, it's far from big enough to circle all the way around the thickest part of my tit—and muffling myself when he squeezes and I cry out.

He dips his head and takes a swollen, hard nipple into his mouth, and my eyes roll back. A fresh wave of arousal crashes over me, and I moan, feeling strangely freed by the gag I'm voluntarily holding in my teeth.

His tongue swirls around the tip, and his teeth scrape against it. I feel like I'm spinning. "Harder," I plead, but it's not the sound that comes out through the lace and satin in my mouth.

If he understands what I want, he ignores it, and sucks gently. Then, he moves to the other breast, leaving one nipple taut and pebbling in the cold air. His fingertips roll the sensitive bud as his mouth takes the other, repeating the pattern of smooth tongue, scraping teeth, cold air.

I'm wet at this point; I have to be. My body doesn't normally make much lubrication on its own—thanks, anxiety meds—but I've quite literally never been this turned on. My hands dance around in their prison, wanting to touch and feel and grab onto something so I don't float away.

He straightens. "Eyes on me, love. You'll watch me as I touch you."

In response, my whole body clenches at once. As his fingers dip lower and lower, leaving a wake of goosebumps, my pulse races, and I widen my stance for him so he can get between my thighs. I almost drop the bra from my mouth as his fingers skim over the lace covering my pussy and every muscle in my stomach quivers in anticipation.

His eyes widen as he feels the wetness that has seeped straight through. "Fuck," he whispers, reverent and desperate.

He hooks the crotch of my panties with his index finger and moves it aside. We both make choked noises when he slides between my lips. His blunt fingertips strum against the hard little nub of my clitoris, and my body jerks against his hand. A breathy noise escapes me, and the bra slips from my mouth.

He instantly retreats, pulling back. "You want me to stop?"

"No!" I gasp, scrambling through the brain fog and distracting way my body is burning and aching. "No, I just dropped it. Please don't stop."

His lips twitch, and he cocks his head, the confusion melting back into heated interest. "So she can be a good girl and ask nicely for what she wants."

Irritation tightens like a whipcord, and I start to argue, but I'm cut off.

As though from out of space and time, a shrill alarm suddenly sounds, piercing right through the cloud of arousal. We both stiffen, and he pulls back, letting me go. He gives his fingers an almost perfunctory suck—like he needs to clean them, and how else would he?—before he reaches for his back pocket to grab his phone. Apparently he has two.

Reeling as if I just woke in the middle of a dream, I fix my bra as he reads something that makes him curse. "It's one of my alarms at the safe house."

I know that look. He's going to leave. Right in the middle of what we were doing. "Something... urgent? Life or death?" It must be if it's more important than this. Than me.

He glances up from his screen, and his scowl melts off his features when he sees the look on my face. He reaches out to cup my jaw, stroking the edge of my mouth with the side of his thumb. "I'll be back as soon as I can. Stay here—inside. You'll be safe for now, just... Stay away from the windows and don't answer the door for anyone but me."

I can't stop my eyes from rolling as I jerk away from his misplaced pity and concern. I'm not *afraid;* I'm wound so tight I might snap. I'm fucking *trembling* with need, and he's going to leave me high and dry. He's not going to finish what he started. Again.

"Bold of you to assume I'll answer the door for you."

He eyes me, but doesn't try to argue. He must be in a hurry. "At least load your gun, all right?"

I make a noncommittal noise. I mean, obviously I'm going to—I'm not stupid—but I don't want him to think it's because he told me to. And I still want to know how he knew it wasn't loaded.

I shuffle out of the way of the door as he shoves his feet into his boots and collects his jacket. As he grabs the knob, he throws me a look over his shoulder. "And Madison?"

I brace myself for the sheer devastation I know is going to follow whatever he says next.

"Be a good girl for me and keep those hands to yourself. At least until I tell you otherwise, yeah? Your pleasure is *mine.*"

I roll my eyes and jerk away. "Oh, fuck all the way off," I say, flipping him the bird as he opens the door. "You probably wouldn't have been able to get me there anyway."

He freezes. "Is that a challenge?"

Trying to tune out the heat in his tone, I examine my nails. "Just a fact, baby. SSRIs are great for anxiety, but not so great for the libido."

Quicker than I can react, he whips a hand around the back of my neck and tugs me towards him. His kiss is hard and quick but full of meaning—a statement of ownership, a promise, and an apology—and he lets go before I can really get a taste. "We'll see about that."

He disappears through the doorway, and I'm left totally unbalanced once again. I'm starting to really loathe the sensation. "Next time at least buy me dinner so I'm satisfied in one way!" I call after him, physically incapable of not getting the last word.

His chuckle echoes down the hallway as he exits the building, and I slam the door.

Once everything settles, the silence of my apartment is almost oppressive. Some Bills and I stare at each other in wide-eyed confusion, both wondering what the fuck just happened, but for different reasons. Probably.

Okay, that was... a lot.

The man I've been dating showed me hints of this, but *this* is the man I always hoped was in there. Don't get me wrong, I loved the chivalry and the teasing banter and the careful choreography of two strangers getting to know each other, but it doesn't hold a candle to *this*. He's the proverbial cat to my mouse—the predator who wants to play. He knows how to tease, how to provoke reactions out of me, how to keep me wanting more... how to make me want to give in.

And honestly, if he hadn't been pulled away, I probably would have—consequences be damned. And it probably would have really complicated everything because I still need to figure out what's going on, and being sex drunk makes that kind of difficult.

So... maybe it's not such a bad thing he left. I can cool off and do some research of my own about this so-called hit list. Part of me believes SpyderMan's story, but I still want proof. And if someone wants me dead, I know a few people who might know something about that.

18

MADISON

*It's exactly what the SpyderMan I miss talking to
so much would do.*

SpyderMan never came back after he left to check on that alarm. I half-expect to find him waiting for me outside my door in the morning, and I'm equal parts relieved and disappointed that he isn't there.

Just as well—I'm in pretty rough shape. I spent all night in various dark web forums, discreetly asking questions, and at about 3 AM the worry in the pit of my stomach turned into full-fledged panic.

He's right. Someone wants me dead. Someone who is only spoken about in the wrong parts of the internet with terrified, hushed reverence—my contact wouldn't even speak his name, as if it would summon the boogeyman himself.

How do you fight the boogeyman?

Well, research is half the battle—you Scooby Doo his ass, rip off the mask and reveal that he's just a man. Men are flesh and bone. Men can be blackmailed or exposed or sent to prison or—if worse comes to worst—killed.

Still, I have to think about more than just my own safety. I told myself a long time ago that I wouldn't let Abuela become collateral damage. I won't let the danger of my choices impact her. I need to lead whoever is after me away from her. That means getting the hell out of Dodge.

There's only one problem, and he's about 6'1", inked, infuriating, and so fucking dominant that my knees quiver a little thinking about it. He wants to *protect me*. Be my bodyguard. And sure, *swoon*—but I don't want to be protected. I want to get this motherfucker who thinks he can put a hit out on me. And I can't do that with tattooed Q on steroids breathing down my neck, telling me to stay away from the windows and only answer the door to him. Controlling me. Telling me what to do.

Okay, I fucking loved when he told me what to do. Yes, *Sir*.

But that's part of the problem. He wants to protect me, and I'm so hopelessly drawn to him that part of me wants to let him. But that would be making a deal with *el Diablo*. He's got a concerning amount of power over me—I'm practically wet just at the memory of his voice so close to my ear.

I'm going to claim and worship every inch of you until you're dripping and writhing.

I'm going to make you come until you beg me to stop.

By the time I'm done, there won't be any question of who you belong to.

The fire in his eyes and the feeling of his hot, heavy hand on my throat make me shiver in longing. *Dios mio,* it's always the quiet ones—the nerdy guys you'd never suspect. The ones with their pocket protectors and tousled hair and quick fingers.

I'm beyond disappointed that I finally met the spy of my dreams and I can't stick around long enough to try his spotted dick.

Then again, if SpyderMan is half as good as he thinks he is, he'll find me. I'm already vibrating with excitement at the thought of the chase—of more cat and mouse games.

After last night, something tells me he isn't going to let me go without a fight. So, I need to stay a few steps ahead of him and slip away before he realizes I'm gone. I just need to take care of a few things—one of which is pretty easily solved with a quick text.

```
mermaidav: Will you take care of SB for me?
I'm leaving town for a bit, but I'll come by
to drop him off and chat with you before I go.
```

NoBody: Sounds like you probably know what I need to talk to you about, then. Yeah, okay enana. Be careful. Talk soon.

As much as I want to bring my cat with me, it'll be a lot easier to lie low if I don't have to worry about him. I don't want him getting hurt, so I'll send for him when I'm settled. If only my other responsibilities were settled so easily.

There's a reason Abuela is in the system with a different last name than me—and it has nothing to do with my stupid bio-dad and his legacy. I've been paying for her care from a dummy account with money that gets cleaned overseas. No one will be able to connect her to me unless they know me personally, and I picked a care facility with the strictest visiting rules I could find. No one gets in to see her unless they're approved.

Dread and guilt twist in the pit of my stomach because it doesn't feel like enough to keep her safe, but it's the best I can do. She'll be okay. I just hope she remembers our conversation. It makes me feel sick that she might wake up next week, wondering where I am.

As I make my way down the hallways of Sunset Hills, I see Manny isn't at the nursing station. So when I approach Abuela's room and hear masculine laughter, it brings a smile to my face. Some of the nauseating anxiety dissipates.

Good, okay. It's obviously a good cognitive day, and she sounds like she's in a good mood. Maybe this will go better than I thought.

Thank you, Manny, for buttering her up.

I shift the bag with two bagel sandwiches to the hand holding my coffee so I can have one free to push the door open, and nearly drop everything as I gasp.

¡El Diablo!

SpyderMan turns in his seat to face the door, wearing that same infuriating smirk that's officially burned into my memory.

"Madison!" Abuela greets me with a larger smile than I can remember seeing in a long time. She's sitting upright in her puzzle chair, eyes sparkling and alert as they dart between me and the man sitting next to her.

And dammit, he's just as handsome as ever, even though he's forgone the badass biker disguise and today he's wearing a suit. With a *tie*. Like he's some sort of businessman or CEO. He's so... buttoned up, with layers of grandmother-approved silk and wool hiding all his gorgeous tattoos. Almost like he knew she wouldn't like them.

Kiss-ass.

Trying to shake off the sudden boss-secretary kinky roleplaying scenario occupying every single one of my misfiring brain cells, I glance between the two of them, back and forth a few times, trying to make sense of what I'm seeing. There's an assassin in my abuela's room, and he's... helping her with a puzzle.

She seems fine—better than fine, actually—but my heart thumps hard and heat rushes to my face because I'm so caught off guard by his presence that I'm embarrassed by it. And angry.

How did he find out about her? What the fuck is he doing here?

"This is Wesley. He works here," she says, sending me a sly look while his back is to her and he can't see. She waggles her eyebrows. Deep in matchmaking mode, it would seem. "Wesley, this is my granddaughter, Madison."

Wesley, eh? Wonder if it's his real name.

"Lovely to meet you. I'm just doing the rounds on our favorite residents," he says, turning back and winking at *my* Abuela.

Her lips curve into a flirty smile, and she giggles like a schoolgirl. I roll my eyes, swallowing down a gagging noise because I need to be cool. I can't freak out at him in front of Abuela because I don't want to upset her or have to explain the real reason I did.

"Nice of you," I manage.

Silently fuming, I enter the room, plopping the bagels down at a free spot at the table, but remaining on my feet to make a point that he's not welcome to join us for breakfast. I need to say goodbye to Abuela but I'm sure as shit not doing it in front of him and revealing my plans.

"Sit, Madison," Abuela urges.

I open my mouth to argue, but she cuts me a look. So, I dial back my planned retort in favor of something less antisocial. "I assumed *Wesley* was just leaving?"

"I only just arrived, actually," he counters easily, then gestures to the empty chair. "Please enjoy your meal. I don't mind."

Oh, he doesn't *mind*? This... jerk! He sits there, all smiles and charm as he lies through his teeth, and I'm the one left standing, grappling for a good excuse and coming up totally blank. Anything I say would either make *me* look like an asshole, or would make my obviously smitten grandmother leap to *his* defense. Frustration boils under the surface as I take my seat.

Okay... fine. One point to SpyderMan. Well played, jerk.

His leg brushes against mine as I settle in my chair, and I jump at the contact, nearly knocking over my coffee. He swipes it—those damn lightning reflexes again—and instead of just righting it, he gives it a sniff, takes a sip, makes a face and puts it back down.

"Not sweet enough for you?" I guess.

"It's not lavender. I was hoping to get a taste of something that would change my life," he counters.

Damn, that was a good line. I kind of hate how good that line was.

His eyes dip to the cleavage below the neckline of my sweater, and he freezes, making me tense. My cheeks heat when I realize what snagged his attention. Fuck, I should have thrown this stupid necklace he won me at the arcade in the damn trash—I just couldn't bring myself to throw away this reminder of our time together. In my defense, I didn't exactly expect to run into him today.

Oblivious to the sexual tension, Abuela launches right in. "Wesley was telling me all about himself," she says as I unwrap and set the bagel in front of her. "He's new to the facility, but has lived in America for four years, and he isn't married," she emphasizes, clearly proud of her detective skills to have learned how *available* he was after just a few minutes of conversation. She adjusts the greasy paper in front of her.

I'm listening, but I'm trying not to care. It's probably all made up anyway. I mean, I *know* he doesn't work at Sunset Hills. My eyes drop to the little badge clipped to his breast pocket that proclaims him Wesley Parker with the Sunset Hills logo. A functioning electronic badge, no doubt.

I wish it didn't impress me. I wish I didn't immediately get the Peter Parker reference. I wish it didn't make my insides squirm, because it's exactly what the SpyderMan I miss talking to so much would do.

"How do you like working here?" I ask pointedly, taking a bite of my bagel.

"It's an excellent facility," he says, flashing a grin. A lie wearing the truth like a hat.

"It is!" Abuela echoes. "I love living here."

I nearly glare at her. Traitor! Only last week she was ripping out my heart by telling me how much she hates it here. But a handsome man shows up, and suddenly she's the poster child of happy residents. I guess it's not her fault—she's just excited about the prospect of a setup. She doesn't know that the man in front of her is a sham.

Well, Mr. Parker, you like lying so much? Let's see whatcha got. Rapid-fire hot seat. "Where are you from originally?"

"Manchester."

"I thought they had different accents—harsher. You sound like the Queen of England."

Amusement dances in his eyes. "I went to school in London."

"How long did you live in the UK?"

"All my life until I moved here."

"And how long was that?"

He smiles. "I'm 31."

He could be—he's got some fine lines cutting through his forehead and bracketing his mouth that aren't deep enough for him to be much older than that. That makes him four years older than me.

"Do you like it here?" Abuela pipes in, deconstructing her breakfast and ripping off a small piece of bread.

"It's recently become very interesting," he answers her, staring straight at me.

"What's your favorite thing?" she presses.

"Probably the locals," he says, still staring.

My stomach twists, and heat rises to my face. "Siblings? Parents?"

"No family."

"So, what's your job here?"

"I'm on the board of advisors."

"What do you do *on the board of advisors*?"

"We make some financial decisions and facilitate projects for the overall success of the business and comfort of the residents."

So, so full of shit. "What—"

"Madison, let the man breathe," Abuela chides, laying a delicate hand on his suit sleeve. With a small glare, she hisses at me in Spanish, *"¿Qué haces? Esto no es una inquisición. ¡Vas a asustar al hombre guapo!"*

I snort and glance at Wesley, who's wearing that blank, slightly awkward look people always get when someone is speaking in a language they don't understand in front of them. *"Si se asusta tan fácilmente, es demasiado blando para mí."*

Her smile is coy. *"A mí no me parece blando..."*

"I don't mind the questions," Wesley cuts in, flashing that smile around like it's free. Ugh. It's so white and clean and bright...

I narrow my eyes at him. "Do you have more teeth than normal people?"

That earns me a sharp look from Abuela. "Madison!"

"What? All I'm saying is, he smiles and all I see is teeth."

"Don't be rude," Abuela chides me before sending Wesley a look that might have been coquettish, like, 40 years ago. What a little hussy! "My granddaughter is just being smart. You look like you have the right number of teeth."

"I do," he says proudly, showing them off yet again. "And I am happy to use all 28 of them to fight that ghastly stereotype about Brits having poor oral hygiene."

28? That doesn't sound right. I start running my tongue across the inside of my molars, and he winks at me. "You're counting, aren't you?"

I suck my tongue back to the bottom of my mouth and roll my lips inward. At the flash of humor in his eyes, I push my chair away from the table, feeling only a little bit like a petulant child. But I'm done with this. I really don't want to leave without saying goodbye to Abuela, but I need to slip away from him.

"I'm going to get another cup of coffee from the cafeteria."

I stand, creating a small commotion in the room as Abuela sees the future she has planned for me and *Wesley* slipping away. "Oh, well... um, Wesley, maybe you should show her where it is."

Damn. I was banking on her wanting to keep him around to bat her eyes at him. "No, that's okay! I know." I start slinking towards the door.

But Wesley stands, reminding me of just how tall he is and just how close we are. Of their own volition, my eyes travel down the length of his dark gray suit that's perfectly tailored to his stunning body.

Christ. The man could wear a potato sack and I'd drool all over him, but this suit? Devastating. He's less wholesome superhero and more sexy villain. He looks like he'd ruin me and make me thank him for it. And

I'm so turned on by the mere thought, my nipples pebble in my ugly beige bra.

What I wouldn't give for a little lace and silk boost right about now. Should have worn my big-girl panties.

"We can't have her getting lost, can we?" he says to Abuela, but his eyes are only for me. A shiver works its way down my spine under the intensity of his gaze. It's just a flash of the real man hiding under the mask he wore for Abuela, and damn if it doesn't make my pulse race. "May I escort you?"

I think I hear Abuela sigh happily in the background. She's such a sucker for manners. And my hand is effectively forced.

That's another point to SpyderMan. "Sure, fine. Whatever," I grumble, defeated.

"Drop by whenever you like!" Abuela cries after us as he gestures for me to go ahead of him out of the room. She chuckles. "I'm always here."

He nods at people as we walk down the hallways, like he actually knows them. Like he's the King of Sunset Hills. I adjust my grip on the strap of my bag, gnashing my teeth and biding my time until we're in the parking lot and far enough away from prying eyes and hearing aids.

I start rummaging around in my bag for my keys as we approach my car, and I can feel him looming behind me, following.

"Don't you have rocks to kick? Maybe some sand to pound or a hike to take, *Wesley*?"

"It's not a lie."

I stop, glancing up at the softness in his voice. "What?"

"I realized after I left last night that I never actually introduced myself. My name really is Wesley."

Of *course* it is. It's sexy and playful, and it sounds amazing in his accent. Frankly... rude. I wish his name was something I could never imagine screaming out, like Gilbert or Donald. "Well, I'm fresh out of Boy Scout badges for not lying to old ladies, so I'll have to mail it to you," I seethe.

"Everything I told you just now was true. It's poor form to lie to your future wife's family."

Future *what now*? I narrow my eyes at him, not sure I want to fully process the squirmy feeling in my tummy at that. His eyes are twinkling in that impish way, and I can't tell if he's making fun of me so I'll just assume he is. I whirl on him, scowling. "What exactly were you hoping to accomplish by going after my *abuela*, Wesley?"

He smiles. "She likes me."

I shake my head. "This was just between the two of us. I can't believe you dragged her into it. Low blow, Peter Parker."

The expression on his face is neutral as he begins working the knot in his tie loose with the hook of his index finger. My eyes are glued to the motion, and I swallow hard. Not because I'm affected by the ridiculously erotic show of his hands flexing underneath the tattoos, but because... another reason. A convincing one.

"It's not my intention to involve her in our affairs—I knew you'd come here."

How? How did he know that? It's on the tip of my tongue to ask, but I don't want to give him the satisfaction of getting yet another one over on me.

He must see the question in my eyes anyway. "I knew you'd want to see her before you left town," he finishes, confirming that he figured out my next move.

My stomach swoops behind my belly button. Am I that predictable? "You really think you have me figured out, huh? He's so smart," I mutter sarcastically.

He cocks his head, and the hair he slicked back to achieve his cleaned-up businessman persona falls into his eye. I fight the urge to brush it aside for him. "I know *you*," he corrects. "You're going to run. Don't."

"You told me someone wants me dead—that they hired people to kill me. Why would I stay?"

"I told you I would protect you."

"I don't need your protection."

I only get the driver's door open a couple of inches before it slams closed, jerked out of my grip. His massive hand is gripping the top corner, and I know he'd hold it closed if I tried to open it again. I spin, outraged, and find him way closer than I expected. I have to lean back, tilting my head so far that I nearly fall backwards.

In the blink of an eye, I'm pinned against the door of my car, pressed hopelessly between the cold, rigid metal at my back and the searing heat of the man in front of me. He leans into me, bracing himself with a hand by my ear, letting me feel the hard press of his firm muscles and heavy weight. I'm gasping for air, making my chest heave and brush against his at the apex of every breath.

"Is this your kink? You like boxing me in?" I quip.

When I feel his hand on my waist, I nearly jump out of my skin. I'm not sure if he's steadying himself, or holding me so I can't get away. Both, I hope. I can feel his warmth, since he snuck right into my unbuttoned sweater, and he's practically burning a hole through my tank top. And he's not being overly gentle, either—he's gripping me hard, and his palms fit perfectly just above the flare of my hips. His hands tighten, forcing a gasp out of me, but his thumbs move gently, stroking the base of my ribcage.

"Let me go," I whisper, hoping he doesn't.

He shakes his head. "I can't do that. God, Madison... the thought that someone wants to hurt you... I'm going out of my mind. Please don't go. Stay. Let me help you."

There's a world of sincerity and anguish in his tone—he sounds scared and truly concerned. I swallow down the tenderness that wants to bubble to my lips and console him. "I'm a big girl, Wesley—I can take care of myself."

"How about this, then: *I* need *your* help."

I go still at the softness in his eyes, my stomach jolting as if a rug was literally pulled from under my feet. After how charged our exchanges have been, I never thought he'd ask nicely. And I *never* thought asking nicely would actually work.

"I need your help to find him."

I inhale sharply at that. Wait... does that mean he's not cutting me out and asking me to put my life in his hands—he's offering to let me be part of it? "I can find him on my own," I protest, but it sounds half-hearted, even to me.

He smiles. "I have no doubt," he says, and my heart lifts. I didn't realize how badly I needed to hear him confirm that until now. "But surely you can see that this is a better option—you don't know what you're up against, and you have a very blatant soft spot for a very vulnerable person. Someone could take advantage." He gestures back to the building with a jerk of his chin, never taking his eyes from mine.

He's got a point. Of course I *can* do it myself—just like I always do—but it would be much easier with his help. He has answers. And what's more, he has *resources*. Plus, it might help to have someone like Wesley on my side if the worst-case scenario happens, because I've never killed a man but... apparently, he has.

"I can't do this without my favorite spider. We'd make an unbeatable team."

I tilt my head back, lips spreading into a smile. A team. Just like old times. And even better, we'll be side by side. "Okay, Wesley."

His brows tip up in the middle, an entreating look full of tentative hope. "Okay?"

"Okay."

The tension blows out of him with a long breath. "Okay. Good. Go finish your visit with your grandmother. We'll talk after." Releasing me slowly, like he doesn't want to, he steps back and tightens his tie around his neck. "I've got an appointment with the vice president of Sunset Hills."

"What? Why?"

"Because I'm on the board," he replies simply, winking. "I made a sizeable donation, and they made me a member."

I feel my jaw drop. He... actually wasn't lying? "Why did you do that?"

"Because the board gets special treatment, and now Rosemary Vazquez is a VIP client. I'm going to get her moved into a room with a bit more luxury and special attention. Phillip mentioned a contract with a security company; I was thinking we could get a guard for her door. How does that sound?"

I swallow down a thickness in my throat that feels suspiciously like happy, relieved tears. He's... taking care of Abuela? Making sure she's safe? "You... um... maybe two guards—one in with her as a companion so she doesn't miss my visits quite as much. She likes Manny."

"Done," he nods.

My intake of breath is a sharp slice through my lungs. "Really?" I croak.

He cocks his head. "She's important to you. And you're important to me," he replies simply.

With that, he turns to head back into the building, but stops and glances at me sideways. He offers his hand out to me, and I know it's not just a silent offer to escort me back inside. It's a question. A test. My stomach flops as the importance of the moment settles on my shoulders.

I take his hand, and we walk back inside together.

19

MADISON

He is so unbelievably charming.

I don't know how long it's going to be before I get another chance to visit Abuela, so I decide to spend as much of the day with her as I can. I'm even in the room when the VP of Sunset Hills drops by after his meeting with "a board member" and breaks the good news that she's getting an upgrade. In true Abuela fashion, she takes the news with a show of polite gratitude for him and prickly old lady cynicism to me, once his back is turned. Manny kicks me out when visiting hours end, and I shoot Wesley a text that I'm going home as I head to my car.

As I pause at my mailbox, I inhale the amazing scent of someone's dinner, and my stomach growls. Must be my upstairs neighbors, the Morettis, because it smells like tomato sauce, garlic, and home-cooked Italian love. Maybe I'll dig out that packaged lasagna in the freezer... unless Wesley wants to order takeout.

Warmth smacks me in the face as I throw open the door to my apartment, and I register a few things at once: the lights are all on, that smell is getting *stronger*, and... Wesley's in my kitchen, leaning on his elbow on the counter and giving Some Bills a scratch so thorough that his purring is audible from here.

"What... the fuck?" I manage.

"Hello Madison."

"Wesley? You... Did you break into my apartment again? To... cook?"

With a smirk on his lips, he straightens, ignoring Some Bills's meow in protest of the interruption. "You wanted to be *satisfied* in all ways, yes? Well, I have a chef friend who gave me a recipe 'simple enough a child could do it.' And if it tastes half as good as it smells, I'll be quite chuffed."

"You can't just…" I trail off, heaving a breath.

Damn, it really does smell good in here. My stomach flips over, both in hunger and at the thought that he took my offhand comment to heart, and now he's doing something about it. He *cooked* for me. He *surprised* me with it. And, yeah, he totally broke in to do it, but it's not like it's the first time…

My ability to rationalize creepy behavior ought to be studied.

"I knew it was a waste of money to get the locks changed," I sigh dramatically, hanging my purse on a hook.

"It was," he smiles, like he knows how half-hearted my protest is. "It won't matter soon anyway. We'll be leaving for the safe house tomorrow morning."

"Oh, will *we*? Good of you to let me know what *our* plans are."

He chuckles. "My pleasure."

"Hmm. Getting a bit high-handed there, *Sir*."

His lips quirk up, but he refuses to rise to the challenge. It's like he knows I'm needling him, trying to evoke a reaction. "Do you want to sit and relax while I finish up? I've got a bottle of red wine."

"Fancy," I drawl, though my heart is hammering at this ridiculously sweet gesture. I consider him as he turns back around and stirs something on the stove. I know if I sit and watch this gorgeous man cook, I'm going to want to jump his bones. And I really need to do some prep work before that happens. I'm a hairy girl—it grows thick and fast—and I swear my pussy has a five o'clock shadow by noon. "I want to shower."

He nods, looking a little disappointed.

Inexplicably, that excites me—it makes my blood pump a little harder. How far can I push him? "It's not gonna be a quick shower, either," I add.

"Take your time," he says lightly.

I start replying, but cut myself off as he reaches for a wine glass. Wait, where the hell did that come from? I don't have wine glasses... Did he *bring* it?

"But first, come here."

At the order, arousal and anticipation knot together in my stomach. Damn, I love that *don't argue with me* tone. Makes me want to argue real bad.

I approach tentatively, and he sets the glass aside. When I'm within reaching distance, he wraps a hand around my hip and jerks me against him. A gasp slips out, and I have to catch my balance on his chest. He slides his index finger into the choker and uses it to pull me in as he curls down and slants his lips over mine.

There's zero ramp-up to this kiss. As he fuses our mouths together, I find that he tastes earthy and acidic from the wine and tomato sauce. It makes me smile against his lips—a smile he returns against mine.

He strokes his hands down either side of my torso and lets them land on my ass. I moan into his mouth as my core electrifies from the contact so close to where I want him to touch me. That moan turns into a whimper when he grips me tight, squeezing and kneading as he pulls me even harder against him—something I didn't think was possible until it happened.

Just as I'm trying to get my legs around him, he pulls back. "In case you were wondering, love, *that's* a proper greeting."

I hum thoughtfully, lips stretching into a grin as I unwind from around his neck and drop back fully onto my feet. "Not 'what the hell are you doing in my house'?"

He shakes his head.

"Not 'hands off my pussy'?"

"I hope not," he chuckles, glancing over at Some Bills. "I think he quite likes me."

"Well, then... Pip pip, my apologies," I tease, attempting a British accent and failing miserably.

With a soft smile, he reaches out to tuck a lock of hair behind my ear. "What do you think 'pip pip' means?"

I shrug.

"It's a farewell, and it's quite old-fashioned—mostly said ironically, now."

"Oh," I say. Backing away, I move towards my bedroom door. "Well... Pip pip, then. I'll see you in about an hour."

He nods and turns back to the stove. "When you're finished, we'll eat, then we'll discuss the important stuff—logistics, our plan, etc—and *then* we'll play."

A thrill zings through me. I love how casually his dominance comes out sometimes. Because he just said it like it was a foregone conclusion. Like there's no room for argument. "You mean you actually plan to try to make me come this time?" I taunt.

Once again, he refuses to rise to the bait. "I do. And you will."

That simple, straightforward reassurance replays in my mind while I shower, making me shiver despite the boiling temperature of water I prefer.

After the everything shower that leaves me languid and tingling, I take a quick peek into the main room and my heart does a happy dance. He's sitting on the couch, reading something on his phone and stroking a totally blissed out cat.

I duck back into my room to dry my hair and consider my next move. I'm liking Wesley's little delayed gratification game plan less and less. I just... I need to know what he feels like inside me. I'm not sure how I'm supposed to sit across from him for an hour when I know the night is going to end in my bed.

Do I go along with the plan that means I get what I want, but not exactly how or when I want it?

Nah, not really my style.

I have a lot more pretty underwear he'd probably like, though I wonder if that's enough to tempt him to veer from his little plan. And, I mean, if we're just going to get naked after dinner, I don't really need to put on clothes...

Oh, *ding ding*. That's the one. We've got a winner.

When I emerge, Wesley is still on the couch. He doesn't look up as I step into the room, so I clear my throat pointedly.

He glances up, then does a double take. His phone nearly slips from his hand as his jaw drops and his eyes go down, up, then back down my naked body. I watch as he takes in the decorative ink that I love so much, then locks in on the swells of my breasts. My nipples pebble under the attention, and excitement thrums in my veins as I recognize the same look he wore when I dropped my dress last night.

"I want to play first," I explain, sensing he's going to be speechless for a little while longer.

That snaps him out of it. "First?"

"Before dinner. I'm not that hungry," I say lightly. But it's like the thought of food activates my stomach, because in that instant it betrays my lie and lets out a loud growl. My eyes widen, hand going to my middle.

He shoots me a knowing look. "No?" he teases, lifting a brow.

"Okay, so I *am* hungry. But I'm hungrier for something else." I let my gaze drop meaningfully to the front of his pants, where the fabric has tented around a very impressive, very mouthwatering hard-on.

He reaches down and adjusts his cock, making me smirk in anticipation. Fuck yeah. He's excited. I bet he's spent the day in just as much painful anticipation as I have. He'll give me what I want. Score one for the brat.

Setting Some Bills gently aside, he stands, brushes some hair off his pants, and starts rolling up his sleeves in a move that would light my panties on fire if I were wearing any. I track the motion, mouth going dry at the slow reveal of ink, pale skin, and veins.

I didn't *need* to be more turned on, but here we are, I guess...

"No. Sit. I'll get you a plate. Once you've eaten and had plenty of water, then we'll play. You're going to need the calories, and I don't intend to stop for a snack break."

So caught up in the forearm burlesque show, it takes a second for his message to sink in. I heave a playful sigh and roll my eyes. "Fine." I turn.

"Madison," he says sharply, halting me in my tracks. "I told you to sit."

"I know, I was going to—"

He pulls out one of the stools and gestures to it. "Before you showered, I explained how the night would go. You remember?"

Tentatively, I nod.

"But you decided you wanted something different, so you came out here naked to tempt me to get what you wanted?"

I nod again, slower this time. It's not dread mounting in me, per se, because he's so calm. But there's an odd, fluttering, nervous feeling in my chest.

"Then sitting here naked while you eat the lovely meal I made for you is the appropriate consequence, don't you agree?"

That taut thread of tension snaps, and I nearly laugh in relief. I didn't realize until now that I was a little nervous about how he'd react. My lips twitch as I take a half step towards the stool. "If I say no, will it get me punished?"

He chuckles. "I will never punish you for honesty or telling me what you really think, only for trying to manipulate me or bend the rules that have been clearly stated and agreed upon."

Oh okay. So it's gonna be like that. I think I'm starting to understand what kind of dynamic this is—and it fills me with excitement because he's deliciously dominant AF and seems to really like the bratty flavor of my submission. We're a match made in heaven, slowly descending into hell.

"I think I'm picking up what you're putting down. I had to try, though, you know?" I say with a rueful smile and a shrug. "I've been thinking about it all day."

"We have that in common."

I wriggle as I settle bare, throbbing skin against the cold, unyielding, rough wood of the chair's seat. Knowing I have to sit here like this because he told me to... fuck, it gets me going.

I'm often naked in my own apartment, but I still feel exposed and sort of on display for him like this. I hope he's got some butter for all these rolls—he can lick it off. He looks like he wants to; his eyes are practically burning holes into my skin, they're so hot with desire.

Dios, he makes me feel so damn sexy. I fully believe that the hottest thing a person can be is self-confident, but it's just so much fucking easier when the person you're with is so open about their appreciation.

Hopefully, it's a quick meal.

He pours me a glass of wine first, grinning in what must be self-satisfaction as I shift around, trying to find a comfortable position. I eye the glass. He went out of his way to buy it, and it's probably perfectly matched to the dish or something... Maybe I can be a classy bitch for one night.

"Thank you," I say demurely, reaching for and taking a large sip of the wine. I nearly cough instead of swallowing. "Yup. Confirmed. Don't like wine. It tastes like sour grapes and feet."

He laughs as he places my plate down. "What should I get instead next time?"

Next time. Swoon.

I shrug as I pick up the fork. "Not sure I understand the concept of drinking alcohol for the flavor. I've done, like, shots. But that's about getting drunk. None of it *tastes* good. Except margaritas," I amend.

"I'm more partial to champagne, myself." He grabs a plate for himself and slides into the chair next to me.

Huh. An even classier bitch.

Now that he's seated, I load up my fork. "This is really good!" I say, eyes wide and mouth full. Frozen lasagna can suck it.

"Thank you," he inclines his head and takes a bite.

"Not to sound ungrateful for the meal, but you know you didn't actually need to wine and dine me, right?" I smirk, twirling another noodle.

"That was fairly obvious from the seduction attempt, yes. But I wanted to. We're starting over." He sits back and gestures to the meal, his smile filled with pride. "This is our first date."

"I thought our first date was tacos and stories of our misspent youth."

"That was Peter and Madison's first date," he counters. "This is SpyderMan and mermaidav's first date."

Gah, he is so unbelievably charming. I hide my smile in another bite of noodles. "So, SpyderMan, tell me about yourself. Is it true you're an assassin?"

"I am—only the wankers who really have it coming, though, I promise. And I usually refer to myself as a hitman. It feels less formal somehow."

"How are the benefits?"

He quirks a smile. "The life insurance sucks, if I'm honest." When I laugh, he joins me, and the moment feels 10 times lighter.

"I meant to ask earlier, how did you know my gun wasn't loaded last night? Part of your hitman training?"

He takes a bite and chews thoughtfully. "About six months ago, you told me that guns scare you and that you'd never keep one loaded in your home."

"Six months ago?" I repeat, disbelief creeping into my tone. "You remember a conversation we had six months ago?"

"I've told you before, Madison. I remember every conversation we've ever had."

His voice is so sincere, goosebumps crawl down my arms and across my chest. "I think I'm starting to believe that," I murmur, almost too low for him to hear.

But he does hear, and he grins. "All right, my turn. Operating system: Windows or Mac?"

"Trick question."

His grin turns sly. "Is it?"

"You know it is. The correct answer is Linux."

"Only for those of us who can't build their own."

"Oh, fuck off," I cry. "You built your *own* operating system?"

"Several, in fact. My first when I was 18."

I laugh and roll my eyes. "You are *such* a nerd."

20

WESLEY

Knobheads can learn.

It's been the most difficult test of my self-control I've ever endured to sit across from Madison's perfect, luscious, curvy, naked body and not reach out and touch. I've pictured grabbing her and dragging her onto my lap at least a dozen times. My cock is aching, and it hasn't gone below half-mast since she got home. Not even when the topic takes a turn towards the darker, more concerning stuff.

"Not to bring up the elephant in the room, but we should probably talk about the whole *my name appearing on a hit list* thing..."

I set aside my wine. "I expect you want to know where the list came from." At her nod, I launch in. "My team and I have been working for a man we know as the General for several years now. He's the one pulling the strings. He's the one we need to find and kill."

She inhales sharply, a line appearing between her brows. "So he's your boss? That can't be good. The General," she repeats, like she's tasting the word. "How do you know killing him means I'll be safe?"

My smile is almost rueful. "Always asking the right questions. The General runs a dark web interface for hitmen and criminals. It's how he contacts us with the jobs, how we send our proof, and how he pays us."

"Sure," she nods, playing it cool though I can see her eyes widen as she looks down at her nearly empty plate. And I don't blame her. Even having been on the fringes of the dark underworld like she has, I doubt she ever imagined something like this. "No General, no interface, no money. I can't imagine a hitman would bother to do a job without the promise of payment. It's not like it's personal or something. It's work."

"Precisely."

"So you want me to help you ID the guy, right? You're thinking he's probably related to some intel I sold?"

"Precisely," I repeat, lips twitching. Am I even needed for this? I bet with the right push, she'd do it all on her own.

She cocks her head, and her hair spills down, coiling temptingly around a tawny nipple. "How does this guy contact you? How do the hits come? Is it posted on that forum or something?"

Eyes locked on her breast, I shake my head. "In an email directly to me."

"Only you?"

"Until we decide whether to take the hit. I've always assumed they went out with some sort of priority based on track record."

Seeing where my attention has landed, she grins and shifts back in her chair, spreading her thighs to give me a glimpse of more. "When did you get the email?"

My throat is dry. "About a week and a half ago."

"Be more specific."

Loath to look away, I quickly pull out my phone and call up the message. "The 25th at 2:49 PM."

"That was the day I quit SmarTech. That was just a few *hours* after I quit—and waltzed out their front door with a panda's ass full of stolen information," she breathes, excited about a lead. "There's absolutely no way that's a coincidence."

"SmarTech?" I repeat, brow furrowed. I ignore the panda's ass bit, assuming she'll explain later. "Interesting. There may be a connection there. Some of our other hits have used SmarTech encryptions. You stole data from them?"

"Yeah. The guy who hired me to do it—my *tío*—should have some answers for us, too. At the very least, he's got all that data I stole."

Odd. There was no mention of extended family in her background check. I file that information away for later. "Do you know what he wanted? Why he sent you?"

"He never tells me," she says, rolling her eyes. "I just copied over everything I could get my grubby little raccoon paws on. Client files, employee files, program files..."

"You are thorough," I say approvingly, finishing my meal and collecting both our plates. As I move into the kitchen to place them in the sink, she watches me with a heavy-lidded stare.

"Then it's settled. Tomorrow we can fake my death, head to your safe house, and we'll grab the USB drive on the way. Love it when a plan comes together."

I give the plates a cursory rinse, then wash my hands. When I'm done, I head back around the counter.

"It's settled," I agree. "And are you satisfied with your meal?"

I watch the question land, watch the fire burn a little brighter in those warm, caramel brown eyes, watch how her pulse thrums in that vein on her neck. "Yes," she breathes, shifting in her seat and pressing her thighs together. "Does this mean it's time to play?"

"Yes. But first, I brought you something," I say, reaching into the bag dangling off the back of my chair and producing a box.

Her eyes light up. "Something sparkly?"

I laugh. "What are you, a crow?"

"Caw, caw!" she giggles.

It's settled. I'm getting her the biggest ring I can find.

I hold the box out in front of her face, letting her slide the lid off. She peers inside curiously, then stares at the curved device.

"You bought me a... really weirdly shaped vibrator? I have plenty of toys, Wesley."

The admission makes my stomach twist in excitement. "None like this. It's one of a kind."

She glances up. "Why? Did you make it or something?"

"Modified it." I lift it from the package, discarding the box, so I can show her some features more closely. "I did some reading and found out that SSRIs disrupt dopamine and norepinephrine, as well as spinal reflexes that can impact nerve sensitivity. Multiple articles recommended stronger vibrations and multiple types of stimulation simultaneously, so I combined this part here that sucks and this part here massages inside, but I wanted to ensure it was still waterproof so I—what?"

She's staring at me, not the device, her jaw slack. "You… looked it up? You read articles?"

"Yes…"

"You made me a vibrator?" she asks, her voice high-pitched and a little squeaky.

I know she's pleased, but when I nod and her eyes fill with tears, I panic a little. I put down the vibrator and cup her cheek. "It's important to me that you enjoy yourself, my love. It's not enough to simply *satisfy* you—I want you mindless from the pleasure, screaming my name." I grin.

She sniffles and laughs, blinking away the mistiness in her eyes. "Is this your way of apologizing for leaving me with the worst case of blue clit last night? I mean, even though there was no penetration, I feel like last night qualifies as pulling a hit it and quit it."

I wince.

"Love 'em and leave 'em?" she suggests, as if the phrase she picked were the reason for my reaction. "Smash and dash—"

I cut her off with a laugh and a kiss. She meets my lips eagerly, instantly trying to deepen it, but I pull back. "I'm not apologizing because I'm not sorry—that implies that I regret touching you, and I very much do not; not for a second—but I didn't want to leave you like that. I hoped this would show you that I intend to finish what I started. And I can recognize when I've been a knobhead."

"You *were* a knobhead," she agrees, the barest twitch of a smile at the edges of her lips.

"A proper knobhead. But knobheads can learn—and I promise I'm a fast learner."

She throws her hair over her shoulder. "Okay. Just so you know, there's no guarantee this will work—but I really, *really* want to try it."

I was hoping she'd say that. I tap the countertop. "Hop up. If it doesn't work for you, you can let me know what kind of modifications you'd like."

"Now?" her brows lift and her smile slants into a teasing smirk. "You sure there isn't something more important you have to do?"

"Wild horses couldn't drag me away this time, Madison."

With a single laugh, she climbs the rungs of the chair. The instant she's on her arse, I step between her legs and pull her to me. Her breasts press against my chest, her hard nipples poking me.

This kiss needs no time to ramp up; we're both desperate for it. She clutches my shirt, balling it into her fists as she breathes a sigh into me. As I deepen the kiss, pushing into her harder and taking ownership of her mouth with my tongue, she whimpers. The sound goes straight to my cock, making it jerk and swell and pound. I love the way she clutches and holds onto me, like I'm a lifeline. It makes me feel like she wants to depend on me—like she trusts me to keep her upright and safe. I feel strong. Powerful.

Her teeth nibble at my bottom lip, drawing me back in when I pull away. I smile against her mouth and adjust my hand so it's around her throat instead of under her chin. Instantly, she stills. I need to remember this—how pliable she becomes with a gentle but firm hand around her neck.

I reach for the toy I made. She watches, excitement making her pulse thrum in the veins on her neck.

"There's lube in my bedside table."

"I have a better idea." I grab the closest counter chair, take a seat, then slide both arms under her thighs and pull her towards me in a quick, jerking movement that forces her down onto her elbows. Since I'm still seated, her pussy is at nearly the perfect height. I won't even have to bend down too far. Her scent—musky, tangy and heady—invades my senses.

She squirms in my grip, though. "I don't... um... Never mind."

As she trails off, I frown and tighten my hold. "Tell me," I urge, voice dropping.

I think I see a faint darkening of her cheeks as she mumbles, "Well, I suppose you did research it..."

"I did. I promise nothing you say will shock me." I need this, I realize. I need her honesty and vulnerability. I need her trust.

She heaves a sigh. "It's just... um, remember how I said at the arcade that it wasn't going to happen for me? That's kind of just oral in general for me. The meds make it hard for me to get out of my own head, you know? I know what I like, so I can usually come when I touch myself, but when someone else tries with their hands or mouth... I dunno. I guess I get too far in my head about it, and I'm worried it's taking too long, or you're getting bored or something." Her eyes dart away.

My heart seems to swell. I feel oddly thrilled by her confession, like it created a possibility I didn't dare hope for.

I want to be the only one who knows how to please her—to be the only one who ever really has. I want to be the only one who can make her scream, who can evoke primal reactions from her body. I want to be able to turn her on with nothing but a whisper of a memory. I want to be inside her in every way—body and mind. I want her to feel me in her marrow.

My head pounds as my desire rises in my veins in a hot wave. My cock swells against my leg, tight and painful with nowhere to go. I lean into that flash of discomfort, because this isn't about me right now.

"Madison, look at me."

She does, and the soft, shuttered fear in her eyes burns me. She needs to relax—there's too much psychological pressure for her around the idea of orgasming. Perhaps in the past, someone made her feel like her pleasure was just an achievement to be collected by whoever made it happen.

Pleasure is often the goal, but for the naturally submissive—as I suspect Madison is, deep down—there's a release in the simplicity of giving in. When a world of choice narrows to *obey* or *resist*, the brain shuts off. It reduces anxiety. It triggers relief.

But it requires trust. She needs to let herself feel anchored to me.

"Madison," I say. The repeated use of her name and unflinching eye contact are two important steps in making myself into the anchor she needs and that I'm desperate to be. "I'm going to taste you because I can't get the thought of it out of my head. If you come, I'll be thrilled, but I want you *wet*. Because once you're ready for it, I'm going to do my very best to use this toy to make you scream. If it's not in the cards, well... it'll be a hell of a lot of fun trying, won't it?"

Her small, genuine smile feels like a win.

"Now," I say, squeezing her thighs in the creases of my elbows until she gasps, "use your safe word or lie back. Up to you."

Goosebumps prickle across her skin. "What's my safe word?"

"Red and yellow should suffice," I say, knowing she'll understand the traffic light system if she doesn't need clarification on the concept of safe words.

"Boring—" she sings.

"Classic," I counter.

"—but it'll do," she finishes, settling back.

"There's my good girl." I wink.

She shivers, and I don't think it's because she's cold.

I've been dying for another taste of this—of her. All others have been far too brief. I take my time, pressing a trail of kisses along her inner thighs and smiling against the softest skin I've ever felt as she twitches under my light touches. It's only once her breath starts heaving in and out that I finally make contact, and she hisses at the touch. I groan into her, my lips vibrating against her tender spot. She tastes so fucking divine—it's a goddamn honor and pleasure to have her in my mouth.

I'm thorough and languid as I lick around her clit, keeping my touch indirect to keep her on the edge of anticipation. When her body starts producing slippery evidence of her arousal, I have to tear myself away.

I grab the vibrator. I designed it to stay in place hands-free, and the shaft end that goes inside is flat and smooth enough that I'll still be able to fuck her when we're using it. Not this time, though, and not just because I promised to take my time with her—I need to be able to focus and watch how it affects her. I'll never be able to think straight with my cock inside her. Especially not if something is vibrating next to me while I am.

That does give me another idea, though. Dual control. Perhaps a remote option as well...

I slide it inside her, line it up with her clit, and start it with a click of the center button. She gasps, and the sound is deep, guttural, and accompanied by an instantaneous full-body spasm. "Whoa," she cries, reaching down as if to move the vibrator away.

"Too much?"

She giggles, wiggling her hips like it tickles. "Yeah, a little. Start gentler, maybe build to the more intense setting as my nerves adjust."

I press the button twice more, making a mental note to add some more variability in speed. Right now it only has three. She settles against me, her giggles melting into low groans and musical whimpers. I catalog how her face screws up and how tightly she shuts her eyes as I move the device around to find the right spot. It takes a moment, but I can sense the shift as her body wakes up and she starts to truly get into the sensations. When I change the setting to medium, her eyes fly open and meet mine.

"Wesley," she cries. "*¡Dios mio!*"

Pride swells, and my whole body tightens at the raw desire caught in her throat. I was already so fucking hard, but now my cock is straining, impossibly harder and leaking precum all in my trousers. Good thing the cameras are streaming this right to my personal cloud—I can already tell I'm going to play this back again and again.

I lean forward, stretching my body over hers, and smooth her hair back from her forehead. I rest my palm on top of her head and smile down at her. "You like it?"

"This thing... fucking rocks!" she manages. Her body is jerking, making the words come out stilted and choppy.

"Shall we try the highest setting?" I ask, running a hand down the length of her torso, pausing to pinch one of her tight nipples.

"Yes!" she cries out, bowing and pressing her breast harder into my hand. "Wait, no. No! I'm gonna... fuck! Don't change it. It's so good!"

I move to take the tip of her breast into my mouth, but her hand flies to my head, fingers threading into my hair, and she tugs my head towards hers. Our lips meet in a hard kiss, both demanding more than we're willing to give. We nip and suck and bite at each other, vying for control and getting lost in the intimacy of being connected. Pleasure courses through me, collecting at the base of my spine and tingling with the need for release.

She breaks away and shrieks. "I'm..."

"Say my name," I growl, reaching down and gripping her nipple hard between my fingers. "Scream it. I want everyone to hear you."

Her whole body tightens, and her limbs shake. She wails, and it's like the sob is being ripped from her chest. "Wesley! I'm coming! Fuck, Wesley! Wesleeeeey!"

Any man who thinks he "can tell" when a woman is faking it, but doesn't get this level of response from an orgasm is a muppet. This is raw, ugly, and not trying to be anything it's not. It's honest. It's perfect.

It's the hottest thing I've ever fucking seen.

She's panting, squirming, and softly moaning "noooo," so I switch off the vibrator. Once she's caught a few deep breaths, I help her into a sitting position.

"That was stunning, love."

"Wow," she breathes, reaching down and pulling the device out of her pussy. It makes an entirely obscene, wet sucking sound. "You *made* that? In, like, one day?"

I barely hide the grimace. In truth, I've been working on it ever since the day I listened to her masturbating from the closet.

But she doesn't wait for confirmation or an answer, breezing right past her own question with a contented, "This thing is gonna be huge with the depression/anxiety girlies. It needs a name. Branding."

"I'm open to suggestions."

"*Clitty Clitty Bang Bang*?"

"Definitely not."

"*The Sham-oh-oh-oh-Wow*?"

"I hope that's not a proper suggestion."

"*The Boyfriend Replacer.*"

"*The Brat Tamer,*" I counter.

She grins and cocks her head to the side. "I dunno," she says, a mischievous kind of mirth twinkling in her eye. "I don't feel very tamed."

"You will," I promise, making her giggle.

21

MADISON

Don't you think we've delayed this gratification long enough?

My knees are still shaking from Wesley's little miracle vibe as we move into the bedroom. He's so hard and seems so keyed up that I kind of expect him to immediately reach for me when we're within dwarf-tossing distance of the bed, but he holds up a finger and disappears. When he returns to the room, he's holding a big glass of water that he hands to me as I settle on the bed.

"Drink it," he instructs.

"Bossy," I mutter, but don't hide the smile as I do as he says.

When he looks up and sees my glass is empty, he holds out his hand for it and sets it aside. He starts carefully unrolling his sleeves, eyes downcast and focused on the task. "Now that we've settled that, are you ready to begin?"

A thrill zings through me. "Say that a little more ominously. I don't think *all* the blood in my body is in my crotch quite yet."

He ignores my joke, dark eyes glittering. "Stand up, please."

Dios, that tone. And for some reason, it's the *please* that gets me. A totally unnecessary courtesy. A demonstration of restraint through politeness. A reminder of the need for mutual respect.

I stand. Suddenly, I feel exposed—I'm acutely aware of my own nudity once again, and my nerves are alive with it.

"Turn around and spread your legs."

"Oh, we're not messing aro—"

"Do you want to be gagged for this, Madison?" he asks, voice dropping.

I shake my head. My nipples are so hard they could cut glass, and my pulse is pounding in my throat. "Maybe if you use your dick," I mutter as I spin.

What can I say? I'm physically incapable of relinquishing the last word.

He heard me, and his laugh is just as low and dangerous as his Dom voice. "Don't mistake me: I love that smart mouth—I can't wait to fuck it. Before we get to that, I just... I want to look. Lean forward. Grab your ankles if you can."

My insides clench so hard it hurts. There's an intense kind of vulnerability in being naked while the other person is still dressed, and this takes that hot, twisty feeling up to 11. No hiding. A display just for him.

Feeling a little dizzy, I slowly lower myself and grab my ankles. I have to shift my hips back to maintain balance, and I know it opens me up almost lewdly. I can feel the draft of cool air against my throbbing, hot, tender skin.

His breath heaves out, stuttering towards the end of the long breath. "Fuck, Madison."

My face heats, and it's only partially because the blood is rushing to my head in this position. I bite my lip and throw him a look over my shoulder as I straighten. "You say that, but you're still standing all the way over there."

It's a dramatic overstatement, but I think I'm going to die if he doesn't close the four-foot distance between us and just fucking *fuck* me already. His sleeves are down and he started unbuttoning his shirt, but he's still totally covered up. And he doesn't make a move towards me.

There's a small shift in his expression as his eyes rake over me. A frisson of uncertainty, of longing so sharp it pokes holes of doubt all over.

"Wesley?"

Snapped out of a trance, his eyes bore into mine, dark and intense.

He makes a contemplative humming noise. "Honestly, I'm... at something of a loss. There's so much I want to say, but I... I don't have the right words for you. For me. For... this."

I suck in a breath. "Wesley—"

My breath catches in my throat, and my stomach twists. The reverence in his voice slips right through all the cracks in my walls—suddenly, I'm rooted in place, watching him look down at me as emotions bubble up that I'm a little scared of.

We're... here. Together. It's real. It's *him*. Between the impossible situation and the repeated setbacks, some part of me never thought this would really happen, so I don't feel ready for it.

Before last week, SpyderMan only existed as words on a screen—and somehow, despite that, he's got a piece of my heart anyway. Because at the end of the day, who are we, really, beyond the words we choose and use? His words have made me happy. They've inspired me, comforted me, teased me, challenged me and *changed* me. I fell for his words a long time ago, and I was prepared to let him keep that piece of me, even if we never met in person.

But now... we're finally together.

I understand exactly how he feels—I'm at a loss, too. I don't know whether I want to stare or touch or taste him first, because I want it all. And there's this strange pressure hanging around us, like expectation and fear. We're not afraid of each other, exactly—we're afraid of this moment, because it feels so *important*. It's one of those rare occasions when you know ahead of time that everything is about to change.

"Kiss me. Please."

His breath heaves out, and he closes the distance. When he reaches for me, I brace myself, but instead of feeling his palm hitting my throat, as he's so fond of doing, he tucks a lock of hair behind my ear and lets his fingers slide down the length of my jaw. His thumb gently caresses my bottom lip.

"You're so beautiful, Madison."

Goosebumps prickle on my skin, though it's a toasty 70 degrees in here. I press harder into his hand. "So are you."

He continues stroking the callused edge of his thumb across my cheek, almost absently. After a few seconds of intense eye contact, I start getting antsy. "Don't you think we've delayed this gratification long enough?" I ask, knowing how frustrated and hopeful I sound.

His lips quirk, and he kisses me. Barefoot, I feel every inch of the height difference as he spins us and walks me backwards towards the bed. When the back of my thighs hits the mattress, I break away, gasping for air, bending backwards in his arms until he has to let go of my face to catch me around the waist. Even then, he pursues, following and burying his face in my shoulder. There's a sharp sensation as he bites the skin there, and a spasm of need wracks my body.

When I make a pathetic little whimpering noise, he pulls away and releases me. Realizing he wanted the space so he could start undressing, my mouth drops into a little O and I fall gracelessly onto my ass, totally transfixed. Butterflies start fluttering around like mad, making my insides roil and tingle.

This is it.

He's meticulous and deliberate as he unbuttons his shirt and drapes it over the edge of my office chair. His pants get the same treatment, and then he's standing only in a pair of boxer briefs, looking like he's trying to smuggle a traffic cone.

Holy. Fucking. Shit.

The first thing I notice is the tattoos, but only because they're so bright and so *copious*. This is a man who understands patience and can sit still through days—weeks, most likely—of discomfort and outright pain of needles depositing ink under skin. Shapes and colors draw a continuous pattern, though a few stand out images strike me—a British flag, a gravestone, a red rose in the mouth of a skull, an ace of spades...

"Beautiful," I breathe, pulling back on the need to run my fingers over them. "Did the same artist do them all?"

"Most," he says, looking down and smoothing a hand across his flat abdomen. Somehow the tattoos accentuate the ridges, making them look even harder and emphasizing the cut of the V that disappears under the band of his boxers. "I had to find someone new when I came over here."

I can't wait to touch every single one, but there will be time for that later. And it's fitting because his body is a different kind of work of art. He looks so... strong in a way that's thoroughly exciting. Solid. Firm. He's all rock-hard hills and valleys, with a smattering of light brown hair across his chest. My eyes drop to his package, and I stare unashamedly as he pulls down and steps out of his boxers. His cock springs up, curving slightly towards his body. Excitement coils and uncoils deep inside me at the sight. I was right—it's pretty.

Like, I know that objectively, dicks usually aren't. His is.

He smiles wickedly, seeing the intensity of my focus. "If you want this, show me what a good girl you can be for it," he instructs, reaching down and gripping his length at the base. It makes it jut out from his body further and look even longer. "Lean back and open your legs."

That normal bristling feeling I get at the phrase *be a good girl* is nowhere to be found. Just eager submission—like my need for this man overwrites any resistance to being told what to do. "Yes, Sir."

I scoot back a few inches and lean my weight onto my hands so I can draw my legs apart for him. He takes a stiff step towards the bed, and my stomach drops in a pure rush of excitement. Then, he stops himself, meeting my eye. The intensity there is almost scary.

"Tell me what you need now, Madison," he orders, giving his cock a firm stroke that steals my breath. "It's hard not to lose control around you, and once I'm inside that perfect cunt I know I'll be lost. What can I do to make sure you're comfortable?"

It's hard to tell which warms first—my face or my heart.

"Well, we've got that," I nod at the vibrator he made me. Then, I eye his size, stretch to the side and reach for the bottle of lube in the top drawer of my bedside table. I tilt it towards the fingers on my left hand, but as I start squeezing, he clears his throat. With a smile that feels equal parts thrilled and shy, I hand it to him.

"Lie back, my love."

Face flaming at the endearment, I do as he asks. He pours a dollop into his hand, warms it, and leans forward. The first brush of his fingers against my aching flesh makes me gasp and spread my legs wider. He teases me with his touch, too gentle to give me the friction I crave, exploring and ensuring every inch of me is slick. When he dips two fingers inside me, I moan. I can just see out of the corner of my eye how his cock bobs in response to the noise.

"Does that feel good?" he murmurs. Breathlessly, I nod, but he clarifies, "Does it feel like enough lube?"

Grinning, I nod harder. Fingers shaking with excitement and need, I hand him the vibrator and hiss as the cool silicone comes in contact with my searing heat. It slides inside so easily, fits in place so perfectly, that I start rocking my hips in eager anticipation of what's about to come.

I hear the lube bottle squirt again, and open my eyes in time to watch him spread more across the tip of his cock. My heart is racing, and my blood is pounding so hard and loud in my temples that I think I might explode from the anticipation.

Then, he leans towards me.

Finally.

With a moan of relief, I reach for him, but he grabs both my wrists, falling down onto them with all his weight and pressing them into the mattress above my head as he settles his hips between my spread legs. The tip of his cock taps against the device seated along my seam, and I gasp and writhe at the sensation.

"Oh, we're doing this again?" I purr. "You're kind of a control freak, huh?"

Not that I mind. Well... I don't mind *much*. I mean, I want to touch him, too, but I love the feel of being trapped underneath him like this. The weight of him... it's perfect. I couldn't buck him off if I tried, even before his immobilizing grip.

"Well, the last time I let you have control, you handcuffed and pointed a gun at me, you little menace."

"Touché," I laugh, knowing he's not serious about that being the reason.

His weight transfers as he shifts, pulling my wrists into just one hand and pressing them hard into the mattress to rebalance so he can grab his cock to aim it. We're almost perfectly aligned like this—I only need to hook my legs around his hips and curl my spine a little to lift my pelvis.

I try grinding down harder on him, to force the tip inside, but his fingers tighten around my wrists.

"Something you want, my love? You only need to ask."

"I want you," I hiss.

"You have me," he observes wryly, grinning at my frown. "Hmm... perhaps it's not enough? You'll need to be a bit more specific."

I want to cry in frustration as I toss my head side to side. "Just fucking do it. Fuck me."

"Now, Madison, we've already talked about you asking nicely for the things you want," he chides, the softness of his voice belying the tight urgency behind his words.

I open my mouth to scream something at him, then snap it shut before the noise escapes. I breathe heavily through my nose and plead at him with my eyes instead. He wants me to show him I know how to be good. So I'll swallow the smart comment if it means I get to swallow him.

"I want your cock. Fuck me, Sir. Please."

"There she is. There's my good girl," he praises, pulling back his hips to align himself at my entrance.

Like he's some sort of sex wizard, the vibrator inside me buzzes to life just as he slams into me fully in one stroke.

Fucking. Finally.

I literally see stars. The breath whooshes out of me on a keening kind of wail, and my whole body tenses around the intrusion. True to his word, he doesn't stop—doesn't give me a second to catch my breath or adjust to the size of him. He pulls his hips back and snaps them forward again. I hear the tone of my cry change from relief to shock to hopeless arousal. I'm glad he's got such a tight grip on my wrists and hip, because as much as I thought I was ready for this... I fucking wasn't. The combination of him and the intense vibrations is almost too much.

"That's it. Don't hold back, love. Be loud for me. I want everyone in this fucking building to know who you belong to," he grits out, voice wavering under the strength of his rhythmic thrusting.

"It's so fucking amazing, Wesley! F-feels so good!"

I throw my head back and squeeze my eyes shut, like it'll somehow help with the assault of sensations. And it does. Between the size that fills me right to the edge of pain, that upward curve that has him dragging the tip against the device pressed against my g-spot, the intense sucking on my clit, and the way he's hammering into me in an unbroken rhythm...

"You like knowing that I'm using this tight little cunt? That I'm taking what's mine?"

An unfamiliar sound spews out from deep in my chest—half groan, half whimper—and my entire body convulses in a wave of arousal that his words sets off. My nipples prickle painfully, brushing against his chest, and my skin suddenly feels too tight. I'm so turned on, I actually feel tears leaking out the sides of my closed eyes.

Between the feel of him stretching me deep inside, and the way he's pinning me... I've never been so completely overwhelmed by someone—he's everywhere. Nothing exists outside the feeling of his lips forcing down on mine, his fingertips digging into my waist, and his cock splitting me open.

Fuck, I wish he'd start moving again. I'm so close to the edge—to tumbling headfirst into that liminal headspace of mindlessness and pleasure—that I can barely believe it. But I won't get there unless he starts fucking me again, despite all those lovely vibrations.

But in that moment, I can't bring myself to break away and demand what I want. The fight is... gone. All I can do is lie still and just... *take* whatever he wants to give me. Though, that doesn't seem like such a bad thing anymore. Was it ever? I can't remember.

I kiss him back as fiercely as I can, pouring all these complicated emotions into it, but otherwise I let myself go limp. I let go.

It's like he senses that he's gotten what he wanted—my true submission. He rears back, studies me for a beat, then starts thrusting again. He releases my hip, trailing his free hand up to hold, massage, then grab my breast. I release a stuttered moan as the squeeze gives the pleasure an edge that makes everything feel *more.*

"You look so pretty when you're taking my cock, Madison," he groans.

At the edge of my vision, I can see as the muscles in his abdomen contract around each controlled movement. "*You're* so pretty," I mumble incoherently. "So good. So fucking good. Feels so fucking good... Oh, *Dios.*"

"Fuck, you're so tight. The way you grip me... fuuuuck. I'm close," he says, and I'm not sure if he's letting me know or asking me if I am too. I don't care which.

"Close," I echo.

He gives me more and more, taking just as much from me with each back-and-forth of his torso. The movements jostle the vibrator, making my body tense and quiver. It builds and builds and builds... Suddenly, I'm not falling over that cliff—I'm hurtling towards the edge at 100 miles per hour, and I'm about to smash into a million pieces at the bottom.

"I'm coming!" I shriek, the release of words and breath and noise just as cathartic as the release of pressure and tension.

His rhythm breaks, and he grunts, finding his own pleasure at the same time that mine explodes. I barely register him as light sparkles behind my eyelids, a roaring noise fills my ears, and my soul levitates. For a breathtaking instant, I'm weightless, breathless, unbound by the laws of reality.

When I come back down, the tickling against my clit gives my laughter a manic edge as I wiggle my hips to escape it. My eyes find his through the hazy confusion that always follows having your mind completely blown. He releases my wrists. Still breathing hard, he clicks off the vibrator, pulls it out and tosses it onto the bed somewhere behind me.

Rolling off, he lies next to me—shoulder to shoulder with our legs hanging off the bed, it's still somehow so intimate that it makes my heart hammer for reasons unrelated to sexual sprints.

"You are..." I pant for a second, unable to finish the thought until I've caught a little more oxygen, "kind of a dick. But *Dios*, do you have a nice one."

Chest heaving, he chuckles, and it vibrates through layers of fabric and padding in the mattress, through skin and bone to settle deep in my core like it lives there. "I'll take it."

I turn to look at him and find his face close to mine. "And the mouth on you? Fil-thy. Filthier than mine, I think."

He grins, and I think I light up from the inside at the purity of how happy he looks. He presses his face closer, finding my lips like he has a map. His kiss is languid, somehow both a thank-you and a reminder of his ownership. Or maybe that's because he reaches up a hand and circles my throat to hold me still for it.

Like I never even came, blood rushes to my pussy and fresh arousal joins the post-orgasm pulsing. My face must show just how much I like his hand there, because he grins.

"Sir?" I rasp as he pulls away.

"Yes, my love?"

I shiver under the weight of the word. Love. *My* love. *His* love. It's suffocating and freeing at the same time, and I have no clue what to do with it.

I grab the vibrator and hold it up, gesturing to it with my free hand. "*The Religious Experience? Screamin' and Creamin'? It's A Whole Vibe?*"

His laugh shakes the whole bed, then his expression shifts to something dark and delicious. "Put it back in, Madison. You haven't begged me to stop yet, so we're just getting started."

22

MADISON

I'm changing his contact from "Sir" to "Sir Nerd."

Dios, last night was perfect.

Luxuriating in bed, I watch Wesley as he moves through the room, collecting his clothes and pulling on his pants. The sunlight streaming in through my curtains has the harsh brightness of mid-morning, and I can smell the coffee he must have started wafting in from the kitchen. It's a good try to get me out of bed, but I'm not falling for it.

"He fucks like a god and he makes coffee in the morning," I say with a little hum of contentment, covering a yawn with my hand.

He flashes me a smile over his shoulder as he sits on the bed to button his shirt. "Don't forget that you have some packing to do," he reminds me.

"Right. Safe house." I readjust my arm under my pillow. "I need some more sleep. And a shower. Okay, maybe shower first. Care to join me?"

"Tempting," he says, reaching out and rubbing my upper arm. "But we need to head to the safe house this morning."

"Then you probably shouldn't have fucked me for, like, half the night."

The sound that rips from his chest is suspiciously like a growl. My eyes widen, going from his sternum to his lips to his eyes. When our gazes collide, the surprise in mine melts immediately to excitement and heat.

"Want to try that one again, love?" he lifts a brow, sliding his hand up my arm until it's a vague threat, resting on my shoulder just inches from my throat.

I think we both know if he closes that distance and grabs me how we both want, he just wasted his time getting dressed.

So I give him my brattiest, most pleased-with-myself smile. "The best-laid plans—derailed by laying the plan," I say, grinning. "It's me. I'm the plan. You laid me. So much. *So* well."

He laughs and moves until he's propping himself up with an arm on either side of me. He presses a kiss to my temple. "We'll go when I get back. Rest, take your shower, have some coffee."

"Where are you going?"

"I need to pack up my stuff from the hotel where I've been staying. And I thought while I was out, I'd grab some things for Some Bills. I need to make sure the safe house is cat-friendly—or at least has a litter box. Plus, if I stay here, I'll never be able to keep my hands off you."

I beam at him. "What a good cat dad. I mean, I know my pussy calls you Daddy now."

He shakes his head, but he's grinning at my joke. "Take your shower, you little menace. I'll be back in a few hours. Don't answer the door while I'm gone. And load your damn gun, Madison."

I smirk. "Yes, Sir."

A minute later, I hear the door shut. Alone and free to make an ugly noise, I do a full body stretch that I can feel in every inch of muscle I've got. *Dios,* I'm sore. Like, in a "smiling through every wince" kind of way. Last night was the best night of my life. No one has ever been so interested in or attentive to my pleasure. He built me a vibrator, for fuck's sake! And it's so much more than the perfect gift or his hot, dirty mouth, or the way he treated learning what I liked as if he were a scientist collecting data from trial and error.

Show me how to touch you, love.

Like this?

Yes. Fuck yes. That's it. Come for me.

He's... everything. Everything I hoped he'd be. Everything I could want. Our online chemistry was good, but our in-person chemistry is off the fucking charts.

But as I take a quick shower and dress myself, I sit with a strange feeling in my chest. It's a fizzy happiness, sure, because Wesley is literally amazing, but why am I not *just* happy? Why is there this lingering sense of... dread?

Maybe it's because if the potential with Peter was exciting and terrifying, it's 100x worse with Wesley. My heart is already involved. It has been for two years.

And I'm not used to being vulnerable. I'm used to being badass hacker Madison, who makes terrible men cry and doesn't need anyone. It's simple. Safe. No one can hurt you when you don't give a shit about what they think.

But I give a lot of shits about what Wesley thinks. And it's really fucking scary because that gives him so much power over me—so much power to hurt me.

That's future-Madison's problem. Present-Madison's problem is... packing—and the fact that I've only got one suitcase, and it's still in my car from yesterday morning. I packed light in anticipation of being on the run, and since that doesn't matter anymore, I'd like to fill the rest of the space with important stuff. The entire contents of my toy drawer, for example.

Just before I head out I remember to grab my pistol from its drawer and roll my eyes as I tuck it in the waistband of my skirt. "Load your gun, Madison," I mock in my best British accent.

Wesley's bike is still parked next to my car, so I assume that means he took that van he pointed out on the street out front. It made me snicker last night as I considered and discarded about a dozen inappropriate jokes. But I can't ignore how ironically polar opposite the two sides of his persona are—on the one hand you've got a panty-dropping motorcycle and on the other you've got a pedo van.

As I open the back door of my car, my phone vibrates in my pocket. Grabbing it, I check the screen and see a text. Of course, he put himself in my contacts.

First chance I get, I'm changing his contact from "Sir" to "Sir Nerd."

Sir

It's not safe, Madison.

Get back in your flat until I return.

I haven't rolled my eyes this hard since I was a kid, and I distinctly remember being told they'd get stuck that way. I start tapping out my response.

I'm not a total idiot. I've got my gun.

But just before I can press send, someone grabs me from behind.

23

WESLEY

When the game is life and death, you might as well stack the odds.

Madison left her flat.

Muttering a curse under my breath, I call up the tracking app on my phone. Her car is still in the lot behind the building, which eases my worry somewhat, but I don't like that she left. I don't like the panic that threatened to swallow me whole when I realized I didn't have eyes on her. And now she isn't answering my texts.

The only real solution I can see is having her by my side at all times—otherwise I might go out of my mind with worry. I'll wait with her while she packs, then we'll go together to pack up my things and continue on to the safehouse.

Most people aren't so blasé when you tell them there's a price on their head. And while I don't want her living in fear per se... *some* fear would be nice to see. Fear makes people careful, and I want her to act with caution.

I park my van in the spot it feels I literally just left—I didn't even make it all the way to the hotel before getting the notification that she left her flat and turning around—and wander to the back. A narrow alley separates her building from its neighbor, and I know from practice exactly where the cameras are to avoid.

But when I get to the small car park in the rear, there's no sign of Madison. I frown and double-check my phone—I didn't see a notification from the cameras that she'd returned inside. And I don't see her at her car. I see... Why is there a suitcase on the back seat? I reach for the door handle and find it unlocked—and my stomach sinks.

A high-pitched yelp sends ice through my blood. I whip around, trying to determine where the sound came from, and my feet start moving before I've fully processed. The area back here is closed off by the surrounding buildings. There are a few security cameras, but it's dark and much more private than the front street. Several alleys snake away from the lot, and I charge in the direction the sound came from.

My heart nearly stops in my chest when I round the corner and see Madison in some bloke's arms. About five yards away, he's dragging her backwards towards a waiting vehicle blocking the entrance—one hand around her mouth, muffling her screams and profanity, and one arm wrapped around her, trying to subdue her as she fights him like a wildcat.

I recognize Madison's gun on the ground between us, so I dart for it, lift it and aim it at him. Luckily, he's at least a full head taller than her, so she's not directly in the line of fire. "Let her go!"

When he sees me, he stops, frozen by an unexpected witness. Madison, however, renews her struggle. I see a flash of her teeth just before he howls.

In that instant, when her attacker is distracted enough to loosen his grip, I watch, dumbfounded, as Madison totally flips the situation. It's like seeing Eleanor or Nicole practicing the moves Dimitri has been drilling into them for months. She gets her feet under her, drops into a strong base, brings her arms together and flares her elbows. With enough room under his arms now, she slips from his grip, dropping to the ground and twisting to land on her back.

No time to be amazed.

As soon as she's completely free of him, I aim the gun at his stomach, flick off the safety, and pull the trigger. The hammer falls and the gun snaps, but the kickback feels wrong. There's no ringing in my ears from the muzzle blast. The gun didn't fire.

Bloody hell.

Madison recovers from the confusion before the attacker or I do, landing a kick to his groin from her position on the ground underneath him that makes my body jerk in totally uncontrollable sympathy. The man goes down, and Madison scrambles away.

"It's not loaded!" she squeaks, darting towards me and safety.

"I gathered," I growl back, tossing it to her as I close in on the man, who is recovering quicker than I would've from a kick to the dick. As he gets to his feet, he pulls a switchblade from his back pocket, making me falter.

I reassess the situation, falling back on Dimitri's training more easily than I would have thought. It's calming, this feeling of knowing what to do in a high-stakes situation.

Assess, plan, and act. Be quick so your opponent does not have time to do the same.

He's a massive bloke, thick around the middle and a few inches taller than me. He's also got a knife. I'm quick and I can throw a punch, but I don't have a knife.

Mistakes will be made in every fight, but losing your upper hand is usually the last one. That's one of my favorite "Dimitri-isms" from the running log we keep to document his unintentionally poetic, violent advice. And he's right, so it's a good thing I haven't lost the upper hand. I've still got a trick up my sleeve.

I charge, taking advantage of my speed. Predictably, he slashes at me, but his elbow flares before he moves, and it's easy to tell what trajectory the assault will take. I'm there, ready, blocking him and ramming my fist into the inside of his wrist. It causes the nerve there to spasm, and his knife clatters to the ground. I get behind him so I can wrap an arm around his thick neck. He starts thrashing against me instantly, and I have to flex with all my might to keep my hold.

A hard jab to my liver steals my breath in a white-hot burst of agony that radiates outward. As I reel from the blow, the man breaks free of the chokehold and turns on me. He smiles with the gleeful menace of a man who knows he's going to win a fight he didn't start but very much wants to finish.

Unfortunately for him, this one's over—he just doesn't know it yet.

I was never really trying to overpower him; I prefer to outsmart them, anyway, and I'm partial to a bit of sleight of hand. When the game is life and death, you might as well stack the odds.

While he focused on the bicep against his windpipe, he missed the prick of the micro-needle from the custom-built ring I always wear, and the double dose of etorphine straight to the side of his neck. The fast-acting opioid is normally used for bringing down animals, but right handy in a pinch.

As he settles into a pose meant to threaten, intimidate, and ready his own attack, I watch the effects of the sedative settle around his eyes, causing them to flutter closed. He shakes his head, confused by the sudden, unexpected sensation of darkness closing in.

He reaches for me, but he loses his balance and his entire body pitches face-first into the ground. The crack of his head against the pavement rings down the alley, a disgusting, violent sound that's a relief. If the sedative hadn't gotten him, that would've.

As I heave huge breaths, I wince and clutch my abdomen. Fuck, that smarts. Dimitri's training involves learning how to take a hit, but every time I think I'll be prepared for the breathtaking pain that accompanies a sharp elbow to a relatively soft organ, I'm proved a liar.

"Wesley?" Madison asks behind me, voice wavering.

Her voice stirs that creature inside me that's all instinct and violence. I turn, grab behind her neck and pull her into a rough kiss meant to remind us both that she's all right. She's in one piece. "Are you hurt?" I demand, scanning her body for blood.

She grabs my biceps tightly, digging her nails in. "I don't think so," she chokes out. "I'm okay. Thanks to you... Is he dead?"

"Heavily sedated," I reply, releasing her against my will and crouching down to check the man's pockets. Empty. My stomach sinks—he's a pro.

I stare down at him. The urge to take his life for daring to put his hands on my girl is strong—and it would be so easy—but there's a reason I left him alive. There's a reason it's always part of my plan to leave them alive. Dead men tell no tales. "We need to question him—to find out why he attacked you," I tell her.

She nods, understanding. "How long will he be out?"

"A few hours. But we have to get out of here," I say, throwing a nervous look over my shoulder. More could be coming. Since we don't know what motivated him, we have no way of knowing what the danger is. "I'm going to send my team in to collect him."

Her lower lip wobbles. "He c-came out of nowhere while I was getting my suitcase out of my car... I got away and I ran, but he caught me..."

I grab her wrist, rubbing the inside with my thumb. "We don't have time for explanations. We have to go. Now."

We hurry down the alley, back towards our vehicles, and I go to my bike. Madison hesitates.

"Get on," I urge, holding out the helmet for her.

"I've never..." she begins, taking the helmet and eyeing the motorcycle with fear. She glances behind her at her car. "Can't I just follow you?"

I shake my head. We can't risk it. We don't know who that was, or who sent him. What if they have her car's information? What if there are more? Motorcycles are the perfect getaway vehicle. They can weave through traffic, fit down tight alleys, and they accelerate faster than most cars.

Madison glances up, then goes pale. "Gun!" she screams, pointing behind me.

I whirl. At the mouth of the alley, a man gets out of a tan sedan and crouches behind his door for cover.

I grab her, curling around her protectively, and drag her down just as a gunshot rings out. The metallic plink tells me it went wide and hit her car. A second later, a car door slams closed, and I know we have seconds until he's on us.

I haul her up and hop onto my bike. This time, there's no argument. She throws her leg over, falling gracelessly onto the seat behind me, and leans her full weight against me, hugging me so hard around the middle it makes breathing a challenge. But it's good. I need to feel her to balance us, and if she's hugging me, I know she's all right. I hit the starter, and the engine roars to life, revving and drowning out her screech of alarm as I peel out of the alley where the first assailant's car is blocking the path. The gunman won't be able to follow us past that car.

Moving too fast to pause, we careen out into the street, cutting off a small lorry and eliciting angry honks. I speed up even more, weaving through traffic and avoiding red lights so I don't have to stop. The blood is pumping so hard in my veins it's audible over the sound of the wind rushing in my ears. There's so much adrenaline and fear and panic, I can't even enjoy the experience of having Madison as my backpack.

I keep checking my mirrors, but we're not being followed by anyone. So I zigzag across town, arriving at the Ulysses Grand and pulling right into the parking garage under the building. Usually I find a spot on the top level for easy access, but now I keep going until we're several levels down, in an area where no one parks unless they have to. Down here, the agility of a motorcycle will outmaneuver that of a car if we get into a tight spot again—and it'll be obvious if someone is lying in wait, since there are only a handful of occupied spaces.

As I pull into the furthest corner and gently slow our momentum, I realize that Madison is trembling. Her grip on me is tight, right up until the instant she senses it's safe to dismount. Then she's gone. Not waiting for assistance, she scrambles off my bike so fast that she falls onto her arse.

"Fuck," I curse, shutting off the bike and putting down the kickstand. "Are you all right?"

I swing my leg over just as she picks herself up. I reach for her, and she backs away a step, her usually warm eyes darker than normal in the low light of this parking cave.

"Madison—"

That's all I get out. She launches herself at me, wrapping her arms around my neck and dragging me down so she can smash her lips onto mine. The adrenaline in my veins roars its response, shifting from fear to desire in an instant. I clutch her tightly, wrapping my arms around her and squeezing her to me, letting my instincts take over—the ones that need to hold, touch, take and claim. She's here. She's safe. She's mine.

My need for her becomes an overwhelming thing. I need to be as close as possible. I need to be inside her. That's the only way to satisfy this urgent terror. The only way to prove to myself she's all right—that we're both all right.

I start to thread my fingers into her hair, but she pulls back, gasping. Her pupils are so dilated that her eyes appear black. She stares at me, chest heaving, then drops to her knees without a word.

"Madison—" I choke out again, this time in shock and surprise as I stumble back half a step and hit the side of my bike. The stand is sturdy, so it barely jostles.

She doesn't say anything, but there's an edge of mania in her eyes as they stare up at me in a silent plea. The fear is being edged out by lust and relief so acute and potent it must feel like love. So I don't stop her as she reaches for my zipper.

There are so many sensations throughout my body; my system is confused and a little numb.I'm fairly certain I'm not all the way hard, but Madison doesn't care. She takes my cock out of my trousers and immediately takes the tip into her hot, wet mouth.

I shout and weave my fingers into her hair. The sensation is powerful, and the knowledge that she's on her knees for me is heady. My legs give, and I land on the seat of my bike before I can recover to stand on my own. Her tongue swirls around the most sensitive part of me, stroking the nerve endings and eliciting a deep, rough sound from low in my chest.

Her lips are so soft, and her tongue is wet and silky against my skin—this is so much better than the roughness of my palm—so it's not long before the blood shifts, moving to fill my cock. It grows in her mouth, making her hum in desire and approval. The vibrations of the sound shoot straight up my spine.

She releases me with a fleshy *pop* of her lips. The sight of her staring up with those warm brown eyes through her lashes is nearly enough to do me in. And that's even before she makes her demand.

"Fuck me," she says, rasping and breathy. "Need it. Need you."

24

MADISON

Will you let me take care of you?

So many emotions—sour, terrible ones—were immediately silenced the second I dropped to my knees. All that existed was the two of us, and I'd never wanted anything more than I wanted him. I needed him inside me so badly; I didn't care how or where. I needed to inhale that feeling of safety and get lost in the taste and scent of him until I couldn't hear any other horrible thought. And now that he's hard, he can fucking do something about this ache that's trying to burn a hole in my insides.

Releasing my head, Wesley reaches down and grabs my waist. I gasp as he lifts me off the ground. There's an instant of an odd, bottomless feeling in my stomach as he jerks me around, pulling me forward and pivoting so I'm against the bike and he's behind me. I catch myself on the seat, gripping the edges and digging my nails into the leather.

He flips my skirt up and reaches between my legs, hissing at the heat coming off me.

Rrrrrrrip.

The sound of fabric yielding to hunger so desperate, rough, and urgent electrifies my nerves and brings a rush of moisture with it. I can't see what he's doing; I can't even reach back and touch him. I feel open, helpless, and it goes right to my core. All I can do is lean here—bared, holding myself up—and wait for him to stick his dick in me.

Dios mio. This is so fucking hot.

"You want this?" he asks through his teeth.

His words send a zing through my stomach, pebbling against my nipples and sparking an ache deep inside my cunt that demands to be filled. He rubs the head of his cock against my entrance, sliding easily through my soft, smooth skin from the saliva I left on his length.

"Oh fuck," I hiss, nodding eagerly, then letting my head hang between my arms which are wobbling as they work to hold me upright.

"Do you want this, Madison?" he repeats emphatically. "Tell me: yes or no."

"Do it. Fuck me. Right now."

With a strangled groan, he spits in his hand, then shoves a boot between my feet, kicking them apart to make room for himself to stand. I nearly cry with arousal. He grabs my hips, lines himself up, and slides into me in a long, smooth, forceful stroke that makes both of us moan. The sound echoes around us, amplifying and then fading as it travels along the concrete.

Fuck. He's so deep. *Fuck*. I'm still so sore from last night, but that pinch of pain is like a reminder that I'm alive. That he's filling me. I clench around him.

The first snap of his hips rips the air from my lungs. I feel that stretch and forceful push from my hair to my toes. The rasp of fabric against the backs of my legs sends a shiver through me. He wanted inside me so badly; he didn't even pause to drop his pants. This kind of half-clothed, desperate, dirty sex in a public place is exactly what we both need right now.

"Harder. More," I beg.

His fingers curl around my waist, gripping hard enough to bruise as he thrusts faster and harder. He's rough, and the pace is punishing, and I love every damn second of it. He fills me so perfectly, so completely, and the head of him dragging against my g-spot feels both *so* good and not enough at the same time.

Even though he's not being gentle, it's like a feather-light touch that hints at pleasure but doesn't stimulate enough to actually cause any. I need to be able to touch myself, or to have something vibrating against my clit. The slap of his balls isn't enough. The tip of him deep inside isn't enough.

Fuck.

I'm not going to come. Not like this.

Fuck!

The realization makes me squeeze my eyes against the prickly tears. I tamp down on the wave of uncontrollable shame—it's *not* my fault, and I have *nothing* to feel bad about—and try to focus on how good it feels. Fuck, I wish this were as easy for me as it is for other people. I need the relief of a release. I need to lose myself in this...

After another few minutes, he groans, coming to a stuttering, shaky stop behind me. His cock pulses and flexes inside me, and I know he's filling me up. The thought is erotic enough on its own to make me clench and moan.

We're both breathing hard when he pulls back and out of me. With a noise of surprise—I didn't realize how much he was actually supporting me—I nearly fall face-first into the motorcycle seat, but he catches me with his hold on my waist.

He brings me up into his arms, back against his front, and curls around me, chest still heaving and rocking both of us with the deep inhale-exhale. His arm snakes up my front, gently circling the front of my throat. Unbidden and unwelcome, memories from my attack surface. That man held me from behind like this. His body was bigger, his hands rougher, his scent wrong, his intent to hurt me, kill me...

I choke down a sob and shiver. The shiver doesn't stop as I come down from the high of the adrenaline. It was temporarily shifted into hot desire, and now that we're not fleeing or fucking, my nervous system is shot. Shivers turn into shakes, and I'm suddenly trembling from head to toe, and I can't control it.

I go rigid in his arms as paranoia creeps back into my consciousness. There are cameras down here. We're exposed.

Wesley realizes the same thing. "As much as I want nothing more than to drape you back over my bike and eat you out from behind, I refuse to give a security guard that show. Let's go get you cleaned up."

The journey up from the parking garage into the hotel is a blur. He ushers me from one elevator to another with a hand low on my back. I'm so focused on the odd, slippery sensation of his cum leaking out from my pussy that I miss all the details. He asks for my phone at one point, and I hand it over on autopilot. And then we're safe behind a closed, locked door in a room where every surface is covered in different kinds of electronics. It makes me smile faintly because that's how I know this room is his.

He parks me in the short hallway between the door and bed, disappearing into the bathroom. A second later, I hear running water and I peek inside. He's seated on the edge of a large tub, leaning forward and checking the water temperature as it pours out.

Oh, he meant, *let's get you cleaned up* literally.

Satisfied with the adjustments of the taps, Wesley stands, wiping his hand on his pants. His eyes are on me as he closes the distance. "I'm going to go erase the security footage from the garage."

Numbly, I nod. "Good. That's... good."

I expect him to breeze past me, so when he pulls me into his arms and presses a soft kiss into my hair, I have to squeeze my eyes shut against the onslaught of emotion that makes them prickle with unshed tears.

"You're safe now," he murmurs. "I've got you."

I inhale sharply, and the breath breaks in the back of my throat. I lean into him harder, willing that vague sense of relief to crystalize and chase away all the rest of my emotions.

He's got me. *Safe*. I'm safe. I'm safe because he's here...

"Wait!" I gasp. "Some Bills!"

"I used your phone to text your upstairs neighbor to retrieve him. He's safe with her in her flat now."

The breath that blows out of me is shaky and full of gratitude. My eyes water with it. He thinks of everything. "Thank you," I whisper.

"Get in the bath when it finishes filling. I'll erase the footage, then I need to check in with my team quickly, let them know about the sedated man in the alley. I'll be in when I'm done."

He leaves the bathroom, taking that feeling of peace with him, and all I'm left with is a highlight reel of terror.

Someone grabbed me from behind and dragged me backwards. Someone covered my mouth and nose and deprived me of air for long enough to make me see stars and almost pass out. Someone shot at me.

Someone tried to kill me.

Wesley swooped in like my hero, but watching him fight that guy was terrifying–especially when he took a hit to the liver that made the blood drain from his face. And then we got away, but riding on the back of that bike was horrible. Every turn we took made my stomach bottom out, and I was frozen in fear, too scared to shut my eyes.

What if we were followed? What if they're watching us right now? What if whoever it is out there that wants to hurt me knows where I am?

Calmate. *This is the anxiety, Madison.* I coach myself the way Dr. Cora told me to. *Anxiety makes your thoughts race and your emotions hard to regulate. Wesley said you're safe.*

It's been a while since I had a bad episode, since the meds I'm on do such a good job. Guess even SSRIs can't compete with the sheer terror of nearly dying.

I shove those thoughts away, shut it all out and move to the tub. It helps to have something else to focus on instead of the swirling thoughts. Right now, I can focus on getting clean, because I can see the grime all over my face. He must have had dirt on his hand when he wrapped it around my mouth...

Don't go back there. Stay here. Stay present.

The tub is half filled and desperately in need of bubbles. Shampoo and body wash create a lame amount of suds that float on top, but they smell nice and it's better than nothing. I peel off my clothes, listening for sounds that Wesley is coming back. All I can hear are the low tones of his voice, muffled through the door. He must be talking to his team.

I disrobe, tossing my ruined tights and underwear into the trash and piling the rest of my clothes in the corner, shivering when I remember how the zipper of my sweatshirt got caught on that man's sleeve...

Here. Now.

I heave a breath and start making observations—another Dr. Cora trick. I've never been in a bathtub this big before. I settle at one end and wrap my arms under my knees to hug them as close as I can to my chest. I marvel at how much more room there is than in the tub in my apartment. It's big enough for two—maybe even three. I wonder if people have sex in it when they stay here.

I get so lost in thought, I don't hear Wesley open the door. "Madison?"

I turn as he crosses the threshold, his socks barely making a sound against the white marble tile floor. "You're still shaking, my love."

Not sure what to say to that, I just nod. "I feel cold."

The look on his face is full of so much concern, I have to look away or I might start crying. "Will you... Madison, will you let me take care of you?" he asks, holding up the half-empty bottle of shampoo.

"Why?" I hear myself ask woodenly. He said it with a certain emphasis, and I'm not sure if it's because I'm in a kind of shock, but I don't think I fully understand the question. Why would he want to do that?

"I... well, I'd say I want to, but it's a bit deeper than that, I'm afraid. I need to."

As long as he's touching me, I'm fine with it. I just need his hands on me or I'm afraid I might float away. "Okay."

As he settles onto his knees on the tile just on the other side of the bathtub, that missing piece snaps into place. Oh, *that's* what he meant. Wait, he's going to... bathe me? Like I'm a kid? I don't like that.

I must make a face, because he hesitates in the act of rolling up his sleeves. "Is this all right?" he asks, brows tilting up in the middle in concern.

I shrug one shoulder, but don't unwind from my tight ball. If I let go, I'll just be sitting here, wet and naked, while he's out there. I don't *like* that. "Um..."

"Tell me," he murmurs.

Oddly, the softly spoken order gives me permission, making me feel free to say what I want without fear of how he'll react. He asked. I'm just doing what he wants. "Will you... get in here with me? You can wash my hair if you want, but I want you to hold me," I say, feeling so ridiculously small and childish that I want to suck the words back in. Only a child asks to be held for comfort; I'm a grown-ass woman. So I clear my throat and explain, "When you hold me, I feel a lot safer." I need to be so surrounded and consumed by him that there's no room for the bad thoughts.

His smile is kind, almost indulgent. "I can do that."

He's meticulous and deliberate as he unbuttons his shirt and hangs it on the hook on the back of the door. His pants get folded and placed on the counter. And then he's naked.

I feel my face flush as I look my fill. He's a work of art.

When he starts moving closer to the tub, I release my legs and scoot forward to give him room to climb in behind me. The white flash of his tight ass as he climbs in makes me bite my lip. Suddenly, I can't wait to have my hands all over his lean muscles and hard body again.

How appropriate that lust is what breaks me through this cold shell of shock.

Water sloshes around as he maneuvers into place, stretching his long legs on either side of mine. I feel one of his hands against my waist, and a flash of fear sends a shiver down my spine.

Suddenly, I'm being grabbed from behind in the alley...

But then I look down and I see the tattoo on Wesley's hand. I smell his delicious, strange scent all around me. I feel his warm, solid body holding me with such gentleness.

And then there's his cock digging into my back.

I'm here. I'm safe. He's got me.

The fear melts away as we sit silently, and eventually I realize I've matched his deep, measured breathing without meaning to.

There's something odd about the eroticism of this—being naked together, being in the bath—that only occurs to me when I realize that he doesn't intend to do anything about his hard-on. Even though we're both willing and turned on. I'm not sure I've ever been naked with a man with no expectation of sex.

"Turn on the faucet and hand me the wand, please," he instructs, tone firm but gentle.

My stomach flips at the demand, blood immediately rushing between my legs and an urgent kind of tingling sweeping across the tips of my breasts. Oh, the fun I've had with showerhead wands.

Okay, it turns out there is *some* expectation of sex. It's just coming from me.

Dutifully, I reach forward, pluck it out of its holder, turn it on and hand it to him. He smooths a hand down my hair, encouraging me to lean back, and runs the water along my hairline like they do at salons. Once he gets my massive, thick mane nice and wet, he starts gently working the shampoo into my scalp.

I close my eyes and surrender to the tingly feeling of someone else's fingers in my hair. As he washes, I can feel my erratic pulse evening out and my nervous system slowly releasing the last of the anxiety and fear. He's calming me. Grounding me. Making sure I feel safe.

He rinses, then conditions without me even having to tell him to.

"Someone knows the rules of feminine haircare," I tease, eyes still closed.

He chuckles. "It says right on the bottle: wash, rinse, repeat."

"You don't have to repeat," I tell him with a small smile, knowing he knows.

"Noted."

He finishes working the conditioner through, rinses that out too, then encourages me to lean back against him. I sigh, settling against his chest with my fresh, clean hair. He's warm and solid, and I just want to melt into him. I tend to float, but Wesley wraps his arms around my middle and keeps me anchored to him.

He uses the wand to rinse the soapy water off my arms and chest. My back bows, offering him my breasts to touch, but he holds back.

"I feel like a prat for using you like that earlier," he says softly.

"What? Don't," I reply immediately, hating the hints of self-condemnation in his voice. "No, that was me. I'm the one who jumped all over you. Besides... I liked it. I wanted it."

He's quiet for a few seconds—enough to make me a bit self-conscious—then the arm around my waist moves and his hand strokes lower, down my belly.

"I know you didn't come." His breath is hot on my ear when he leans close and whispers, "Would you like to come for me now?"

I shift my hips up, opening for him as his fingers trail down my tummy. He's so close to where I want him to touch me. But just like it wasn't going to happen for me against his motorcycle, it's not going to happen like this, either. I know my body, and the manual approach just usually isn't enough.

"Maybe, um..." I start, then chicken out.

"Tell me," he urges.

"Use the showerhead," I say, glancing over my shoulder to watch how the words land.

But there's no condemnation or reproach on his face—only a dark kind of heat, desire and excitement. I realize with a jolt that he's not put off by the request. He's not irritated because I need something more powerful than fingers or tongues, and he's not doing it to humor me or hurry to get me off so he can stick his dick in me. He wants to do this. A lot.

Suddenly I realize what I want.

"He... in the alley, he... grabbed me from behind," I confess softly.

Wesley goes rigid. "Do you want me to—"

I shake my head. "No, actually..." I inhale. Do I dare ask for this? It feels so... wrong. So exposing. Who goes through something horrific and then asks their partner to recreate it?

"You can tell me anything, Madison," he says.

"Normally, I like being restrained... I like when you hold me like this—and I don't want to think about him when you do it ever again. I want you to erase him. I want you to replace the awful memories with better ones. I want you to take that violence and turn it into something I *want,* where I have control and I can stop it."

He nods and, if possible, that dark look in his eye shifts to something even darker. "What's your safe word, Madison?"

"Red," I recite dutifully, the word a kind of security blanket.

"Good girl. Lie back."

When I settle back against him, his free hand slides up my ribcage, up between my breasts and circles around my throat. I gasp against his palm, letting my head fall back. My pulse roars in response, arousal tingling between my legs, making me squirm.

He uses his grip to shift my head to the side and drops a line of kisses along the line of my stretched neck, from shoulder to just under my ear.

The sensation goes right to my swollen, thrumming, throbbing core. That ache deep inside me is like an itch I started scratching and stopped too soon, leaving it itchier than when I started.

"Like that?" he croons into my ear, making the fine hairs on my arms stand. "Do you like the feel of my hand on your throat, my love?"

My eyes drift shut. It's like he's talking to me so I can remember it's him back there. "Yes Sir."

He drops his legs and maneuvers mine over his knees, then widens them until my calves are pressed into the sides of the tub. I'm spread open, wide, and the warm, silky water caresses my aching pussy so softly that I have to clutch his forearm as my body spasms in need.

"I've got you, Madison."

I nod. He tightens his hand, angling my head back so he can cover my mouth with his. Just as I open to receive the kiss, I feel the spray of the wand between my legs, against my upper thigh. My leg tenses, but I'm trapped—not just by his demanding lips, or his legs pressing mine into the cool sides of the tub, or his fingers against my pulse. I'm trapped by his desire. I'm helpless to do anything but give in and obey. And it's such a turn-on that my skin feels like it's on fire.

With a flick of his thumb, he changes the spray setting to the targeted pulse from the middle. And when the focused stream of water finds my clit, I moan, jerking in the erotic prison of his body. The spray is intense, but diffused enough that it hits a wide area, massaging not just the nerve endings but also the area around them. My whole body is alive with the sensation.

"Too much?" he asks, lips brushing against mine with the shape of the words.

Eyes squeezed shut, I shake my head.

"Eyes on me. Look at me, Madison. Stay right here with me," he demands, rolling his hips forward so I can feel his cock pressing into my lower back. It makes me whimper, reminding me of the ache deep inside me, desperate to be filled. My eyes fly open, and suddenly I'm falling into the swirling gray depths of him. "You're mine, you understand that? Mine."

With as deeply as we're locked in, the words land in a way that causes chills to erupt all over my skin. I squirm under the weight of it, and tug uselessly against his hold, sucking in a sob when the fact that I can't move just ratchets my arousal up another notch.

"Wesley—"

"And I'm yours."

Wesley's fingers are hot and firm on my neck, holding me in place. He makes a deep noise, low in his chest, and slams his lips down on mine. I totally lose myself. With the nozzle perfectly aimed at the exact right spot, I'm spinning, weightless and formless, ascending towards a building pressure that sits almost painfully out of reach. I fly higher, reaching closer, and the water pounds relentlessly against the most sensitive part of me.

With a final push, I tip over the edge, and the spinning sensation gets faster and more disorienting as I careen downwards into the open arms of the pleasure that's been waiting to consume me. It takes over my body, tightening and releasing, making me shake with the force of how good it feels. The orgasm wanes, but the echoes of the pleasure still pound against me from the inside out.

I start fighting against him, the water sloshing around us as I twist around, but his hold on me is like steel. My pulse races for a different reason now. Because while I'm ready for the pleasure to end, I thrill in this show of dominance—that we'll stop when he decides we're done.

I asked to be restrained. I asked to be at his mercy. I *want* this.

And now I want it to be over. So, when he pulls back, I gasp, "No more! Red!"

He reacts to the word as soon as it leaves my mouth. Instantly, the strong pulse of water against my overly sensitive nerve endings disappears, and my body relaxes in relief. Slowly, he lowers our legs and slides his palm down to rest over my heart instead of around my neck.

He holds me like that as my breath evens out, and my body stops shaking with aftershocks. I feel myself slump back against him. He's still hard, but I'm way too languid and content to worry about doing anything about it. And for his part, he seems perfectly happy just to take care of me.

Imagine that.

I'm shaking like a newborn deer, knees knocking together when he helps me to my feet. He climbs out of the tub and then holds out a fluffy towel for me to wrap myself in. He knots his own towel around his hips and pulls me against him, kissing me so gently and thoroughly that I can't remember why I was so scared of the sensation of floating away...

25

WESLEY

She gets all of me, and I'm taking all of her.

After the bath and a meal, Madison settles into bed, cuddling under layers of blankets and comforters, and I sit against the headboard next to her. It's early evening, but she's clearly exhausted from everything that happened today. My mind is buzzing, and I know I won't be able to sleep for hours, but I can't bring myself to be more than a few feet from her.

My cock is aching, and it hasn't gone below half-mast since she invited me into the tub. Now, next to her like this, I can barely stand being so close and not being inside her. Made even more difficult as the memories from the tub swirl around my head like soapy water down the drain.

The way she quaked with pleasure in my arms, the way she clung to me like a lifeline, the way she trusted me—both with the truth that was clearly difficult for her to verbalize at first, then with her body as I held her and coaxed her pleasure from her... it means more than she can possibly understand. It was everything to me. That level of trust isn't given lightly; it honored me. It felt like power. It felt like purpose.

I want nothing more than to gather her into my arms, but I want her in the worst way, and I know how rough today was—I can't be sure I'll be able to restrain myself once I have her body against mine. I want to give her space to process everything, if that's what she needs.

She tosses and turns, trying to find a comfortable position, and I grab my phone. First order of business is to check in with Mac and Dimitri. When we spoke before the bath, I let them know about the attack.

Since Dimitri is moving around well but technically still recovering, Mac volunteered to go grab the body. I'm curious if it was still there—if the man shooting at us was that man's partner, I doubt the body was still in the alley by the time Mac arrived.

3 Musketeers Chat

Mac

No body.

I heave a sigh and tap out a response to the minutes-old message.

I figured.

Mac

I'm sticking around for a while to see if anyone comes back. Want me to drop the van off for you in the AM?

Yes. There's a suitcase in the back seat of her car, if you don't mind grabbing it and bringing it when you do. And her cat is with the upstairs neighbor in 2F. She'll want to see him in the morning.

Mac

Can do. You good?

I'm fucking livid. Did either of you take a look at the footage I added to the shared drive? Any thoughts on who the attacker was?

Dimitri

I recognize him. We crossed paths on a job once before. He goes by The Butcher.

> Fuck. That means the General sent someone else after her.

Mac

> We'll get him, Wes.

> If it helps, I know exactly how this feels and can confirm it fucking sucks.

Dimitri

> You will feel better when we kill him.

Dimitri's unusual contribution has my lips quirking up, despite all the frustration and rage. He doesn't normally suffer any off-topic discussions, and talk of *feelings* has been known to make him leave our group chat altogether.

Smiling and shaking my head, I drop a pin at the hotel for Mac so he knows where to leave the van for me.

I glance down at Madison as she flops over onto her other side. The cover has slipped down over her shoulder, and I itch to right it for her. But I know it wouldn't be just an act of care. If I let myself cross this divide, I'd also let myself trail my fingers down, following the curve of her neck, sweeping her hair out of the way to reveal that soft tan skin...

Exhaling noisily through my nose, I flick through my apps until I get to my email. I check for a note from the General, but the last I have from him is the automated confirmation of my bid for Madison's job.

I tap over to a private browser and type in the exact URL I need. It's the only way to access anything on the dark web; that's what differentiates it from the regular internet. You don't need a specific browser or anything, but there's no Google. Nothing is searchable. You need to already know where you want to go.

The website throws my login credentials back at me, stating the account doesn't exist. I scowl and type them out again, slower. It doesn't work. One more time to confirm...

My stomach plummets. I'm locked out of the General's system. He must have removed me. *Fuck.* Fuck!

"Wesley?"

Shaken from my swirling panic by her soft voice, I look down. "Yes, my love?" My tone is tight, and it takes every ounce of my willpower not to let her see my agitation.

She rolls over and faces me. "You were right."

"I usually am. You'll need to be a bit more specific."

Her smile is sleepy but amused. Closing her eyes, she nestles down further on the white cotton, dark hair coiled in inky, wet tendrils against the bright white. "I should have loaded my gun."

"Yes," I agree softly. An unloaded gun is the least of my concerns, but I'll be pleased if the outcome of this is that she's never armed with something useless like that again.

"Thank you," she whispers, shifting back and spearing me with a look that's so full of emotions it would knock me on my arse if I weren't already there. "It was dumb to leave my apartment, like you said. But you were there when I needed you. I had no right to hope you would come, but I did. And you did."

My heart jerks in my chest. She had every right to hope I would come, and it cracks something deep inside me that she thinks she doesn't. I set my phone on the bedside table and scoot down until we're face to face. I'm on top of the covers and she's underneath, so hopefully that'll be enough to help me keep my hands to myself.

Still, I can't resist reaching up and brushing the hair from her eyes. "I will always come, Madison. I told you—you're mine. Do you understand what that means to me?"

Her eyes flick back and forth between mine instead of answering. There's some confusion there, as well as something guarded that I can't identify. After a second, she shakes her head.

"It means that I take care of you. I protect you. I don't let anyone hurt you."

Her brow twitches, settling into a slight frown. She swallows, nods, and looks away, but she seems confused—perhaps only content to let the conversation drop because she's not sure she's ready for it.

And it's just as well, because I'm not sure I'm ready either. I can't put this feeling into words yet; it feels too soon to say the words out loud.

Because I've never wanted anything the way I want her. I've never needed something to be mine this way. It's like she's awakened another side of me—one that considers lines something to cross and rules something to break. I'd do anything for her.

I've joked about Mac's stalking and Dimitri's kidnapping from the view atop my high horse, but now I know that I'm no better. My single-minded determination would have resorted to much darker means if she'd managed to slip away from me this morning—stalking and kidnapping would have seemed the milder option.

I've already been less than honest; I let her think we'd be working together, knowing full well she thinks that means something very different.

I simply can't let her be involved in my search for the General. I need the information she has—now that we know what information it is, that part's sorted—and then I just... I need her to be somewhere that I can keep her. Where I can take care of her and know she's safe.

I wish I could be a normal man. I wish I could come to her as is, bare myself and let her take whatever parts of me she wants. But I can't—this is all or nothing. No half-assing it.

She gets all of me, and I'm taking all of her. Every part.

"Does it mean you're my own personal hair washer, too?" she teases, lifting her eyes. The shuttered fear is gone now, like she's buried it and decided to try to move on. "I gotta say, I think I'm ruined for showers now. It's going to be baths only from now on. The logistics will be a nightmare, but I'm willing to put in the work to give you what *you* need."

I'm gratified by the ease in her tone. It's only been hours, but it feels like it's been far too long without bratty, lighthearted Madison. "Go to sleep, you little menace."

Her smile crinkles the corners of her eyes as a lock of green hair falls sideways across her face. "Yes, Sir."

I can recognize this for what it is—a deliberate shift to a lighter topic. It's too soon for a declaration of feelings. Too much has happened today. She's not ready, but instead of shutting down she's dispelling the tension.

God, I love how her mind works, and how easy it is for her to analyze and sort through information. I love how she uses every tool and weapon at her disposal to vie for power—power I have no intention of relinquishing, but it's such fun watching her try. I love the way her lips tip up at the corners in anticipation of my laughter whenever she says something clever. I love her beautiful, soft body. I love her confidence in it.

I love... her.

She turns back onto her other side so we can spoon. I drag her against my chest and hold her tighter, just as I intend to do going forward. I nearly lost her today. I nearly let her down.

I have to be better. Have to try harder. *Have* to figure out what's going on. And until I get this mess sorted out with the General, I'll need to hold Madison tighter.

Being locked out of the system is concerning—any lack of information is concerning—so, first chance we get, we'll need to retreat behind the 12-foot gate and the safety of the group.

In the morning, we'll head there first thing. For now... Like this, with her in my arms, I think I could sleep through the night for the first time in years.

26

MADISON

I'm taking control this time.

Light wakes me, and I'm instantly blinded when I open my eyes. I shout in pain and roll away from it, only to bolt back in fright when a sharp yowl protests the movement. I sit up, finding an irritated, ruffled cat stretching in the center of the bed. Immediately, I scoop him up and hug him to my bare chest, burying my face in his soft fur. He wriggles in my grip, but eventually starts purring at the attention.

I don't know how Wesley did it, because I doubt this fancy-ass hotel allows pets, but he reunited me with my son. My heart feels so full it might burst as I sit with the rush of emotions, calmed by the gentle sound of a contented cat.

When Some Bills starts wriggling to be released again, I let him go, and he saunters to the end of the bed to groom himself.

The light that temporarily stunned me is sneaking in through a thin crack in the middle of the thick curtains, but the room is dark otherwise, and I can't hear Wesley moving around in the bathroom. But the evidence of him is everywhere—mussed sheets, clothes neatly folded on a chair, electronics on every available surface. Yeah, no way he's leaving all this behind.

My eyes snag on a familiar suitcase on the chair near the air conditioner.

Okay, seriously. This man is... almost too perfect. He literally thinks of everything. It's amazing how much small gestures matter.

It feels like a million years ago when I packed it, but it was only two days ago. I throw off the covers and go to grab some clothes, making a face at the sight of my appearance in the mirror as I pass—as a lifelong wavy/curly girl, I know better than to go to bed with wet hair. Wind-blown lion isn't my best look, so luckily I packed a hairbrush when I was planning on skipping town.

Wesley's not back by the time I finish dressing, so I grab my toiletries bag and head into the bathroom to brush the fuzzy socks off my teeth and tame the mane.

As I brush my teeth, I gape at all the fixtures and amenities that I was too distracted to notice last night. In-room espresso bar, heated marble floors, a bidet toilet... This is the nicest hotel I've ever been to. I mean, not that it's a huge list—we were way too lower middle class growing up to go anywhere—but you gotta have big money to stay somewhere like this.

The sound of the door opening makes my heart leap, but it quickly settles when I hear that familiar British voice, "I brought breakfast."

I clutch the edge of the sink, inhaling deeply to calm myself. Normally I'd be irritated with myself for being so jumpy, but I'd say considering the events of the past 24 hours, it's the appropriate response. "Be right out. Is there bacon?"

"There is."

"And coffee?"

"Café Bustelo."

That stops me. I trade my toothbrush for a hairbrush and poke my head out of the bathroom. Wesley has a tray balanced on his forearm as he's locking the door behind him. My mouth waters at the scents wafting off the white plates, but bacon isn't what's making my heart race. *Dios*, the man can wear a pair of jeans.

"They had Café Bustelo here?" I ask, letting my eyes linger on how the denim hugs his legs all the way around.

"No, I had the concierge get it." He strides into the bedroom and lays the tray on the edge of the bed. I follow him, still dragging the brush through my tangles.

"Why?"

"Because it's what you drink," he says, turning.

Shocked, I glance from the steaming white mug to his face and find an expression I recognize. He was wearing the same one last night when we were lying in bed, facing each other. When I desperately wanted to cling to him, but was too restless and hesitant to do it.

You're mine. Do you understand what that means?

It means that I take care of you. I protect you. I don't let anyone hurt you.

I suppose it also means that he notices things. That he goes out of his way to do things just to make me happy. And I suppose that all adds up to one simple truth—he cares. Though, it doesn't feel simple; it feels like a lot. More than I know how to handle right now, if I'm honest.

I swallow the lump in my throat. "Thank you," I say on a whispered croak, my voice thick with emotion.

Dios, I want to jump his bones. I don't really know what to do with all these big feelings, but wanting him is the only part I've never really questioned—the only thing that's easy.

He sits on one side of the bed and gestures to the other end of the tray, effortlessly redirecting Some Bills, who seems very interested in the bacon and eggs on his plate. "We need to talk about what's going on."

Oh, right. Hitmen after me. Life in danger. It's not quite time for the good stuff. *Down, girl.*

I take my seat and pull a plate over to my side of the tray. "So, to the safe house we go?"

"Not anymore. The attack yesterday changes things—I got locked out of the General's system, so I'm flying blind."

I made a sympathetic face. He must hate that.

"All I know is that the bloke that grabbed you was another assassin in the area, and he's still out there somewhere. So we're going to my center of operations. I need my team for support, and all my best equipment is at the mansion. And it's a fortress—we were safe here for the night, but I'm not taking any chances with your life."

My smile is quick, then I shove an entire length of bacon into my mouth before Some Bills can swipe at it. "Your team?" I ask, intrigued.

"Mac and Dimitri. And then there's the girls."

My eyes widen, and I can't stop the grin. "There are girl assassins on your team?" I ask, breathless with excitement.

"Eleanor and Nicole are not assassins," he says, almost chagrined to let me down. "But they live there too, and they're lovely. You'll like them."

Irritation prickles that he's describing another woman as "lovely" but I decide to table that irrational jealousy. "Well, we should stop at my *tío's* on the way. We need that data."

He considers that with a frown, taking a thoughtful bite. "I'll go."

"*We'll* go," I correct.

He cuts me a look. "We don't know who might be out there looking for you. It's safer if you stay here."

Yeah, that might be true, but it won't matter to Tío. He's not exactly friendly to strangers—especially ones who know his business. "If I'm not with you, he isn't going to give you the data. He doesn't trust people he doesn't know."

"I don't like the idea of bringing you somewhere I've never been."

With a soft smile, I reach out and lay my hand over his. "Don't worry. We'll be safe there."

He heaves a sigh, flips his hand over and squeezes mine. "Fine. But we're taking the bike." When I make a face, he explains, "Quick getaway if things go sideways. And with your face hidden and hair tucked up in a helmet, no one will know it's you."

"Fair enough," I compromise, pushing my empty breakfast plate away. "When do you want to leave?"

"No sense waiting," he asserts, standing. He grabs the empty tray and places it on the desk, taking the last sip of his juice. "Are you ready to go?"

I consider his ass, so perfectly in my line of sight. "We're safe here now, right? For a little while anyway?" At his curious nod, I smirk. "What if we left in 20 minutes?"

"Something you want to do first?" The look he throws over his shoulder is adorably curious, and I realize he's so deep into problem-solving mode that he totally missed the innuendo.

With as much deliberate seduction as I can possibly manage, I bite my lip and let him see me scan his body slowly, up and down. I stand, closing the distance between us, unbuttoning my sweater. "I'm still hungry."

He watches me, jaw slack as he drags in a shaky breath. His hands flex at his sides, making the veins along his muscular forearms pop. "Madison," he says, infusing my name with so much desperation and longing that it makes lightning spark between my legs. "Don't look at me like that. There isn't time for that."

"It's only 30 minutes," I negotiate.

"I don't want to rush—I want to really take my time with you."

That squirmy feeling in my tummy is back. Elation and excitement. "I know. And I'm really looking forward to it. But now *I* want to take my time with *you*. I really liked having you in my mouth yesterday, but it wasn't enough. Give me, like... 45 minutes," I amend with a smirk.

I let my sweater fall and step up to him. His eyes rake over my breasts and, like he can't help himself, he lifts his hands and cups my face. It's both an invitation and a deferral, when what he clearly wants is to rip off the lace cups and grab a nipple between his teeth.

"I don't need you to service me—to do this when I can't reciprocate." He's trying so hard not to give in.

With a little laugh at the irony, I turn my head and suck his thumb into my mouth. When I did this at the arcade, he lit up like fireworks. This time is no different. "I know. That's *why* I'm offering," I point out. "If you were selfish, I wouldn't want to give this to you. If you were inconsiderate or mean or greedy, I wouldn't want to please you or submit to you.

"And the way you took care of me last night was so amazing. You were gentle, then you gave me exactly what I needed. You make me feel so special, Wesley. So... cherished."

Lifting his hand and tucking a lock of green hair behind my ear, he nods, face serious. "I cherish nothing more," he murmurs.

I bite down on a smile. "And I cherish you, too. So I'm taking control this time—I'm *thanking* you. And you, Sir, are going to sit back and let me."

That does it. Decision made, he cups the back of my head and pulls me in for a bruising kiss. The instant our lips touch, he cradles the nape of my neck and fuses his mouth to mine. He bites at my lips, plunders my mouth with his tongue, and our teeth hit each other almost hard enough to make me pull away. I can feel how badly he wants to tear off my clothes and flip me over. I can taste how badly he wants to take control.

I place a hand on his chest, feeling his warmth and the steady beating of his heart against my palm. "On the bed."

While I like being on my knees because of the interesting feeling of the power dynamic, I can appreciate the comfort of a soft mattress. I take his hand and pull him with me, waiting as he gets settled propped against the headboard.

I climb onto the mattress straight into his open arms, straddling him, putting our faces close enough to breathe the same air. He's so handsome. I could live in his gray eyes, could spend hours tracing lines between the faint freckles on his nose that I never saw until now. I love white guys—between the freckles and random tiny moles everywhere, they're covered in brown spots, like tortillas.

As we kiss, I grind on him, rocking my hips to tease him. When I can feel him stiffening against me, I shift back, off his lap. My eyes drop, and my hand slides down his hard chest, skating over the ridges of his abdomen through his button-down, and settles on his belt buckle.

"I'm in control now, Sir. Your safe word is 'don't stop,'" I joke with a wink.

I open his fly with a flick of my long nails. I watch and salivate as his cock pops out of the hole in his boxers, hard and shining with precum. Once he's settled in place, I lean forward and lick that pearly drop. He hisses and his abs tense, but to his credit he doesn't grab for me at all.

My hair follows the trail I make as I flip up the bottom of his shirt and press a soft kiss to every tattoo I can see and dip my tongue into every ridge where muscle meets muscle. I take my time, feeling his desire shifting into something more urgent. After a few minutes of lips and gentle brushes of my hair on the most sensitive part of him, he's panting, sweating, so tense it's like he's going to snap at any second. I glance up and see that his eyes are squeezed shut so hard that it's carving deep lines between his brows and around his eyes. I blow some cool air on the head of his cock, and the whole thing jerks.

"Fuuuuck," he hisses.

I grin. "Be as loud as you like. Scream my name, Sir," I croon, teasingly throwing his words back at him.

"Fuck, Madison," he breathes, emphatic with the rush of air he was holding in. "You're having too much fun with this."

The agony in his tone is music to my ears. I smile against his skin on the next kiss. "I'll take *What not to say to a brat when she's in control* for $800, Alex."

"Bollocks," he whispers through a broken laugh, and the word itself sends shivers down my spine.

"This is hard for you, isn't it?" I ask, cocking my head as I gaze up at him.

"I think you'll find it's hard for *you*," he grits out.

I giggle at my unintentional double entendre. "I meant this," I gesture to the way he's gripping the sheet with white knuckles instead of my head. "Not being in control."

After a second, he nods. "It's not... my normal way. Only for you," he says softly. "I'd only do it for you."

That bowls me over. I guess I didn't realize how deep that dominant streak went. I suppose it makes sense, though. He's a man used to controlling everything, including a network of informants and the information itself. It shows in little ways, too, like how clean and meticulous and organized he is.

And that is *so* exciting. Because while I'm having fun, I'm just a tourist. Giving the orders doesn't get me going nearly as much as taking them. Or, rather, playfully deciding whether or not to follow them.

It's only fun for me now because he's not truly submissive—I'm just borrowing the power. Honestly, the real rush I'm getting is from teetering on the edge of his control. If I tease him hard enough, will he flip us over and take what he wants? It's exhilarating.

"I guess it's lucky that I'm much more of a bottom than a top," I assure him.

"Could've fooled me," he groans. "What are you going to do? Tell me."

"Ah ah," I chide, rearing up and shaking my head like I'm admonishing him. "You're the one who's supposed to be making noise, not asking questions. Now who's the brat?"

His laugh this time is edged with mania and turns into a whining noise as I let my hair brush against his length. It's gotten almost impossibly harder with all my teasing. He *loves* this, and the intensity of his desire for me is fucking *everything*. His hips buck, and I press my hand against his lower abdomen, tsking.

"Madison," he growls, reaching for my hip.

With a grin, I take pity on him, kneeling over him, gripping the base of his cock, and swiping my tongue across the slit at the top. His moan is low, primal. I take the head into my mouth and swirl my tongue around the tip, pressing hard against that spot just under the flare on the back part, where most guys are sensitive.

And he's one of them. He practically jack-knifes as his thighs lift off the mattress. "Oh fuck! Madison, my love, that feels amazing."

I close my eyes. *My love.* I let it wash over me like a warm wave of bliss. I push deeper, drooling all over his cock to ease my way down, reveling in every helpless, desperate noise he makes. I know he's trying so hard not to grab my head...

His restraint nearly breaks at one point, and I nearly ask him to just do it—to fuck my face like he wants—but I suppose this is better. I'm a gal who enjoys a good face-fucking, but bent over like this is not the best position—that's how you lose your breakfast.

"Fuck, you're so good at that. You're taking me so well... *fuck.*"

If I had to rank my favorite sex acts I've done with other people, giving head wouldn't be at the top, but there's something different about having this kind of power over Wesley. Giving him pleasure makes me feel *so* good about myself. It doesn't hurt that he tastes and smells incredible.

So I give him everything I've got—I suck and roll my tongue across his shaft; I use a hand when I can't fit more of him in my mouth without gagging, and I use the other to reach into his pants and cup and play with his balls.

I lose myself in the repetition of bobbing my head, and the feeling of the smooth skin on my tongue. Just as I'm about to pull away for a break, he groans and jerks under me. My mouth fills with the earthy, salty taste of him.

"Swallow it all," he orders, sounding transfixed as he finally gives in and weaves his fingers into my hair. Brushing it back so he can have a view. "Good girl. That was such a good job. Goddamn, Madison."

My pussy pulses at the reverence in his voice and soft praise. I sit up, and he follows, placing his warm hand around my throat, like a comfort. I welcome its presence, reaching out to clutch at him. We stare at each other with soft smiles.

"Ready to go?" I ask brightly.

He chuckles and tucks a green forelock behind my ear. "After the blood returns to my brain, sure," he jokes, leaning forward and pressing a kiss to my lips.

Once he recovers, we head down to the garage. I give him the address; he types it into his phone's GPS and lifts a brow at what comes up.

I shrug. "That's where he'll be. Two birds with one stone—we can grab lunch!" I enthuse.

"I'm not sure I've ever had a proper, authentic tamale."

"Then you're in for a treat."

With a smile, he sets the phone into the holder clamped to the handlebar and kicks the bike into gear.

And then I'm clutching Wesley for my damn life. I really thought motorcycles would be cool and fun, but I'm just cold and terrified. My stomach bottoms out every time he has to lean and shift his momentum to take a turn. And even the powerful rumbling between my legs and Wesley's soft stroking of my thighs as a comfort whenever we stop at a red light can't bring me out of it.

It almost works, though.

Wesley rolls to a stop. He dismounts first, glancing around as he helps me off. I can tell he's assessing his surroundings, and I wonder if he's ever been to this part of the city.

On the whole, Ulysses is tired and underserved by a local government stacked with corruption. City Hall sits in the northern part of the city, in streets lined with old elms and metered parking. The southern part of the city is where they shove all the ugliest parts they don't want to think about. But there are a few blocks, right in the middle of it all, that are a bright spot amidst the dereliction and decay. None of the buildings here are crumbling, and the cars on the street have all their tires.

After all, when you're at the top of a crime-adjacent empire and you employ half the neighborhood, no one would dare graffiti *your* building. People don't care how dirty the money is when it's poured into the local community; they'll deny ever having heard your name when the cops come around.

The people who live here are like one big family, and Mama B is a second *abuela* to me. She'll cluck over my outfit and tell me I'm not eating enough beans. Oh, shit... I didn't brush my teeth after what Wesley and I did...

I lift my hand, cupping it in front of my face, and do the breath-sniff test. All I can smell is my own skin. Why do I bother? It never works.

I nudge Wesley and murmur, "Does my breath smell like dick?"

"What?" he asks, throwing me a look over his shoulder.

I blow air in his face—or as close as I can get, 10 inches below him—and he makes a face of surprise. "Dick breath?" I ask.

A grin splits his face, and he chuckles. Suddenly, I'm pulled into his body with a thick arm around my waist. "Yes," he says fondly, leaning down, kissing me and promptly sticking his tongue in my mouth. "And now so does mine. That'll really confuse them, don't you think?"

I throw my head back and laugh with my whole body.

We climb up the concrete steps, and I inhale deeply as the warmth spills out, meeting me in the doorway. *Mama B's Tamales* is like a warm hug from my childhood—the air is fragrant with *chiles y tomates*, the walls are covered in colorful murals, neon-colored paper cutouts hang from the corners of the drop ceiling, and the travertine tile floor smells like lavender Fabuloso.

Mama B greets me with a deeply lined smile and a tight hug.

"Hi Mama B. Good to see you. This is Wesley," I say, jerking my thumb at him. She waggles her brows at me, a silent approval.

After giving him a motherly pat on the cheek, she lifts her voice, calling towards the back. *"¡Hijo! Madison está aquí y trajo a su novio. Iré a buscarlo, no me oye desde esa oficina,"* she says, releasing me and heading towards the back of the restaurant, where Tío keeps one of his many offices. As she goes, she urges, *"¡Siéntate! Te traeré tortillas."*

Wesley seems surprised at her abrupt departure. "She'll be back. Her first instinct is to feed everyone. I've known her all my life," I explain.

Wesley and I are choosing a table to sit at when a familiar face appears in the hallway. Dark hair, dark eyes, tattoos, a permanent smirk...

"Tío," I say, stepping to the side so I'm not blocking Wesley. "I'd like you to meet—"

"You," Tío says from the doorway, eyes wide in shock.

"You!" Wesley echoes, grabbing my arm and tucking me protectively behind him.

I scowl, but before I can ask what the fuck is going on and how they know each other, Tío Felix produces a gun and points it at Wesley. "Madison, why don't you step away from the nice hitman?"

27

WESLEY

Is it weird that I'm kind of... proud?

I feel like I've been tossed into a frozen pond and the ice has sealed back over my head. What the fuck is Felix doing here?

This is bad. I guess I was wrong to assume Felix didn't know what I looked like.

Madison tries to push away my arm, to get out from behind me, but I refuse to move. I don't care how familiarly he said her name—he's a threat. He has a gun, and I don't. And I don't care that I'm blocking its path; it's pointed a little too directly at someone it shouldn't be, and bodies don't always stop bullets.

"Want to point that somewhere else, mate?" I suggest coldly, jerking my chin at his weapon.

"I will if you move away from her, *mate*," he replies, mocking me with the last word.

We eye each other up. We're evenly matched, height-wise. He might have a bit more muscle on me, but I'm fast, and Dimitri's taught me how to fight as dirty as I need to.

"*Dios,* will you two chill?" Madison cuts in, exasperated as she tries—and fails—to get around me again. "The tension in here is making me jealous. Like, just kiss already. Put the gun down, Tío."

Felix snorts, but doesn't move. We glare at each other for the span of a few breaths.

Madison makes another irritated noise, elbowing me lightly in the side. "Wesley, let me go."

Bristling, I tighten my hold on her arm. "Not happening until he lowers that gun."

Felix laughs. "*Tu novio es el que está celoso, enana. Llama a tu perro.*"

She rolls her eyes. "*Lo estoy intentando, pero no me ayudas. Y él no es mi novio, Tío.*"

I'm somewhat mollified by the fact that she calls him uncle—it's familiar without being intimate—but I can't control the growl that escapes my chest when his eyes settle on her, dark and glittering.

And I hate that she said I wasn't her boyfriend, even though I'm not. I despise that term; I'm much more.

"*Estoy lo suficientemente cerca. Ahora, apunta con tu arma hacia otro lado, lejos de ella,*" I grit out.

Both of them turn to me. "Wait, you speak Spanish?" Madison asks, eyes wide. Then, a line appears between her brows. "Wait, *close enough*? What does *that* mean?"

Felix doesn't let me explain. "I know you like to piss off your *abuela*, but sleeping with a murderer is taking it too far, *enana*." He smirks at her, and my hand fists into a ball, ready to punch it off his face.

She turns her ire on him. "Mexican grandmas and their fucking double standards, I swear. Like that's so much worse than regularly destroying evidence for them, or *being* a murderer," she hisses.

So she knows exactly the kind of man he is—the full extent of what he really does for a living. Interesting. It explains why her first instinct was to diffuse the situation and not question why her uncle was pointing a gun at me.

I suppose she did tell me that she does jobs for him—that stealing data from SmarTech was his idea. And now that we know about the connection to the General, there's no way it was a coincidence that he sent her there. He must have figured it out.

That pisses me off. I've spent years trying to find any sort of lead, and Felix finds one in a matter of months?

"His boss—*El General*—wants me dead. His boss wants you dead too, Mads. That's what I was saying in my message."

"I already know that," she replies easily.

Felix makes a noise of disbelief. "Did he tell you he *took* the job?"

How the fuck does he know that? No one should know that. The channel between the General and the hitmen he contacts is closed. I'd know.

"It was the only way to ensure no one else did," she says.

I never told her that part explicitly, but of course she figured it out. Clever girl. I've never been more pleased to have been honest with someone—because Felix looks quite put out that he doesn't get to be the one to break that news to her and use it to drive a wedge between us.

"He's not going to kill me. He saved my life, Tío," she says, taking a step to the side and lowering her voice. "And since *you're* the one that got me into this mess, I suggest you put that fucking gun away so we can all talk like fucking adults."

Felix tries to stare her down, but I've never seen her look this fierce—not even when she was on top of me, pointing a gun at me. Felix only lasts two seconds before he makes a noise by sucking on his teeth and lowers his arm.

That's right, you smug fuck.

"Doesn't mean you should trust him," Felix jerks his chin at me. He glances up out of the window behind me, stretching his neck to see down the street. "That your bike?"

"Yeah."

"You came alone?" he asks, lifting a brow. "No scary Russian in the van or sniper with a rifle on a nearby rooftop?"

Fuck. My stomach roils as I try to think of something to say that wouldn't make it seem like I walked into the proverbial lion's den without backup. But Madison speaks for us. "We're alone. Now will you please chill the hell out?"

In an instant, Felix is smiling. It's not pleasant—more the knowing smirk of a man who thinks he's reclaimed the upper hand—but he tucks away his gun and takes a seat at one of the bright tables. Madison joins him and, loath to be outside of touching distance, I follow.

It feels quite wrong to be sitting across from him like this. This temporary truce is a tenuous kind of peace, held together by a thread that might snap at any second.

"Okay. Good. So, other than his boss wanting you dead, how do you know each other? Because that wasn't just *you tried to kill me* energy," Madison points out, gesturing between us. "There's clearly a history here."

We eye each other appraisingly. I lift my brows and motion for him to explain. I can't wait to hear his version of this.

He leans back in his chair, arms crossed over his chest and biceps bulging against his jacket. "We have a few... mutual acquaintances. We run in some of the same circles."

"You're not normally so circuitous, Tío," she drawls. "Quit filling the air and get to the point."

God, I love this woman.

"We may have gotten entangled in a job a few months back," Felix says, shrugging.

I snort. "That's one way to put it. I'd call it accessory to kidnapping."

"Simple miscommunication," Felix protests, eyes flicking to her and going soft, like he's trying to convince her.

I frown at him and lay a hand on her thigh protectively under the table, gratified when she reaches down and threads her fingers through mine.

"What did you do?" she accuses him, delighting me further.

I don't even bother to hide the self-satisfied grin. She has a close relationship with Felix that I know nothing about, but she takes my side so easily. And perhaps it proves that she knows him well enough to assume his implicit guilt, but it also means she trusts me enough to believe me about it without question.

He has the good grace to look sheepish, reaching up and scrubbing the back of his neck awkwardly. Madison looks between the two of us with undisguised suspicion, sensing how much is going unsaid.

"He helped a man kidnap my friend last autumn. She's not part of this world; she's a nurse—never did anything to hurt anyone."

Madison gasps and glares at him. Without warning, she grabs the closest thing—a paper-napkin-wrapped silverware set—and chucks it at his head, hurling all kinds of insults about his manhood in Spanish while she's at it. Felix ducks, and the silverware sails over his shoulder and clatters on the ground behind him. Hands raised protectively, he tries to defend himself in Spanish with all the same shitty excuses he told Mac—that he didn't do it, didn't mean to, didn't know—but she continues shouting about how he promised he'd never hurt innocents until he stops fighting back. Looking cowed but pissed, Felix turns his head and takes the abuse with a sour face.

"He's not really my uncle," she tells me, switching back to English and grimacing. "We're not related. He's more like a friend of the family we can't get rid of."

That explains why he didn't show up on her background check.

Felix adjusts his position. "*He's* just deflecting," he says, gesturing at me. "It's not even relevant here. Doesn't have anything to do with the General."

"It's pretty fucking relevant to us," I shoot back. "Because we're after the General too, and we might've been able to combine efforts, but some wounds run too deep."

"You're after him, too?" he repeats, the look on his face shifting.

"Yeah, well, I'm not going to work for the bloke after he puts a hit out on the woman I—" I swallow the rest of the sentence. Fuck. I'm not saying it for the first time to prove a point to someone else. That's privileged information, for her ears only. "—plan to protect. As far as I'm concerned, my contract with him is over."

"Interesting. And knowing how tight the *tres amigos* are, I'm assuming this means you're all out." He strokes his chin.

"We're aligned," I confirm.

"Hmm... You know that means we have a common enemy now," he points out. The tilt of his head is appraising, but not hopeful—we both know a temporary alignment is not the same as a truce.

I just shake my head. "How did you know the General sent me her name? How did you know we took the job?" I ask. What I really want to know is how he even knows about me, but that's less important. Right now, Madison's safety is the priority, and he might be able to give me some insight.

He cocks his head and studies me with a faint smile. "You mad I know something the spider guy doesn't?"

"It's SpyderMan," Madison corrects primly.

A pit forms in my stomach. She didn't tell him about me back when we were just mermaidav and SpyderMan, did she?

"It's the same way you knew about Alfano and those other jobs you intercepted, isn't it?" I say. It's an assumption I'm testing. We don't know for sure it was him...

Until he sits back with a smile. "What, you didn't like my little Russian present? I figured the big guy would be thrilled to take out another Volkevich after him and his nurse. Heard it didn't go so well for him, though."

My scowl snaps down harder. He really does have ears and eyes everywhere.

He cuts me an unimpressed look. "SpyderMan," he repeats, rolling the word around. His stare is a challenge. "Some kind of comic book hero kid, right? This is the *mierda de hombre* you want taking care of you, *enana*?"

"Be nice," she warns.

Felix snorts. "You should stay here. We'll keep you safe."

The implication that he thinks he can take care of her better than me makes me gnash my teeth. But to my immense satisfaction, her laugh is derisive. "No thanks. Now, quit avoiding the question. How did you know Wesley took the job from the General? It might help in our search."

He flashes her a grin, and the gold capping one of his back molars briefly gleams in the light. "Same way I know anything. I've got a man on the inside."

He refuses to elaborate further, but that doesn't surprise me. A man on the inside? Interesting. That must be how he knew there was a hit out on him, too. "Do you have access to the platform?"

"Maybe."

"We need access. We need to know why another assassin attacked her yesterday."

"Because there's still an open job for her," Felix answers easily.

My jaw falls. "Even though I took it?"

"It's a fucking free-for-all."

Madison grabs my arm to steady herself, gripping me tightly with cold fingers. "What?" she croaks, eyes wide.

Felix nods, all traces of humor gone. He pulls his phone from his pocket, unlocks it, calls something to the screen, and slides the phone across the table to her. "This went out yesterday to anyone registered as US-based."

She leans forward, and I tilt my head to read over her shoulder.

It's a screenshot of an email. All identifying information has been erased, but the words are clear enough.

Madison Cooper Ulysses 27 5'2 brwn/brwn. 10MM for proof.

"This went out to everyone?" I breathe, fear coiling in my gut. At Felix's nod, I feel the blood drain from my face. "This is... unprecedented. I've never seen a hit go out wide like this. The names only ever went out to one of us at a time."

"Ten million?" Madison says softly, rereading the short note. "Damn. I'd kill *myself* for that much. Is it weird that I'm kind of... proud?"

"Yeah, Madison. It is," Felix says, shooting her a look. "This *cabrón* is right—this isn't how *El General* usually does things."

"A broken pattern always means something," I mutter. "In this case, it implies urgency. I'd wager it means that whoever is running this operation is really threatened by you."

Madison gestures to me with a pointed expression directed at her uncle. "See? They're *that* threatened by me. Tell me you're not just a little impressed." At Felix's head shake, she grins. "10 mil. I bet you're only saying that because my death was worth more than yours."

Felix rolls his eyes. I can't recall the figure, but I'm fairly certain Madison's right. And that's another data point proving how badly the General wants her dead.

"We really need to fake your death," I tell her. I appreciate the efforts to cut through the tension, but I'm not interested in making light of the situation.

"On that at least we can agree, *cabrón*," Felix echoes darkly. "I'll take care of it. *Me deberás un favor, enana.*"

I inhale sharply, a warning on the tip of my tongue—Felix knows what he's doing, but he isn't known for his generosity. Owing him a favor has proved to be a terrible idea in the past. But I needn't worry. Madison apparently knows just how to handle him.

"Oh? You want a favor? After it was *you* who put me in danger in the first place?"

I watch Felix realize his own mistake, arrogance faltering as his smirk freezes.

"How about I don't tell Mama B that you gave me a job that almost got me killed?" she drawls, lifting a brow and crossing her arms. "Or that you apparently *kidnapped* a nurse."

"I didn't!" he protests, but cuts himself off with a sigh. Felix glances between us, like he still wants to fight. "Fine. Deal."

I can't help but gloat a little. Trust Madison to understand how powerful the right information can be, wielded like a weapon at just the right time.

"Abuela can't think I'm dead," she warns him. "I won't put her through that."

"*Claro.* I'll handle it. I'll manufacture the proof the General will want, but you won't officially be dead to the police. You'll be missing. They don't immediately assume you're dead when there's no body."

"All right. It's settled, then," Madison beams. "Just give me my panda back and we'll be on our way. You know how it is—assassins to evade, criminal masterminds to track down..."

With a final glare directed at me, Felix gets up from the table and disappears back down the hallway. While he's gone, Mama B drops off a large tied plastic bag with several styrofoam containers, taking a moment to kiss Madison on the forehead and pat me on the cheek again. He returns a few minutes later with a silly purple panda keychain that I now know to be a USB drive—the "panda's ass" she referred to.

But Felix doesn't hand it over. Instead, he closes it in his fist, crosses his arms, and regards me. "The General dies?"

I nod.

He narrows his eyes. "Can I trust you, *Wesley?*"

It's an interesting conundrum of a question. A smart man never asks something when he won't trust the answer, and I do believe Felix is a smart man. In fact, he'd be smarter *not* to trust me.

But I can recognize the potential here. We might need him yet, and if he's on Madison's side, then he's on my side, as far as I'm concerned. I'd wager he feels the same.

"I would do anything to keep her safe. Whatever it takes," I promise.

"Oh yeah? You'd die for her?" he challenges.

But I don't hesitate. I don't need to. "She's mine to protect. I would give my life for hers."

Out of the corner of my eye, I see her turn to look at me, but it's the wide grin on Felix's face that grabs my attention. "*Yours*, huh?" He flicks his eyes back and forth between us a few times, then shakes his head, chuckling. "Good fuckin' luck with that."

"Be *nice*," she hisses, reaching across me and punching him in the arm.

He laughs, rubbing the spot. Just before we leave, Felix lays a heavy hand on my shoulder. "If you hurt her, I'll feed you your own *cajones, sabes?*"

The implication makes me see red. I take a step towards him, fists clenching, but Madison effortlessly dispels the tension once again. "Oh, stop. If he hurts me, not only can I feed him his balls myself, but I'll be genuinely pissed at you if you deprive me of the right."

28

MADISON

Restriction and protection aren't the same thing.

Well, that was... a lot.

A $10 million bounty on my head and a hitman free-for-all.

Tío Felix having a history with *my* SpyderMan, and being involved in a kidnapping plot.

Wesley jumping between me and a gun... telling my *tío* he'd die for me. *Die* for me?

I shiver and glance over at him, and find him squeezing the steering wheel so tightly that the leather creaks under his hands.

What a mind-fuck. We've both been stuck in this loop of disbelief and trying to process ever since we left Mama B's. We went back to the hotel, but we only stayed long enough to load my suitcase and cat into a surveillance van that's jam-packed with so much tech and equipment I nearly creamed myself. And now we're on our way out to the 'burbs.

It's kind of funny, but of all the things that have happened in the past few days, it's the fact that we're on our way to Mansion Row that feels the most unreal.

Streets widen, trees appear, and suddenly there's room to breathe. It's flatter out here, with parking lots instead of rows of two-story buildings right against the sidewalk. People have yards, and homes are set back off the street.

Wesley turns into a neighborhood, and I am momentarily stunned by the sight of homes bigger than entire apartment complexes near where I live. We drive past plots of land that are probably called *estates* or some shit. One has its own tennis court. One has a series of buildings—I bet the help lives in one.

And Wesley lives *here*? Shit, I've been in the wrong business...

We pull up to a huge iron gate and I watch, completely awestruck, as he inputs his *fingerprint* and the gate slowly swings open for us.

Now that we're here, I realize we made the entire journey in silence. I wonder where his head's at, because mine is spinning. "*Dios*, you weren't kidding, huh?" I joke, trying to break the spell. "This place really is a fortress."

He looks over suddenly, eyes wide with surprise, like he's just remembering I'm here. His expression shifts quickly through contrition, then relief, and I watch as his body language completely changes. As the gates close behind us, the rigidity in his posture melts away, and he reaches for my knee.

When he rubs his thumb along my inner thigh, the gentle touch sends a spark up to my core that makes me shift in my seat. *Put it away, Madison—this isn't the time.*

My stomach starts twisting into excited knots as we head up a driveway so long I wonder if it has a street sign. We pull up to an eight-car garage, and the door rolls up silently, apparently motion or weight activated. The van fits in a spot between a big, shiny SUV and a Mustang. The cars keep going down the row, with a silver Mini Cooper and blue sedan that's the most normal of the bunch.

Neither of us moves when Wesley cuts the ignition.

"Is it because of Tío Felix?" I ask softly.

"What?"

"This... distance? I'm assuming you're not sure what to say to me—I mean, we just drove in complete silence for, like, half an hour."

He looks like I've struck him. "What? No! No..." he sighs, runs his hands through his hair and gives it a frustrated tug. "Fuck. I'm sorry. I..."

He reaches for my knee, covering it. "I have a tendency to close off when I'm processing."

Grateful for the warmth and contact, I cover his hand with mine. Just another example of how we know each other, but we don't *know* each other. I'm sensitive to being shut out, and he processes in silence. We'll have to be aware of that moving forward. "It's okay. It was a lot," I agree wryly. "Are you okay?"

"I am now. Now that we're here. Now that I can finally do my job and protect you properly," he says, tightening his grip. The feeling of his huge, warm hand squeezing me somewhere so delicate sends a zing of excitement to my core.

You're mine. I take care of you.

I would give my life for hers.

He keeps saying stuff like that. And I know they're not just words and empty promises. He literally stood between me and a gun—even though my *tío* never would have shot at me, *he* didn't know that. And the memory of the grim determination on his face twists up my stomach and sends a little thrill shooting through me because no one has ever cared so much about my life.

But still, I can't let him shoulder this burden. "It's not your job to protect me, you know."

"Agree to disagree," he counters, eyes boring into mine. "I just want to keep you safe. Always."

"Always safe," I repeat with a little breathy laugh. "It's a nice concept, but there's no such thing."

"Agree to disagree," he repeats.

I crack a smile, but I'm confused. "Where is this coming from? I mean, don't get me wrong—it's hot as fuck when you claim me like that. I mean, damn," I say, fanning myself and making his lips twitch. "But promising to give your life for mine is... It's"—*too much*—"not like it's your fault I'm in danger."

"It *is* my fault your life is in danger."

I roll my eyes. "Why, because you're a hitman? Wesley, I'm not exactly innocent in all this. *I* stole that data. I chose a dangerous path in life, and I always knew this might happen." When he doesn't look convinced, I try another angle—teasing him. "What are you gonna do, wrap me in bubble wrap? Take away my internet privileges?"

When he answers my playfulness with a contemplative look—like he's fucking *considering* it—I scowl and level my finger at his chest, poking hard. "Let's get one thing straight, nerd: my life is not your responsibility; it's mine."

He opens his mouth to argue, and I poke him again. "Shh. I'm not done. You are not going to blame yourself for things that happen that are out of your control. *We a*re going to take this data point—thank you very much, General—and use it to be smarter."

"You're right about that, of course... but this world is so dangerous," he says softly, gesturing around him at what he clearly means by *this world*. And obviously he's not talking about an eight-car garage. "You're a target now. And if something happens to you..."

I know he means well. I feel some of my outrage wash away like a wave on the sand. The sand's still wet—I'm still left with the emotions—but the reason is gone. "You know I'm smart and capable, right?"

"Of course."

I smile at how readily he answered. "Well, sometimes the smartest thing you can do is acknowledge when you don't know something. And I know that *you* know better than me about what's going on and the inherent danger. I mean, you *saved* me—I'm not making light of that. I know that you're trying to help me and keep me safe." His shoulders sag, and he looks relieved, but I'm not done. "*But...* I'm an adult, and my own safety is a discussion I get to be part of. Okay?"

Abuela—as much as I love her—controlled me for years with *it's what's best for you*. How do you argue with *I'm just trying to help*? You can't. The best intentions are like a warm jacket that doesn't fit. You know why someone would want you to wear it, but it's not right.

It took me a long time to embrace who I wanted to be, just because it was different from who she thought I should be.

"Restriction and protection aren't the same thing. That's called benevolent control, in case you didn't know. I learned that one in therapy," I add with a smirk. "Okay?"

"Okay," he repeats.

But I can see in his eyes that we've only put a pin in this conversation. That'll have to be enough for now.

He collects my bag from the back, I take the cat carrier holding Some Bills, and together we head towards the *mansion*.

First impressions are important—they set the tone. You can't take them back, and most people are judgmental enough to hold the first five seconds of meeting you against you—I know I am. Abuela has drilled this into me from birth. It's why we have car lipstick. It's why I don't leave the house with wet hair. It's why I feel naked without my gold hoops and pretty nails.

And it's probably why my heart is pounding now. Some combination of heading inside to meet Wesley's team of trained assassins and *lovely girls,* and the fact that this place is like a cathedral of excess. As if the fingerprint access gate or eight-car garage weren't enough, the walk across a flagstone patio towards carved, polished hardwood front doors really drives it home. They look like they should be answered by a butler.

"Wait, do you have a butler?" I gape, adjusting my hold on Some Bills's carrier.

"What? No," he chuckles as he offers his thumb for another fingerprint reader.

No wonder he called it a fortress. This place is *secure*. Even I can feel some of that $10 million tension leeching out.

I follow him into a fuckin' foyer with marble and brass and *two* sets of stairs. I swear, everything about grandeur is designed to make you feel small. The sound of the wheels of my suitcase is like nails on a chalkboard, the grinding and squeaking reminding me I got it for $5 at Goodwill. My head falls back as I take in the sparkling chandelier, smiling in spite of myself at the dancing rainbows the crystals cast on the wall.

Shit, I've *definitely* been in the wrong business...

"One second, I'm going to pop into the loo."

"Take your time. I'll stay right here," I mumble. My voice comes out dampened through my stretched throat as I crane my neck to try to see the landing at the top of the stairs. Is something... moving up there?

One of the narrow doors behind me shuts, and I glance around just in time to miss which one it was, since there are two. That probably means one is a closet. I wonder if that's created any drunken mistakes—if anyone has ever accidentally peed on a coat.

Some Bills hisses, the noise echoing off marble and metal and shocking me. I lift the cage in my arms, spinning it around to the opening to see what's got him worked up. "What—"

Something comes bounding down the stairs, and I don't have time to do anything but suck in a breath to scream as an enormous blur of brown launches itself at me. Protecting my child first, I half-turn to shield the cage, and land hard on my knee and then hip. The carrier falls from my arms and skitters across the marble as I finish the rest of my descent with about 150 lbs of something following me down.

Luckily my arms are free to protect my head from the fall, but I land hard on my elbow, skidding a few inches. Stretched out on my stomach, it takes me a second to get my bearings before I realize that the smell and hot feeling on my neck is dog breath.

Over my shoulder, a Great Dane smiles a dopey dog grin down at me. It leans down and promptly begins licking as much of my face as it can reach. I turn my head with a little squeal of disgust and try to shrug it away, but its enormous paws are digging into my back and I can barely move.

"Nice to meet you, too," I wheeze when it stops. "Now get off me."

There's a sharp whistle that makes the dog look up. Seeing something more interesting than me, it dismounts and trots over to whoever made the noise.

"Who are you? How did you get in?" a deep voice thunders.

His accent is so thick, it takes me a few seconds to register what he said. This must be Dimitri—normally I don't like to stereotype, but in this case I think I'm safe assigning that identity to the man with the Russian accent so thick you could chip a tooth on it.

"Door was open," I joke, painfully rolling over and rising into a sitting position. When I look up, my stomach drops and fear spikes at the sight of the big, mean-looking giant of a man standing at the bottom of the stairs.

Now *that's* an assassin. He's probably the tallest person I've ever seen, built like a refrigerator and, judging by his scowl and icy stare, just as frigid. As if his size and bulk alone weren't enough, he's got a gnarly old scar that made a mess out of an otherwise damn handsome face.

The noise he makes is full of disbelief and scorn. "That is not possible," he replies, totally straight-faced.

Wait... is he for real? Yeah, obviously the door wasn't open. Wesley gave his fingerprints to two separate scanners and needed an eight-bit code to get into Fort Extravagance. "I was just kidding," I mutter.

I'm almost afraid to take his hand when he offers it, looming over me and bending at the waist to get his arm down low enough. He helps me up, nearly lifting me clear into the air when he miscalculates my size. But as he settles a giant paw on my shoulder, I realize he's not being helpful. He's keeping me from getting away.

And maybe it's because he's so fucking enormous that I'm basically eye-level with it, but I have to resist the urge to put my hands up like I'm surrendering when I see the outline of the *weapon* in his dark sweatpants.

"Jesus, is that a gun in your pants or are you happy to see me?"

He scowls harder—how?—and digs into his pocket. "It is a banana," he replies simply, showing the fruit. He shakes my shoulder lightly. "Now tell me who you are."

I almost laugh at the dry delivery of what is objectively the funniest thing I've ever heard anyone say, but the tightening of his fingers makes my bones creak, and I wince instead. "You are one scary motherfucker, you know that?"

"Yes," he booms.

Wow, he can really project. Or maybe it's all the marble that his voice can bounce off. "Relax, I'm with Wesley. I'm tech support. Here to help you catch all those bad guys—"

And that's when Wesley opens the bathroom door. "Madison? Dimitri, what's going on?"

"Oh, she is Madison," Dimitri says, voice full of recognition. He releases me with an apologetic look. I mean, I think it is. I literally can't see his face because he's too tall. I can see up his nose, though.

I reach down and scoop up the cat carrier. Some Bills seems wary of the dog and a little ruffled, but otherwise fine. I'm so glad I put him in the carrier for this—I'd hate to have lost him somewhere in this labyrinth of luxury.

"I texted you that we were on our way—" Wesley cuts himself off as his eyes land on the Great Dane panting at the bottom of the stairs. "Is that a dog?"

"No, it's a mini horse with personal boundary issues and a very enthusiastic way of saying hello," I say, wiping the side of my face on my shoulder. I feel like I've still got drool on my cheek.

Wesley crosses the foyer and lifts a hand to turn my face to the side, like he's checking for damage. "Are you all right? What happened?"

"I'm fine." I shrug off his concern, though I grab the bottom of his shirt so he won't go anywhere. I feel a lot less like I'm gonna piss my pantaloons in front of Dimitri with Wesley bolstering me.

Dimitri gives us space, turning and laying a hand on the Great Dane's head. The picture it paints is genuinely surprising—next to each other and from further away, they almost look like a regular-sized man and his regular-sized dog.

"You got a dog? When did you get a dog?" Wesley demands, rubbing his temples.

"Recently. Wesley, this is Small Dog." At Wesley's look of slack-jawed astonishment, Dimitri's chest puffs out. "It is funny because it is not true. He is quite large," he explains needlessly.

My eyes widen, and I turn to Wesley to gauge his reaction. Okay, this guy *cannot* be for real.

But Wesley is just lifting a brow at the dog in disbelief. "Nicole let you name him that?"

"She hasn't yet. We're putting it to a vote. My entry was Doobie Scoo," says another newcomer.

When he steps into the foyer, my breath whooshes out. This guy is warm where the Russian is cold. Tan skin, smiling eyes, tawny hair flopping casually. Even though he's shorter than Dimitri, he's still way too fuckin' tall, if you ask me. But his smile seems permanently affixed, and it's so damn charming on his handsome face that I nearly swoon before I remember myself.

"Fuuuck me," I breathe in, swallowing my drool. With this many inches of raw masculinity on all sides, I think I just got pregnant. "What's a girl gotta do to get spat on around here? Should I fry some bacon?"

Wesley pinches my ass, and I start laughing. I know it's not nice to tease him like that, but I couldn't help myself. It's been a series of very long days, and I think I'm starting to get loopy.

"I'm Mac," the hot guy says.

"I'm Madison. And this is Some Bills," I gesture to the carrier, glancing up at Dimitri. "It's funny because it *is* true."

There's a beat, and then Dimitri lets out a loud bark that I only realize is a laugh when his lips settle into a twisted half smile. "Because pets are expensive and do not create value! I agree. That is a good name. Very clever."

He *is* for real. Okay. Good to know. This could be a lot of fun.

"Is she here?!" someone calls from behind Mac.

The patter of bare feet against polished stone precedes a woman into the foyer. A few more measured steps behind her is another woman.

It's a foyer party, apparently.

They're both gorgeous—plus size baddies that make me feel so comfortable in my skin in this weird, unfamiliar, austere place that I'm instantly nervous because I want them to like me so badly. One is pale, with bright blue eyes and a round face that's open and friendly. She's got food all over her apron. The other is a tall, bronze goddess with wild golden curls haloing her head like a crown. No food on her.

Dios, is all they do in this house have giant orgies? I mean, I'm not opposed, but you also couldn't pay me to go near Dimitri's anaconda. He'd split me in half.

"Hi!" the one with the apron says, crossing the distance. "I'm Eleanor."

"Nicole," the goddess waves, going to Dimitri's side. She leans down to pet Small Dog on the head, and he gives her an adoring look that somehow echoes the one on Dimitri's face.

"Madison," I say, taking Eleanor's hand as she extends it.

Jesus Christ, is there something in the water here? Every single person standing in this room is somewhere near or over six feet tall—I can't tell exactly, because it's hard to estimate from way down here. I feel like I'm about to be sent to the kid's table.

"This is probably weird for you," Eleanor says with a friendly, understanding smile. "But we've been waiting for you to get home. To meet you."

"Weird is..." I glance at Wesley, who's watching our exchange with a hint of a smile, "not the word I'd use, but that about covers it."

Eleanor chuckles, then cocks her head to the side, taking in my hair. "You know, you look kind of familiar."

"I was *just* thinkin' the same damn thing, darlin'," Mac adds.

Eleanor's blue eyes widen. "Hey wait, didn't you used to work at the Rouge Elephant—"

"Oh! You were the girl at the flower shop—"

Mac and Eleanor cut each other off, exchanging a look and then a laugh when they realize they both remember me from different places.

"I've had a lot of jobs," I explain wryly. Working at the flower shop was to help someone Abuela knows through church, but the seating hostess gig at the Rouge Elephant was because I needed some credit card information on a few of their high rollers for a job.

"You're the green-haired seating hostess who tried to steal my man," Eleanor says, still smiling widely. Out of the corner of my eye, I see Nicole stiffen.

I swallow. Fuck. Now I kinda remember her, too. I'm a bit thrown off by her persistently friendly face, which seems so at odds with her fighting words. She doesn't *seem* mad, but I turn to the side and tuck myself against Wesley a little harder, hoping to show her exactly where my loyalties lie. Wesley lifts a hand and gently rubs my upper arm in a move so possessive and supportive it makes my uterus do a little flip.

"Doesn't look like he can be stolen," I note, hoping I didn't step too hard on anyone's toes.

She laughs, and I feel the steel in my spine melt. "Nope!" she agrees brightly, going over to him. He holds his arm up, and she slots into the space he creates seamlessly, like they've done it thousands of times.

Now we're all coupled up, standing in a strange triangle. I shoot a little smile at Wesley, who's been a comforting presence but stood back and let me handle things. He's been so quick to step in up until now—I wonder if it was my little lecture in the car, or if he just doesn't think I need protection here.

Either way, I get the sense this introduction was important to him, so I hope I passed the test.

I blow out a long breath. "Is there somewhere we can put SB?" I ask, lifting the carrier in my hand.

Eleanor gasps jealously. "You have a cat!" She turns to Mac, lower lip dropping into a pout. "Now everyone has a pet but us."

His gaze turns appraising. "You know I'll get you whatever you want, darlin'. As long as you don't want a parrot."

"Oh, I wouldn't want... wait, you have a problem with parrots specifically?" she wonders. "Why?"

"Because it's fucking creepy that they can talk, and frankly, more people should be concerned about that. I don't trust 'em."

"Any bird that can talk is definitely spying on you and sending your secrets to the government," I agree seriously.

"Thank you," Mac says, gesturing to me like I'm the only sane one for believing him.

"Ravens can talk, too."

Mac's smile of teasing amusement falls instantly. "What?" he croaks.

"I'll show you a video later that will blow your mind," I offer, eyeing Eleanor just to be sure I'm not encroaching. Again. "Both of you," I amend, just in case. *I promise I don't want your man.*

She's pressing her lips together to suppress a smile. "Let's go into the kitchen. Are you hungry, Madison?"

"Madison, you're bleeding," Wesley says before I can answer, gently taking my forearm and examining the back of my elbow. The stinging sensation when my skin pulls against the handling probably means I've got a strawberry from my fall.

Nicole straightens. "What happened?" she asks in a low voice. And if her no-nonsense medical professional tone wasn't enough to convince me, the way she instantly crosses the room in concern when she's been so standoffish would.

That means she's probably the nurse Tío kidnapped. Great.

"Just hit the ground a little hard," I explain, lifting my forearm and feeling like a kid at the doctor when the Amazonian Queen gets close enough to examine the scratch.

"Go with Nicole," Wesley urges. He holds out his hand to take the cat carrier from me. "I'm going to put him in my office."

My eyes cut to the dog, still sitting like a good boy at Dimitri's feet. "He wasn't exactly a fan of Small Dog," I say quietly.

"No dogs allowed in the office," he assures me with a wink.

Still holding my forearm with her gentle, cool touch, Nicole turns to shoot Dimitri a look over her shoulder, to which he ducks his head. "Small Dog," she rolls her eyes, but her lips twitch in playful exasperation as she turns to me. "They named him George at the shelter. I just don't want to confuse him."

This is the strangest place I've ever been.

As if he heard my thought, Wesley chuckles, presses a kiss to my temple, takes the cat carrier, and lets Nicole lead me further into the mansion.

29

MADISON

Usually it takes people a whole interaction before they decide they don't like me.

Eleanor, Nicole, and the mini horse lead me into the kitchen, and I try—and fail—not to audibly react to the splendor. But this is some serious Iron Chef shit, with gleaming stainless steel appliances and polished stone. The island lives up to its name—a large entity in the center of the room. I can see several half-started projects, with a flour-covered rolling pin, half-diced vegetables in piles on different cutting boards, and stainless steel bowls filled with shredded meat. It's like being at Abuela's for Christmas tamales, when all my *tías* would make an assembly line with stations for each phase of the labor-of-love process, and it smells so good that my stomach immediately starts growling.

I want to examine what's on the stove, but Nicole leads me to a big glass table along the wall and sits me down. "I'm going to go get my kit."

"It's really just a scratch," I protest.

"Yeah, but George probably drooled all over it, right?" Eleanor says, then starts cooing at the dog, "Yes you did, because you're a big, dumb, slobbery sweetheart, yes you are."

He pants back with a dog grin, a glob of said drool falling to the floor with a wet slap.

"Oh, maybe," I say, though I'm sure soap and water would suffice.

"Better safe than sorry," Nicole says before she disappears through the big French doors that lead out to a patio with what I assume is a covered pool. The mini horse follows her to the door, presses his nose against the glass and whines once, then settles into an enormous dog bed in the corner of the room.

I glance around, grappling for something to say. I'm not great with new people—especially when I'm not sure where to find common ground—but I want to try, since it seems like everyone in this house is so important to Wesley.

But Eleanor saves me from having to come up with the small talk, and it's such a relief I could kiss her.

"I still can't believe you're the girl from the Rouge Elephant," she says, shaking her head as she resumes what I assume was her position before all the hullabaloo—between the stove and island, in front of a large wooden cutting board with half-chopped stalks of celery.

"Small world," I agree, thinking about how Wesley and I have lived so close all this time. "Do you guys still go to dinner there?"

The smile freezes on her lips. "Not so much anymore. It was our favorite restaurant for a while, but... something happened. Made it kind of hard to go back."

"Someone spat in your food?"

She laughs, but there's no humor in it. "I wish." Just as I'm about to ask her to elaborate on that weird as hell comment, she gasps. "Oh my God, I love your nails!"

I look down and grin at the colorful designs. They needed a fill, like, last week, but I've had other priorities. "Thanks, I love my girl, Natasha. Want her info? She makes house calls."

She casts a disparaging look at the tips of her own fingers. "As much as I wish I could be that girl with the cute nails, it never works for me. I'm too hard on them in the kitchen. The acrylic always pops off."

I make a noise of commiseration. "You gotta try hard gel. The same thing used to happen to me since I type so much, but this stuff is great. I haven't had one pop off in ages."

Her eyebrows lift, and she reaches for her phone. "Hard gel, you said?" she asks, tapping like she's looking it up or adding it to her notes app.

I grin and nod. "I can send you what she uses, if you want."

"Oh!" she smiles brightly. "Yeah, once you get your phone back, definitely send it to me."

I frown, confused, and lean forward to dig into my pocket, just in case she knows something I don't because she sounds so sure. But, nope, my phone is still there, so I pull it out and show it to her. "Or I could do it now?"

She gapes. "They didn't take your phone?"

I clutch it against my chest, an odd flare of panic rising. "*They* can try…"

Laughing at my reaction, she sets the knife aside and disappears behind the island for a second, reemerging with a large steel bowl that clangs loudly against the marble when she sets it down. "No, sorry, not like that. I meant they'd take it temporarily until everything blows over. It's like a safety thing so no one can track you that way. They put mine in a little metal box and got me a new one. Nicole's fared a bit worse," she grimaces, then lowers her voice. "She said Dimitri threw it out the window of a moving car."

"Oh," I feel myself relax, then I chuckle. "Yeah, no one's tracking me with this phone. No need for a Faraday box—that metal box they put yours in that blocks the signals," I explain. "I added a whole bunch of goodies to it for my personal safety. Hazard of the job."

"That's right, you're a tech genius like Wes!" she says, wiping her bangs with the back of her hand. "Ugh, I'm so jealous. I've never been good with technology. I think I actually heard my laptop sigh when I googled how to take a screenshot last night. I always forget."

Okay, I like her. A lot. She's so… easy to be around. "Well, I can write code, but the only thing I can cook is breakfast tacos, so I'm pretty jealous of your skills. What are you making? It smells so good."

Her enthusiasm only grows as she delights in the opportunity to talk food. "A couple of things! Some freezer meals and quick protein for the guys, and dinner tonight is wild mushroom risotto with pan-seared chicken breasts in a white wine sauce with a garden salad."

My jaw falls as she casually drops the most gourmet meal on a random Wednesday. Despite how my stomach grumbles, I resist the urge to demand how long I have to wait. "*Dios mio*, girl, you can't just say things like that to me. I'm over here salivating now. Is this place a safe house or a Michelin-starred restaurant?"

Her grin is so happy, it's infectious. "I'm a chef," she says proudly. "But enough about me. I want to hear how you got into your line of work with Wes—I bet it's a hell of a story." She considers that, then asks, "That's your meet-cute, right?"

"We—"

Her head comes up. "Oh, shoot, wait a minute," she says, leaning forward and craning her neck to see out the wall of windows. "I meant to wait to ask so Nicole could hear the story, too. Here she comes."

The nurse in question breezes back into the kitchen and settles on the seat at the head of the table. Her mini horse lifts one drooping eyelid in interest then perks up, his tail thumping twice when he sees her, and promptly drops his head back onto his paws like it weighs too much to hold it up. I bet it does.

Nicole smiles to herself as she lays the first aid kit on the table in front of her and begins unzipping the bright red bag. "I didn't realize all Great Danes did was eat and sleep," she muses.

"What a life," Eleanor agrees, then gestures my way, pointing at me with the tip of her chef's knife. "Madison was just about to tell me how she and Wes met."

Nicole threads the loops of a mask around her ears and pulls on a pair of gloves. "Dimitri said you're one of Wesley's spiders?"

"Is that what he calls us? I guess it makes sense since his handle is SpyderMan. The man loves a pun." I laugh, bending my arm and offering her my elbow. "*Such* a nerd."

"Can confirm," Eleanor laughs. "So? The meet-cute?"

I wince at the stinging sensation on my arm as Nicole swabs the area with an alcohol wipe. "Ah!"

"Oh, sorry."

"No *problemo*, just warn a girl, eh, Nurse Ratchet?" I joke, trying to lighten her mood.

But it doesn't land how I thought it would, and my stomach nearly falls out of my butt as Nicole's brows lift and she says, "Of course. Sorry again." Her voice is muffled by the crinkling noise of the mask, but her tone sounds tight.

"I didn't... um..." I grapple with how to backpedal effectively. "Sorry, I didn't mean it... It was supposed to be a joke. Obviously, it was a bad one."

She won't meet my eye; she just says, "It's fine. You were saying?"

"Um..." I hesitate, but there's not much I can say to undo it, so I'll just move on and hope she's not really offended by stupid jokes. "About two years ago, I found him in one of the forums I was using at the time to sell tips. He posted a job, I had the info he was looking for, and the rest was history," I finish lamely. I'm not usually trite, but I'm nervous.

"I didn't realize you'd known each other for so long," Eleanor remarks.

"We've talked almost every day since we met," I admit, feeling a little heat rising to my cheeks at the admission, for some reason.

It only burns hotter when Eleanor cries, "Aw! So this is like a friends-to-lovers situation?"

"More like... intentionally anonymous internet coworkers secretly pining for each other... to lovers."

"I'd watch the hell out of that Hallmark movie," Eleanor declares.

But focused Nicole isn't nearly so romantic. "Just a Band-Aid," she says, an exaggerated warning in her tone as she starts unwrapping it.

It just about kills me to do it, but I bite back the retort. Once the bandage is in place, she collects all the trash and gets up from the table. After tossing it, she slides onto one of the counter-height stools that I know I'm going to have to leap onto, and turns to study me with a tilted head. "What does it mean to be an informant? Where do you get your information?"

It's not that I'm not proud of what I do, but I try not to air all my dirty, illegal laundry with people I just met—especially ones who I've accidentally already offended. With a teasing grin, I waggle my finger. "It's classified."

Eleanor giggles at my joke, but Nicole's eyes narrow. She shrugs, like she doesn't really care, and reaches towards the fruit bowl in the middle of the island. Peeling a clementine, she says, "I guess you don't really have to talk to us about it... but if it's the reason someone's trying to kill you, we kind of already know. Stuff like that's not really classified in this house."

I catch a whiff of something guarded in her tone, and I glance at Eleanor for her reaction. Eleanor's smile has faltered, and she's looking at Nicole with gentle censure. "What Nicole means is that we're close knit. But whatever happened to you is your business. Tell us if you feel comfortable."

I glance between the two of them. "I can totally tell you the whole story... but maybe after I've been here for more than three minutes," I promise.

"That's totally fair. Right?" Eleanor prompts Nicole, who nods with a kind of contrition that makes me feel a little better.

In the awkward lull that follows, I glance around, realizing that I expected Wesley to be back by now. How long does it take to put a cat in an office? And what happened to the other two? "Where are the guys?"

"Probably still in Wes's office," Eleanor replies, resuming her chopping task. "I'm sure they're having a meeting."

"A meeting? About what?"

Nicole slides her peel across the counter, and wordlessly, Eleanor sweeps it into the trash can at her side. It's coordinated, but unspoken—a dance of familiarity—and it makes me feel out of place and oddly jealous of their easy companionship. "You. Your situation."

I frown. Eleanor is still absorbed in cooking, and Nicole has started eating her peeled fruit. Neither seems particularly bothered or interested in what's going on in the other room. "Are we... shouldn't I... go in there?" I ask, starting to rise from my chair.

"Why would you?" Nicole asks.

"Because..." I'm so thrown off by the genuine confusion in her voice, I have to try twice to get the words out correctly. "You just said they're talking about my situation."

"Yeah. Because they're going to handle it."

"But... But it's *about me.*" I glance between the two of them and tap my clacky fingernails on the glass tabletop for emphasis. We're clearly mis-communicating, here.

Eleanor and Nicole exchange a meaningful look that goes over my head. "You don't have to worry," Eleanor says, smiling brightly. "They're pros. And you're safe here."

"I'm not *worried,*" I say slowly, trying to make sense of this. "I'm interested. I'm invested. This is about my life—why wouldn't I want to be part of the discussion?"

Eleanor stops chopping and stares into the middle distance, like she's trying to remember something fleeting. I seem to have stumped Nicole, too, because she's frowning down at the counter. "I guess..." Eleanor starts, like she's figuring out how to end that sentence as she speaks. She looks at Nicole, making me feel like this is perhaps a shared memory. "I didn't know how to handle my life being in danger, but they did. So I let them."

"Yeah, same," Nicole agrees.

Ah, okay. I get it now. "Well, I *do* know how to handle my life being in danger," I explain. "I'm not just, like, a chef or a nurse. I'm a hacker. I can help."

Nicole's mouth flattens into a line. "Down the hall. Last door on the left before the conservatory."

I get up from my chair slowly, trying to gauge the faintly displeased look on her face. "Are you guys going to come with me?"

"No thanks. We'll be in here, being unhelpful chefs and nurses."

Fuck. I grimace and glance at Eleanor for support. "That's not... you know that's not how I meant it, right?"

Eleanor rolls her eyes so hard her irises disappear under her bangs for an instant. "She knows. Right, Nicole?" she asks pointedly. Nicole shrugs in a way that's vaguely an agreement. "If you can help and you want to, you *should* go. I bet Wesley will be chuffed. That's British for excited," she adds sagely.

I'm locked in indecision—clearly I made a misstep, and I want to fix it, but I don't know how. I feel like Nicole doesn't like me for some reason, and it seems to run deeper than a few bad jokes. I just don't know why—after all, I *just* got here. Usually, it takes people a whole interaction before they decide they don't like me. And she doesn't even know about my preexisting relationship with the man who helped kidnap her...

I probably should ask Wesley how to handle that grenade.

Which, honestly, is fine. People don't like me. I get it. And normally, I'd say *screw it* and let it roll off my back. But she's Wesley's friend. I want to make a good impression. I was kind of... excited at the thought of them being my friends, too. And if we're all going to be living together until someone's not trying to kill me anymore, I'd like to get along.

So I'm trying, damnit.

"Hey, I'm not sure what I said or did—if I did say or do something—but I'm grateful to have a safe place to stay, and that you looked at my cut and that you're making me dinner," I say, nodding at Nicole and Eleanor in turn. "I'm sorry I flirted with Mac a million years ago... and for the inappropriate joke about Dimitri's dick. But I make inappropriate jokes when I'm nervous—it's kind of my thing—and *his* thing looks like it could level a small town. Congratulations, and you terrify me." I nod at Nicole.

Eleanor laughs. Gratifyingly, there's a small twitch to Nicole's lips that gives me hope before they settle back down into a flat line.

"Madison, it's okay. We're cool," Eleanor says. "Now get out of here so we can talk about you."

I'm so tempted to pause on the other side of the doorway to eavesdrop, but I doubt that would endear me to my new *besties*, so I continue down the hallway.

I'm a little indignant and my ego is a tad bruised, but I can sort of see things from Nicole's perspective (even though it's waaaaay up there). A new person always changes the dynamic—I guess it's not that surprising that at least one person would be resistant to it. I bet she's an earth sign. Virgo, if I had to guess.

My journey down the hallway towards the last door on the left before the conservatory—where, presumably, Colonel Mustard committed murder with the lead pipe—is waylaid by the artwork on the walls. Suddenly, I feel like I'm in a gallery. These paintings are insane... is that a Mondrian?!

30

WESLEY

This isn't black and white anymore.

I let the cat out as soon as the door closes, and he promptly slinks across the room to hide under the desk. I don't blame him—my hair's raised about finding a dog here, too—and Madison already explained that he'll come out to explore once he feels safe.

Hopefully she'll do the same, though I'm far less concerned about Madison coming out of her shell. If she keeps making comments about being spat on, I'm going to give her exactly what she wants in front of everyone like I'm marking my territory.

Swiping a hand down my face, I stifle my groan. I'm not normally such a damn caveman. It's not as if I'm genuinely worried about Mac or Dimitri making a move. They're so settled and happy, it's frankly maddening. Nor am I particularly worried that Madison means anything by it—she's probably the most overtly flirtatious person I've ever met. It's how she is. I know that. I *like* that.

Nothing gets me going more than seeing someone covet something that's mine. Except maybe getting to teach her a lesson about who she belongs to...

"You're moving around well," I say, noting Dimitri's single crutch as he heads towards his spot in the room. He's not even leaning on it heavily.

"*Da*. I have always been a quick healer."

Mac pulls his chair up to the edge of my desk. "Don't keep us in suspense, Short Round. I feel like you've been gone for weeks. Catch us up; tell us what happened. The General put out another hit on her after you took the job? And it's open season, to top it off?"

"Very unusual," Dimitri remarks.

I nod, blowing out a long breath. So much has happened. Where to begin?

Probably with the part that they'll think is the most important. "Yes. And there's been a... development."

"Good or bad?"

I won't even bother trying to figure out how to answer that one. "Felix is Madison's uncle."

As predicted, Dimitri goes stiff and still. "What?" he demands, anger lacing his tone.

"They're not strictly related, but that's just semantics, I think. The point is they know each other very well. He's faking her death for us to get the other assassins off our backs."

There's a second of stillness and silence, then Dimitri straightens. "You are saying that you know where he is at this very moment?"

Yeah, I figured Dimitri would hear that and want to take action. I take my seat at my desk, taking care not to accidentally step on a tail or kick the cat. "I am... but I'm also saying he's helping us—her."

"So we will go there later and kill him?" Dimitri guesses.

"No..." I sigh. "He knows more about the General than we do. He's the one who made the connection with SmarTech I mentioned—he sent Madison in. He could be useful."

Dimitri scoffs, waving his hand dismissively. "This is not enough to save his life."

Mac jumps in to help—likely because he was never completely sold on the idea of killing Felix. "Wasn't it you who said that it's poor form to kill a neutral, useful man?"

He narrows his eyes at Mac but jerks his chin in a reticent nod. "He was no longer neutral the moment we discovered he had kidnapped my woman."

"I know. But," I say, holding up a hand when he would argue, "he's not *not* on our side. He abandoned Kyle instead of finishing the job and taking the payment months ago. He got Eleanor *out*. And if he helps us with the General, then we're more or less on the same side—at least temporarily. Perhaps the situation ought to be reexamined from a new angle."

"And what angle is that?"

"The one where he's family to someone who's important to me," I answer flatly.

Dimitri makes a face, then blows out a long breath through his nose. He turns his head to the side, and I almost miss the small nod that shows he'll hear me out. "You and Nicole deserve your revenge, and I'm not saying Felix deserves to simply be forgiven. But this isn't black and white anymore."

"I suppose having information makes him useful," Dimitri admits after a few seconds. He doesn't seem particularly happy about it, but it's a start.

But then he shakes his head. "His information is not useful if we do not trust him. That is the issue with men like him—trust is a bridge made of cards. Constructing it takes time, and problems cannot be fixed because instead they bring down the whole structure."

"Google doc," Mac interjects, grinning at the surprisingly accurate metaphor.

"You're right," I agree with both of them. I smile, but it tastes bitter. "But I think there's one thing we *can* trust about Felix—that he'd never hurt Madison."

As much as I hate to admit it, Felix's protective instincts towards Madison make me feel oddly better. Sure, he's a dickhead, and he got her involved with SmarTech, and part of me wants to kill him for it... but he also keeps tabs on her and obviously considers her part of his family. He's been protecting her on this dangerous path she chose, and now that the dust has settled, I find I'm oddly... grateful to him for that.

Dimitri frowns. "So she is... a hostage? We use her to control him?"

I cut him a look, knowing he doesn't really think that's an option. "No... I know it's a wild concept that a woman be brought to the house both willingly *and* aware of what's going on"—Mac scoffs loudly and dramatically—"but Madison isn't leverage to be used against someone for our own personal vendettas."

Dimitri considers this for a few seconds, then crosses his arms. "I do not like it. This is creating a situation where the choice will be Madison or Nicole—spare the man because of what he means to your woman, or kill him for what he has done to mine."

And there he goes, cutting to the heart of the matter. As usual. "For what it's worth, I agree. And I don't like that it's come to this."

But Madison's words in the car ring in my ears and buzz around in my chest, refusing to settle without acknowledgment.

I'm an adult, and my own safety is a discussion I get to be part of.
Restriction and protection aren't the same thing.
That's called benevolent control.

"Will you do me a favor?" I ask. He nods instantly. "Speak with Nicole and try to put aside your own anger to see how *she* feels about it. She's the one who was injured, after all. She deserves a say in her revenge."

Dimitri takes a second to think, then inclines his head. "That is a good idea."

"Now that you two have hugged it out," Mac interjects, rubbing his hands together. "Let's talk shop. Where are we? What do we know?"

"From what I understand, Felix sent Madison to SmarTech to copy and steal their secure files. Right after she finished the transfer and quit, the hit came out on her. The timing is too coincidental, especially combined with the fact that so many of our other jobs have used SmarTech tools. They're involved somehow—someone at that company could very well be our man."

"She stole data from a company that makes its business in security?" Dimitri asks, brows lifting. "This is impressive."

I can't fight the grin. "Massively impressive. She went undercover on the inside to get it, then snuck it out right under their noses. She's got guts. And skills. Fuck, I couldn't have built a more perfect woman for me," I gush. Because I can. Because after listening to these lovesick fools talk about their women all this time, it feels good.

"All right, save your not-so-floppy disk for her," Mac says, rolling his eyes. But he grins at me, obviously happy for me. "So, you're going to start with this SmarTech data, I assume."

I nod. "Madison has the files."

Mac considers that, scratching at his short beard regrowth. "So where do we go from here?"

I think about the book in my top drawer, hidden in its locked compartment, and all the notes I've been keeping for a decade about my search. Do I tell them? We're getting close—this is closer than I've ever been. And this next part will be tricky—knowing would give them some additional context about what we might be up against...

Or it would upset them, like it did when I told them how I parse out the names. Perhaps it's best to stick with the original plan, and the plan has always been to wait to tell them until it's over.

There's a soft knock on the door. Dimitri, who's closest, goes to answer it. "Oh, hello, Madison."

"Hey!" Her head pops out to the side as she leans around him, and she waves with her fingers. "Whatcha doin'?"

"We were just speaking about the data from SmarTech. Come on in," I wave.

She disappears again as she straightens, totally eclipsed by the man in the doorway. "Should I go back and get a running start, or is this more of a Great Wall of Dimitri situation? Is there a toll?"

"Of course there is no toll," he replies simply, moving aside to let her in.

Her eyes bug out as she looks all around, taking note of the line of Raspberry Pis and single-board computers on my back desk with an impressed whistle. "Sweet setup, SpyderMan."

I grin, glad she approves. "Sit," I gesture to the chair Mac's in. "Mac can stand."

With a chuckle, he does just that. "Sure can."

A feeling of rightness settles into my chest as she takes her place next to me. Then she gasps at the sight of the transparent walls of my desktop. "Is that the most recent NVIDIA RTX graphics card?"

My grin widens. "It is."

"Why do you have the best graphics card money can buy? You don't play any games."

"Because it's the best graphics card money can buy," I repeat her words back, heavy with the implication that she answered her own question.

She snorts and rolls her eyes. "That's such a price-tag-flex goon move. ASUS GE Force would have gotten you there for a quarter of the price. All the performance you'd need—"

"Not when I'm streaming multiple sources of video simultaneous-ly—"

"Dear God, there's two of them," Mac declares, locked in on our back and forth. I look over in time to see him elbow Dimitri, who raises an eyebrow and nods his agreement.

Madison and I smile at each other.

"Well, in our own Wes's words, if nothing needs shooting or stabbing, Big D and I aren't much help. You two clearly have things under control." Mac waves, heading for the door. "Call us when the action starts!"

"*Da*, and I will expect you at our regular training sessions. I accessed the security footage you saved and watched your fight in the alley by Madison's apartment. You need to work on your footwork and blocking. Your entire left side was wide open; it is no surprise he got in a hit."

I roll my eyes as they turn to leave. "It's always 'work on your footwork, Wesley,' and never 'good job taking down the giant bloke, Wesley.'"

"It was not good work; it was sloppy work," Dimitri argues. "Mediocrity is not to be admired, even if the outcome was favorable—mediocre assassins are simply dead men."

A giggle slips out from Madison as Mac cries from the hall, "Google Doc!"

"You're going to love the Google Doc," I explain to her, bringing it up in my browser.

Her laugh is bright as she leans in and scans through the first couple of lines. "*A blanket of snow hides many sins.* That's beautiful."

With a long-suffering sigh, Dimitri follows Mac out, shutting the door softly. A few seconds later, Some Bills pokes his nose out from underneath my knee, surprising me with a cold, wet hello against my shin. I lean down and give him a scratch with a fond smile.

"USB?" I prompt, holding out my hand.

She digs into her pocket, producing the little panda keychain, and places it in the center of my palm. "There's a ton of data on there. Transferring it is going to take a while. A few hours, maybe."

I stick it into the port, initialize the transfer, and sit back as my computer calculates. She's right. "Well, then, it looks like we've got some time. How about a tour?"

"Sure." Her lips quirk as she glances around, then she tilts her head. "Think I can bribe the tour guide to show me your bedroom first?"

39

WESLEY

Yin and yang

Bathed in the golden light of morning, Madison's sweat-slicked body writhes and shakes. The green front pieces of her hair are dark with moisture, sticking to her forehead in a wavy, irregular pattern as she tosses her head back and forth against the pillow. The wet sound of my fingers pumping in and out of her soaked cunt, coupled with the low hum of vibrations, has faded into the background like sweet music—music that's been on replay all night.

We did take a break after midnight, since the toy I made for her needed charging—a modified prototype, one of the earlier designs, since the real thing is still in her flat—and then she taught me exactly how to touch her to make her come. I coaxed one orgasm, then wrung another from her pleasure-drunk body.

"W-Wesley," she moans, voice hoarse from overuse.

"Is this going to be seven? Or eight?" I ask darkly.

She huffs out a reticent laugh—a noise she didn't mean to make—then clenches around my fingers, gritting her teeth and tossing her head. "This doesn't add to last night's count. It resets when we sleep."

"Even if we only got a few hours?" I tease.

Her eyes snap shut and she shudders, perhaps remembering what it felt like to wake up this last time, pressed back to my front, my fingers sliding into her well-used pussy and my thumb working into her tight asshole.

The rhythm of her breathing changes, her nipples peak into hard nubs, her stomach muscles tense, and her toes curl inward. She doesn't need to tell me she's about to come—I know from how her pussy clamps down on my fingers so hard I can barely move them, and how hard she's clutching my shoulders. It's a beautiful thing to watch how she fights it at first, then gives in, powerless against the wave of pleasure she can't stop and doesn't want to. My name is a prayer that whispers between lips that are red and swollen and a little chapped.

Before she's even fully come down, she's rocking her hips and chanting, "Fuck me. Please fuck me, Wesley. Right now. While I'm... oh my fucking *god*... Please, please, please, please. I want your cock. I love how it feels when you fuck me while this thing is inside—"

I don't need to be begged twice, let alone four times, and my perfect girl has gotten so good at asking nicely for what she wants.

I slide out of the bed, grab her ankle and jerk her to the edge. I love this angle—the power and control, and the height advantage giving me a perfect view of her torso as it follows the momentum of my thrusts. Those bouncing tits alone are nearly enough to make me spill myself.

Her legs spread to the right width to cradle me—we've practiced enough that her body knows mine instinctively. She's plenty wet, and I'm leaking like a bucket with a hole, so when I sink into her exquisite heat, we both groan. She grips me so tightly, spasming around me with an irregular pattern, caught in the throes of her body's reactions. The device buzzing away next to my cock, her wet warmth, the all-consuming knowledge that she's mine, that she's being satisfied, that I finally have her after all this time...

The orgasm starts to build, heavy and urgent in my balls, and I know I'm not going to last.

No way. I refuse to be a two-pump-chump.

I withdraw, and she cries out, a deeply displeased noise. The noise gets even sharper as I pull the toy out of her. She squirms, like she's trying to sit up, so I reach for her throat with my free hand and hold her down. "You're not going anywhere, Madison," I growl. "Lie still."

With an erotic little sob, she grabs my wrist, steadying herself since I'm not pressing against anything I shouldn't be. "Wesley," she whines, swallowing hard against my palm. "Sir!"

The title sends me spinning into a mindless black hole of urgency. I flip the vibrator around so it can attach back onto her clit where it belongs, and thrust my hips forward at the same time. Since it won't stay in place on its own, I grab her hand and force her fingers around it so I can still maintain my grip on her neck.

"Hold it," I bark.

She cries out in relief and satisfaction, and it vibrates against my hold. I tighten my fingers, applying pressure to the veins that supply blood to her brain. Then, I turn up the sucking action to medium. She screams through another release, tightening and loosening around me, and I let my hips take over. Without the electrical pulses so close to my most sensitive parts, I can fuck her nice and hard and let the orgasm build slowly.

Her legs hook around my hips, pulling me in deeper, and she clutches my wrist like it's a lifeline. "Too much," she moans hoarsely, brows slashing upwards as her eyes roll back.

"You have a safe word," I remind her, snapping my hips against her harder. She knows exactly what to say to make it stop if she really wants it to.

When she doesn't say it, I know she's not ready for it to end. My smile darkens. I continue to pound into her, holding her down and controlling her pleasure. Forcing it. Feeding on it. Basking in it. Her pleasure is *mine*. Those noises are for *me*. Every gasp and moan slides along my spine, prickles against my skin, seeps into my blood, and settles around my bones. She's inside me; I'm inside her.

She clenches around me, completely lost in another wave of pleasure, and I watch the tears gather in the outer corners of her eyes and slip out. I don't know why that's what does it, but my orgasm suddenly explodes out of me. It's a rocket of sensations—of pleasure so good it hurts and the disorienting feeling of satisfaction and physical weakness at the same time. The release takes a piece of my soul with it, giving it to her as if she doesn't already have the rest of it.

I'm shuddering against her, riding the aftershocks when she rasps, "Stop, no more. Red."

I jerk away so quickly that the toy nearly flies from her hand. There's no censure or displeasure in her tone, but I'm sensitive to the use of her safe word. I release her throat, take the vibrator from her, click it off, and set it aside.

"Are you all right, my love?" I ask, trailing my hands down the side of her body and grinning as she giggles and shivers at the light, tickling touch.

Her eyes are closed when she smiles and hums her answer. "Oh yes. I'm fucking fantastic. And you're a fantastic fuck. We're like... one of those circles... with the swoopy parts." She pants, drawing meaningless shapes in the air with her pointer finger.

"Yin and yang?"

"Sure. Yeah. That."

Sex drunk. I chuckle and take a step back to give her room to sit up. Her half-closed eyes are fuzzy, and her hair is a mess, her skin is wet with sweat, but she's never looked more beautiful. When I lean down to kiss her slowly, she meets it with languid satisfaction. The press of our mouths lacks all the hunger of the times we've kissed before. This time it's intimate, not a precursor; it's sealing the connection, not setting expectations. Affection. Aftercare.

She's the one to pull back with a throaty noise. "Enough," she rasps. "I'm tapping out. I'm sore and sticky and tired."

"So the sass can be fucked out of you. Good to know." The bed dips next to her as I kneel on the mattress, flipping so I'm sitting upright against the headboard I've hardly ever used. I claimed this room back when we first moved in—it's the master, so it's roomy and has an attached bath—but the mattress is still so new we had to cut it out of the plastic and make the bed. And now that I've spent some time on it, I realize how much more comfortable it is than the couch in my office where I nap throughout the day and night.

She laughs, and it's such a light, joyful sound that I close my eyes and bask in it. Her arms come up over her head in a stretch that makes her wince and curl inward slightly in a protective move. "The sass and the sense, apparently. If I don't take a shower, I'm going to get the worst UTI of my life."

I watch, stretching an arm behind my head in a relaxed position, as she stands and grabs my towel from the hook on the back of the door. My body feels well-used and depleted. My abs, forearms, and thighs are so sore I can tell they'll hurt for days. My dick is practically raw. I'm starving and thirsty and exhausted.

And I wouldn't have it any other way.

I roll out of bed and reach for my pants.

"Should I come down to your office when I'm done?" she asks. "I bet the data was done transferring last night."

The sudden reminder of the situation hanging over our heads is a jolt to my heart. The data is certainly done transferring, and I'm eager to get stuck in, but...

Madison can't help me. I can't have her in my personal space, so close to so many secrets. I can't have her watching as I sift through the data, and I can't tell her what I'm really looking for. She's far too clever to accept half-truths or poor explanations, and I'd rather not lie to her at all, let alone outright. I'd hoped she would want to spend some downtime adjusting to her new surroundings, but I should have expected this.

"It might be," I say, keeping my voice even. "But you've been through a lot, and you deserve to rest. Sleep, relax, have a few nice meals, watch some telly, play a computer game if you like. Maybe get to know Eleanor and Nicole, too?"

She narrows her eyes at me, then shrugs, and I swear all the air whooshes out of me at once in relief. "I am still pretty tired. It would be nice to get some more sleep."

I nod. "I'd like to see you happy here, Madison. Think of it like a vacation. Let me take care of things for a bit—I can handle the initial data filtering."

"Okay. You'll come get me when you need help?"

"I will."

Not a lie, I tell myself. I won't be coming to get her because I don't need her help.

32

MADISON

Welcome to the Hitmen of Ulysses.

It's been a couple of days, and I think I'm starting to get into the rhythm of the house—this group is sort of like a family, but they lack some of the togetherness habits I'm used to seeing. They don't have meals together every day or do puzzles in front of Mexican soaps. They have an easy camaraderie, but they're not in each other's business. It's more like a group of independent adult couples who have their own interests and things to do. Which, frankly, is kind of awesome.

I keep checking on Wesley, but he keeps saying he doesn't need my help, and he acts sort of weird whenever I come into the office to hang out. When I'm sitting on the couch with Some Bills on my lap, he'll answer my questions with short answers, but eventually I start feeling like I'm bothering him, so I leave. He did say he closes off when he's processing, but I'm starting to get kind of antsy. And it's not just because we haven't acted out my fantasy of being bent over that desk...

I want to help him. But I also want him to *want* my help.

I'm a little worried this is more of that *I just want to protect you* bullshit. He said he'd let me know when he needed me. I guess I just have to take him at his word.

Eleanor is my unofficial house sponsor—mostly because she's so friendly, but also because I always know exactly where to find her when I have a question, like where the extra toilet paper is, or which button on the Italian espresso machine makes the coffee come out. She's always in the kitchen, making something that smells too delicious to pass up.

Mac seems to have endless energy as he drifts through the house; when he's not working out or running the perimeter, he's pestering Eleanor or they're sneaking upstairs to bone. And they're *not* sneaky. Once, they started before they got all the way to the attic, and their love echoed through the house. Made me so horny I took Wesley's showerhead for a spin.

I haven't run into Nicole much, and I wonder if it's because she's introverted or if it's personal. I see her walking George outside, training him with endless patience, and sometimes I see her curled up in the library in one of those massive, cushy chairs. I tried to strike up a conversation with her once—trying to get to know her, like Wesley requested—but she gave monosyllabic answers and then made some excuse about it being time to check on Dimitri's wound. I mean, I assume it was an excuse. Maybe it was a euphemism, and they're way more discreet when they bone.

When he's not with her, Dimitri spends almost all day in the gym. I've gotten so used to the sight of him going up and down those stairs, I didn't realize he had stopped at the landing at the top of the stairs this morning as I was heading into the office for a visit with my man.

"Madison. Come," he said. The words were barked at me, and I nearly looked around to figure out who he was talking to, to see if he confused me with Small Dog.

"Everyone who lives here must train," he explained.

And since Dimitri's "explanation" was nowhere near enough, Wesley helped fill in the blanks. Everyone in the house takes self-defense lessons from Dimitri—even if you don't want to. Even if you don't need self-defense lessons. Even though I'm a world-class hacker "helping" process gigabytes of data from SmarTech. None of that gets me out of gym class, apparently.

So 45 minutes later, I'm red-faced, heaving breaths, already looking disgusting as I climb off the treadmill, while Eleanor and Nicole are at most a little winded. I didn't come prepared for a workout, so I'm double-bra'd, in borrowed bike shorts from Eleanor that go past my knees, and wearing my Converses that made Dimitri's lip curl in disapproval.

"Now that we have warmed up, we can begin," Dimitri booms.

I don't feel warmed up. I feel like I'm going to die. *Dios,* I'm out of shape.

We shuffle after him towards the corner of the room like ducklings. The floor is lined with "sparring mats" over here, which is frankly terrifying. They look... well-used.

"Because Madison is new to this, we will return to the basics of self-defense."

"I know the basics of self-defense," I cut in. If he'd let me explain myself earlier, we could've avoided wasting time. "Don't backtrack on my account; I'm sure I can keep up."

Nicole makes a noise of disbelief, and Eleanor elbows her arm with a meaningful look. My stomach twists at the unspoken exchange that makes me feel like such an outsider.

Nicole turns to me. "We've been training with him for months. And no offense, but you look like they have to measure you before they let you go on the Ferris wheel."

I almost laugh. Now, I've heard a lot of short jokes, and usually they annoy me, but that one was pretty good. Not overtly offensive or derogatory. I rock back on my heels, considering her—maybe I was wrong about her. Maybe she *does* have a sense of humor; it's just frozen underneath that cold demeanor.

All right, Ice Queen. Imma melt you yet. Watch me.

Dimitri nods. "Nicole is right. You are very small, Madison. Often, the men we must face are large and well trained. Not all techniques will work, so we study a wide range to combine the most effective."

Small? I mean, I *feel* small around these people, but I'm short and wide, and usually the world doesn't let me forget the second part. "By that logic, pretty much everyone is bigger than me," I offer with a shrug. "If I say I'm not a beginner, don't you think that means I know how to accommodate a taller opponent?"

Dimitri crosses his arms as Eleanor and Nicole exchange a look, and, once again, I'm under the microscope, very much an outsider in a group that isn't actively trying to make me feel that way. But it creeps in every once in a while like this—a shared look that implies history and has a meaning that I'm not in on.

I square my shoulders. I was expecting to have to prove myself, but I was kind of hoping I could do it by showing everyone a few quality of life tricks on their computers, like browser add-ons for internet shopping or widgets that create schedules and digital calendars. Dimitri seems like the kind of guy who likes schedules and lists.

Guess I'm going to have to do it this way.

"Fight me," I challenge.

Dimitri cracks a smile. Well, not a smile—more of a half-step above a grimace. "That will not end well for you."

"I might surprise you," I argue.

"It's hard for him to hold back," Nicole intervenes, and I can't help but wonder if she's trying to protect me or if it's a humble-brag about her man's skills. I'll be generous and assume a little of both.

I glance at her, then go back to sizing up the big guy. "He doesn't have to."

He drops his arms from their crossed position, shaking his head, and I know what he's going to say before he does. So I don't let him. I close the distance, catching him off guard, and bring my elbow out around my body with as much force as I can. I'm not trying to hurt him too badly, so I clip him in the stomach instead of the groin.

He makes an *oof* and there's a surprised gasp behind me.

"If I could reach and put force behind it, I'd have thrust the heel of my hand into his nose. Instead, my strike zone is solar plexus, groin, knee, instep," I explain to the peanut gallery, pointing to each area as I say them.

His brows go up an instant before he lunges for me, darting to the side. I dance away, staying on the balls of my feet, never giving him my back. That's the biggest mistake someone my size can make—the only reason that assassin in the alley got the drop on me was because he snuck up from behind.

There's a spark in his eyes as he realizes what I'm doing. Another almost-smile. "Yes, good, Madison. You see how she keeps me in front of her? If I am able to grab her from behind, that is the end of the lights for her."

"Endgame," Eleanor corrects at the same time Nicole says, "Lights out."

"That is what I said," he dismisses.

Lightning quick—quicker than anyone his size has any right to be—he snakes out and grabs my wrist. I have a flare of panic, but my training kicks in.

I throw my elbow again, hitting him in the solar plexus this time, hard enough to make him double over. He reaches for me as he gasps for air, but now I can get both arms around his neck since he's so much closer to my level. I jerk his head back, twisting, pulling with all my might so he follows the spin. Once he's off balance, I release and step back as he falls hard on his back.

Someone claps—Eleanor, I'm guessing—and I almost laugh. I lean over and brace myself on my knees to catch my breath as Dimitri rolls into a sitting position.

"Good," he puffs, clearly stunned to have had the breath knocked out of him. "Then what would you—"

I mime kicking him in the groin, stopping just short of making contact, but close enough that he flinches and Nicole makes a nervous noise of protest. I toss her a look, frowning. "I wasn't really going to kick him in the balls, Nicole," I say.

She has the grace to look sheepish. "Of course not."

Dimitri waves off my offer to help him up, getting to his feet gracefully. "Where did you train? You have combined the moves from judo and taekwondo and boxing—"

"I have friends in low places," I say evasively. "There... may be an underground MMA somewhere in Ulysses, and I might know the guys in charge."

"You know of an underground fighting ring?"

I purse my lips. "I can neither confirm nor deny its existence."

"Hmm," Dimitri muses, staring at me. "You will bring me."

Nicole makes a sound of protest that makes me wince. I don't know the way to melt her exterior yet, but I'm pretty sure it's not by bringing her husband on field trips she disapproves of. "Sorry, big guy. But if the wife thinks it's a bad idea—"

"I'm not his keeper," she cuts in, bristling. "It's not a good idea because he's a wanted man. We don't know how many *bratoks* are still out there looking for you, Dimitri. Underground anything means gambling, and gambling means Russians. That's what you said, right?" Her voice gets high at the end of the last sentence, charged with emotion.

She doesn't strike me as the type to start crying to manipulate the situation, so when I see a tear fall from the corner of her eye, even I'm alarmed.

Dimitri nods and crosses the distance between them, pulling her into his embrace. He places a kiss in the center of her forehead and murmurs to her. I hear, "You are right, my *med*. I was not thinking," before his voice drops too low and listening starts feeling like eavesdropping.

Without meaning to, I've made another misstep. Fuck.

Once they finish their discussion, I try again. "If you'd like, I can teach you a move—I can't do it, but you can probably manage because you're so tall. It'll land with you sitting on his face," I offer, waggling my brows, hoping to dispel the tension I didn't mean to create.

She smiles, but it's wobbly. "No, thanks."

"We will resume tomorrow," Dimitri decides, sweeping his palm up and down her back.

She and Dimitri leave the gym, and I turn to Eleanor, kind of at a loss. She makes a commiserative face at me. I can see in her eyes how much she hates this—people being at odds, feeling like she has to pick a side.

Definitely an air sign. My money's on Libra.

We decide to finish our workouts. After I show her a few moves, she demonstrates some of the ones Dimitri has drilled into her. An hour later, we're both sweaty and sore, but it feels good. Nothing like punching someone wearing boxing mitts to work out some of your irritation at being the outcast who can't find the right thing to say.

"Want a beer?" Eleanor suggests as we climb the stairs.

I chuckle. "I'm no expert, but don't they recommend water after a workout?"

She shrugs. "Mac says the first one is hydrating."

"I'm good, but I *am* hungry."

"I can help with that."

We head to the kitchen, but of course there's no such thing as a simple snack with Eleanor. She immediately puts me to work: sous-chef onion chopper. "You just didn't want to cry," I accuse, wiping a tear on my shoulder to avoid touching my eye with onion hands.

I'm going to have to find Wesley's secret stash of chips—he's always pulling a bag of something crispy and delicious out of nowhere. I just can't seem to find a time to look when no one else is in the kitchen.

"Can I ask..." I begin.

"She'll come around," Eleanor answers with so much certainty, I almost wonder if I *did* finish the rest of that sentence.

I chew on my lower lip. "You sure? She seemed pretty upset, and I just..." I sigh. I don't want to turn this around and imply that it's only Nicole's problem, since I feel like we got off on the wrong foot and that's on both of us, but I'm genuinely at a loss at this point. "I don't know what I did, so I don't know what to do. Ya know?"

Her smile is sympathetic. "I do. And trust me, it wasn't about you. She was kidnapped a few months ago," Eleanor tells me somberly, her eyes dropping to the pan she's stirring. "She's been having panic attacks since it happened."

"Oh," I say. I nod, like I understand, but secretly my stomach twists into a knot. Once the truth comes out about the kidnapping situation, it's only going to complicate things.

But, as Abuela always says (even though she means it about cleaning houses), one mess at a time...

"Nicole is a really good person, and she's probably my best friend at this point," Eleanor says, and I tamp down on a flare of jealousy. I want her to say that about me. I want Nicole to say it about me, too. I just... I want in. I want to wedge myself in the middle and turn this into a trio where we laugh together and support each other.

I want it so badly I can taste it. And it tastes kind of like onions.

Eleanor continues, oblivious to my reaction. "But she's complicated. I won't go into too much detail, because it's not my story and I don't talk about my friends behind their backs... but I'd say this to her face. I have said it to her face, actually," she amends with a little laugh. "Nicole is so far in her own head sometimes, she can see out her ears. She had a rough childhood, I think. It made her so kind, but it also makes her doubt people's intentions."

The words hit a little too hard in a way I doubt Eleanor meant them to. They sting as they settle. "I can relate to that."

"And she's pretty guarded. She's afraid of rejection, so she rejects people first. She's working on it."

Oof. She's two for two here. Sounds like Nicole and I have more in common than either of us would like. It's not the kind of common ground you find easily with new people, but it does help put some things in perspective.

I regard Eleanor out of the corner of my eye. "You know, you've got this whole... wise beyond your years thing going for you. Kind of freaks me out."

"I know," she agrees, suddenly somber. "I'm actually 30."

"Really?"

She sighs and lowers her knife, swiping her hair out of her eyes. "It's the bangs, right? Makes me look younger? It's kind of hard to take me seriously?"

I laugh, shaking my head at the ridiculousness of it. "Yeah. It is the bangs."

"I knew it," she laments. "I keep thinking I should let them grow out so people will take me more seriously, but I just hate my big, dumb forehead."

"I'm sure it's not—"

She lifts her bangs, showing me. "See?"

Mac chooses that instant to stride into the kitchen, chuckling when he sees what we're doing on the other side of the island. "Is she showin' you her forehead? Darlin', I keep telling you, it's a beautiful forehead. Sexy even, because it's got your brain in it."

"Boo!" She scoffs and reaches for the bowl in the middle of the island. She throws an apple at him, which he easily plucks out of the air before it can hit. "I know you love me and you're trying to be sweet, but you sound condescending. No one has a sexy forehead. That's not a thing."

He takes a bite, kisses her cheek as he passes, and leans down to whisper something in her ear that makes her blush chin to hairline, disappearing right under those hotly contested bangs.

"I'm in the middle of something, but I'll find you later, darling," she says, a polished, northern pronunciation of every letter that almost feels like a mockery of his slow drawl when he calls her the same thing.

I consider the two of them, letting my mind drift back to Wesley. There are some similarities in how they act that I can't help but notice. In fact, I've seen the way Mac looks at Eleanor reflected in not just my man, but also in the occasional softening of Dimitri's scowl. The three of them are cut from the same cloth.

"Can I ask something else?" I say once Mac is clear of the room.

The secretive smile she's wearing doesn't falter. "Shoot."

"The way Mac is with you, and how Dimitri is with Nicole... it's sweet how protective they are, but doesn't it sort of grate on you? Doesn't it seem kind of..."

I trail off, considering how Wesley's been since we got here. He's so much more relaxed now that the danger isn't imminent, but he's also so focused. He's got a mission, and I feel like he's shutting me out.

"Controlling?" she suggests.

My shoulders round as she puts the word out there so I don't have to. Clearly, she gets it. "Yes! Doesn't that bother you?"

"Oh, Mac can totally be a controlling asshole. But it comes from a good place."

I narrow my eyes at her. "So that makes it okay?"

She shrugs. "It does for me. I know better than to stick my nose into this particular argument, though, so I'll just say this: you're the only one who gets to decide if that makes it okay for you."

I open my mouth to change the topic, then snap it shut, considering her. Eleanor knows Wesley—has known him longer and maybe knows him *better* in some ways since they've lived together this long. Maybe I can... share how I'm feeling with her. Maybe I can actually open up to a girlfriend and get advice.

It's something I've never done. I've never bared myself to someone like that—never sought advice for my love life. Never had someone so close to the situation. Never felt like someone would understand, or care enough to listen.

And it certainly doesn't hurt that she's so wise.

"He's just so possessive!" I blurt.

Eleanor snorts and dissolves into knowing laughter that's so bright and happy, I have no choice but to join her. "Welcome to the Hitmen of Ulysses. For the admission price of your life being in mortal danger, you get a growly, possessive Neanderthal who loves you out loud, fucks like no one's business, and might plant a tracker under your skin."

My eyes widen at the specificity of that last one. "Did Mac—"

"No," Eleanor giggles, totally unbothered. "Well, not yet, but he's made too many comments for it to be a joke."

"I think if I even casually mentioned that to Wesley, he'd start designing one from scratch."

She nods. "He would."

I sigh. "It's like, he's so demanding. And, I mean, sometimes it's really hot. I mean *really* hot—"

"Wait!" she cries, trotting into the pantry and emerging with a bottle of champagne and two glasses. "This is the kind of conversation you have over a glass of wine."

I don't have the heart to tell her I probably won't like it, so I hop up onto the stool at the island and watch as she tilts the glasses and pours one for me. When she's done, she takes a long sip, smacks her lips and sets down the glass. It makes a little tinkling noise on the marble. "Okay, go." She leans forward onto her elbows, propping her chin in both hands.

I use the stem to spin my glass, putting off taking the first sip. "It feels weird to even complain because he just wants to... *take care of me*, but it feels more complicated than that. I don't know; I've never been in a serious relationship before—let alone one like this. It feels like... he wants so much from me."

"Too much?" she asks, taking another sip, tone completely free of judgment.

"I don't know. I mean, I *want* to give him what he wants, but I don't think I know how... I think I'm afraid. And I'm not even sure why. It's stupid to be afraid, right?"

"No, it's not," Eleanor counters immediately. "I know what you mean. It's like, what if you give him so much that you lose part of yourself?"

Not even thinking about it, I take a small sip from my glass. The bubbles burst on my tongue, and it feels odd, but the taste is... interesting. Better than communion wine, I'll give it that. "Yeah, kind of. I feel like he wants me to *need* him. But I don't need anyone to take care of me. Frankly, I don't really understand why he wants to."

She takes a sip, thinking. "Need and want aren't the same thing. And letting someone take care of you doesn't mean you can't do it yourself," she points out. "And it doesn't mean you have to let him either. You have to talk about it and find some kind of middle ground, where you're both happy."

"Talk it out," I repeat, shaking my head. "Easy as that, huh?"

She grins. "Communication. Frankly, that's my answer to most problems." She spins her glass, takes another sip, and refills it. Mine is still mostly full. "Wesley's pretty good at communicating though, right?"

"About some things," I agree. "But..."

But lately, there's something kind of off. Why did it feel like he was so much more open with me before we got here? Why did I feel so indispensable when I was mermaidav to his SpyderMan, but ever since we got here I feel like nothing more than the Brat to his Sir?

"I think you're right. Things were different before—online—and then I think we jumped straight into this physical relationship and this really rigid sexual dynamic." Eleanor's brows go up at that, but I roll my lips inward on the smile. I'm not quite ready to share *everything*.

"We need to figure out how to be just Madison and Wesley," I decide.

33

WESLEY

Traviesita

The office door opens unexpectedly, and I'm suddenly a teenager, caught with my hand around my cock by my mum. I slide the black notebook into the drawer as Madison steps into the room. "Oh, Madison."

"Hey," she says brightly, eyes flicking up to my face from the drawer I've just gotten closed. "Eleanor says dinner will be ready in two hours and there's nothing left to chop, so I came to see if you needed any help."

"Just about to take a break, actually," I decide instantaneously, rolling backwards in my chair.

"Oh, good." Her smile is cat-like as she reaches behind her. I hear the lock turn, and blood rushes through my body, collecting low.

Before I can stand and meet her halfway, she starts sauntering towards me with her arms behind her back in an innocent posture. "So, what's new?"

Taken off guard by the abrupt change in temperature, I settle back and watch her come to me. "Well, it appears Felix has followed through on his promises. He filed a missing person's report and sent over the confirmation email from the General in response to the proof of death. You've just made him a very rich man."

"Like he wasn't already," she mutters. She rolls her eyes and pauses in her journey to give her cat a scratch under the chin.

When she bends over, I realize the strategy in the move. Her skirt comes up in the back just high enough that I can see... everything. She's not wearing panties.

She wants to play.

My heart starts pounding, desire pooling in my veins and throbbing in my dick as it hardens within the confines of my trousers. Every muscle in my body tightens, and I nearly stand from my chair. She'd look excellent draped over the arm of that couch.

Then I recall a request she's made in the past—an almost flippant remark about working together and sitting on my lap.

"Madison," I say, voice low in a way that makes her straighten. I can't see her face, but I can imagine the tilt of her lips when she realizes she's about to get what she wants. "Come here, please."

She spins, eyes dropping to the thick outline against my thigh. Doing as I ask, she saunters over, arms still behind her back so her breasts jut forward. An offering.

"Have a seat," I say, gesturing to my thighs.

Trying to hide the spark of thrill, she bites down on her grin and nods eagerly. She turns and shifts her weight back, effectively presenting me with her ass. My palm itches to slap it. But I don't—I let her settle, getting one leg over each of mine. I tilt us back and push my legs together so she can straddle me more comfortably, and when we shift forward again, she's so wide open that I can feel her warmth radiating and smell her desire in the air. God, she smells delicious.

Sitting on my lap, she's still short enough that I can see over her head, so when I spin the chair, my screens are still visible. Not that I'd get anything done with my little distraction getting me unbelievably hard by wiggling what I know is a bald, bare pussy against my trousers—even if I were going to do work with her like this.

"So, this is what you see, huh? This is what it feels like to be Spyder-Man." She looks around and points to the edge of the desk. "You need a big framed picture of me right there."

"Do I?" I ask, dropping a kiss onto her shoulder. She smells so good, and her skin is so smooth; it's an effort to pull away.

"Maybe one with you and me and Some Bills. Like, an awkward family portrait."

Her use of the word squeezes my heart. Family. Her and me. I want that. "Not sure you could look awkward if you tried," I say, placing my lips higher on the side of her neck.

She shifts her hips, her hot slit finding the outline of my cock. I can hear the stuttered exhale, can feel the throbbing in her flesh against mine.

"Madison," I say, letting my warm breath blow into her ear. "Why are my trousers getting damp? Have you been a naughty girl?"

She squeals in surprise as I wrap my arm around her waist. The noise in her throat turns into a long moan as my fingers slide under her skirt.

"No panties," I tsk. "And here I was, thinking I'd shove them into your bratty little mouth. We'll have to do something else to keep you quiet, then, you little menace."

"*Traviesita*," she whispers, and I can hear her smile in the word.

"What?"

"*Traviesita*. It means little menace in Spanish. Little troublemaker."

"*Traviesita*," I repeat, hearing my own British accent attempting to mimic hers.

A shiver crawls down her spine. "*Dios*," she says, her breath heavy.

"Do you like hearing me speak Spanish to you?" I ask, leaning down and pressing another hot kiss on her shoulder in the dip near her collarbone.

"Yes," she groans, letting her head fall to the side to give me more access to her neck. "Say more. Please, Sir."

"You'll have to help me become fluent," I say, punctuating it with a light brush of my lips. I hover over her pulse, sucking on the skin. "As it is, my vocabulary is somewhat limited and textbook. I'll need direction for the dirty stuff."

She nods eagerly. "Yes. Anything. More. Please."

"*Me encanta sentir tu peso sobre mí.*" *I love to feel the weight of you on me.*

She starts rocking her hips faster, grinding her pussy into me harder.

"*Estás tan cálida, y tu piel está tan suave.*" *You're so warm, and your skin is so soft.*

"*Mi piel* es *tan suave,*" she corrects. "Keep going."

I slide her hair out of the way and press a kiss over one of the ridges in her spinal cord. My hands glide up the tops of her thighs, my calluses rough against her smooth skin in a way that highlights our differences and excites me on a primal level. I grab the dip above her hips, using them like handles and moving her in the rhythm I want on my lap. She moans and reaches back for me, but I shake my head, grab her wrists, and place her hands flat on the desk.

"*Eres traviesita. Puedes portarte bien conmigo ahora, ¿verdad?*" *You're a little menace. But you can be good for me now, right?*

"*Sí, papi.*"

Oh, fuck me, I like the sound of that. "Open the top right drawer there," I instruct.

Panting and a bit disoriented by the change in pace, it takes her a second to realize what I asked. Then, she reaches for the pull and leans forward to peer inside. Her delighted laugh fills the room when she finds and retrieves the sex toy I made for her.

"I had a feeling we'd need it in here," I explain.

"And you were right."

"I usually am."

She laughs again. "Can you really call it getting lucky if I'm so down bad for you that I'm a sure thing?"

"Yes," I reply instantly, quite serious. "Because I feel lucky every time I'm with you."

Her hips slow to a stop, and she tosses her hair out of the way to look over her shoulder at me. "Wesley," she says, voice thick with emotion. "That was really sweet!"

The urgency of the moment changes—the thrumming, mounting desire plateaus—and I reach up to take her face in my hand. I pull her head up and back, slanting my mouth over hers. Our kiss is gentle and tender, and I sweep my thumb back and forth across her cheek. She places her hand over mine, holding it tightly.

But it doesn't take long for the press of our lips to turn into something hungry and desperate. Every sound she makes against my mouth vibrates through my chest. Every small motion of her on my lap presses on an already-pulsing dick. Every whiff of her delicious warm scent reminds me how long it's been since my head was between her thighs (this morning).

I release her jaw and trail my hand down the front of her, grabbing the zipper on her pullover and dragging it with me. Not breaking the kiss, I palm her breast and give it a good squeeze. The whimper she makes into my mouth sets my blood on fire, so I move to her nipple and pinch.

Her back bows, causing her breast to jut forward into my hand, following the prick of pain. She's trembling already, legs shaking.

"*Me encanta tus pechos,*" I tell her, pulling away. I have the pleasure of watching her eyes pop open, then glaze over with lust at the Spanish praise. I do love her breasts. I love how they spill out over my hands and how responsive her nipples are, beading and hard for my touch.

I let my fingers trail down her stomach. "*Me encanta tu*... erm... tummy?"

She lets out a little giggle. "*Barriga.*"

"Barriga," I repeat, failing miserably to roll my r's like she did. *"Todo en tu cuerpo es redondo, suave, y perfecto." Everything about your body is round, soft and perfect.*

I give the flesh right over her belly button a knead, making her gasp. I know it puts pressure on the bladder and can heighten the feeling of arousal. Seems to have worked, because she starts grinding on me again. "Please, Wesley."

"And I love this very much," I breathe into her ear, strumming against her clit with two fingers.

She chuckles. "We stole that one. *Clitoris.*"

"I think I can remember that."

I rub a small circle around her sensitive center. She's not very wet, but I've come to expect this, and I don't care a whit. My girl isn't self-conscious about much, but clearly in her past someone made her equate moisture to desire.

I know she wants me. She knows I want her. It's not about that, and the solution is too simple to spend any energy letting it bother my ego—especially when it's a conflation. The more reading I do on the matter, the more I understand that sexual desire and female moisture are only loosely related.

"There's lube in the drawer as well," I say, relishing in her little shakes of excitement. "Let's put in your special toy, shall we?"

"You mean the *Dream Cream*?"

"Absolutely not."

"*Wesgasm 5000*?"

"Worst one yet."

"*Spyder Vibe*?"

I pause. "Actually... that one isn't so bad."

With a triumphant laugh, she leans forward and reaches into the same drawer for the bottle I left next to the device. I realize almost too slowly that she intends to do it herself. That won't do.

I snatch the bottle, silencing her pout with a laugh. "*Traviesita*," I admonish, holding out my hand so she'll give me the other half of the equation, too. "You know I like to do this part."

She sighs, but it's dramatic, and I know she doesn't mean it when she hands me the device and purrs, "Yes, Sir."

Draped over mine, her legs are too wide open and her feet are dangling, so I help her forward off my lap and give her a little push so she braces herself on the desk. I wheel back, admiring the view of her: ass up, on her tiptoes, wiggling her hips desperately for a touch.

Standing, I take my place behind her, feeling her shiver when my trousers brush the naked backs of her legs. I flip her skirt up, laying the fabric on her lower back and baring her to me. Golden, perfect skin. I pull my hand back and give her a sharp smack. She jumps, and her little noise of surprise melts immediately into a groan of desire.

"Oh, fuck," she breathes, dropping her head between the arms holding her upright on the desk. Her hair falls forward, pooling onto the glass top in inky coils, swirled with green.

From her reaction, I'm tempted to spank her again, but I'm not sure how long I'll last. I have an issue controlling myself with her—to the extent that we've started using a cock ring. It helps that I've already been balls deep inside her perfect cunt once today, because I've found it takes the edge off.

So I spread lube between her lips, slow and methodical, until she's panting and begging. Then, I slide the vibrator in place and smear the remnants onto my cock. There's still a bit left on my fingers when I'm done, and I rub them together, staring down at her pliant body beneath me.

I reach down with a well-lubed finger and press against her asshole. She inhales sharply, licks her lips and presses her hips back against me, impaling herself before I can even do it. Her reaction makes my cock jump. Desire creeps up my spine, tingling in my balls so hard that another bead of precum leaks out.

I push the tip of my finger deeper in, spreading all the remaining lube. The ring of muscles in the asshole is firmer, stronger, and when she clamps down on my finger I nearly lose it, imagining her doing it on my cock. With an uttered curse, I withdraw.

"Noooo," she moans, rocking back. "No! Put it back in! Fuck... Fuck!"

Her bratty demands melt into a shout of surprise when I stick my thumb back in her ass and use it as leverage to push her forward and lift her hips up onto the desk. Without allowing for another noise of protest or demand for control she doesn't truly want, I shove myself inside of her, slamming my eyes closed as the full length of my cock is enveloped in her wet heat.

She muffles her own cry, biting down on her forearm.

"What's the matter, *traviesita*?" I taunt, snapping my hips back and forward again, bottoming out and drawing another muted cry. "Don't you want them to know how naughty you are? And how well you take your corrections?"

"Is that what this is?" she fires back, laughing and then moaning again as I buck my hips forward again. "You're—oof!—fucking the attitude out of me?"

I scoff and press my thumb deeper into her ass. "Like that's possible."

"Oh fuuuuck. Turn it on," she begs.

"Do you think you've earned it?" I counter, barely maintaining control over my voice. All I want to do is grab her hips and pound hard, but she's writhing and her ass looks so fucking good stuffed full with my thumb.

She's quiet for a few seconds, then coyly asks, "Do *you*, Sir?"

I grin. She has now—realizing it's not up to her. "Yes," I reward, pulling back far enough to reach the button with my free hand. It buzzes to life, and she nearly sobs her relief.

I'm grateful she seems so close, because with this device vibrating so close to my sensitive tip and how worked up I already am, this won't take long. A few moments of push-pull —I've barely found my rhythm—and I can feel the release gathering in my balls. The sensations pool there, collecting.

"I'm close," I grunt.

"Yes, come for me," she moans. "Feels so fucking good. So amazing. *Dios,* your cock is so good. This thing you made me is so good. I love it."

My orgasm hits me like a freight train, robbing me of my senses for an instant that seems to drag on. The pleasure crests, shooting through me like the fire in my veins—a pleasure so intense it verges on pain. My vision whites out, and my head falls forward.

The comedown is slow, like wading through the remnants of a dream towards consciousness. I can see her sweat-slicked body below me, can feel my release coating me inside her. She bounces, rocking on top of the desk, forehead pressed down. "Please, please, please," she whimpers. "I'm so close... I need this so bad."

I shake my head of the thick, disorienting feeling, and pull back. God, she's clutching my thumb tightly... I pull it out too, reticently. After tucking my softening cock away, I crouch down so I'm eye level.

"Do you want my fingers?" I ask.

"Yessss," she hisses.

"Where?"

She pauses, considering it, and glances over her shoulder at me. "My ass..." she whispers.

"Ask better than that." I slap her cheek. The impact stings my hand.

She cries out, but it has the intended effect because she hurries through her request, and it's as complete and perfect as I could want. "Please fuck my ass with your fingers, Sir!"

I shove my pointer and middle fingers into her cunt first, getting them wet with the combination of liquids, and she gasps and tightens around me. The feeling of the vibrator is quite strange, and I drag my fingers along it as I withdraw, making her breath break in her throat.

Still lubed and a little loose from my thumb, my index finger slides into her ass easily. "Do you like it?"

"Yes, more!"

I work my second finger in, and she gasps and moans around the intrusion. "Take it," I rasp, slapping her other cheek firmly and then taking hold of it. I pull, spreading her and making more room for my hand. "You can take it."

Working her over, building to a rhythm that's hard and fast and re-lentless—it's almost better than fucking her. From the side, I get to see the expressions on her face. I get to watch her eyes roll back. I get to watch her body shake and tense as she rubs her thighs together to find the perfect amount of pressure on the vibrator.

And when her orgasm builds, I get to watch as her body tightens, how her brows screw up, and how her mouth parts to let out the little noises of anticipation.

"Oh, *traviesita*," I mock darkly, enjoying delivering the degradation almost as much as I enjoy giving praise. "Are you going to come? Like this? Spread out on my desk, a desperate little mess, begging me to fuck your tight arsehole with my fingers?"

"Oh my *God*," she sobs. "So... close..."

I sink to my haunches and bite her, right in the middle of her thick cheek, still red with my handprint.

The pinch of pain must be what does it. She screeches her release, only remembering to muffle the sound after a second. Her ass clenches and loosens around my fingers in an unpredictable pattern as she shudders through her orgasm.

When she collapses against the desk, boneless, satisfied and spent, I sit back in my chair and pull her onto my lap. We're both sweaty messes, covered in fluids and lube. I couldn't care less.

"I can't believe you bit my butt," she murmurs.

"Seems like you liked it just fine."

With a little laugh, she cuddles against my chest, humming contentedly with her eyes closed, and my heart soars. After a few minutes of closeness, when our pulses have slowed, and the sweat has gone cool in the air, she rears back. "What were you doing when I came in?"

"Hmm?" I say, stroking her upper arm. I heard her, but I need a second for my brain to come back online.

"When I came into the room. You had a book?"

"Oh, just some notes," I reply, swallowing the sudden thickness.

"Notes about the General?" she asks. "Can I see?"

"They're barely legible," I misdirect. "Just some musings, trying to keep my thoughts straight."

She swallows, eyes dropping. "You said you'd let me know when you needed help. I guess I just thought I'd be in here with you—that we'd be trying to track this guy down together."

I inhale deeply and hug her back to my chest. "I don't want to stress you out. You've been enjoying your downtime, yes? Finding your place in the house?"

"Sure, making dinner with Eleanor and nearly slicing off my finger," she mutters. "What if I want my place to be in here with you?"

Fuck. There's nothing I want more. I just... can't.

"You're too... distracting, Madison. Every time you're in here, all I can think about is doing what we just did."

Not easily deterred, she shrugs. "Well, there are like a million rooms in this house. Give me one to take over, and I'll be like a remote coworker. We already know we make a good team that way."

Another denial springs to my lips, but I reconsider. That territory, I can navigate. I already know how to parse out jobs from a distance. "That's not a bad idea," I say.

"I'm chock-full of not-bad ideas," she teases, grinning. "Some might even say good ideas."

I chuckle. "Of course."

"Look, Wesley, as much as I like *this* kind of work," she says, waggling her eyebrows suggestively, "I'm ready to do something with my day other than bouncing on it, watching weird Japanese horror movies—"

"They're not weird—that's closed-minded."

"—and taking bubble baths. Put me in, coach!" she grins.

I smile back and tuck her hair behind her ear. "I'll work on getting you a setup of your own."

34

MADISON

Caught like a rat in a trap.

Wesley is hiding something. The thought is twisting in my stomach, filling me with anxiety. It's all I could think about every time I saw him yesterday or this morning—the look of surprise on his face when I opened the door. Like he'd been caught.

There's something in that book he doesn't want to show me. Maybe he didn't even want me to see the book at all.

Why won't he let me help him? Surely he knows that two heads are better than one? There's so much data on that drive, it would take him the rest of his life to go through it all by hand. I know he's writing a program to sort it for him. I know he knows that's firmly in my wheelhouse.

So why is he keeping me at arm's length?

I don't know how to reconcile the two sides of him. There's the part that holds me tenderly, fucks me roughly, croons praise into my ear in the worst Spanish accent I've ever heard, and makes me feel like the most beautiful woman in the world. And then there's the part that looks at me with a kind of shuttered fear, like he's some kind of crone who's seen into the future and doesn't like what happens. That part of him is too far away for me to reach, like the top cabinets in that ridiculous kitchen where they haven't gotten a stepstool because "no one has needed one."

I don't care if he thinks he's protecting me. I don't care if he thinks he's taking care of me. I want to know. I want to help. I want him to treat me like an adult and stop assuming he knows what's best for me.

And I really want to know what's in that notebook.

I wait until he takes a trip to the bathroom and slip inside his office. Some Bills greets me with a trill and winds through my legs. "Not now, buddy," I whisper, feeling weird for sneaking around like this.

Tossing a look over my shoulder to ensure I'm alone, I creep towards his desk. I don't remember which drawer he put the book in, so I try a few near the top. Normal office supplies—pens, paper clips, a tangle of USB cords that came with electronics but are too short to be useful—and no notebook. When I get to the top middle drawer, I realize it's one with an extra compartment at the top. A secret compartment.

A *locked* secret compartment. It doesn't budge when I jerk on the handle lip.

"What are you doing, Madison?"

My heart leaps into my throat, and my head whips up to find Wesley in the doorway. He's got a fresh can of energy drink in his hand, so I was apparently wrong to assume he was headed for the bathroom.

Caught. Caught like a rat in a trap.

And what does a rat do? It attacks—it bites back. "Why is your desk drawer locked?" I accuse.

He frowns and crosses the room, setting the can down on his desk and standing over me. He's already almost a foot taller, but he seems bigger right now for some reason. Maybe it's the shame of sneaking around that makes me feel smaller. I square my shoulders and lift my chin.

"Madison, why were you trying to get into my desk?"

"Oh, we're doing a question for a question?" I ask, setting my jaw. "What was that black book I saw yesterday?"

His eyes drop to the drawer, a pretty clear tell. "Notes. I told you—"

"Why do you keep notes locked up?" I interrupt, feeling my indignation rising as his expression closes off.

He opens his mouth, then blows out a breath and shakes his head. "Habit, I suppose."

Not good enough. I ask what I really want to know. "Why are you shutting me out of this investigation?"

He frowns. "Madison, I'm not. I told you I was going to get a computer setup for you—"

"So you can sit in here and only feed me the pieces you want me to see. I'm not stupid, Wesley. You want this to be like how it was, when you were the one in control, managing everything from the middle of your web—when you didn't have to tell me anything and I just did whatever you wanted. That's not how it is anymore."

"Madison, calm down," he says slowly.

Oh, he did not. *He fucking did not.*

I take a deep breath, knowing that the calmer and more rationally I lay out my feelings, the easier it will be for him to hear them. "Do you remember what you said at Sunset Hills? I was ready to handle this myself, but you said we could track the General down *together*. You said *I can't do this without my favorite spider*."

He reaches up and tugs at his hair, clearly hating this confrontation. "It's easier for me to just do it. Only I know what to look for."

"So tell me and we can do it together," I suggest, waving my arm for emphasis. "Divide and conquer—it would be a pain at first when you had to explain it, but ultimately faster."

"It's... not that simple."

"Then explain it to me!"

"I..." he sighs in exasperation. "I know you're trying to be helpful, but I don't need your help—I only needed your information. I'm sorry if you feel misled."

The anger that's been steadily rising towards a boil nearly spills over. I scowl at him. "You're sorry if I feel misled," I say with a shake of my head. What a bullshit apology. "Well, I do. I feel misled. Why am I even here, Wesley?" I ask, shifting away when he reaches for me, responding to the hurt in my tone. "Why did you bring me here?"

"You were in danger," he replies instantly, the excuse locked and loaded. "This is the only place I could keep you safe—that we could be together and not have to worry about other assassins or attempts on your life."

"That we could be together," I repeat, feeling like the words are somehow hollow. "Oh, I see. I'm here to be your little sex doll—stress relief for you. I'm good enough to fuck, but not to tell the important stuff."

His face twists, and I realize how horrible that was.

"I'm sorry, I didn't mean that. You don't treat me like a doll. You never have." I sigh, feeling even worse now. His face is still a mask, hiding his genuine emotions behind the excuses and deferrals. "Just... be real with me. That's all I want. Tell me what changed?"

"Nothing changed," he argues. "It's never been safe for you to be part of this. Your work has exposed you to certain things, but it's different on this side of it. Nicole and Eleanor understand—"

Having their names thrown at me in this moment of anger is what does it. I snap. "What if I don't want to be like Nicole and Eleanor? What if I don't want to be just some helpless damsel, sitting uselessly on the sidelines of my own life—"

"Wow." The word is a soft exhale, and we both spin.

Nicole is in the doorway of the office, hand poised like she was about to knock. I don't need to ask how long she's been there, because the wide-eyed look says it all. She heard what I said in anger, completely out of context.

Fuck. *Fuck!*

"Nicole—" I start.

She turns her head to the side, avoiding eye contact as she clears her throat. "Um, Dimitri asked me to come get you for training. Don't worry. I'll tell him you don't need any of us."

"Nicole!" I beg, feeling hot, prickly tears behind my eyes. I'm torn as she turns to leave, wanting to chase her and explain myself, knowing it probably won't matter, and feeling tethered because this isn't over with Wesley yet...

"Fuck! That's just... great. Perfect. Just another reason to hate bitchy Madison, who thinks she's better than everyone else." I press the heels of my hands to my eyes to try to hold back the tears.

I wanted to like it here. I wanted so badly to be part of something, to have friends, to be one of the members of this tight-knit group. I even kind of thought this time it could work out because I had an *in*—I was Wesley's girl.

But apparently I'm not. Or, I can't be fully. Just like everything else, it has to be on his terms. And I'm not part of the group, either—I'm stuck outside, saying all the wrong things and making people who already don't like me even more pissed off.

To make it all worse, it's my own fault because I let my guard down. I let myself believe it would work.

This is what happens when you care about what other people think. They make you feel stupid for it.

I feel his hands on my shoulders, a clumsy comfort. "Stop," I grit out, pulling away. "I won't be with someone who doesn't care what I want because they think they know better. So either tell me what's going on, or I'm leaving."

"Leaving?" he repeats, voice dropping. It's like a question and a warning all at once.

"I'll go sleep outside with George," I threaten.

When he smiles at that, I almost slap him across the face. It's full of relief, not humor, and I realize he thought I meant I'd leave the mansion. And that just makes me mad all over again. "Oh, don't worry, *Sir*," I hiss. "I'm not going anywhere. You made sure of that."

I whirl and storm out of the room.

"Madison!"

"*Don't* follow me!" I call back.

He calls after me once more, but gives up when I don't even pause. He probably realizes I need to cool off. And honestly, if he did try to come after me right now, I probably would slap him.

Not that I condone violence against your partner. Just... I'm all fired up and not feeling very rational.

I glance out the kitchen window, finding George's doghouse on the other side of the pool patio. He's asleep, head resting on his front legs. Despite the swirling anger and hurt, I smile to myself, remembering my threat. Maybe it's not such a bad idea—that house looks roomy. Plus, I need to lick my wounds anyway.

My phone buzzes, and I grab it from my pocket. It's an... alarm notification from my security app. When I swipe over to the live video footage to see what triggered it, my stomach and jaw both drop.

Is that... Todd? Is that Todd hefting my desktop computer over his shoulder and trying to sneak out my front door? What... the... fuck? What the fuck is he doing?

My feet start moving immediately, Wesley's name forming on my lips, but I stop myself.

Todd works for SmarTech. He's got a connection to the company we know is part of this. Maybe he even *is* the General...

That one almost makes me laugh out loud. There's no way Todd is the General—the one with a network of hitmen at his disposal; the one not even SpyderMan could find. My dumbass neighbor, who can't even come up with insults that hit? That just... doesn't fit. He doesn't have that reach. He's not capable of that kind of cunning and skill...

But he's just stealing my computer for some reason. And while it's definitely the most valuable thing in my apartment, it's the *only* thing he's taking. That computer has all my private files and years of stolen intel, including everything I took from SmarTech. If the General works at SmarTech and I became a target after I stole that data, it seems logical to me that the guy wants it back. And Todd has 'disposable henchman' written all over him.

Or maybe Todd is just being a douchebag.

Either way, the point is, if I tell Wesley, I won't get to find out what's going on. The fact that there's a connection here to SmarTech and the General means that I get cut out *for my own safety*.

But... if I check it out myself...

A plan starts to form, and I know I need to act quickly. If I can catch Todd red-handed, it would be best. Since Tío already faked my death, I probably don't have to worry about assassins hanging around my place, but the police think I'm missing, so I can't be stupid. I need a disguise, a car—Eleanor probably won't mind if I borrow hers—and a gun.

A *loaded* gun.

I fly up the stairs to the room I've been sharing with Wesley and change into some different clothes. First rule of a disguise is not being recognizable, so my usual uniform is out. I shuck on some of Wesley's sweats, trying to ignore how tight they are across my hips. I look like a curvy teenage hoodlum. If I grab a hat from the coat closet downstairs, and some big shades, it won't be immediately obvious who I am to any of my neighbors, let alone strangers on the street.

Checking the hallway to ensure I won't get caught sneaking out, I descend into the foyer and pull what I need from the closet.

For the most part, this place keeps people *out*—but I'll need a code at the gate. Lucky for me, Eleanor is the type who uses the same code everywhere, and I watched her type it into her phone the other day. So I grab her keys from the communal dish by the door and waltz out to the garage, feeling like I'm breaking all kinds of laws. My heart is racing.

The car starts with no issues, and I barrel down the drive. Holding my breath, I type Eleanor's code into the keypad. When the gate swings towards me, I bite down on a smile.

While I make the drive back across the city, I consider my plan. Getting inside the building will be easy enough, but to be most effective I'll need to surprise Todd. That means breaking into his place. I don't know how to pick a lock... so how do I get in?

I find a spot right out front, check my reflection in the mirror to ensure the hat covers my hair and the glasses are doing what they should to hide my face. Satisfied, I trot up the front steps. Going to my own door is an autopilot response, so I force myself to walk to the next door down the hall. And I stare at it.

I mean, I could just *knock*... right? I could cover the peephole and point my gun at him when he answers the door. But there are lots of ways that could go wrong—he could see it and scream for help, he could slam the door, he could be overly cautious and open it with the chain so I can't slip through, he could be wearing headphones and not hear my knock...

Or... I eye the door handle. It can't... it can't be that easy, can it? No way that douchebag sits in his apartment with the door unlocked—

The knob turns in my hand.

Fuck. Yes. Badass spy Madison, reporting for duty.

Since the immediate living areas are empty and our apartments have the same layout, I know exactly how to get to his bedroom. I find him in there, sitting on the floor with a screwdriver, my computer propped between his legs. He looks up when I step into the doorway, and his face turns bright red, then pales out completely.

"M-Madison?" he croaks. "You... you're supposed to be dead!"

I grin, because he genuinely looks like he's seen a ghost, and lift my gun. "Boo!"

35

WESLEY

What?

My phone buzzes, but I ignore it.

"She'll come around."

I close my eyes and drop my head into my hands, refusing to look at the open doorway and see the sympathy and pity on Mac's face that I can hear in his voice.

"You heard that?" I ask, mostly for confirmation.

"I think the entire house did," he observes with a quiet chuckle. "I'll tell ya, man—she's little, but she can really holler."

I sigh as he enters the room and drags the red chair next to my desk, like he always does for our meetings. He kicks out his legs, crossing them at the ankle, laces his hands behind his head, and fixes me with a look. "Wanna talk about it?"

Yes.

No.

I sigh again. "She's got a right to be mad," I offer lamely. "I love that she wants to help, and I know that she *can*—that she's capable—but..."

"You want to keep her out of it because it's safer for her," Mac finishes for me, nodding. "Been there."

"You haven't been *here*, exactly. Eleanor didn't fight you tooth and nail to be involved," I point out wryly.

His grin is easy. "Nope," he says, popping the p. "And, if you'll re-call, when she wanted to help, I *let* her. Obviously, I was the better boyfriend."

"You mean that time when she helped and ended up carjacked and nearly shot by the man we were after?" I return evenly, wiping the self-satisfied smirk right off his face.

"Well, that's what happens when we go with your plans. People tend to get shot." He shrugs after a second. "Especially Dimitri."

Both our phones buzz—his making a sound that I know to be the no-tification from the gate when someone leaves—and Mac grabs his from his pocket. He swipes through, eyes flicking across the message. "It's Eleanor leaving. She said something about grocery shopping earlier."

"Can it be that simple?" I wonder. At Mac's raised brow, I nod at his phone, indicating Eleanor's departure and Mac's ease. "She leaves the house and you're just... all right with it?"

"Oh, I seem all right with it?" Mac asks, brows shooting up. "Nice. My poker face is getting better."

As intended, I crack a smile.

"The only way I maintain any chill whatsoever about her leaving is that she wears a tracker in her watch, she's got one in her purse, and there's one in that cute little Mini Cooper she wanted so bad. If I could get her to swallow one every morning, I'd do that, too."

It's on the tip of my tongue to offer to make a subdermal tracker that wouldn't hurt too badly and would last years before the battery needed to be replaced, but it's not really in the spirit of the current conversation. "But it works for you?"

He shrugs. "For now. I'm not stubborn enough to think it can be like this forever. I guess..." he rubs the back of his neck. "I guess that's why I'm not too torn up about this. You know—taking down the General and everything. The end of it all."

The end. I suppose that's what this is—what it will be. I've been too focused to really think about it, but without the General, what's keeping us together?

"It's my out," Mac continues. "It's my chance. *Our* chance."

I'm taken aback, but his words ring a bell. It's been a while since he brought it up, but Felix got Mac thinking about his exit strategy at the restaurant all those months ago.

I wonder if Dimitri sees it the same way—that this is his chance to get out and start his life with Nicole properly, or if the threat of the remaining Bratva members who want him dead casts too long of a shadow over that possibility.

Then I wonder why I *haven't* seen it that way. Has my single-mindedness, thinking only of my goal, eclipsed the potential for life after I've achieved it?

"This life has been great in a lot of ways. I... I got a family out of it. I got my girl out of it," he adds, tone dropping with seriousness. "But I'm not just *me* anymore. I've got Eleanor to think about, and she doesn't want to be jailed here because some fucker out there wants to hurt me. We worked it out as best we could, compromising until we were both happy enough, but I... fuck, man. I don't want to compromise on this anymore. I'd rather just know she was safe and not go insane with worry every time she leaves the house." He heaves a breath. "If the choice is *this life* or her, it's not a choice. It's her every time."

"Yeah," I say softly, feeling it in my bones.

Mac leans forward and claps me on the shoulder. "It'll be all right, Short Round. You and Mads'll figure your shit out."

My lips twitch at the nickname.

"Now, since I'm here, why don't you give me an update? Whatcha got?"

"Fuck all," I say, impossibly more miserable. It's a reminder I didn't need of the fact that if I just gave in and did what Madison wanted—brought her in, accepted her help—I'd probably be much further along.

"Really?" Mac asks, shocked.

"I've got all this data, but it's difficult to refine. Unsurprisingly, my initial search combinations for 'the General' yielded nothing. Obviously it's an alias, and there are plenty of people within the SmarTech framework who have some relation to the word."

Mac chuckles, but it's not with humor. "Sure. Makes sense."

"And once I filtered out anyone with a history as a 'general' of some kind—post masters, general education, etc—I'm left with a handful of names who lead me down dead ends. People with no connection to the previous hits, or no access to the kind of resources the General would have."

"You're going through SmarTech's client files?" he asks, scratching his jaw with his knuckles.

I nod. "And employee files. I think it's more likely it's an employee."

"But you checked the client files for previous targets?"

"I did. They're all in there, Mac," I say, seriously. "Even the names we didn't take. It's still possible it's a coincidence, since SmarTech is used by half the country, but the likelihood gets smaller and smaller with each confirmed name. We're sitting at around 0.001%."

He whistles. "So the General is someone working at SmarTech, finding hits from a database of people who use their software? Fuck, man. That's bonkers."

If he only knew... "It is."

"He'd have to be pretty high up the food chain, right? To have access to all the data—everyone's names?"

"Certain roles at the company would have access to more, but essentially yes. I'd expect so."

He leans his elbows on his knees, threading his fingers in the space between. "You think someone is... executing a personal vendetta?"

I give a half shrug. "I must admit, I'd begun to agree with Felix's assessment—I thought perhaps it was a criminal, paving the way to sit at the top."

"Does that still fit if they work at SmarTech?"

I sigh and rub my eyes. "I don't think so. I don't know. It's clear SmarTech is somehow involved. I just don't quite know how. I don't know who's pulling the strings. I don't understand the motive. I feel like this investigation is all over the place—it's not following normal patterns I'd expect to see."

"You'll figure it out. I've got faith, man."

"Thanks."

Just at that moment Eleanor breezes down the hallway, bottle of water in hand, headed for the stairs. Mac throws her a fond look, then does a double take. I do the same.

"Wait, Eleanor? If she's here, who was at the gate?" I ask, terror rising in my throat because I already know.

"It was her car," Mac says slowly, connecting the same dots.

I pull my phone out. The notification I ignored a moment ago flashes across my screen—an alarm from Madison's flat that the system was disabled and someone went inside. I pull up the feed from all the cameras I left in there ages ago and rewind to the time of the alarm.

Son of a bitch.

"Fuck!" I cry, shooting out of my seat.

"What?" Mac wants to know, moving out of my way then following me as I charge through the hallway, into the foyer.

"What?" Eleanor echoes from the landing of the stairs leading down to the gym, purely confused.

"Madison's neighbor broke into her flat. Stole her computer."

"What?! Fuck," Mac says.

"What?" Eleanor repeats, panic rising and mingling with the confusion. "What's going on?"

"Madison just left," Mac tells her. "She got the same notification Wes did—probably went to go get her computer."

"What?! With all those bad guys still after her?" Eleanor gasps. "Oh my God! Go get her!"

"I'll take my bike; it's faster. You follow in the van," I bark out to Mac as I jerk open the front door. I don't even stop to make sure he heard or confirmed.

I shove my helmet on, tear out of the garage and fly down the drive, only pausing long enough to enter my code and to let the gate swing open just far enough for me to slip through. Then I take to the streets. I'm going out of my mind, caught in a loop of horrible possibilities.

A hitman lying in wait, despite the job appearing complete.

A police officer stationed outside her flat recognizes her.

She gets into a fucking car accident.

Fuck! Worry twists every possible terrible outcome and makes it seem not only possible, but likely.

I drop my bike to the ground when I arrive, and I certainly don't take the time to remove and store my helmet. I'm up the steps and through the front door in moments, so pissed at needing a key to get through the inner door that I nearly break the glass. I'm reaching for my picks when someone comes through the front, on the phone and blithely unaware as I slip in behind her.

I slow, considering Madison's door. If I know her, she went right for Todd. So I do too, reaching for the gun I shoved into the back of my jeans on my mad dash out of the mansion.

The door is shut firmly, but unlocked. I creep in as silently as possible, my heart pounding so loud in my ears I almost can't hear her voice.

"Oh, you really did it this time, Toddy-boy. Hot Toddy. T-bone. Can I call you T-bone?"

"It was my f-football nickname," Todd replies shakily.

"Of course it was; your name starts with a T."

Oh, thank God. She sounds unharmed. Almost bored.

I move far enough into the room that I can see them. Todd is duct taped around the ankles and—I assume, since I can't see them behind his back—wrists, sitting in the center of a bed with no covers or pillows, and Madison is on the other side of the room, her gun pointed lazily in his direction. Her computer lies on the floor between them, missing several key pieces that indicate someone has begun disassembling it. The floor creaks under my foot, and I remove my helmet.

She whirls, her eyes widening at the unexpected interruption as she hides the gun behind her back. She realizes it's me and relaxes—then realizes what my being here means, and tenses all over again.

She swallows. "Hey, buddy…"

"Madison," I reply calmly.

She's not hurt. She has the situation under control. If I seem upset or worried or angry, I'll take her credibility away from her, and that might make Todd stupid or brave. I've seen it before.

But fuck, I'm practically shaking with anger and fear…

"Would you step out here with me for a moment?" I say, forcing an evenness into my voice.

Todd senses an opportunity and leaps in. Perhaps he doesn't recognize me. "Dude, help me! She's crazy! She came in here with a gun and tied me up—"

I hold up my hand. "Shut the fuck up," I tell him, then crook my finger at her.

She presses her lips together and spins back around to Todd, flashing him a saccharine smile. "Would you excuse us for a moment? And remember, if you scream, I *will* shoot your dick off."

"She will," I echo seriously.

She follows me into the main room, closing Todd into his bedroom amidst the sound of his soft sobbing. "Wesley!" she whispers excitedly, barely containing herself. "You'll never believe what I found out—"

Letting my helmet fall, I grab both of her upper arms in my hands. "Madison, what the fuck were you thinking?!" I whisper back.

The excitement in her eyes dims, realizing I wasn't actually fine with what I walked in on. "I... I'm sorry, but you've got to hear this—"

"I don't. We're going. *Now.*"

Suddenly outraged, she fights against me, twisting until I'm forced to let go or risk hurting her. "Stop! Listen to me!"

"No, you'll listen to *me*," I fire back, livid. "This was unbelievably stupid, Madison. You put yourself in so much danger, I'm shocked I didn't find you dead on the ground. You want me to think you're smart and capable? Well, fucking act like it! Every second we spend here is another second you're at risk of being discovered. Of being *murdered.*"

She scowls back, matching my fire. "Todd confessed to me," she hisses. "He told me that my old boss, Fred, told him I was dead and bribed him to steal my computer by offering him a promotion. That means Fred is part of this—he knows something, or maybe *he's* even the General."

I grind my jaw. "Or maybe he was just acting on orders, unaware of what's really going on."

She shakes her head. "No! He thought I was dead. But I haven't been *declared* dead—someone on the outside of this would think I was just missing. Fred knows about the hit. He knows someone took credit for my death. Todd said he had specific details, like that I'd been shot. Pictures."

I pull back. "That..." That's actually a good point.

She sees my hesitation, and the excitement sparks back in her eyes. "He told Todd to steal my hard drive and bring it to SmarTech. And I was thinking, what if we let him?"

"He'll tell Fred you're still alive," I argue.

"He's already seen me," she fires back. "What are you going to do, kill him to keep it a secret?"

I sigh harshly. "If Fred is the General, or knows him, we'll be back where we started with a $10 million price on your head. Probably more. Not to mention, it will get Felix's contact removed from the system if it's discovered he faked that hit. The General might even put out a hit on him in retribution."

"Oh," she says, shoulders dropping. "I didn't think of that."

I watch as she pulls out her phone and starts tapping out a message to—presumably—Felix. She waits a few seconds, then scans his reply. "Tío says it's fine," she assures me, tucking her phone back in the pocket of her—my?—sweatpants. "His guy who faked it can just get back in if he's kicked out, and he used an alias so they won't be able to track him to put a hit out on him."

I sigh. I really need to find out how Felix knows all this shit. "So you want to let Todd tell Fred?"

"I want to let him bring my hard drive to Fred *with* a listening device attached to it," she suggests, eyes bright, pleased with her own cleverness. "You've got some in that van, right?"

"Mac's bringing them," I say, realizing I've just lost. It's a good idea—even I can see that.

It doesn't make what she did any better, though, and the only thing that mollifies me is that she clearly realizes this discussion isn't over. But she smiles at me with grim resolve and opens Todd's door.

He straightens immediately, pretending like he wasn't just trying to saw through the tape on his feet with the blunt edge of his bedframe. Rookie move—always start with the hands.

"Good news, T-bone. We're gonna get you that promotion."

Todd looks baffled, and a bit terrified by the news. "W-what?"

Madison grins. "We're giving you the hard drive."

The fear shifts to utter and complete confusion. "What?"

36

WESLEY

An impossible choice

Mac rolls in some time later, and I bring Madison's computer out to the van while she babysits her neighbor with the gun—her suggestion, in order to limit the number of times she's out on the street. I disassemble her machine, retrieve the solid-state drive, and take apart one of the earpieces I have on hand to make a tiny listening device. I'm not terribly pleased with my work, since it sticks out against the wire connections and obviously doesn't belong, but it also doesn't look like a listening device. It ought to buy us at least some overheard personal conversations—until he tries plugging it into a motherboard, anyway.

I just hope we hear enough that it's worth the consequences.

After Madison untapes her victim and offers him the SSD, she threatens to shoot off his dick if he tells Fred she's alive—though she fully expects him to—and we leave. Mac agrees to bring Eleanor to pick up her car, and heads back with the van.

Wordlessly, I hand Madison my helmet. Perhaps it's my imagination, but she hugs me tighter than she ever has on the ride back.

She follows me from the garage without a word, nervously clacking her nails against each other and chewing on her lower lip. I can't tell exactly what she's feeling, but I'm fairly certain that if I'm hoping for genuine contrition and an apology, I'll be disappointed. And I'm right.

"I know you're mad," she starts as soon as the office door closes firmly behind her. "But that went so well! This is the biggest clue we've had yet, and we're so close now!"

The rage that was so sharp moments ago has dulled into something quieter and controlled. "The ends do not justify the means when your life is at risk, Madison." I shake my head as I drop to the couch. Some Bills promptly stands from his curled position, arching his back in a stretch, and sits, regarding us with sleepy eyes.

"If I hadn't been there to question him, he never would have spilled the *frijoles*. And it's fine, right? I'm fine. I took precautions. I *loaded* my gun. I knew you were coming, and I knew you'd bring the..." She trails off, then frowns. "Wait, I never sent you that text. How *did* you know?"

No sense denying it now, I suppose. "I installed cameras in your flat when I was watching you to determine if I wanted to kill you." I reach out and scratch Some Bills behind the ear when he rubs against my arm.

"That's..." She falls back a step. "Um... I don't know exactly how to feel about that."

"I also watched you masturbate from your closet before we ever even met in person."

"What?!" she hisses. "Wesley, just because you're mad at me, that doesn't mean I'm not allowed to be mad at you for something else—"

"Be mad. You ought to be. Because men like me are *not good people*," I say slowly, emphasizing the words. "I don't know how else to get it through to you. Your life is in danger, and you don't seem to care."

She rolls her eyes. "Of course I care. Come on, Wesley—you don't genuinely think I just charge into things with no regard for my own safety. That's not what this is about."

"You're under my protection—"

"You mean your control," she snorts.

"—and it's on me if you get hurt!"

"Stop saying that! It's not your fault if I get hurt! Stop trying to... take responsibility for my actions! It's so weird."

"It *would* be my fault. You have no idea." I blow out a long breath and drop my head into my hands.

The couch shifts under me as Madison drops onto the adjacent cushion, leaning in with a desperate look in her eye. "Then how about you just fucking tell me? Tell me why you won't let me help you sort the data. Tell me why you're really after the General. Tell me what that black notebook you hide in your drawer is. Tell me why you won't trust me!" she urges, finishing on a cry.

I want to. The guilt that's been keeping me awake at night for years bubbles to my lips, wanting to spill over and spill out.

Tell her.

God, I want to. I've wanted to for ages. But after all this time, I... I don't know how.

Keeping unnecessary details from Dimitri and Mac is one thing—even if they had known the truth, it wouldn't have changed anything about what we've done or how we did it—but keeping the truth from Madison is quite another. The omission feels much more like a lie with her, and not just because it was my actions—my mistake, my worst shame—that ultimately wrought all this, but because I want nothing more than to have her at my side, bouncing ideas with me and teasing my coding choices. Acting as a partner. *My* partner.

But secrets are tricky things, and they can sit so heavy that it feels like they're part of you. It's like a boulder nestled in a perfectly shaped divot—trying to move means working against gravity, and the boulder falls too easily back into place. It belongs in that space, just as the lie belongs, covering and crushing the truth, its weight borne by the conscience.

And the reason for holding back is the same as it ever was. It's not safe for her to know; it's not safe for *anyone* to know. Especially before I'm certain I've found the man I've been looking for.

"It's not that I don't trust you..." I run my hands through my hair and sit back, glancing over.

She sees the decision on my face, and her shoulders round in defeat. "You say that, and I think you might even believe it, but I know that's what it is. At the end of the day, though, it's all about trust. You've been keeping the truth from me in one way or another since the very first day we met," she says softly, eyes downcast. "And I know you had your reasons, and I know you think your reasons are good, but... I have always been honest with you.

"I have always been 100% myself with you—and only because *you* made me feel safe enough to do it. You are the only person who's ever had all of me—not just the real me, but my loyalty and my respect and my trust. You *saw* me. You made me feel seen, even when we'd never even actually seen each other."

She shakes her head and wipes under her eyes, getting rid of a tear before I can see it. "You were the only person I wasn't supposed to have to worry about. And now I feel like I never really knew you at all," she finishes. The final twist of the knife.

My heart cracks, splintering into a thousand pieces, an echo of the broken look on her face. I've hurt her. Deeply. And I know only the truth can fix it.

This is the cost of a lie. I always knew there would come a time when the price was too steep. But as much as I want to tell her... it goes against every fiber of my being.

All my life, I've controlled the flow of information. It's what I do. It's more than what I'm good at—it's who I am. I'm the spy master. The keeper of secrets. My web of lies is woven from the finest gossamer, hiding in plain sight. It's exhausting. Isolating. Lonely.

But this is an impossible choice. If I tell her, I risk losing her violently, like I lost the others. If I don't tell her, I risk losing her heart.

What is the point of a life that she's not part of? What am I protecting if I can't have her at the end of all this? Only one of those outcomes means losing her forever—the secret can only hurt her if she were to tell anyone, and if I were ever going to trust someone to keep my secrets, it would be her.

With a deep sigh, I stand, move to the door, and click the lock into place. If I'm going to do this, I can't risk an interruption. She frowns at me, suspicious of the ominous sound.

"All right, Madison," I say, going to lean against the desk in the spot Dimitri usually occupies. I'm only a few feet away, but no doubt she'll be happy for the distance when she learns the truth. "I'll tell you everything. It can't leave this room."

Her expression irons out, and she sits back, nodding to me to proceed.

"In my early 20s, I was recruited to a project. It was top secret—government, I assumed. We were a team of five, held to a very high standard of confidentiality. We worked independently—everyone completed a different piece of the project—and were monitored to ensure we didn't accidentally reveal anything to outsiders or each other."

"That sounds like government work," she agrees.

I inhale shakily. "That was what we all believed. I was recruited for my bit, based on my dissertation—"

"Wait, are you a doctor?" she pipes in, a grin forming at the corners of her mouth. God, it feels like it's been ages since I saw a smile from her.

"PhD, yes."

"Doctor Nerd. Nice." She fishes her phone out of her pocket. I see out of the corner of my eye as she calls up my contact on her phone and changes the title name from Sir to Dr. "Go on. I'm listening."

"Essentially, I created software for data mining and pattern recognition. Very powerful—capable of taking most inputs, sorting massive amounts of information, and producing results that were very easy to refine. That was my part of the project."

She nods, understanding how impressive a tool like that would be—even more so a decade ago.

"Matilda was from the banking industry. She was an expert in cryptocurrency and was writing her second dissertation on identifying patterns for money laundering and illegal transfers. Derrick and Fiona, working together, had created an anonymous messaging platform and a third-party vouching system that created a foundation for trust between participants. They'd intended for it to become a service exchange platform, mostly between neighbors. I'll wash your windows if you'll watch my dog—that kind of thing.

"Xavier—or X as he preferred to be called—was our criminal element. We weren't privy to the details, and he never would have told us himself, but after..." I trail off, my voice breaking. I don't want to get ahead of myself. "I hacked the system and found him. He was... a hitman. I believe they must have used him for his contacts."

All lightheartedness Madison had infused into the room dims suddenly at the mention of hitmen.

I watch as my brilliant mermaid starts piecing it together on her own. I watch her eyes work back and forth, seeing nothing, and a frown line appear between her brows. "So... You're saying you worked on a project that was assembling a database of hitmen and other seasoned criminals, giving them a trusted platform to communicate anonymously, finding dirty money to pay them without being caught, and..." she swallows, making eye contact at last, "had a way to process huge amounts of data to find exactly who you wanted dead."

I nod.

"Whoa." She sits back, shock and horror written in the lines of her face. I nearly wince. I deserve her horror. God knows I've spent these last years regretting every moment I spent on that project.

"None of us put it together quite so succinctly, but then again we all believed—apart from Xavier, I suppose—that we were working on a project for the government. We thought we were doing something for the greater good. Derrick used to make jokes about chiseling it on his gravestone because it was sure to be his greatest accomplishment."

"What happened to him?" Madison asks softly, eyebrows slashed up in the middle in concern. I assume she's picked up on the use of the past tense.

"I was late to work that day," I say, rubbing at my bottom lip, locked in a memory I haven't willingly relived in a long time. "I remember being so upset that the tube was late, because it was the day we were turning in our projects. We were going to get lunch to celebrate. Sushi, because Fiona had never had it before. Odd, the things you remember...

"I was in a hurry, so it didn't occur to me that the building was oddly quiet. When I got to the second floor... The carpet squished under my foot—that was what alerted me. I thought I'd stepped in spilled water or something but... It was blood."

"They killed everyone on the project?" she asks.

"They killed everyone," I correct. "The janitor. The receptionist. The security guards."

Her lower lip wobbles. "How did you escape?"

"Luck," I laugh bitterly, hating the word almost as much as I hate the memory. "The janitor had similar tattoos. I think they must have assumed he was me."

"You must have been so scared," she whispers.

I nod vaguely, still locked in the awful memory. "I got out. Changed the coroner's records, so it appeared I had died with everyone else. I started digging and found out more about the company that commissioned the project. I found a few of the stakeholders—asked my questions; had my revenge. One of the idiots told me the plan—I was too blindsided by rage to even figure it out on my own, then. He's the one who connected the dots for me, told me the grand idea of a private hitman for hire platform. Turned out they'd sold our work to the highest bidder, and neither party wanted any loose ends or witnesses or possibility for replication."

"Who was the buyer?" She swallows. "SmarTech?"

I shrug. "I couldn't get anyone to tell me who the buyer was, so I took on the search myself, primarily on the dark web. A few years ago I stumbled upon something that felt familiar and I realized I'd found the platform Derrick and Fiona built. From there, I followed the process for verification, got myself into their list of contacts, and I've been working for 'the General' ever since, hoping that eventually if I collected enough pieces of the puzzle, I'd learn who he was and I'd know who was responsible for what happened." As if on cue, my computer fan powers off due to inactivity, making the silence in the room feel more oppressive.

"And now, after everything we've learned since your name came up... it seems as if someone at SmarTech was the buyer, yes. They're using SmarTech's database of personal information about their customers to identify targets."

She digests that. "Mac and Dimitri... are you going to tell them?"

"I planned to. I always planned to tell them. But... after—once we killed the man responsible. I can't predict how they'll react. I'd much rather ask forgiveness than permission."

"You think they'll abandon you when they find out the truth?"

"No," I say sadly. "But knowing about this project got everyone who worked on it killed. I couldn't let that happen here. Until I was sure, it was safest for everyone if I didn't say a word—especially because knowing the truth wouldn't have altered the plan in any way. It doesn't make it any more or less dangerous that we've all decided to kill the General."

She nods, but chews at her bottom lip as if her agreement is begrudging. "Okay, but that's..." she blows out a long breath. "That's so crazy."

I fight the grimace. Her reaction is better than I'd hoped for—she hasn't looked at me in horror for what I've done—but it's not forgiveness either. I can hear the gears turning as she works through the information.

"So, you see now. You see why it will be my fault if you're hurt because of this. Everything that's happened... it's *all* my fault. Every death is on my head, even if I didn't pull the trigger or wield the knife."

When her head lifts, her expression is almost haunted. There's horror—but it's on my behalf, not directed at me. "Wesley, that's a lot of guilt you're holding onto."

"Survivor's guilt," I agree. "But it doesn't change the fact that it's my responsibility to right the wrongs that wouldn't have happened without me. This tool is much too powerful, and it's gotten into the wrong hands. I have to destroy it."

She's silent for what feels like a long time, and when she speaks her voice is almost too low for me to hear. "You guys have taken a lot of really bad people off the streets. I know that saying it could have been worse doesn't mean much when you're carrying so much guilt, but it's true."

"I know," I nod. "It's one of the few comforts I've had."

"Okay." She stands, approaching me slowly and lifts a hand to reach out for me, but pulls back. That aborted gesture might as well have pulled my heart out with it, but it's no more than I deserve. "I need to... um... I need some time. I need to think about this."

"Of course."

"I won't say anything to anyone. I promise."

"Thank you."

She heads for the door. Hand on the knob, she turns. "Wesley? Thank you for telling me."

Her tone is too sad for me to take any comfort in the words. I nod, and she nods back, then gently closes the door, leaving me in the office with all my darkest thoughts.

Some Bills headbutts my shin, demanding attention, and I smile down at him. "At least she left me some comfort," I say, folding over to scratch behind his ears.

37

MADISON

Well... my flabbers are gasted.

After I apologize profusely to Eleanor for "stealing"—her word, not mine—her car, I hole myself up in one of the guest bedrooms. There's only one that has a full setup with a bed, and I vaguely remember Wesley telling me Dimitri slept on the same floor as him before Nicole. I grab some blankets from the linen closet, lay on the bare mattress in the unfamiliar, empty room, and wrap myself up in a burrito of emotion.

I'm trying to process the depth of everything Wesley told me, but I think I've reached the end of my capacity to think. I just keep turning the same things over and over in my head—that he helped make this software, that he narrowly escaped with his life, that he's been carrying this secret for almost 10 years...

I can barely comprehend the full brunt of the guilt he's been dealing with—the sour, poisonous emotions that he's kept carefully hidden away. I can understand why he feels like it's his fault—the General never would have existed without his work. But he didn't know what would happen. I'm sure he feels like he *should* have figured it out, but that's hindsight.

All his overbearing tendencies make sense now—it makes sense why he'd feel like it was his fault that I was hurt. It makes sense that he'd react to potential threats by trying to shield me from them.

Frankly, I don't even care about the software and all that. I'm stuck on the lies. I'm stuck on the fact that instead of taking my trust and giving me his, he shut me out. Secrets are part of who he is—it's his instinct to close off instead of sharing.

Can I be with someone who's so shaped by deceit?

If he'd done things differently, we might never have met. So now *I'm* feeling guilty because despite all the death and loss, I can't bring myself to regret what happened or wish things had turned out differently.

Ugh, now I feel like a bad person.

I'm on a weird sleep schedule anyway, so when my brain finally shuts off and I fall asleep at the crisp hour of 7 PM, I'm not really surprised to wake up and find that it's dark out.

My stomach growls, so I unwind, wipe away the crusted tears, and head downstairs. Poking my head into the hall, I see Wesley's office door is closed. Good. I'm not sure I can face him quite yet.

I creep into the kitchen, almost afraid to make noise. I think... it's empty. For the first time since I got here.

Fuck yeah. This means I get to search for Wesley's junk food stash! Man, I could really go for some empty calories right now.

I'm about halfway through raiding the drawers in the pantry when I hear the French doors open. I freeze, hoping that whoever it is will leave me in peace, but I hear the fridge open and then the screech of chair legs against tile and I sigh, knowing someone is settling in for a midnight snack.

I suck another sigh back in when I see it's Nicole.

She sees me too, and my heart flops over at the odd expression on her face. I remember the last thing she heard me say, and the shuttered look of hurt. She probably doesn't want to see or speak to me right now.

"Um, I was just leaving—"

"Wait," she says softly. "Please. Don't go."

Whoa. *Please?* Bitch, I'm rooted in this spot. They'd need a forklift to move me.

"I was hoping to talk to you, just the two of us."

Her tone doesn't give me pause for once—it's entreating and gentle. Hope swells. I push away the self-doubt that tries to cut it down and head over to the island to take the seat next to her. "Because you *do* want to know how to do that move where you land on Dimitri's face?"

She smiles, and it's much more genuine and much less guarded than I can ever remember. "No. Well... maybe eventually. Not for a while, though. I wanted to say that I'm sorry."

Whoa. My flabbers are gasted.

I was all ready to swallow my pride. I thought at most, she would tell me she was open to hearing *my* apology—and even that would have been cool. I thought I was going to have to explain myself and apologize for what I said... Never in a million years did I think those words would be coming from her!

"I'm sorry too, Nicole. I didn't mean what I said—"

"I know," she nods, then grimaces. "I heard enough of your fight to know what it was really about. It's my fault you've been walking on eggshells, and probably why you were sensitive about it in the first place. I'm sorry for how I've been acting. I've been cold to you, and you really didn't deserve it."

"It's okay," I say casily. "You're protective of this little family you guys have here, and I was an outsider."

She nods, looking down at her hands. "That, and I was... jealous, I think."

"Jealous?" I repeat, stunned out of my smart comments.

She looks uncomfortable. "Yeah. It's horrible of me—again, so sorry—but I knew you'd been attacked and you... you saved *yourself*. It made me feel weak and so pathetic, especially because I've been having these panic attacks. And you're... not weak or pathetic. At all. You're just as smart as Wesley—"

"Smarter, actually," I interject with a wink, making her smile.

"—and you can help them. You... picked at a scab you didn't know was there. Frankly, I'm just realizing it's there." She licks her lips, grappling with her final thought. "The way Dimitri and I met was *tumultuous*. Passionate, but difficult. We had a hard time adjusting to each other, and part of it was because I never felt like I belonged in this world. Still don't, really."

"Ah," I say as the final puzzle piece clicks into place. No wonder she was so sensitive when I called out her profession and argued for my seat at the boy's table. "And I waltzed in—the crazy hacker who can put a guy twice my size on his ass."

"Yeah," she agrees with a little self-deprecating smile. "And it didn't help that you're so cute and charismatic, frankly. But that's my thing. That's not about you and I really shouldn't have made it your problem. I'm sorry about that, too."

I sit back, eyeing her. Her body language is stiff, and her head is hung, like she's truly contrite. I'm betting she's harder on herself than anyone else would ever be. She seems like the type.

"Let me guess..." I say slowly, and Nicole presses her lips together in a grimace, expecting some kind of scathing indictment of her character that she thinks she deserves. I grin, since she's confirming my theory. "September 12th."

Her head comes up, and she frowns. "What?"

"Your birthday."

There's a second of silent confusion, then her lips tip up. "It's the 16th, actually."

I snap, making her jump a little at the sudden noise. I level my pointer finger at her. "I fucking knew you were a Virgo."

At that, she laughs. "Why? Cause all Virgos are total bitches?"

"Yup!" I agree, laughing too. When we settle, and she seems more relaxed, I toss my hair over my shoulder and lean back in the chair. "Of course you're an earth sign. You hate having emotions at all, especially the unpleasant ones, because it's harder to rationalize them and create distance. Makes you lash out sometimes. Don't sweat it; my *abuela* is a Capricorn. I'm used to it."

She sits back and stares at me for a few seconds, her lips falling into a little O. "Whoa," she says softly. "Do you and Eleanor read the same books or something?"

"Depends. Does she read the ones about dudes with giant dongs and bat wings?"

Nicole smiles. "I think so."

"Cool." Not exactly sure what fictional pickles have to do with the science of astrology, but I'll take any opportunity to connect with one of my new housemates. "But seriously, don't sweat it. Honestly, all I heard was that you think I'm cute. Because you are the most gorgeous, sexually intimidating person I've ever met, babe. I'm super duper in love with Wesley, but 10/10 would let you ruin me and call you Mommy any day of the week."

Her cheeks flush a deep red color that makes her look even prettier, then her eyes widen. "You love him?" she asks, totally sidetracked from her own embarrassment at my compliment.

I... oops. Fuck.

Well, yeah, I love him. His confession earlier doesn't really change how I feel. I think that's what's so confusing about it all, if I'm honest. I *want* to choose him. I want to let myself love him. Desperately. I'm just scared.

But I want to. And that's what matters, right?

I grin, feeling impossibly freed by the truth. I love Wesley. I fucking love him!

Glancing back at Nicole, I see her expectant expression, and table my enthusiasm.

Oops. I probably should have told him first. "Um... I mean, yeah. Maybe don't say anything to him?"

She nods, instantly serious, and I know that she'd take any secret I told her to the grave. Another thing I love about earth signs. They're so stinkin' loyal.

"Well, I'm glad. Wesley deserves happiness, and you guys are literally perfect for each other. And I'm sorry again about being so damn territorial. My emotions have been all over the place."

"Why, are you pregnant?" I joke.

When her eyes widen instead of laughing along, the blood drains from my face. "Oh.. Uh..." I panic. Fuck! Not again!

When the hell will I learn? It's supposed to be: think, *then* speak.

She licks her lips and looks around, like she's expecting someone else to pop out from behind a doorway. "Maybe don't say anything?" she repeats my words back to me in a hushed tone.

"I would never," I assure her, feeling like we ought to seal the bond with a secret handshake or pinky promise or blood oath. Wait, that's probably not good for pregnant people... "It explains even more why you reacted that way, though."

She nods. "Yeah. This... bean," she euphemizes, eyes dropping to the curve of her stomach under her flowy pajama shirt, "makes it hard to do anything other than worry about the future."

"Okay, first of all, *bean*? That's adorable. And second... You're worried?" I ask.

"Yeah. I'll... never fit into Dimitri's life like you fit into Wesley's."

I study her. "Yeah, but you don't want to fit into this life. And that's what matters."

"I'm not sure it is." Her hand rests idly over her belly button. "I don't want to, and he's never asked or expected me to. He says he'll leave it all behind. But... it's all he knows. What if he resents having to leave?" she asks quietly, like she's afraid of saying the thought too loud and making it true.

"Does he have to? You're *making* him?"

"What? No! Of course not. He says he wants to. And with all this stuff with the General, it seems imminent—like it's really going to happen. But what if, once this is all over, he's not content with a quieter life?"

"Hmm... he says he wants to, but... He lies a lot? Says stuff he doesn't mean to make other people happy?" I guess, knowing it's not true. I haven't known the guy long, but I watched him spit food into the trash right in front of Eleanor, impervious to her glare. He doesn't give a fuck about lying to protect other people's feelings.

Her eyes narrow. "Okay, you've definitely been talking to Eleanor."

That makes me grin. "Or maybe I can recognize the signs of a girl who thinks she doesn't deserve someone who puts her first because no one else ever has."

Nicole looks like I've slapped her.

"Maybe I was her, too," I add, before she goes back on the defensive.

Sucking her lips in, she digests my words for a few seconds. "Cute, charming, self-aware, and eloquent. Damn, girl. You're the complete package."

I beam, almost more excited by the source of the compliment than the words themselves. "Want to hear the most freeing thing my therapist ever told me?" At her nod, I continue, "You have to trust other people when they tell you how they feel—because you're not a mind reader and they have no right to expect you to be."

As soon as the words leave my mouth, I draw an immediate parallel to my situation with Wesley. He's told me how he feels—he lied about the situation, but never about that. I've always known exactly how he feels about me. He didn't tell me why he was so obsessed with keeping me safe, but he never lied about wanting to do it. That's... not a lot, but it's something. It's a start.

She looks away. After a few seconds, her voice is hoarse as she says, "I think I need the name of your therapist."

I lean forward and grab her hand, squeezing it. "You're gonna love Dr. Cora. She does virtual appointments."

Nicole sniffles and wipes a tear with her free hand, then squeezes mine back. "I'm so glad you're here, Madison."

I'm so glad you're here.

I sit back, reeling. Such a simple phrase, but has anyone ever said it to me before? Sure, I think it's implied with family—my Abuela is certainly glad to have me around—but family has an expectation and obligation. It's different when it comes from a friend. It hits different when it's someone who doesn't *have* to choose you and chooses you anyway.

What would happen if I... chose her back? Not just her, but all of them? Could I? Is that something I'm allowed to do? Is a place in this odd little family something I'm allowed to want?

I don't know what's going to happen after we take down the General. Presumably, without a boss or a job holding them together, things will change. Will the group fall apart? Go their separate ways?

Will Mac and Eleanor leave to start their happily ever after?

What will Nicole and Dimitri do about the Russians on their backs? What will they do about Tío, and the part he played in it?

Worry curls in my gut, and I feel the dread creep up the back of my throat. Fuck. I can't let her leave without telling her about Tío—I don't want to undo anything we've built, but I'll feel like such an asshole if she finds out later and feels betrayed because I didn't say something when I had the chance.

"There's something I need to tell you," I hedge, withdrawing my hand in case she needs physical space when I break the news.

"That Felix is your uncle?" she guesses.

My jaw falls. Bunch of damn mind readers in this house... "Uh... Yes?"

"Dimitri told me." Her eyes drop back to her stomach, and I feel my whole body tense and go cold. She's so hard to read. "Honestly, I'm kind of relieved. I'm a nurse. I'm a healer. I don't want things to end in bloodshed unnecessarily."

It's like a weight being lifted off my shoulders, and I breathe a deep sigh. "Good. Me either."

"Well, maybe with you involved... they don't have to. Maybe there's another path? I don't know enough about it, but I think you do."

I nod, feeling at once both humbled and intimidated by her faith in me. Is this what it feels like to be *in*? To feel like people trust you and believe in you? It's a lot of pressure, but it's also kind of motivating.

"I think I can figure something out," I assure her.

"Good." She slides off her stool and heads for the fridge. "Hungry? I'm feeling snacky; we could split one of those prepped meals."

"Um... Okay, don't get me wrong... I'm still pinching myself about the five-star meals every night—but sometimes I just want..."

"Junk?" Nicole guesses with a glint in her eye. "I think I know where Wesley keeps his stash."

I groan, rolling my eyes back for effect. "Goddess. Lead the way!"

We find several bags of chips in the back of a cabinet I would have needed a step stool for. We finish the Doritos, sitting on the floor of the pantry and swapping stories. She's got some awesome, gnarly medical anecdotes from working in the ER, and she's fascinated by my history and how I got into hacking and how that led into becoming an informant.

As she heads back to bed, I can't keep the grin off my face.

But now it feels like something is hanging over my head. So, I grab my phone and text my *tío*.

Promise?

Neither will my son.

Now wait just a goddamn minute. That's not fair. You can't withhold your cat's visitation rights. I'll call PETA on your ass.

Fix it.

How the fuck do you suggest I do that?

Oh, I see. You only don't know everything when it means you have to do something you don't want to do.

Fine. But you are actually going to owe me one for this.

Are you telling me that getting three hitmen off your back isn't reason enough?

I tried that olive branch shit with them already. Didn't work. Sorry, enana. Piper's gotta be paid for this one.

Fine.

Really? You've never agreed to a deal before.

Never for myself, no. But some things are worth sticking your neck out for.

38

MADISON

Do you know what I mean when I say you're mine?

The door creaks as I open it, and I find my man in a dark room lit only by the semicircle of screens surrounding him.

"Careful. *Gringo* like you, you're gonna need sunscreen for all that blue light," I joke.

He looks up. "Madison."

"I'm turning on the light, so gird your loins," I warn him.

He winces as the room brightens suddenly, shielding his pupils from the pain of rapid dilation. I wonder how long he's been tied to that office chair—my money's on hours. I bet he hasn't gotten up since I left him there yesterday afternoon.

I settle onto the couch, and he spins, watching me with a careful look. His hair is askew, like it's been ruffled and tugged in frustration, and his dark circles are stark slashes under his eyes. Yeah, he didn't sleep a wink. Poor guy. I beckon him with a wave of my hand, patting the cushion next to me. "Come here, please," I say, dropping my voice and imitating his accent.

Some of the dread leeches out of his face, and he crosses the room. The second he's settled in his seat, I throw my leg over his and straddle him, facing him. We're nearly eye to eye like this, and he reaches up to tuck a green forelock behind my ear, like he always does.

"Hi, Nerd," I say, smiling softly.

He grabs my waist with both hands, squeezing. The rest of the tension relaxes off his face. He's finally realized this conversation is going to go well for him. Good—I wasn't trying to leave him in suspense. I don't want him listening with half an ear because he's worried about what I'm going to say. I want him locked in.

"Hello, my love," he replies, a whispered entreaty.

It's a question. Am I? Am I still *his* love, after all this?

I lean forward and snuggle into the side of his neck. Skin to skin, grounding ourselves in each other. I inhale his scent, feeling a stirring between my legs that's basically Pavlovian at this point. But that's not what this is about.

"I've been thinking about your past." He stiffens, but I continue, zagging when he's expecting a zig. Being the one to apologize when he's expecting to have to do it—call it the Nicole effect. Not that I'm apologizing, I'm just... making things right so he doesn't have to. I'm a giver like that.

"You let me in, and it made me realize that I've never let anyone see all of me, either. You know the most, but even you don't know everything. But... I think it might help. I think knowing this might help you understand where I'm coming from."

I inhale deeply and launch in.

"My parents were teenagers—my mom was 16 when I was born. I was just a baby and there was a car accident... she died. My bio dad apparently decided he couldn't do it—didn't want to, most likely. Obviously, Abuela stepped up. She raised me. She was strict, but I've never doubted that she loves me. She always told me I was a gift from God, but I heard the whispers. To everyone else in the community, I was the unwanted bastard of a loose, immoral girl who deserved the wrath of God."

Wesley makes an appalled noise.

"Some Catholics can be pretty judgmental," I shrug. At this point, I'm over it—it's a fact about the world that's too exhaustingly true to be worth any more emotions. "I think it made me... angry. Closed off. I didn't understand how people could be so unkind and hate me for something that wasn't my fault. The kids at school were mean, too, and it really only made me lean into the *prickly bitch* persona.

"Eventually, I got into computers and started making online friends, and things really changed for me. I found more acceptance from strangers who were miles away than I'd ever experienced from the people close to home. And once I realized I could learn anything I wanted? Game over."

"It was similar for me," he says, sounding pleased to have this in common. "Bullied in school, and found my niche in computers."

"I knew that, I think. You have that way about you." I smile against his collarbone. "Abuela started having memory problems when I was about 18. It started small, but it got bad kind of quickly. Then she had a fall and couldn't walk or take care of herself, and I... I had to step up. It was more than supporting both of us—I became her nursemaid and only companion. When girls my age were going to college and exploring what it means to be an adult, I was helping Abuela go to the bathroom.

"Do you know what people call you when you're orphaned as a baby, bullied in school, grow up lonely and then have to take care of your grandmother—the person who's supposed to take care of you—on your own by the time you're 20?"

He shakes his head.

"Resilient. They mean it like such a compliment, too. Resilient," I repeat, wanting to spit out the bitter taste of the word.

"Being resilient is good, right? Instead of breaking, you bend. You adapt. You grow."

"Yeah," I agree with a sharp laugh. "Yeah. But... I'm so fucking tired of being resilient. I just don't know how to be any other way."

He sweeps his hand up my back in comfort, and I shiver against the touch and clutch him tighter. "I'm tired of being strong. I'm tired of proving myself. I want acceptance, and I don't want to have to hide or change who I am to get it. And I'm so tired of pretending not to care." My voice takes on a wet, musical tone, and I rear back. I let him see the moisture pooling in the corners of my eyes. "I like it here. I like Nicole and Eleanor and Mac and Dimitri. I like you."

He smiles and reaches up to brush away a tear for me.

I inhale shakily at the tender contact. "I'm tired of not letting myself want things. I want this. You and me."

The earnestness of my declaration is reflected back to me for a long moment, only to crystalize into a steely kind of resolve. I know he's decided the same thing I have—that we'll do whatever it takes.

I smile. "Secretly, I kind of love that you want to take care of me, but I don't know how to let you. I'm willing to learn what it means, but you *have* to be open with me. I've been the only one in charge of everything for a decade. I want to give control to you, but it doesn't come easy."

"I think I understand that now. I'm sorry," he whispers.

"I know," I say, loving that it's as easy for me to forgive as it was for him to apologize. It'll make fights much simpler between us. "Do you remember what you said to me in the bathtub when you were taking such good care of me after I'd been attacked and I was shell-shocked?"

It's not what he was expecting, so it takes him a second to adjust. "Erm... I remember saying some things," he admits.

"It's okay; it was a leading question. I'm going to tell you," I wink. "You said that I was yours."

"I did." He nods.

"But," I add, lifting a finger. "You said that you're *mine*, too."

His lips twitch at the corners, and I slide my hands up to cup his jaw. "Do you know what I mean when I say you're mine?" I say, repeating his words back to him.

He shakes his head.

"It means that we trust each other. We fight for each other. We're honest about everything, even the stuff that's embarrassing or makes us feel unlovable. We *see* each other. Okay?"

It's on the tip of my tongue. *I love you.* And I can feel that he loves me, too. But... it's not quite the right moment. When I tell him that I love him, I want it to stand on its own. I want it to be the only emotion, not on the heels of an apology.

He slides his hands around me, dragging me forward until I'm resting my forehead against his. The smile he offers is so full of relief and hope, I almost start crying again like a total dweeb.

"Okay."

"Good. Now give me one of your spare laptops—because I know you've got at least four, you nerd. We're going to get this fucker."

39

WESLEY

How the 3 Musketeers got together

We don't get much done for the rest of the night—despite Madison's declaration, we quickly passed out on the couch, tangled in each other, exhausted by our emotions—but in the morning, Madison proves how foolish I'd been.

Working with her is seamless. I'm comforted by her quiet presence next to me—the only sounds are a periodic, thoughtful noise or puzzled muttering, and the soft clacking of her keyboard. I feel energized. More productive and focused because she's here. Having her at my side, speaking the same language, being so entirely and completely understood and supported...

Working with her is a dream I don't want to wake from.

"So you tried searching his alias, obviously. I think a top-down approach makes the most sense, given the breadth of the data, don't you? Let's start filtering things until we get a more manageable list. Age, physical location, background..."

It's hard not to smile. "That's what I've been working on. I'll continue. You look into Fred."

"Roger that," she salutes me and gets to work. "I'm going to look for Todd, too, just in case. I don't think he's involved too deeply in this because he's kind of an idiot, but you never know."

It's just before noon when Madison's plan pans out.

The listening device we sent to SmarTech with Todd has been mostly relaying static and the muffled sounds of being carried around in a pocket. I've been able to hear voices, but the tones have always been of a polite greeting or casual conversation. Until now.

I lean forward, shut off my headphones and turn up the volume on my speaker so she can hear it.

"—sure this is it? It's from her computer?"

"That's Fred's voice," Madison confirms.

"Yeah... and... uh, she wasn't dead, like you said she was." Todd's voice is awkward, but accusatory.

I lift a brow at her and she shrugs. "We knew he'd tell," she points out.

"What?" Fred is surprised. *"How do you know?"*

"Because she caught me with her computer and tied—uh, she threatened me with a gun." Todd narrowly avoids admitting to being tied up by a woman smaller than him. *"I don't know where you got your information—"*

"She caught you, but this is her SSD? I... I'm confused, Todd. Tell me what happened."

As Todd launches into a completely fabricated tale of his own heroism, fighting off the cowardly attacker and stealing the SSD card to bring to SmarTech with his own prowess and cunning, Madison chuckles. "Such a *pendejo*. At least he didn't mention you, or what we did to the card."

"So she's alive," Fred repeats, sounding distant and lost in thought.

"Yeah, but that's not my fault. I did what you wanted, right?"

"Sure, yeah..."

"So, my promotion?"

"What? Oh, of course. Thanks for this. I'll shoot a note to Nancy in HR letting her know about the title change by the end of the week."

"Awesome. Thanks, Fred." He clears his throat awkwardly. *"I mean Mr. Harvey."*

"You're welcome, son. Now, excuse me, but I have an important lunch meeting."

We wait in silence, listening hard as the door closes Fred in. A few seconds later, he speaks again. *"I have it, but she's still alive. It was Todd. Yes. Yeah, I agree. We don't need him anymore. I'll take care of him."*

Madison and I exchange a look as he hangs up. We hear the creaking of an office chair and heavy steps across the room, and the door shuts.

Madison grimaces. "Poor Todd. He's a world-class tool, but he doesn't deserve to *die*."

"Yes, 'taking care of him' is probably not a good euphemism in this case," I agree.

She gives it a moment of contemplative silence, then moves to the heart of the matter. "So Fred is in on this, but he's answering to someone," she assumes.

"Do you think they're just using SmarTech's data?" I wonder.

"What's the alternative?" she asks. "*SmarTech* is controlling a hitman website? Why would a security company be ordering hits on people? It still doesn't make complete sense to me... Although... I mean, the resources required to run the hitman forum are massive—even just from a power consumption standpoint."

"True."

"It's gotta be SmarTech. And from the sounds of it, it's multiple people there."

I feel the certainty settle in my gut, and I know she's right.

That means we have the confirmation we need to start planning our next move. "Who does Fred answer to? You and I can start there. And we can get Mac and Dimitri started on surveillance—learning Fred's routine. If we can get our hands on him, I'm sure we can get him to tell us what we still need to know. Like how they're running the program and where they're keeping it."

"And the why. That's what I still want to know," Madison adds. She thinks for a moment, then shakes her head and stretches, leaning so far over the back of her chair that I hear her spine crack. "Let's take a break—we've been at this for hours. I think I smell lunch and I'm kind of starving."

"Chock-full of good ideas," I say, smiling.

"Now he gets it." She winks, stands, and holds out her hand to me.

Hand in hand, we head out to the kitchen and find the four others together, sitting around the glass table in the kitchen, chatting and eating some sort of casserole I can see on the stove. All of them turn to look at us as we enter the room.

Mac grins, arm slung over Eleanor, lounging. "Wes! Mads! Sit. We were just talking about how the 3 Musketeers got together."

Eleanor pipes in, "Yeah, I realized I've never heard the story."

Nicole nods, taking a hearty bite of her salad. "Me either. I bet it's really interesting—three hitmen, from such diverse backgrounds."

"Color me intrigued as well," Madison agrees, loading up a plate and joining the group. I follow her lead, taking the seat next to her.

Mac rubs his palms together. "Right, so. How far back you want me to go?"

Eleanor shrugs, picking at her steaming pile of veg.

He grins. "Okie doke. I was born on a stormy April night at 10 pounds, two ounces—"

"Feel free to skip forward some," Eleanor interjects.

"10 pounds?" Nicole repeats, wincing. "You owe your mom an apology."

"That's what she says!" Mac replies, grinning. "Okay... skipping forward... Well, I was a Special Forces sniper for eight years, and when I got out, I hopped from job to job. Lots of guys end up in private security details, but you have to put some time in before any of the good companies will look at you. I was bouncing at a club when this guy," he claps me on the shoulder, "showed up. Offered me something way better. Better pay, better hours, better life. All I had to do was what I was best at—shoot the bad guys. What was I gonna do, say no?"

He grins at me, and you'd have to know the whole story to even detect the brief tightening around the corners of his eyes.

Because I know the whole story, I see it. I smile back like I don't.

"It was similar for me. Wesley came to me," Dimitri says, shoveling a giant forkful of plain chicken into his mouth.

"I know you're not a storyteller, but you can do better than that," Eleanor teases.

Dimitri chews, swallows, and narrows his eyes at me. I'm not sure if he's trying to remember, or if he's deciding how much to tell. "I had to flee Russia for… reasons I can neither confirm nor deny," he says, throwing Madison a look that makes her grin. I'll have to ask about that inside joke between them later. "When I got here, I was still on the run. My contact who helped bring me into the country was caught and sent to prison before he could provide the documentation I needed to start over. I had nothing except a name I could not use and the wrong sort of men after me.

"There is not much you can do in America without the proper paperwork, but I found odd jobs. I was on one such job when I received a curious note under the door of my motel room."

I smile at the memory. I saw Dimitri's stats in the file I found in the Russian prison database, but panicked a bit when I came face to face with the real thing. There's a world of difference between reading 6'8" and seeing it up close. Frankly, I was concerned my offer wouldn't be enough for him, and he'd wring my neck with his bare hands.

"He offered to buy me pie," Dimitri continues, a faint smile on the corners of his mouth.

"He bought me a cup of coffee," Mac interjects. "Did he take you to a terrible diner, too?"

"*Da*. It was very bad pie—too sweet."

I laugh. "What can I say? American diners fascinate me. And pie is supposed to be sweet, by the way."

Dimitri's lips twitch. "Over terrible pie, he told me of this job, and he told me his handler would pay handsomely for the same work I was already doing—and that they would create a new identity for me. But what convinced me was the offer of a team. At this point he had already recruited you," he adds, nodding at Mac.

Mac and I exchange a look. "I didn't know that," I say. I'm oddly touched.

But Dimitri shrugs dismissively and starts cutting off a new bite of his chicken breast. "I was used to the *Bratva*, where everything is done with a partner or in a small group. I missed having someone to look at my back—"

"Watch your back," Nicole corrects.

He nods at her, and I'm so taken aback by the lack of a defensive, knee-jerk *that is what I said* that I almost miss the next bit. "I did not like being alone. I knew there was a possibility that this team would be bad, but I joined and found it was not so bad. We work well together. We *watch* each other's backs. It has the camaraderie I wanted in the *Bratva*, with an additional benefit that no one is trying to kill me for my position."

Dimitri takes another bite, apparently done with his story. All eyes turn to me, clearly expecting me to go next.

I consider each person in turn and settle on Madison.

Yesterday, Madison offered me an alternative outcome I hadn't dared hope for. I always assumed that when I told Mac and Dimitri the truth about my beginning, it wouldn't matter because the ending had already been written. I always assumed it would drive us apart, which wouldn't matter because the job would be finished. It would hurt, but ending up sad and alone would be no more than what I deserved.

But yesterday, I showed her the deepest, ugliest, most shameful parts of me, and she showed me acceptance. Perhaps it's not too much to hope that they might do the same.

My heart thuds hard and heavy in my chest, and an odd flipping sensation forms behind my navel. It's time to come clean.

"I've been keeping something from you all."

The silence of the room is palpable. There's an expectation in the air—a nervous energy as they wait for my story after such an ominous lead in. I try to start, only to have the words fail me. "It's difficult to know where to begin," I say ruefully, wishing suddenly I hadn't set the tone so dramatically.

Suddenly, I feel Madison's hand in mine. I look down at it, then smile gratefully at her. She's doing for me what I did for her—anchoring me. Giving me something to hold onto.

Boosted by her support, I begin. Having told the story once already, the words flow more easily this time. No one speaks until I get to the end. Until I get to the part where I reveal how I assembled our trio.

"Wait, so the General never..." Mac realizes with a hard edge to his voice. "It was *you* who recruited us. Not him."

I nod.

"Why?" Mac asks, rubbing the back of his neck.

"I knew I needed a team to help maintain my position in the forum and help me take down the General when the time came. I wanted to keep the team small and tight—one person to handle the digital and research, one to be the feet on the ground, and one to offer support from afar. I found Mac's name first in a data breach of some confidential government files."

"What files?" he asks, voice low.

"Files that made me think you might be amenable to returning to a life of violence on your own terms," I reply vaguely.

His eyes narrow, and I know he knows what's going unsaid. But I'm not about to air his dirty laundry in front of everyone. Those files with the Army therapist were meant to stay locked away and redacted.

"I wasn't responsible for the leak. And I burned every trace," I tell him seriously.

Scowling, he nods, a reticent gratitude for allowing his deepest shame to remain buried until he's ready to face it. Lord knows I put my own off for long enough—now is the time for my reckoning, not his.

"I got Dimitri's name from someone in the hitman forum—likely someone from his old *Bratva*. They were looking for him. He had the right skill set and temperament to be the man on the ground, and once I learned about why he had to flee Russia... well, I took a chance. And I'm very glad I did."

The silence that follows grinds me down. Eleanor is staring at Mac, face full of concern, and he rubs his eyes harshly. Nicole and Dimitri are solemn, but Nicole is also holding Dimitri's hand under the table like Madison is holding mine.

"I kept your names off the General's radar. You've never worked for him—you've been working for me all along. And perhaps I should have told you earlier, but... I couldn't tell you."

"You could've," Mac counters. The hurt on his face breaks my heart.

"It's not that simple."

"Not if you make it complicated," he snorts.

"Why pretend it's not complicated?" I return. When he stubbornly sets his jaw, I know he's refusing to understand. I sigh. "I couldn't risk the truth getting out—the fewer people who knew, the better."

"But we're not just *some people*. We're... a team. I thought we were a team."

"We are," I insist, voice rising. "Mac, do you remember when we were discussing the complications of trying to find the General when I first realized Madison was one of my spiders? Do you remember how we questioned what role he might play in her life, whether she spoke to him without realizing, if he knew about her internet usage or had put sleepers in her life?" I watch Mac make the connection before I reach my conclusion. "When you don't know where the danger comes from, it could be anywhere. The smartest thing to do is to treat it like it's *everywhere*."

But Mac still shakes his head. "Then why tell us now?"

"Because we found it," Madison says.

I nod. "The General is someone at SmarTech, using SmarTech data and resources. So now that I know where my project ended up, I'm going to destroy it."

"But it's done some good, right?" Eleanor asks softly, like she's almost afraid to intervene. "You've taken so many bad guys off the streets."

"Yes," I agree sadly. "But no one should have that kind of power. Whoever bought it—whoever is controlling the hit list now—has gone completely off script. They targeted Madison, and journalists and other people who don't actively cause harm. It went from a way to balance the scales to a weapon in the wrong hands. That's why it never should have existed."

Dimitri speaks up for the first time. "This is..." he blows a long breath out through his nose, his brows lowering further as if the release of oxygen is pulling them down. "Unexpected."

"I know I kept it—"

"Not that," he cuts in. "Well, yes, the fact that you kept important information from us is irritating. But if you had told me the truth at the beginning, I would not have joined you. If you had told me earlier, I probably would not have stayed on the team. And I would not wish for my life to have turned out differently." His eyes cut to Nicole and soften. "Regret is pointless when you are happy in the present."

"Google doc," Mac says faintly, his own eyes cutting towards Eleanor. She reaches for his hand.

"If anything, it is a relief," Dimitri continues thoughtfully.

"What?" Mac demands, his ire rising again as he directs it across the table.

Dimitri lifts a brow. "I would rather work for a man I know and trust instead of this anonymous General. Wesley kept this secret from us, *da*, but he had a reason. Just as I have reasons for my secrets, and you have reasons for yours."

Mac crosses his arms, leaning forward onto the table on his elbows.

"Does it really matter that we never worked for that *svo lach'*—that we were always contractors through Wesley?" Dimitri wonders in that relentlessly straightforward way of his. "The jobs were done. The money was paid. The choices we made about the targets were our own."

"Of course it doesn't matter," Mac fires back through his teeth. He hangs his head for a second, then turns to me. "It... it just kinda sucks that you thought you couldn't tell us."

"Not through any fault of your own," I promise. "But you have to understand... the only people who knew anything about this were dead—were killed *because* of what they knew. I had no idea who was responsible, or where they might be, or what they might know about me and the two of you... I thought the truth might get us all killed, so it was safer to keep the secret until I knew what I was up against."

With every point, some of the lines of tension in Mac's face iron out. By the end of it, he's sitting upright and wearing a look more akin to compassion.

"That must have made you feel so alone," Eleanor says softly.

Her heart is so damn big that it tugs a smile to my lips. "Sometimes," I admit. Then I glance sideways at Madison. "But sometimes strangers on the internet have a way of making you feel much less alone."

She lets out a choked laugh.

"All right," Mac says, scrubbing his face with his palm. "Fine. I get it. I'm... well, I'm not *not* mad, but I understand why you did what you did."

I nod, knowing that's the best I can hope for at present. He'll come around.

"So you're telling us now because you found the guy? You know who the General is?" Mac asks.

"We know where to start. Who to target."

Mac tosses his fork and shoves his plate away. "Then what are we waiting for? Let's fuckin' go."

40

MADISON

Well, that's fuckin' terrifying.

I'm in the shower when it hits me.

"*Dios*," I breathe, eyes widening and then wincing as a stream of sudsy water falls right into my surprised expression. "Ah, fuck!"

I'm so excited by the realization, I can't get my hair rinsed out fast enough. I nearly trip over the lip of the shower and slip on the wet tile as I climb out. The near brush with death makes me pause and catch my balance.

I can't die because of something stupid before I get a chance to tell Wesley what I just figured out. And I suppose that means—since I have to go downstairs—I should probably also put on clothes first. Everyone is downstairs, and I don't think Wesley will be very receptive to what I have to say if he's anxious I might accidentally drop my towel.

No time for undergarments. I throw on a dress over my nudity and fly down the stairs, hair dripping in my wake. Just as I'm about to turn the corner towards the office, I skid to a stop, my feet literally making stuttered squeaks on the marble.

I poke my head into the kitchen. "Hey!" I call to Eleanor and Nicole.

Nicole spins, and Eleanor looks up from her knife work and the enormous, beige lump on the counter in front of her. "Madison, you're... wet?"

"I thought you'd—are you butchering a whole turkey?" I interrupt myself. I shake my head. "Doesn't matter. I figured it out! Come on!"

I turn and sprint down the hallway.

After a second, Nicole and Eleanor follow. Nicole's voice echoes after me. "That was way too dramatic not to pique my interest."

"Hell yeah. I want to know," Eleanor agrees.

I jerk open the door, feeling Nicole's presence at my back. "It's a project!" I shout into the office, making all three men turn to me with identical expressions of shock.

Okay, so *I* know what that means, but I can see how it makes no sense without context. I rush over to the laptop Wesley set me up with and hurry to log in before I lose my train of thought. It's a weird feeling to have everyone watching over your shoulder as you type—like being on display. The contents of one's computer are a deeply private thing, and even though this isn't really my personal machine, I can't shake the itchiness under my skin.

Or maybe that's just nerves. *Dios*, I hope I'm right about this...

Eleanor appears in the doorway, wiping her wet hands on her apron as I type my epiphany into the search bar, holding my breath. The result comes back, and I cover the elated laugh with my hand as I spin the screen towards Wesley to show him. Goosebumps erupt all over my skin.

He goes very still next to me. "Why didn't that come up in my search?"

"Because it doesn't say 'General' it says 'Gener-*AI*.' It's SmarTech's generative AI machine learning project. It's *Fred's* project," I emphasize. I want to kick myself for not realizing it earlier. "It was all very hush-hush; I wasn't there long enough to work on it, but obviously I snooped," I add, chuckling when Wesley gives me a knowing look.

Shower thoughts for the win.

The software itself isn't in the file, but there are some confidential documents. I see out of the corner of my eye as he pulls up the project documentation and starts skimming.

"What is it?" Eleanor asks, eyes round.

I cut her a grin before pulling up a Google search and sending an article I read a month ago about SmarTech's project—Safe-T Keeper (still the stupidest name, ever)—to the group chat. "You know how they say things are cutting edge if it's advanced and state-of-the-art, and they call it bleeding edge if it's newer than that—more experimental, more exciting?"

"Oh, yeah, I *totally* knew that," she says, resolutely shaking her head at Nicole, making Nicole grin in amused agreement.

"This is ahead of *that* curve. It *is* the edge, I suppose," I continue, losing my metaphor in my excitement. "It's a software that's supposed to be a kind of support tool for city governments to make better, data-driven decisions for the safety of their citizens. That's how they're selling it, anyway."

"This is it," Wesley confirms. His hands are shaking. "I recognize the patterns in the architecture this lays out. It's my data filtration, and this describes the same platform I've been logging into for jobs and contacting the General."

"They will sell it to cities to use?" Dimitri asks, tone rising in concern. "They will put the mayor or some such self-serving politician in charge of a program that could target and end lives at will? That is insanity. Even in Russia, they would know better."

I shake my head. "That's the thing—it's being sold as a fully set-it-and-forget-it, AI-run thing. *No one's* running it. It's supposed to run itself."

"It's making decisions? *The program* is choosing people and sending out hits?" Nicole looks totally terrified as I nod.

"Are you tellin' me the robots are deciding who lives and who dies?" Mac asks, dead serious despite essentially summarizing the plot of several excellent sci-fi movies.

"With some human input initially, but yes. Essentially," Wesley says. "Someone programmed the criteria to use; the program is filtering their massive amounts of personal data to find targets and sending them out to an approved list of hitmen. The AI handles payment when the job is complete."

Mac shivers. "Well, that's fuckin' terrifying."

"All the things that didn't make sense about how the General acted and made decisions, all those behaviors we couldn't account for... it's because they weren't *human* behaviors. The motive was just to reduce crime—it wasn't a man trying to benefit from the death, or someone who had a personal vendetta. There was never any urgency or disorder to it. It was a computer. It didn't have *desires;* it had a pattern."

"Until me."

He looks at me. "They must have programmed it to protect its own secrets. When you stole the data, you triggered a fail-safe protocol."

"Yeah," I agree.

"How long has the AI had full control, do you think?"

"I don't know. They've probably been testing it for years. You might have always been working for the AI." I exhale long and slow, looking around the room at the serious, concerned faces. "SmarTech is launching this tech soon. Next week, I think? The launch party is on Saturday. They probably already have buyers."

"We can't let it get out. We have to stop it before it goes live."

"Did these assholes learn *nothing* from movies? You never give the machines the power to kill," Mac growls. "What do we do?"

I turn and am shocked to be at the center of attention. "We..." I falter under the weight of everyone's anticipative stares. Are they all expecting *me* to know? "Uh... I'm just the devastatingly beautiful, brilliant mind who put it all together. I'm not the ideas guy. Wanna take this one, SpyderMan?"

He frowns and sits back, steepling his hands, deep in thought. "We need... to find where it's being kept. Before they start releasing the project to any buyers, they'll be holding it in a private server. If I were them, I wouldn't use the cloud for backups—too unsecure—but we can't rule it out. If we can get in and get onto a network computer that would have access to the confidential software files, I'll be able to determine if there's a cloud backup."

"And once we're in, we can delete the source code, overwrite the backups, corrupt critical dependencies," I suggest.

He nods, excitement growing. "And even if we can't get access, it would have a kill switch. They'd never release it without some kind of failsafe."

"You're right," I realize. "This program could potentially be a danger to them as well, so they'd never release it without some ability to control it internally…"

"Are you getting a word of this?" Nicole stage-whispers to Dimitri.

Dimitri's answer is a grunt.

But I'm staring at Wesley. Watching him think out loud—having a front seat to his incredible mind doing its thing… well, if I weren't so caught up in the moment and my excitement at figuring it out, I'd probably drop to my knees and unzip his pants right here and now.

Fuck me, he's hot. I press my thighs together, squeezing to give that dull thrumming in my blood the pressure it's craving.

"Fred would know," I assert confidently, finishing his thought. "Even if it runs itself, it's still his project. He should know all the details, or at least have access."

"Then we need to have a little chat with Fred Harvey."

"Right, about that…" Mac cuts in. "We've been following him for a few days now. Short of nabbing him from the parking lot—"

"Which is a terrible idea," Dimitri interjects, making me think they've already had this exact conversation.

"—the guy is never alone. Always protected, always with his phone in his hand. It's like he knows we're after him."

"He might," Wesley observes. "He knows Madison's alive—he might assume she would come after him."

"Or he's paranoid as a side effect of being a terrible person," I add, grumbling.

"You said there's some kind of launch party?" Mac asks, excited like he's got an idea.

I grin. "Yup."

"That could be our in. It's weirdly easy to nab someone in a room full of strangers, if you do it right," Mac says.

There's some silence after his revelation, and I consider that. He'd be surrounded by strangers at a launch party—I suppose that's when it would be the least conspicuous to get close.

"I want to help!" Eleanor says. Mac cuts her a look, and she shrugs at him with one shoulder. "What? You said it was going to be a party. Guess what parties have: caterers. I can totally get in unnoticed."

Looking suitably proud and impressed with her, a smile splits his face. "Damn right you can, darlin'."

"I want to help, too," Nicole says, her voice softer, but no less determined.

Dimitri swallows, looking at her with a scowl that would make me cower. She just lifts a brow and meets him head-on, daring him to say something. Clash of the frickin' Titans.

"We'll need all hands on deck," Wesley says to Dimitri. "We need a team to nab him from the party, someone to question him, a team to go into SmarTech to access the network computer, someone to find and destroy the servers, and add in someone to take care of the extra security they'll likely have due to the hype and inherent risks..."

"Even with Eleanor and Nicole, that's... too many someone's," I say, watching out of the corner of my eye as Nicole goes to stand with Dimitri and they have some kind of silent exchange. "Just finding the right servers to destroy would take all of us."

"We need more help," Wesley realizes, sending me a meaningful look. *Dios,* I feel like I'm in the man's brain. I love it here.

"I'll text Tío Felix. He promised to help," I say, mostly for Dimitri's benefit, who seems to tense up anytime my *tío's* name comes up. "He wants the General gone just as much as we do."

Wesley smiles at me, eyes shining with hope. "We can do this," he says, and it's an assurance that everyone takes to heart, but I know he meant that just for me. Him and me. *We* did it. Not to minimize what will likely be a bitch of a planning session as we hash out the logistics of finding the Gener-AI program and destroying it before it gets out, but we've done the hard part. We solved the puzzle. We're halfway there.

I chew on my lip, squirming in my seat against a strong, sudden pulsing and pounding between my legs. We're so close, I can feel it.

And now I've got an itch to scratch.

I lock in on Wesley, biting my lip. I'm so horny, I can feel my nipples pebbling against the loose material of my dress. Something about solving the puzzle with the man I love... When I look down, I realize I can see the outline of his dick in his pants, and I swallow the sudden wave of heat. He's getting hard, too.

"Okay, everyone out," I say. I feel the curiosity as everyone turns to look at me again.

Fuck. I can't wait another minute. I start reaching for the hem of my dress, eyes hot on my man. "I mean, I guess you can stay if you want—but if you stay, you play. No spectators."

Eleanor's giggle cuts through the shocked silence.

Wesley's eyes flash. "Everyone out!" he roars, reaching for me.

49

WESLEY

A truce that comes with snacks

Madison's eyes narrow when she sees the black bag in my hand. "You're heading out to the meeting with Felix?" she asks, knowing the answer before I nod in confirmation. She moves into the open doorway, blocking my path with all five feet nothing of her, arms crossed and toe tapping in irritation. "If you think you're going anywhere without me, you are coo-coo for Cocoa Puffs because he's *my* Tío, and I was the one who set up this meeting—"

I close the space between us, looming over her, and she cuts herself short when I circle her throat with my hand. "Shut up and get in the van, *traviesita,*" I jerk my chin towards the vehicle in the driveway behind her. "I'll brief you on the way."

Her grin turns into a laugh that bobs against my palm. I tighten my fingers, holding her still as I lean down to brush my lips over hers.

"Are you guys gonna rip your clothes off and have crazy hot nerd sex all over your laptops again?" Mac asks dryly behind me. We're blocking his path.

"How dare you?" Madison shoots back. "I'd never have sex on a laptop. That's how you get an STV."

His brows snap down, not getting the joke.

I bark a laugh. "Sexually transmitted virus."

Madison joins my laughter, and Mac shakes his head as he squeezes past us, muttering about how we've got a secret language. He's halfway to the van when he stops and hoots into the air. "Oh! Like a computer virus! Ha! Good one, Mads."

Once we're finished loading a few more things in, Mac and Dimitri climb into the front while Madison and I step into the back. I take my usual scat. I've already put another stool in and created some space for her at the wall of monitors so she can plug in her laptop. Not that we need that today—just future planning.

"You and I are going in," I explain to her as Dimitri putters down the driveway—the slowest, steadiest driver among us.

"You're not in the van?" Mac asks, surprise in his tone.

"Not today—Dimitri is taking over. I showed him how to operate the equipment this morning."

"Hey, look at you! You angling to be the new Short Round?" Mac asks, elbowing Dimitri.

"This nickname makes even less sense for me than it does for Wesley," he replies dryly, leaning forward to check before making a turn onto the main road.

"That's why it's funny," Mac replies easily.

"Then why is it not funny for George to be named Small Dog?" Dimitri demands, like they've had this argument before. If they did, I wasn't there—a damn shame.

"Dunno," Mac shrugs. "Maybe it's too..."

"Blunt?" Madison suggests. "I mean, for the record, I don't really think Mac's nickname is all that funny either—"

"Thanks for that."

"—but jokes need to have layers. You can't just blatantly call a thing something it's not—people will think you just misunderstand. Like, for example, Short Round is a pop culture reference, too."

"Hmm," Dimitri replies, digesting this newest insight into how humor works.

"Anyway..." I reach behind me for the silver hard-sided case and set it onto the limited tabletop space on the fold-down desk. I snap open the clasps and relish in her swift intake of breath, seeing the devices nestled in the foam cutouts. Her eyes follow as I point to each in turn. "I've got your standard secret agent package. Watch with a biometric scanner. New ID's—license, et cetera. Earpieces with built-in microphones."

She lifts one of the earpieces gently and whistles as she inspects it, cushioning it between thumb and pointer finger and gently tilting it to see all sides. "Built-in microphone? It's so tiny! Bone conduction?"

Not even surprised she's familiar with the tech, I nod. "Long tap to turn on and off, short tap to mute or unmute yourself, double tap to mute or unmute these guys. I usually put Mac and Dimitri on different channels so I can have one in each ear because they tend to try to talk over each other."

She collects her new IDs and replaces the ones in her wallet, handing them to me for safekeeping. Then, she puts in the earpieces.

"One more thing," I say with a grin, pulling a box out of my back pocket.

"What the fuck, Wes?" Mac interjects, eyes on me in the rearview. His tone is high with alarm. "Are you... are you fuckin' *proposing* back there?!"

Madison hears Mac's question and whips her head around, eyes wide. There's excitement there, but there's also a bit of fear. It nearly makes me laugh. "No, we're not quite there, yet," I tell her, chuckling when she heaves a sigh and relaxes in response. I lean closer and lower my voice. "But it *is* sparkly."

Her gasp as she lifts the cover makes my chest warm. I let her take the necklace out of the box so she can examine it. It's the Tiffany's equivalent of what I won her at the arcade—a buttery soft leather choker with a gold heart pendant. The heart has a single diamond offset in one of the curves that winks at us intensely, even in the low light in the back of the van.

Her eyes lift to mine, and she clears out some thickness in the back of her throat. "You just had that in your pocket, huh?"

"The rest of the tech comes back to the case when we're done—but not this. This is yours. It's a personal tracking device, so I'll always be able to find you."

Her smile lights up her face, competing with the diamond. "Put it on," she whispers, handing it back to me, spinning on her stool, and lifting her hair out of the way. The buckle makes a very faint tinkling noise as I slide the prong home, and she shivers as I brush my fingers against the nape of her neck.

She spins back around, fingering the gold, and moves her hand out of the way so I can see how it settles against her throat. "Stunning," I say, meeting her eye so she knows I mean the whole package.

"I fucking love it," she beams, radiant.

"Let's see, Mads," Mac says.

Eyes on me, she turns her torso and stretches up so Mac can see it in the mirror. I know he's seen it when he sighs and grumbles, "Showoff. Thanks a lot, man. Making me look bad. Eleanor's gonna want one of those now. It's gonna be all *how come my tracker isn't made of diamonds? Am I right?*" he elbows D.

Dimitri grunts. "Nicole does not wear jewelry. Her tracker is something discreet that clips to her bra, which is far more practical. It looks like one of those devices that count your steps."

"Step counter? Pedometer," Mac offers with a snap as he thinks of the word.

"That is what I said." Dimitri waves him off. "And you should simply tell Eleanor that hers is inferior because Wesley is in charge of making the trackers and obviously he is saving the best ones for his own woman."

Madison giggles in delight, clutching the heart around her neck. "Being in the van with you guys is *so* much fun."

Pulling us off to the side so we're out of sight of the rearview mirror, I hook a finger under the collar and tug her in. Her pupils dilate, eyes flashing with heat as her chair rolls forward with her body, her knees fitting perfectly between my own spread legs.

"Do you know what this collar means, my love?"

She pretends to think. "That you think I look good in diamonds? I agree."

I hover over her lips, close enough to feel her warmth. "Try again."

"That it'll be way easier for you to stalk me?"

I shake my head. "One more time."

"That I'm yours?" she guesses, tilting her head up and saying it against my mouth.

"There it is."

She fists my shirt and tugs me down. As we kiss, we ignore the hooting and groaning from the front of the cab, pulling apart before either of us can really get too involved. It won't do to meet Felix with a hard-on.

Playing with the pendant, Madison studies the spy case. "Going all out for this, huh?"

"It's all just a precaution. And Mac and Dimitri are simply back-up—we know better than to do this sort of thing on our own by now, even though it's a white-flag ceasefire. We're helping him; he's helping us. We have the same goal. We're sharing information."

Dimitri huffs but doesn't disagree. Even though Nicole sanctioned this forgiveness, he holds a grudge.

"And that's why he's in the van," I mutter to Madison, who giggles.

Mama B's Tamales is just as delicious-smelling and bright as I remember. The short, elderly woman seated at the first table behind the host stand shouts in Spanish when she sees Madison, hauling herself to her feet and opening her arms for a hug with a warm, deeply lined smile.

They start speaking to each other too rapidly for me to follow reliably, and as soon as I hear the heavy pounding of boots against travertine tile, my attention is on the door anyway. Felix emerges from the back room with a large man shadowing him.

Madison and Mama B turn when he enters. Mama B hisses at him, admonishing him for his empty hands when there are guests. With a deep sigh and a roll of his eyes in response to her chiding, he turns on his heel and disappears. When he returns, he's got a plastic basket of tortilla chips and a cup of salsa.

A truce that comes with snacks? I could get used to this.

We all settle at a table of Felix's choosing, on the other side of the restaurant from where Mama B is humming to herself as she runs a wet cloth across the plastic faces of the menus. The large man next to Felix looks comical trying to shove himself into the booth. His jacket flap opens briefly, displaying the handle of his piece. I suppose it makes sense that they'd come armed, though it makes my stomach twist uncomfortably. Or perhaps that's just the flat expression of the man's stony face—he's a killer. No doubt about it.

Madison waves at him and makes a motion with her hands that takes me a second to recognize as ASL—one language sadly not in my repertoire.

This woman is so full of surprises, it really ought to stop surprising me.

The man nods and settles back in his seat, turning dark eyes on me with a flat expression.

"Leo," Felix introduces with a jerk of his thumb.

"Where's Isaac?" Madison asks, leaning across the table and dipping a chip into the salsa.

"Fuck if I know. Let's get this over with. You said you figured out what the connection was between SmarTech and *El General*? Share with the class."

Madison claps her hands, brushing off the salt from the tortilla chip, and nods. She digs into her pocket, unlocks her phone, and pushes it across the table. "It's a program using personal data to isolate criminals and threats and then pushing out hits to a network on their privately hosted platform. AI run."

Felix and Leo exchange a look. Leo makes a circular motion with his index finger. "Fuckin' hell," Felix mutters. "That's... fuck."

"Madison said you mentioned knowing something about the SmarTech servers in your message?" I ask.

Felix takes a chip, regarding me thoughtfully as he eats it, as if trying to decide how much to reveal. It feels like he's just posturing when he takes the second and shoves the basket towards me with the tips of his fingers. "Eat, *gringo*, or you'll offend *mi mamá*."

Madison makes a frustrated noise. "Do you know where their servers are?" she asks. "It would save us a lot of time and effort when we go in if we only have to focus on the cloud copies."

I nearly wince, because in a negotiation you don't often tip your hand so early. But I suppose he's her relation, and this isn't exactly a proper negotiation. I can't tell which party holds the power.

He exchanges another look with Leo, then sighs and leans forward on his elbows. "Yeah. I know where their servers are."

A million questions rise to my tongue, but I swallow them back and defer to Madison. Watching me do it, Leo's expression shifts slightly into something that could vaguely be considered approval.

"Well?" Madison demands, reaching for another chip. Taking her lead, I do the same. Leo—who hasn't said a word; who perhaps *can't* say a word—lifts a brow at me as his lips quirk up at the corners.

Felix's eyes flick to me. "Well, what?" he taunts, even though it was Madison's frustrated challenge.

"What is this? Are you stalling?" she demands. "I thought we were going to have a nice casual meeting and talk about what to do about the fact that someone—some*thing*—wants both of us dead."

Felix sucks on his teeth and sits back, eyes still on me. "I did too. Then, this guy rolls in with my buddy Mac and the Russian as backup. They in your ear right now, too, *enana*? Is *la verga del gringo* all it takes to get you to switch sides?"

I couldn't care less about the implied insult to me, but he just insinuated she's some kind of whore—even though I know it's meant to bait me, I fucking fall for it anyway.

My hand on the table closes into a fist, and my heart pounds in my throat. Out of respect, I lower my voice so Mama B doesn't overhear me. "Because we're in your house and I don't want to cause a problem unnecessarily, I'll let that go—but you will *not* disrespect her, and you certainly won't do it in front of me to make a fucking point. Got it?" I grit out.

"Atta boy," Mac pipes in approvingly.

Felix grins, the gold tooth in the back of his mouth flashing in the light from the big window in the front.

Madison lays a hand on my thigh under the table, squeezing just above my knee—a silent thanks and gentle request to let her handle this. I look at her and force myself to swallow my rage. But I can't snuff it out completely—my caveman brain can't let it go until I mark my territory. Conscious of two sets of watchful, untrusting eyes on me, I lean in and kiss her temple.

When I pull back, Felix's expression is different. Less smug, more calculating.

"I can't tell you where the servers are," he finally admits.

"Because you don't know?" Madison fires back, disbelief plain in her tone.

"Fine. I *won't* tell you where the servers are." An outraged noise falls from Madison's lips, and just as she finishes inhaling to lay into him, he holds up a conciliatory hand and glances down at the screen of her phone again. "But... if you tell me that you want to take down SmarTech and make sure this *murder software* gets destroyed, I'm in."

If Madison is surprised by what feels like a complete 180, she doesn't show it. For my part, I think I'm starting to get a handle on how Felix's mind works. He knows he needs to eliminate the threat to his own life and that he needs information from us and our help to do it. But he refuses to relinquish the upper hand, so he's going to do his best to make it seem like he's doing us a favor. It's quite tricky of him.

Normally, I'd never work with a man like him. Anyone who needs the upper hand all the time trusts no one, and that means he isn't trustworthy enough to share information with either. But Madison's connection with him is creating a tenuous bond—perhaps only for the duration of this mission.

She cocks her head at him and reaches for her phone, which he hands back to her. "We need to know where they are."

Apparently, not even Madison warrants a straight answer on that one. He takes another chip, munching noisily. "Why?"

She turns to me, so I take this one. "Because until they release the product, they'll probably be storing it in that server. Our plan is to corrupt the program files or disable the program with a kill switch, but if we can't, we'll need to destroy the servers that host the AI."

"You thinkin' an explosion?"

I purse my lips. "SmarTech has government contracts, and I'd rather not have Big Brother breathing down my neck. So if we can accomplish it without an explosion, that would be preferable."

"Aw, but I love explosions," Mac laments, sounding truly put out.

Madison is barely able to maintain a straight face.

"All right," Felix says after another silent, minimal conversation with his right-hand man. "I won't tell you, but I'll do you one better. If you can guarantee the big guy won't go on a murder spree and try to wipe out my team, we'll help you out."

"Do not speak for me," Dimitri warns.

"How?"

"Just let me know when you're planning on making your move, and I'll make sure we're in place to fuck shit up," he grins. Apparently Felix likes explosions, too. "Tell my ole buddy Mac that I'll be in touch. I have a feeling he's got what I need and, from where I stand, he still owes me one."

"This fuckin' guy..."

He holds out his hand, offering to shake on the deal, but pulls back when I reach for it. "The big guy gets a leash, yeah?"

"Yeah, all right," I say, taking his hand and making Madison roll her lips inward, since she also heard Dimitri and knows I just did exactly what he told me not to.

"Good. We're cool then?"

It's a loaded question—one he apparently didn't expect an answer to as he shuffles out of the booth sideways. As he stands, he tugs on the lapels of his jacket to straighten it. "And speaking of debts," he reaches into a pocket and tosses a small notebook onto the table. "That's for the Russian. Tell him... I'm sorry. That ought to settle things up between us."

Felix is looking at Madison when he says it. She grins at him, nods, and grabs the booklet, pocketing it without looking at the pages.

"Oye, mamá, ¿podrías preparar un plato para llevar para los dos idiotas que están en la furgoneta?" Felix lifts his voice so his mother can hear him across the room. She whips her head around and smiles at the request to make up some plates to go. Even though they're meant for Mac and Dimitri, it smells so good in here that I might need to *check* them first.

"One last thing," he says, leveling a serious look at me. "What do you plan to do about SmarTech—like, the people who work there?"

"We're only interested in ensuring this program never sees the light of day."

His smile turns dark. "Good. But if you happen to cross paths with Craig Pinsley during your mission, you leave him be. He's mine."

"The CEO of SmarTech? Why?"

He rolls his eyes. "Would you just mind your fuckin' biz, already? Christ."

Felix and Leo both give Madison an affectionate gesture—hair ruffle and signed goodbye, respectively—before disappearing to the back of the restaurant. I'm curious whether this is another of Felix's many operations, but I don't want to ask too many questions where I can be overheard. Better to hold them until we're back in the van.

Once we're inside, Dimitri immediately starts making his displeasure known. "You cannot control what I do, so you should not make assurances as if you can," he starts in as soon as I get the door slammed shut. "It will only make you look foolish."

"Yeah, yeah," I mutter. "Won't matter much anyway, considering he'll be off handling the servers for us. You won't even have to *see* him."

"Hmm." The noise is equal parts dismissive and displeased. "What did he give you for me?" he demands, scowling in the rearview mirror.

Madison pulls the little book out of her purse and tosses it up to him.

"I'm curious to know, myself," I say as he catches it just before it hits him in the back of the head.

I glance at Madison, and she shrugs, unrepentant about her aim.

Acting as if each page might contain some kind of explosive, or jump out and bite him, he carefully and slowly flips through, using the very tip of his index finger and thumb.

"Worried about leaving prints?" Mac jokes. "Come on, we're on the edge of our seats."

"It is..." Dimitri's brows lower, and he turns another page. "Names and addresses... Volkevich, Volkevich, Volkevich..."

"Did he give you the name and location of the rest of the Volkevich *Bratva* members?" Mac asks, jaw falling.

"Every remaining rat," Dimitri mutters under his breath, the frown melting off his face as he continues turning pages. After the list runs out, he carefully closes and pockets the book. "We will see if these tips pan out. Until then, I will reserve judgment."

Madison, looking chuffed as hell, wheels over to sit next to me and leans in. "I did that," she whispers with a proud smile.

"Yeah, I had a feeling," I say, pulling her in for a kiss before we reenter problem-solving mode and discuss what just happened with Felix as a group.

42

MADISON

This is when I knew.

As I slip through the opening in the doorway, I hear an exhausted Wesley confirm with the room, "So we're all clear for tomorrow, yeah?" The door closes before I hear any of the responses.

Everyone is clear. I know it; they know it. I'm told that typically Dimitri fills the team lead role, since he's the man on the ground—but not this time. Wesley has stepped up as the orchestrator of our mission tomorrow, and he keeps checking in, making small adjustments and contingencies. Mac openly sighed the last time he questioned whether we needed to review the logistics of the event one more time.

And while Wesley thrives under pressure, I think feeling responsible for any potential complications is stressing him out. I can see it in the new lines in the corners of his eyes—can hear it in the tired determination in his voice.

I need to take care of my man. If nerves are making *me* edgy, I can't imagine what they're doing to him. And with a day as big as tomorrow looming, sleep wouldn't come easily to someone who *can* reliably get eight hours most nights.

Luckily, I know a few things guaranteed to help take his mind off his troubles.

I head into the bathroom and start filling the massive jetted tub that takes up one whole wall. After the bubble bath goes in, I've got some time to kill while I wait for the tub to finish filling, so I start setting the mood. Lights down, candles lit. Too bad I don't have any rose petals...

"Madison?" Wesley calls somewhere in the foyer below, sounding curious and confused.

"Up here!" I cry back.

Fuck. I was going to put on lingerie. I debate letting him find me naked except for this choker he gave me that I've decided never to take off, but a pile of clothes in the corner would ruin my vibe.

I meet him at the door. He's got a laptop tucked under his arm and a tired smile on his lips. "I thought you were going to the bathroom," he says, leaning down and reaching for me automatically when he's within an arm's length.

"I was. I just came up here," I say, lifting my chin so he can plant a kiss on my lips.

"Is that... a bath?" He tilts his head, like he's listening to the water running. When I nod to confirm, he smirks and moves to set his laptop down on the corner of the made bed. "You've changed your mind about letting me wash your hair tonight?"

"No," I say, laughing when his smile falls. I grab his wrist and tug him towards the bubble tower. "Next time. This one is for you."

He appraises the tub as I reach down to shut off the flow of water. "If I nipped down for some champagne for us—"

"Mmm. Wine that tastes like feet and hurts the back of my throat," I joke. After I finished that glass with Eleanor, I decided I hated it. "If you want some, though, I'll go get it."

He grins. "Just the bath, then."

When he moves to unbutton his shirt, I bat away his hands. "I want to do it," I say demurely. When he opens his mouth to argue, I realize asking nicely isn't getting me anywhere, so I level my finger at his chest. "Stop trying to control the situation, you control freak."

Heat flashes in his eyes, and he threads a hand into my hair, cupping the nape of my neck. "Control is kind of my thing."

"I noticed, *SpyderMan*."

"I'll give up control only to you," he says more softly, gaze settling on my lips.

I go up on my toes and press my mouth to his. Before he can clutch me to him, I pull away and settle my fingers on his top button. I can't tell what that shuttered look in his eye means, but he's not letting me put enough space between us to undress him, so I place a soft kiss over his heart. "You've been working so hard, trying to plan and handle everything. Trying to take care of everyone. Let me take care of *you*."

"You're very good to me," he murmurs.

"Only because you're so good to me."

We're so close that I can hear him swallow before he nods and steps back to release me. I want to take my time and make it as slow a seduction as I can. I unbutton his shirt, placing a kiss on every inch of revealed skin, and draw the sleeves down so I can trail my fingers along his arms. I linger on the belt buckle, drifting my touch across the bulge behind his zipper. His swift inhalation goes straight to my stomach, riling up the butterflies. I love how he reacts to my touch. He's a guarded person, but I love how openly he wears his desire for me.

I get down on my knees to unlace and help him out of his boots, then step out of his pants. He's not fully hard, but his cock jumps when my gaze lands on it, so close to my face. Close enough to touch. I lean forward and place a kiss on the tip, giggling when he makes a choked noise and lays a heavy hand on the top of my head.

"Is this meant to be a kindness or an unbearable tease?" he groans.

"Little bit of both," I say honestly with a shrug.

He grins. "*Traviesita*. I never quite know what to expect from you. You keep me on my toes."

Dios, it fires me up hearing him speak Spanish. I get to my feet and gesture at the bath. I perv on him, grinning as his muscles flex as he gets into the tub. I can't wait to run my tongue through every valley of his hard body. I'm almost too excited to undress slowly, since I just want to get in there with him, but I force myself to clip my hair out of the way, then unzip my sweatshirt slowly.

"I like the way you praise me," I tell him. *You keep me on my toes* is still ringing in my ears, making me feel flush with pride.

"Do you?" he asks, his tone distracted as he watches the skin slowly being exposed with a hungry expression.

I nod, tossing aside the sweatshirt and shimmying down my skirt. "Whenever I would tell someone I like being praised, it was like a knee-jerk reaction to hit me with a 'good girl.' And good girl is fine I guess, but it's not very... original."

"You don't like being called a good girl?" he asks, brows lifting. "I happen to know that's not entirely true."

I smirk. "It has a place. It's fine, like I said. But frankly, it's... generic. I want something that feels tailored or authentic and relevant. Like one time my tattoo artist said, 'you're sitting so still for me, I love it' and I still think about it. That's why I like the way you praise me. You call me clever, and make specific observations."

He reaches up to give me a way to steady myself as I climb in. I almost overfilled the tub, so I am very careful as I settle against him, my back to his front. He's warm and solid, and I just want to melt into him. As I start to float, Wesley wraps his arms around me and keeps me anchored to him as always.

I feel his lips against my neck, and his breath is hot on my skin. "You want to be acknowledged for being impressive, not obedient. I'm not surprised."

"Well, that's... okay, yeah, that's fucking exactly it. Damn," I blow out a breath on a laugh.

His chuckle vibrates through my back, settling around my heart and squeezing with the happy contentedness of the noise. "Mmm. I'm going to need the name of that tattoo artist."

"Why, you need a touch-up?" I ask coyly, grinning as his hands tighten against my waist. "She wasn't my type, don't worry. I'm much more into the secretive, British, dominant types with great smiles and super sarcastic senses of humor. So... if you know anyone like that, send 'em my way."

I expect a teasing reprimand, but he just presses his smile into my skin and holds me tighter.

In the silence that falls, I can sense his worry creeping back in. "You want to ask me to reconsider coming tomorrow, don't you?"

I can feel his lips stretch into a smile—can hear it in his reply. "Is it that obvious?"

"Yes. But you get brownie points for holding back. Do you think the others are having a similar conversation right now?"

"Doubtlessly."

"It's a good plan, Wesley. It's going to work. We all want to be there."

We finish our bath in comfortable silence—no showerhead shenanigans—and I get out first so I'm the one carefully creeping across the wet tile to hand him a towel. He still climbs out and wraps it around me, though.

As he rubs the moisture off of me, I pull back enough to see into his eyes. Emotions swirl all around me, only sharpened by the pleasure and sweetness of his touch. This feels like the right moment. Finally.

"Wesley, I love you."

His hand stills, and the softness disappears from his expression.

It's not the reaction I'd have wanted, but I can't take it back now. So I inhale shakily and continue, "You don't have to say it back. You've got a lot on your mind; it's okay. I just... I needed to say it. We've done everything we can to plan for tomorrow, but there's still an unavoidable risk. There's still some danger. So, I... I need you to know."

His smile is faint, and he tucks a lock of hair behind my ear.

My return smile feels tight. I know I told him he didn't have to say it back, but now I'm kind of kicking myself for it. I'm, like, 99% sure he loves me too. Why isn't he saying it?

He steps away, holds out his hand, and I let him guide me back into the bedroom. He sits on the bed, pulls me onto his lap, draping my legs perpendicular to his, and reaches for his laptop.

Uh... He's going to do more work? Now? I scowl at the laptop, fighting the urge to kick it off to the ground.

But I humor him, watching as he pulls up a folder with a few deft clicks. "Do you remember when I said I remembered every conversation we've had?"

I roll my eyes. "Yeah, because you've got a photographic memory or some shit?"

"Not quite... I don't remember because of how my brain works, or just because I'm particularly smart. I remember because I want to—because I choose to." He makes a final click, calling up a document, and it takes me a second to realize what I'm looking at, and when I see the usernames, a shiver runs through me.

"This is the first time mermaidav made me laugh." He chooses another file. "This is the first time you made me laugh so suddenly that I spat out my drink. I had to buy a new keyboard." I exhale an amused noise through my nose, feeling a heavy prickliness behind my eyelids as he pulls up another conversation. "This is the first time we stayed up all night talking—you were in and out, but I didn't budge from that chair, hoping you'd keep coming back. This is the first time you shared a personal detail—your favorite color. Green, obviously. This is when you first told me a secret. And... this is when I knew."

"Knew what?" I rasp.

He meets my eye, turning away from the laptop to face me. "It's always been you—long before we met in person. For me, it's only ever been you."

For an instant, the lines of him blur behind a wash of moisture in my eye. I blink it away.

"It's always been you for me, too," I whisper back, feeling the truth in the words and hoping he can, too, despite that they're his own sentiment echoed back to him.

"Madison, I'm so in love with you, I don't know how to exist without you. If I lose you, I lose everything."

I suck in a breath, feeling the ache in his words before I see the tears welling in his eyes. I hold his face in both my hands, gently running my thumb under the corner of his eye to sweep away the tear. I want to console him, but I swallow down the gentle words because I can see he's not done.

"This is my chance to undo the damage I've caused—to keep more from happening. My chance to make up for the worst mistake of my life. I want so badly to see this program finally destroyed... But I'd walk away from it all to avoid losing you," he confesses.

He's not saying it to manipulate me into backing down—he's letting me in. Finally. Completely.

I exhale noisily through my nose and slide my hands down to rest on his shoulders. "You won't—you don't have to. Because we're all in this together. You're not alone. You don't have to face this alone. It doesn't have to be your fault anymore. It ends tomorrow."

He nods, almost absently. "Tomorrow means no more General. Tomorrow means no more *hitmen*. Tomorrow, it all... ends."

Another piece of the emotional puzzle locks into place, twisting that dread a little harder in my stomach. Tomorrow, Wesley loses the purpose that's been driving him for years. He loses the thing that's been holding everyone together. He's afraid of losing himself.

I have no control over any of that, but I know one thing for damn sure. He's not going to lose me. And if he loses his purpose, I'll help him find another one. If he loses his family, I'll be there. If he loses himself, I'll pick up the pieces and Krazy glue them back together.

There's so much certainty in how I feel about him, I'm a little intimidated by it. He's afraid of losing me? Well, I'm afraid of losing him. We just have to trust the plan and trust each other.

"It's not tomorrow yet," I point out. I shift in his lap, straddling his legs and, pressing the full length of my body against him, wrapping my arms tightly around his neck. "Tonight I want to be just Madison and Wesley. Not SpyderMan and mermaidav. Not Sir and brat. Nothing between us, no roles we're playing or games... just love."

He grins, stroking my upper arms gently. "Oh, there is plenty of love within our Sir and brat dynamic," he counters.

I scowl in irritation. "Okay, yeah, I know. I was trying to be all deep and symbolic, and you're ruining it."

"Sorry," he says, completely devoid of contrition.

"Kiss me, Wesley."

He makes a strangled sound, full of relief and eagerness and greed. The pull of his mouth echoes in all my most sensitive places—the sides of my neck, the tips of my breasts, the dips of the soft skin above my hips, and then finally between my legs. It pulses through my veins, inflaming and filling me with a desperation to be as close as physically possible.

Towels disappear, lube is retrieved from the bedside table, and I find myself on my back. When he sinks into me, I muffle my cry against his shoulder.

"I love you," I tell him, stroking my hands up his back and trying to infuse the words with as much emotion as I can.

"I love you," he says back, punctuating his sentence with a roll of his hips that changes the angle and makes me quiver. Then he stills, so deeply embedded inside of me that we feel like a single entity. He drops his head to my shoulder.

"I love you," he whispers again, then pulls back. His expression is strained.

I reach up and stroke his cheek with the tips of my fingers. "What's wrong?"

"I don't think it's going to happen for me tonight. I'm too..."

"In your own head?" I finish, feeling the words lift off my lips like they've got wings.

"Yeah," he confirms.

A fizzy kind of happiness settles in my stomach. I'm not sure there's anything he ever could have said that would have made me feel more connected to him than that. Because, yeah, I know exactly how that feels—not great—and he's opening up in the moment instead of hiding from it. He knows I know how he feels, so he's sharing it with me.

"I'd like to just hold you instead, I think."

I trace a heart shape on his back with my nail, making him shiver. "I'd really like that."

43

MAC, ELEANOR, NICOLE AND DIMITRI

MAC

It's kind of funny how circular life can be sometimes.

Because I've been to this storage facility before. I've even been at this facility with these same guns before. Last time we were intercepting their movement and stealing the shipment, and this time I'm loading up what remains of it, but it's still the same guns at the same facility.

When the last box is on the truck, I shoot Felix a text that he instantly reads. Guy must have his phone in his hand.

The drop point is only a few miles away, and I pull into the abandoned lot right next to the sedan. Felix is leaning against the door, arms crossed as he waits, and he straightens as I hop down from the cab.

A year ago, I'd have gone in for a shake. Maybe even a quick bro-hug. Too much has changed, but the impulse is still there.

"Hey, man." He nods.

I snort at the strange, stiff greeting. "Felix. You look good. Last time I saw you, you were like a buck eighty-five? You've put on some muscle."

His gold tooth flashes in the light from a street lamp at the edge of the parking lot. "Shit, you wanna fuck me, *mano*?"

And just like that, the tension is broken. I roll my eyes and clap him on the shoulder. "C'mon."

We head around to the back of the truck and I shove the rolling shutter door up, revealing five plywood crates. Felix gracefully climbs up into the truck bed and lifts the top off one.

"It's a fire sale," I tell him proudly.

He cuts me a look. "Was that supposed to be a joke?"

"Yeah," I chuckle. "Get it? 'Cause they're *fire*arms?"

"Oh, I got it; you're just nowhere near as funny as you think you are," he says distractedly, examining the goods in the box. He whistles, lifting an AK-47 out. "Where'd you get all this heat?"

"Been holding it for a while," I shrug. "It's... time to let it go."

In actuality, there were six crates left from the job we did that brought us to Ulysses. The Feds seized most of it, and used it as evidence to close the case on the illegal weapons trading the mayor was doing, and we kept six crates full of explosives and military-grade weapons in a storage facility right under everyone's noses.

Felix gets five because... well, just because I'm getting out of the hit-man business, that doesn't mean I'm going to just give up all my toys.

He grins again, slamming the heel of his hand on the top of the crate to seal it back down. "Well, I'm happy to take it off your hands."

"That ought to cover our debts, yeah?"

Felix's laugh rings out. "Yeah. This oughtta do it."

Dimitri hated this idea, but he didn't want the guns either. None of us wanted the hassle of trying to fence them, or the potential legal nightmare of trying to turn them in. Obviously he's worried about Felix using them against us, but not me. This is the dawn of a new era.

Plus... if he does, thanks to Madison, we have everything we need to nail his ass to the wall. But I don't think he will. Not while we've got his family on our team.

Thank God for Mads.

Felix drops down from the truck bed and tugs the door back into place. I offer him the key, pulling back when he swipes for it. "Don't even think about veering from the plan. I'll be watching."

He takes my key, then my hand, slamming it into a shake with his own. "Oh, I know. You always are."

Not for much longer. "No hard feelings between us, yeah?"

Felix lifts a brow and flashes that grating smile—the one that's at once knowing, judging, superior and private. The one that makes you feel like he's 10 steps ahead of you and he knows something you don't and thinks it's hilarious. "Nah. Holding grudges is bad for business—I cater to other people's, no time to hold my own. Besides, seems to me you three make better allies than enemies."

He tosses the key to the sedan at me, and I climb into the old, beat-up car. As Felix drives off, I reopen the comms channel. "Operation 'we can trust this guy, right?' is a go," I say, grinning when I hear someone—not even sure who, with so many possible voices in my ears now—snort.

It's Mads. Good ol' Mads. The girl who can always be relied on to get the joke. *"A bit wordy for an operation codename, don't you think?"*

"Too late to change it now," I sing. I squeeze the steering wheel in my grip, itching to tap my other earbud and open the line back up with Eleanor. My leg jiggles nervously.

She's got this. She wanted to help. She's not in any real danger. She told you to stop checking in because it was making her more nervous.

Still, I can't help myself.

"How you doin' with your part, darlin'?"

"I'm ready."

ELEANOR

I swear I'm going to pee myself. Or hurl. Hopefully not at the same time.

My heart is racing so hard that I know my face is probably beet red. I keep checking in the reflective surfaces of the trays I stack and windows I pass. And while there's a definite pink flush, it's really no more than you'd expect after running around.

Stay calm, Eleanor.

I like to think I've come a long way since I walked in on a sniper in my apartment. I'm so far from that sad, scared, self-critical girl who was afraid to go after things she wanted. I've learned so much since meeting Mac—about myself and the world—and one of the most transformative realizations was that I *can* do hard things. Taking on a challenge that scares me is an opportunity to prove to myself that I'm strong and resourceful...

But that doesn't mean it's not still scary in the moment. And it definitely doesn't mean I'm any better with this secret agent/spy shit.

With trembling fingers, I adjust the neckline of the black chef's coat, feeling like I'm wearing a nostalgic kind of costume. Only, my chef's coats never had a camera wired through, peeking out and pretending to be a button.

"Can you still see?" I mutter, trying to look like I'm talking to myself and not the group of people listening in and watching my every move.

"Yeah, Eleanor, we can still see," Madison replies with exaggerated patience.

To calm myself, I repeat the plan. Dump the carefully measured vial of sedative into a champagne flute. Put it on the tray with the other cocktails. With her help, find Madison's boss in the crowd. Offer him the cocktail with the sedative. Get the fuck out.

It's one of the rare times I've been alone in the room where the catering stuff is set up, so I grab the sedative vial from my pocket, snap off the top and dump it all into one of the elegant thin glasses. The drink fizzes at the addition, but doesn't bubble over. When it dies down, the flute is a fraction fuller than the others, but with no noticeable change to the appearance. It's the same pale yellow as the others from the lemon juice.

Just as I'm stashing the empty vial in my pocket, Sarah comes barreling through the double doors, slamming down her tray and rubbing her eyes. It didn't take long to figure out who was in charge of catering at this event—it's a surprisingly small, collaborative circle of mostly women—and Sarah from Great Eatz was thrilled for an extra set of hands when two of her staff called in sick. That was sheer luck; I was just banking on the fact that it always feels like there are *never* enough hands.

"I swear to God, they never listen when they're ordering—I always tell them to double however many crab puffs they think they want, and even then it won't be enough. Eleanor, can you check on the crab puffs we have left for me? I've got to go talk to someone with allergies."

I have to bite back the amenable response that instantly springs to my lips. Chef Eleanor has no problem checking on the crab puffs, but I'm not Chef Eleanor tonight. I'm Undercover Eleanor. "I was just about to take out this tray of cocktails."

"You don't need to be on cocktail duty—you should be plating. Give it to Tilly," Sarah suggests, catching the girl by the arm as she tries to scoot by.

Fuck. One minor hiccup and I'm sitting here like a dead fish, mouth agape, trying to come up with some reason to object that makes sense other than *well, I would, but one of these champagne flutes is full of the perfect dose of etorphine and I have to make sure it gets to the right corporate asshole with network access to a murder-for-hire software program that we're going to dismantle before it goes live.*

I'm not quite sure how the truth came to be so unbelievable.

"I, uh..."

Sarah reaches out to grab the edge of the tray.

"I need to do it. I, uh... I need to talk to one of the guests."

Her frown deepens. "What? You can't use this event as an excuse to talk to someone. That's so unprofessional."

Fuck. She's right.

"Tell her you're pregnant," Madison suggests. *"People back down for personal stuff like that."*

"I'm pregnant," I blurt out, latching on to the offered excuse when I can't seem to think of one myself.

Sarah goes still, and Tilly stops mid-step towards the double doors.

"I won't cause a scene," I rush to add, nearly wincing when I realize I've created a whole new problem for myself. I just needed an excuse; instead, I opened a can of worms. "I... I just need to talk to him."

"That's... uh..." Sarah glances around, makes a face of warning at Tilly, and takes my arm, pulling me aside. "Is everything okay? I don't want to pry, but I thought..." her eyes flick down to the giant diamond on my finger.

I'm going to kill Madison.

My cheeks feel so hot that I know I'm blushing at least four shades of red to pink right now. At least embarrassment fits the story. "I just need to talk to him. Really quickly."

"Yeah, okay. You'll be discreet?"

I nod and duck my head. Picking the tray back up, I head back into the party. "The reason did *not* have to be that dramatic," I grumble under my breath, knowing the incredible little devices will still pick up the sound.

Madison chuckles in my ear. *"Yeah, but it's way more fun for me that it was."*

The launch party is a tasteful event. About a hundred people are milling around between black tablecloth-covered high-tops and the low, circular tables where they'll have dinner in about an hour, after the presentation. The screensaver on the display has been cycling through a slideshow with the presentation schedule, pictures of smiling business executives on some kind of retreat where they had to wear matching green t-shirts, and stock photos of people working at computers. Music drifts softly through the air from the speakers in the four corners—something jazzy and light that doesn't compete with chatter. People are dressed to impress, and there's a buzz of excitement in the room.

"There he is. Up ahead. He's the one with the blue tie. See him?"

I take it back. I'm not going to kill her—I'm glad she's in my ear. Because even though I stared at his picture long enough to convince myself I had it memorized, he looks different in person. Way more tan.

I sidle up to the group, grabbing the tray to hold it with both hands when it starts to shake. "Champagne cocktail?" I interrupt politely.

The man and woman across from me take a glass and place their empties on the tray. Fred, who is in the middle of a story, is gesturing with his nearly empty flute. We're trained to ask once and leave, but I can't leave.

My heart is going to pound out of my chest. I hold out the tray towards him, the slightly fuller glass closest to him.

"Sir? Would you like a drink?"

Take it. Oh my God, take it. Please take the right one. That one. Take it!

He frowns at the interruption, then realizes what I said. For a single, suspended second, I have the completely irrational intrusive thought that I'm mentally pleading with him to take the right champagne flute so hard that he can actually hear me.

Then he launches back into his story, giving me the almost-empty and taking the glass closest to him. He drains half the flute in a single massive gulp, making a face at either the faint taste of sedative or the burning sensation of bubbles in the back of his throat.

My knees nearly give out with relief as I head over to the last person in the group to offer a flute.

"Tag, you're it," I whisper as Nicole takes a flute off my tray and gestures at me with it, a cheers of acknowledgment.

NICOLE

If I have to listen to this absolute *tool* tell one more story about the kind of yacht he plans to buy after Safe-T Keeper goes live, I'm going to shove more sedative down his throat.

Luckily, I don't have to.

Fred goes down like something out of a cartoon. He's in the middle of his sentence, then he grimaces and shakes his head, like he's trying to clear the sudden disorientation. Etorphine works pretty fast, and this guy can really shotgun a champagne cocktail.

One second he's upright and slurring about how he doesn't feel good, and the next he pitches forward. The woman he almost falls on screams, and a glass shatters at their feet as he knocks it out of her hand on the way down.

In the panic that ensues, I lift my voice and spring into action. "I'm a nurse!"

Tossing my skirts aside, I kneel down next to him. "Sir," I say, speaking loudly and clearly. "Can you hear me? What's his name?" I ask the group of people huddling over us with panicked expressions.

"Oh, nice touch. She's a natural," Wesley approves.

"Fred Harvey!" someone in the audience volunteers.

"Everyone, please give us space," I say. Dutifully, the crowd immediately nearby takes a few shuffling steps back. I lean over Fred and tap his shoulders. "Fred, can you speak? Mr. Harvey? Can you tell me what's wrong?"

Fred's eyes flutter but don't open completely, and he makes a garbled noise.

"Does anyone know this man? Does he have a medical condition?"

The crowd remains silent until someone pipes in, "Should I call an ambulance?"

I've seen it time and time again, and this was exactly what I told the group when we were forming the plan. A crowd naturally defers to whoever seems the calmest and most confident in an emergency. People won't take initiative from me—he's asking me if he should call an ambulance instead of doing it. Normally, it would piss me off because in a true emergency, there's no time to waste seeking approval.

Not tonight. Tonight, I'm glad for the hive-brain panic mentality. People won't act for fear of doing the wrong thing.

"I'll take him—it'll be faster than waiting for an ambulance. Can someone call the emergency department at Ulysses Memorial?" I ask the crowd, trying to get ahead of the 911 calls by introducing an extra step. Of course I don't really want that—Fred won't be going to the hospital tonight.

Well, maybe... depends on how cooperative he's feeling.

"I will," a deep, Russian voice volunteers. Even after all this time, it sends a shiver up and down my spine and nearly makes me break character because I want so badly to smile conspiratorially at him.

"Tell them an adult man collapsed and is unresponsive. A medical professional is bringing him for treatment. This appears to be a medical issue with no observable trauma. No airway blockage or obvious bleeding..."

A concerned murmur goes around. I don't need any more confirmation that I'm selling the hell out of this. I glance up, then do a double take at the tall, dashing waiter no one hired—just for effect. "You."

His eyes widen as he looks over, phone still clutched to his ear as he makes his pretend call to the hospital. "Me?" he repeats.

"You look strong. Can you help me get him to my car? Call the hospital on the way."

Pocketing his phone with a grim expression, he gently touches the shoulder of a man in his way, who looks back, then does a double take when he sees the size of Dimitri and scrambles out of the way.

My man leans down and slides a hand under Fred's armpit as I take the other side. When we discussed this last night, he fought me tooth and nail.

You are pregnant, my med. *You will not be lifting anything heavier than this glass of water until my* milyy rebenok *is born.*

I looked that one up. Sweet child. It made me choke up a little.

But I argued that if he lifted a grown man into his arms like a baby, no one would ever stop talking about it. It's too memorable for what is sure to be one of the few things anyone talks about for the rest of the night. Me? The bossy nurse who leaped into action? They'll forget about me. The massive, scarred waiter with the thick accent? Yeah, he doesn't need any more reason to burn his image into anyone's memory.

To the casual observer, it would appear that the enormous, scarred server and I share the burden of getting the barely conscious Fred Harvey out of the ballroom of the Ulysses Grand, when in reality Dimitri is bearing the brunt of it.

People clear a path as we make our way through the automatic doors. Maintaining the ruse, I hurry to Dimitri's SUV and get into the driver's seat as he maneuvers Fred inside and slams the back door shut. He hops into the passenger seat, and I back out of the spot.

As I check the rearview, I can hardly believe my eyes. The hotel entrance is empty. No one at the party even followed us out. Either our act was that believable, or none of Fred's coworkers cares enough about him to check and make sure two strangers aren't blatantly kidnapping him.

We're... we're totally pulling this off.

Oh my God, is this what it feels like to be on the other side of things?

I think I finally understand why they do it. What a rush!

"It is easy to become too excited," Dimitri coaches me calmly. "Remember to drive the speed limit."

For some reason, it makes me laugh. Maybe it's that I'm already kind of giddy because I can't believe how well that went. I suppose I knew how thoroughly the guys plan everything, but it's totally different to experience it firsthand. To be part of it.

I look over at him. "I love you so much."

"I love you too, my *med*. More than my life. But not more than yours or that of our *milyy rebenok*. So please return your eyes to the road."

I smile and do as he instructs.

Milly. That's kind of a cute name for a girl.

DIMITRI

I suppose it is human nature to reflect on the beginning when one is at the end. People often say that life is a journey. At the start of mine, I was a man who enjoyed tying someone to a chair and making him bleed while I pried information I wanted out of his lips. Sometimes with actual pliers.

But interrogation is not a skill I ever thought I would teach to someone else.

Fred sits in the center of what was once a large conference room, taped to an office chair and very effectively restrained. He woke some time ago and promptly exhausted himself and angered us all by proving that no one can hear him scream. Now, he is sweaty, mad and very afraid.

In our planning, we discovered that the building next to SmarTech is available for rent, making it the perfect secondary location, since it is empty, isolated, and we are close enough that Madison can access the SmarTech network wirelessly. She set up some equipment I recognize from Wesley's home office in this conference room, taking over the end of a long table.

But she is not at her station—she is on her feet, standing before our hostage, and the sharp crack of her slap rings out around us. She yells something at him in Spanish, and I must assume from her tone that it is an insult since I do not speak the language.

"Madison!" I admonish sharply.

She turns to me, shock plain in her expression that I would scold her when she is trying to be intimidating. But she does not need to be intimidating; she needs to be effective.

"You will injure your hand doing it that way. You must shape it to create a small cavity," I explain, adjusting her hand into the proper position, cupped with a space in the center. "Then, when you slap, aim for the ear. If you can get enough force behind it, you will break his eardrum."

Fred's eyes go wide, and he flinches as she slaps him again, making a grunting noise of pain and dropping his ear to his shoulder to soothe the sensation in the aftermath.

"Oh, yeah, that's way better," Madison says approvingly, turning to Eleanor, who is watching with grim fascination. "You wanna try?"

Her eyes light up. "Ooh, yeah!"

Fred's eyes narrow on her. "You're making a big mistake," he tells her, obviously zeroing in on the innocent appearance of her open face. "You... you don't look like a killer. You don't want to hurt me. Think about what you're doing! This is torture—you're about to torture someone!"

She hesitates and glances at Madison. "He helped create that software? Or, like, he knows what it does, and wants to make a profit off it?"

Madison nods.

"Then, yeah. I don't feel bad about this," Eleanor says, her tone full of a darker kind of purpose. She flexes her hand, then twists to wind up for her blow.

"Wait. You are supposed to ask him something first," I remind her. "This is an interrogation."

Eleanor stops, stumped. Then, she steps up to him and slaps him the same way Madison did, shaking out her hand as she demands, "What's your password?"

"We don't need him to tell us," Madison says. "We've got his phone and his fingerprint. I bet he keeps all his passwords in that app on his phone."

"Oh," Eleanor says. She hits him again. "Where's the Joker?" she demands in a low, garbled voice I have never heard before.

"That was a pretty good Batman, darlin'," Mac compliments from somewhere in a nearby building where he is setting up his rifle.

She slaps him again, and a pathetic whimper slips through his lips with a string of spit that lands on the lapel of his suit jacket.

I chuckle, and Madison turns to me, shocked by the noise. "She looks sweet but is bloodthirsty. It is very amusing," I explain.

Since they clearly have this interrogation under control, I go to Nicole, who is standing in the corner of the room, watching with her arms crossed and wearing a faintly amused smile. I want to shield her with my body from the unpleasantness, but instead I stand next to her. The only reason I allowed her participation was that she agreed to carry a gun and stay away from the danger. She argued that Eleanor and Madison could not be left alone with this man Fred—she claims they rile each other up. It seems she was right.

"You're going to miss this, huh?" she asks as I settle against the wall next to her.

"What?"

"Teaching. Doing something useful with all those skills you've got. Passing them on."

I consider this. Once Wesley has taken the Gener-AI program offline and there are no more jobs to complete, there will be little reason to continue to train with the others. But I have enjoyed training with them very much, so I decide, *"Da."*

For some reason, this causes Nicole's eyes to fill with tears—an alarming occurrence that has become more frequent lately. She assures me it is completely hormonally normal, but seeing her crying fills me with an anger that is pointless, with nothing to kill or destroy for making her cry. She wraps her arms around my middle, hugging me gently, and murmurs into my shirt, "You're going to be a good dad," she says softly—too softly for the others to hear.

The praise warms me, and I must swallow down a thick feeling in the back of my throat. "I will not be passing this information to a child," I say, confused about why she equates teaching Madison to burst an eardrum with being a father.

"No," she agrees readily. "But you... you explain your point of view in this really complete and direct way. And you're patient. You're gentle as a teacher—well, as gentle as I've seen you be," she adds when I lift a brow at her. "I don't know if you know this about kids, but you kind of have to teach them everything. So being a good teacher... it's a really good thing."

I had not considered parenthood in this way. The fear that has knotted my chest ever since I saw that pregnancy test on the bathroom sink loosens slightly. Nicole believes I will be a good father. I did not know how comforting that would be. "I can do anything with you by my side," I tell her, grabbing her hand and pressing a kiss to her palm.

Her smile is warm and soft, much like her.

"Did you ever think that you would go from being kidnapped to assisting me with one?" I ask her, smiling so widely that my scar pulls against the corner of my mouth.

She laughs, a deep, husky noise that stirs in my loins. "No. No, I didn't. And I gotta say, it's kind of a rush. If I weren't already pregnant..." she gives me an ardent look.

"Yes. It is always good to practice," I agree. She laughs again. "But first, we must end this." I tap my earpiece to unmute myself. "Wesley? James?"

"Just getting into place," James replies.

"I'm here," Wesley confirms.

"Then I will meet you at the entrance."

44

WESLEY

This is like being in the ladies room at a night club.

Fred's behavior leading up to tonight made it obvious that he was expecting trouble—him and whoever he's working with at SmarTech, which we assume at least includes the CEO and board. They stand to make millions off this product, and they know the stakes, so it's not surprising they'd want to ensure the launch goes off without a hitch.

So we prepared for it.

"Cameras are down," Madison confirms. *"You have 20 minutes before the alarm goes off and the backups come online. Make it count, Spyder-Man."*

20 minutes to get in, find Fred's office, log into his computer, get into the program files, and shut it all down. We have to pull this off tonight; otherwise, the program will be sent out, it will proliferate and adapt—as AI is wont to do—and we'll lose our shot to contain it before it becomes a juggernaut.

With Madison's help, I can do it. With Dimitri and Mac's backup, I can do it.

I can do it.

SmarTech offices are in a large, stylized glass and metal structure on the outskirts of Ulysses. The entrance is grand, austere and sleek, with doors of glass and chrome that open up into a big room with polished concrete floors and a desk with two guards to direct visitors down the hallway and workers through the turnstile.

But it's 7 PM on a Saturday, and this is a Monday through Friday, 9-5 office building. There's no reason for there to be security guards.

Because they're not security guards.

"Butcher," Dimitri greets the larger of the two.

His chuckle is dark and knowing as he stands from the desk where he's been resting his feet. His accent is just as thick as Dimitri's. "Ghost. It has been, what, eight months?"

"What a ridiculous question. Why would I keep track of this?" Dimitri asks.

There's a single second of heavy confusion following his statement, then all hell breaks loose.

The other bloke who's leaning against the desk reaches into his holster and produces a gun, aiming for me, as the Butcher leaps at Dimitri with a knife. The sound of glass splintering and the sight of blood oozing from a single hole in the man's forehead happen simultaneously as Mac steps in with the kill shot from above.

In the wake of the bullet, glass shatters behind us, falling and ricocheting off the floor in a million sparkling shards. As I duck and cover, Dimitri and the Butcher are locked in, exchanging blows.

"Go!" Dimitri shouts, dodging a hit.

I take a running leap over the turnstile and burst through the internal doors.

"Take the first left," Madison instructs in my ear.

I do, hurrying, feeling exposed. It's eerie in here—dark and silent—and my heavy footsteps are the only sound. Mac can follow my progress through the halls, since the offices lining the outer walls have large windows, but he's a last resort. The clock is already ticking after that first shot—the authorities might already be on their way—and we've only got 20 minutes. 18 now, most likely.

"Janitor, three o'clock!" Mac says.

Up ahead, the hallway disappears to a hard right. I don't have time to wonder if he's really a janitor or another hitman as the bloke rounds the corner and catches sight of me. He freezes behind the large rolling trash and pulls an earbud out.

"Uh... who are you?" he asks suspiciously.

I don't buy the act. It's too dark in here for a janitor. I ignore the question and charge ahead, and the man's dumbfounded expression shifts into one of steely purpose as he reaches into the trash can, producing a large rifle.

It's lucky I didn't hesitate—I get to him before he can get the gun up. He dodges my punch, swinging the rifle into the air towards me, but I drop. A shot goes off, blasting through the drywall corner and echoing in the feedback in my ears. But there's no time to react to the ringing sensation, despite the pain of the too-loud noise. I shove my shoulder into his stomach and force him against the wall. I can feel his head bounce off it as he hits.

Flicking the cover off my ring, I reach up for any bare skin and manage to grab him around the forearm. He uses the butt of his gun to hit me on the back of the head, and my balance falters at the crack of pain. I stumble backwards, nearly losing my footing, and he swings his gun back up with a triumphant smile.

The etorphine hits him suddenly and hard—the dose is for someone much larger—and he fails to aim properly. Another shot goes off, piercing a ceiling tile, as the man keels over.

Chest heaving, I cup my hands around my ears with a grimace of pain. I can hear Madison, but it's like hearing someone's voice while your head is underwater.

"Wesley?" she cries. *"Mac? Is he—"*

"I can see him, Mads. He's fine. Didn't get shot. Probably just hurting from that discharge. His ears'll equalize in a minute."

I shake my head, trying to get my bearings again. "Fuck, that smarts," I complain, rubbing underneath my ears to see if there's any blood. There isn't, thank God.

"Are you okay?" Madison asks, voice full of tearful relief.

"Yes, my love. Which way do I go?"

"Follow that hall, and his office is the last on the left." She inhales shakily. *"I hated that. You handled it super well, but that was so scary."*

"Almost there," I promise, a consolation to us both. My heart is racing, and the adrenaline is making me feel ill. "How's Dimitri doing?"

"The Butcher is handled. I am checking the perimeter for more janitors and security guards."

That at least makes me feel better. Being the boots on the ground and taking care of the close encounters with miscreants is really more Dimitri's forte.

Fred's office is locked, but my pick makes quick work of it. His desk is tidy, with a few ostentatious decorations to prove how impressive he is to anyone seated on the other side—a clock with golden hands, a glass-encased photo of him shaking the CEO's hand, a framed Master's Degree.

I take a seat in his chair, jiggle his mouse, and focus on our next hurdle. "I'm in. Password?"

There's a scuffle and a sound of low, male outrage followed by a sharp slap that nearly makes me grin. *"Okay, got his thumbprint and unlocked his phone... password wallet... SmarTech login... Oh, got it! It's... are you for real, dude?"* she says, accusatory, then sighs like she doesn't want to say it. *"It's Pu$$yDe$troyer69, capital P and D, dollar signs instead of each 's.'"* I can practically hear her shaking her head at him.

Mac's laughter is so instantaneous, he can't get himself muted fast enough and we all hear the first few barks.

"Such a tool," Nicole mutters.

It works—because of course it does—and I'm greeted by a very organized desktop. I head immediately to the main finder folder to see the list of drives he has access to.

Madison, who can see what I'm doing through a camera wired to my shirt, helps me identify the right one. *"Okay, the B-drive is HR, C is projects, D is operational... It's the E drive. R&D is in there."*

I click on it and type in the search terms we decided on. But Safe-T Keeper and Gener-AI don't return anything. Trying to make it harder to find than that, apparently.

"The files in here are named with a code, but I can't tell what it means," I say, shaking my head and scrolling through what feels like infinite files with randomly generated names. Letters and numbers all mixed up.

"What's the project under?" Madison asks, voice low and meant to be intimidating, I'd wager.

"Like I'd tell you!" Fred laughs.

Another slap sounds, followed by a growl from Fred. *"Is that the best you got?"* I hear him seethe. *"Am I supposed to be afraid? What are you girls gonna do next, sit on me? It'd probably hurt more than your weak ass—"*

There's another noise, and this one is much more of a thump than a slap.

"What part of being tied to a chair makes you think it's a good idea to antagonize us right now?" Nicole barks at him.

"Nicole," Eleanor breathes in awe. *"That was such a good punch."*

"Thank you," Nicole replies lightly. *"You were doing a really good job, too. You looked so strong. Good form."*

"Thanks!"

"This is like being in the ladies' room at a nightclub," Madison laughs. *"Oh, wait! Okay, try X026KA0225."*

I type it in, the folder comes up, and I double-click. "This is it," I breathe, scrolling through project files I recognize. The software itself is a small icon at the bottom with a colorful image replicating the SmarTech logo. To be safe, I open it in the sandbox environment first. My heart thumps hard in my chest, a wash of emotion sweeping over me as I come face to face with the ghosts of my past.

"This is it," I repeat.

"You've got it?" Madison breathes.

"I do." I pull up the code in an editor.

"Okay, so now we just need to corrupt the—"

I hear a deep, faraway chuckle reverberate through the earpiece. It's chilling and smug in equal measure. *"It won't matter. You're too late."*

"What do you mean?" Madison asks, her voice becoming shrill in her confusion and alarm. I can't picture the look on his face, but she sounds scared. *"What do you mean, Fred?!"*

I realize why he's laughing a second later, as I get to the most recent additions to the event log.

"You're too late," he repeats.

Fuck. We are too late. The software was sent to fulfill the preorders this morning. I have the list of cities that have bought the tech right here, but that means that SmarTech isn't the only one with a copy anymore. We can delete the backups and destroy the host server, but each of these cities has their own copy, operating independently. There's no kill-switch option because we didn't get here in time.

We can't stop it from getting out.

"It's already out."

45

MADISON

Kind of a fitting end.

"It's already out."

My body feels cold and stiff as I fall back into my seat, which rolls a few inches and throws me off balance. Fred's smile is condescending, and the blood coating his teeth from Nicole's blow gives it a real demonic edge.

"It went out this morning to every city on the list," he says, evil curling around every word and making my skin prickle.

Eleanor gasps, exchanging a fearful look with Nicole.

I'm reeling. How could this have happened? How could we have failed? I turn to him, blinking back tears of rage and horror. "You made a monster," I say softly. "You just put a *monster* out into the world. And you're so focused on the money, you don't realize what you've done!"

"Not the money," he shakes his head. "The numbers. Crime in Ulysses is down 30% since we gave the AI free rein on the data. 30%! That's insane. That's... you can't argue with numbers like that!"

He's the one who's insane if he thinks he can win me over with that kind of argument. "Crime is down, but the murder of criminals is up? You seriously don't hear the contradiction in that?"

He rolls his eyes. "We're making this world safer—"

"No, you're not," Nicole cuts in. "You're making them more careful, or you're driving them to another city that's less protected and prepared. None of this is happening in a vacuum. There are always repercussions."

"And it's still murder!" Eleanor adds.

Fred spits on the ground. "Good fucking riddance. Scumbags are dying. Boo fuckin' hoo."

"Scumbags, now. But what happens when it starts targeting not just violent, destructive crime? What if the AI starts going after anyone who breaks the law? You released something destructive into the world that self-polices. How can you not see how big of a problem that is?"

He turns his head.

"And what if it turns on you? What you're doing is illegal, too. You created a literal killing machine. At what point do *you* meet the criteria?"

He inhales deeply and turns back to me, stone-faced. "What's your game plan, Madison? What's your move? You either have to let me go, or you kill me." Another bloody smile flashes, and I can tell how convinced he is that he knows how this is going to play out. "Are you going to try to make me think you're going to kill me? After all that—your little bleeding-heart display? Yeah, I'm thinking no."

Suddenly, the door to the meeting room creaks open. We all turn with similar expressions of curiosity—there's no way it's Wes or Dimitri returning, they're still in the other building—and *Todd* steps into the room.

He lifts a gun, pointing it right at me.

"Oh my god!" Eleanor screeches in alarm. Nicole gasps, stepping in front of her protectively.

With a terrified noise, I throw my hands up automatically.

"What? What's happening? What just happened?" Wesley demands in my ear, responding to the sounds in the room.

My heart pounds in my ears. Fuck, it's scary being on the wrong end of a gun. I can barely think. "Todd," I say softly, informing Wesley and willing my voice to remain calm and even. "What are you doing here?"

"Todd! Shoot her! The bitch kidnapped me!" Fred urges, sensing his chance.

"No, wait!" I cry. "Wait!"

He levels the gun at my chest with a maniacal smile—he looks truly deranged and ridiculously pleased with himself. "I got suspicious when Fred collapsed. I knew you gave me that SSD for a reason. I always knew you were a cunt, but I had no idea just how big of a cunt you really were."

"Todd, help me!" Fred renews his request.

"Don't help him," I plead. "Fred isn't on your side, Todd. After you gave him the SSD, he put out a hit on you!"

"A hit? Like… a hit to kill me?" At my urgent nod, Todd's brows come down, and his eyes flick briefly to Fred. "Is that true?"

Before Fred can get in there with a lie, I keep going, "Safe-T Keeper is a program that SmarTech created that contracts hitmen to take out criminals or anyone who gets in their way. Remember how Fred told you I was dead? I got in their way. And you know too much! They won't let you live," I promise.

"Is that true?" he repeats to Fred.

"Of course not; she's lying. Todd, don't listen to her! I'll make you a senior manager! Untie me, son."

Todd approaches Fred, keeping one eye on me and the gun pointed firmly in my direction. "She's a crazy bitch. She tied me up, too. What, you have some kind of fetish for men way out of your league, Crunch Wrap Supreme?"

I wince. "He's the one lying. You were never going to get that promotion," I say, my voice dropping in urgency. "I have proof. I can show you!"

I can see it then. The spark of a waver in his resolve. "Proof?"

"Lower the gun, I'll show you the software and the list. I'm plugged into their network, and we just got into the project framework. I can show you that your name is on their kill list."

Looking incredibly suspicious, he glances between the two of us a few times. With a slow nod of agreement, he approaches and leans over my shoulder. He pokes the gun into my back, between my shoulder blades. "Don't get any ideas," he growls.

But my only idea is to show him the proof. So I do. I scroll through, find his name, and point to it with one shaking finger. With an angry noise, Todd turns to Fred. "She's not lying. My name is in there."

Fred pales as Todd turns on him. He starts shaking, trying to back away in the rolling chair with small, ineffectual movements of his taped feet. "I... It... It's not what it looks like."

"I think it is what it looks like," he returns.

"Todd, stop! I can still help you!" Fred screams. "You can still come out on top! You can have everything! Your revenge against the cunt *and* the promotion!"

"Oh yeah? How?"

"I can tell the program not to kill you. I have an override code. I can take you off the list with my phone."

"Fuck," I whisper, glancing down at Fred's phone on the edge of the conference table. The key is in there?

Todd's eyes cut to me. He swipes the phone off the desk before I can make a move for it, then points his gun back at me as he sidesteps towards Fred. "Then do it. Right now. Show me."

Fred's head bobs up and down, an immediate promise. "I'll show you, and you shoot the bitch, yeah?"

"Okay, deal," Todd agrees, sending me a cold look.

I know the phone is still unlocked, so Todd can just hold it up in front of Fred's face and let him direct him through the screen to get to what he needs. "You go into that app," Fred coaches, eyes darting up towards me and the other girls to make sure no one is making a move while they're distracted. But we're all rooted in place, hands up in the air in surrender to the weapon, terrified expressions on our faces. "Go into the messages... yeah, it needs my thumbprint again. Okay, look for your name—that one. Pull that one up. Okay, now reply to it with this exact phrase: Signing key 11 rejected."

Todd eyes him suspiciously. "Simple as that?"

Fred nods. "You'll get a confirmation in a second—it confirms that the hit won't be carried out. You can look back in my sent box if you want, see that it's worked before. It's synced to my phone and my identity."

"A signing key?" I repeat as it all clicks into place.

I fucking knew it. I *knew* SmarTech never would have released something like this without a failsafe. I grin, throwing Todd a look as I sit back and let my arms fall. "Makes sense. Every monster needs a leash."

With a similar confident grin, Todd tosses me the phone, and I flick through the app.

Fred glances between the two of us, confused at the abrupt change in the temperature of the room. His eyes are wide as he glances around, watching Eleanor and Nicole relax, too. "What... what's going on?"

I read the messages he exchanged with the AI, assessing the content. "Looks like the program has a command-and-control function. That's the failsafe. The AI is autonomous, but it checks in with the parent program for every hit. If anyone enters their signing key, the hit is negated. It's how they're protecting themselves. I fucking knew there was no way they'd just let that program out into the world with no guardrails."

"Everyone involved in the project probably has a key," Wesley remarks, entering the room. Dimitri is hot on his heels. "If no one responds, it moves forward with the hit. If the connection is severed, it becomes fully autonomous, and no one is safe. It's SmarTech's self-destruct option. If they go down, they take everyone down."

Our eyes meet from across the room, and I know he feels the same swell of relief.

"You were right," he breathes.

"We can stop it," I say, nodding. "We have his key, so we can keep every hit from happening until we can find and destroy every copy of the program that got out."

"I don't know what that means, but it sounds like we won," Mac declares from the doorway, the last to join the party.

"What the fuck? Who the fuck are you? Who the fuck are you people?!" Fred interjects, raging against his bonds. "You... you... No!" he roars.

Todd steps up to him, winds up and punches him squarely in the nose. Fred's head jerks back, bone crunching and blood pouring out as his momentum shifts forward again, and he flops against the tape, unconscious.

"That's for trying to fucking kill me, you fucker," he yells at Fred, shaking out his hand.

Eleanor lets out a giggle that's as much a noise of relief as amusement.

Wesley crosses the room, holding out his hand, and Todd offers him a half smile before slapping it with his own in a high five. Wesley frowns. "I'm not fucking high fiving you, you twat. Give me the gun."

"Oh," Todd makes a sheepish face, handing it over.

Wesley checks the chamber, then lets out a long breath. I think if Todd had been pointing a loaded gun at me, Wesley would have killed him, regardless of how much he just saved our asses. "Thank you, Todd. For... that. Thank you."

Todd's chest puffs out, and I nearly roll my eyes, but even I have to admit that was well done. "Yeah, thanks," I say. "You acted the shit out of that. Fred really thought you were going to help him."

It was a big risk—the biggest of the night by far. But I knew that Fred would never give up any critical information willingly. Dimitri might've been able to torture it out of him, but I argued this was quicker—and at the time we thought we were up against a time crunch to stop it from getting out.

Todd wasn't initially really open to anything I had to say—still kind of butt-hurt about being duct-taped and threatened with a gun—but once I showed him the proof, he turned out to be pretty reasonable.

We also offered him a bunch of money in exchange for his help. Like, a *lot* of money. We had to make sure to preemptively outbid Fred if he tried to bribe Todd to switch sides.

"Fuck yeah, I did." He grins, then reaches his hand out to me. I do roll my eyes this time, but I give him that high five he's after. "Sorry about the Taco Bell joke, too. I was... uh, going for authenticity. Fred laughed at that one earlier this week—I wanted to make him think I was on his side."

"Authentic, huh?" I repeat, unimpressed. Authentically a *pendejo*, through and through. At least he apologized for it, I guess.

"So I'm safe now, right?" Todd asks, glancing back at Fred like he'd really like to land another punch.

"I'd lie low for a day or two. What are your plans?" Wesley asks.

Todd's answering grin is huge. "With this kind of money? I'm retiring at 32, buying a beach house and filling it with girls and booze."

"Classy," I snort.

"I am who I am," he shrugs. "All right. Well, I'm out. Good luck cleaning... uh... all this up."

As Todd strides from the room, hands shoved in his pockets, humming something happy, we all turn to the last remaining issue. Fred. "What do we do with him?"

Six people regard the tied up, passed out man with varying degrees of anger.

"You will need his fingerprint, *da*?" Dimitri asks, palming his knife.

"You're gonna... cut it off? So we can carry it around? No. Ew." I shake my head. "No, there's a password. The fingerprint is just a secondary authentication option. We'll be able to do it as long as we have his phone. We can clone the app and use his credentials and change them to guarantee ourselves access."

"I know you guys can stop the hits, but is there a way to... I don't know, add him to the list?" Nicole suggests.

I grin, liking this neat bow she's come up with. "Hell yeah. Kind of a fitting end to be a victim of the machine he helped create and sell. But how do we keep the other signing keys from blocking his name?" I wonder.

"I have a suggestion," comes a deep, familiar voice behind me.

I whirl, and Felix is in the doorway. His stance is protective, and the look on his face is a little wild and urgent.

"Felix? How did you know we were here—" Mac begins.

"Your big ugly van is parked outside, and this was the only room with lights on," he replies, like it's obvious.

"What are you doing here?" Dimitri growls.

Felix glances at him, then directs his next statement at me. "So... things... escalated. You're all gonna want to get the hell out of here."

"What? Why?"

Felix's grin is positively feral. "Boom," he says, doing the appropriate hand motion to demonstrate.

"What? Why?" Wesley repeats, much more alarmed than when I just said it.

"Uh... 'cause I want to?"

"I told you, they have government contracts! The military police will—"

Felix cuts in with a noise of exasperation. "You can stay here and yell all you want, but I'm getting the fuck out, and I'm here to make sure she gets out," he nods at me. "The building next door is gonna blow, and you really don't want to be in here when that happens."

With that, he disappears, and we all turn again to look at Fred.

"We could just... leave him here," Mac suggests.

We're halfway home, most of us piled in the van, when the car shakes. I spin in my seat to look out the back window and find a pillar of smoke in the night sky that glows an eerie shade of red as it reflects the fire from the explosion.

"That was it?" Mac pouts.

"If you are close enough to be impressed by an explosion, it will be the last emotion you ever feel," Dimitri returns sagely.

"Google doc?" I suggest to Wesley, who grins and nods.

46

WESLEY

Family dinner

A few days later, I catch Madison in the hallway after the long bath I insisted she take to give me enough time to set up her surprise.

She's been enjoying some true downtime now that her life is no longer in danger. We both have. With Fred's cloned phone plugged into my computer, I set up a program that uses his signing key to automatically veto every message that comes in. It's been working with 100% effectiveness, I'm pleased to say. And now that we have control over the program, we can start tearing it down piece by piece until there's nothing left.

We're both eager to start.

"I have a surprise for you, my love."

Madison gasps, hand going to her tracking necklace. "Something sparkly?"

Remembering that was her exact reaction last time, I chuckle and run my hand down her soft, silky hair. "No. Sort of shiny, though."

"Color me intrigued."

I lead her into the office, where Some Bills has taken up residence in the corner of the couch closest to the windows, where his naps are occasionally directly in the sunbeams streaming through the thick curtains. As soon as she steps into the room, Madison inhales sharply, seeing the alterations I've made.

The desk that used to sit along the back wall and hold all my half-finished soldering projects has been cleared and pushed next to my own.

On it, there's a brand new, ridiculously overpowered and top-of-the-line laptop, a mechanical keyboard, a wireless mouse, a headset, and a double monitor arm.

"When did you…" she begins, trailing off as her eyes zigzag across the tech like she can't decide what she wants to look at first. "How…"

"You're going to need your own setup if we're to track down all the remaining copies of the Gener-AI program and wipe it out."

"Side by side," she says, eyes teary and full of love and hope.

"Side by side," I confirm, then nod encouragingly at the desk. "Go check it out."

With a child-like grin of excitement, she bounds over to her new desk and examines everything with a critical eye. She lifts the top of the laptop, cranes her neck to read what kind of chip it has, and whistles. "You went all out."

"Only the best," I agree. "You deserve it."

"It's all…" she trails off, swallowing thickly, "it's perfect, Wesley. Thank you." When I come around, she leans up and kisses my cheek.

I take my seat and gesture to the one next to me. "Good. Now, get to work. You've got a laptop to set up, and we've got local government systems to hack into."

She nods absently, looking down at her own office chair. It's the same model I use, so I'm surprised when she makes a face. "It's all perfect except…"

"You don't like the chair?" I ask, feeling my brows lift.

"I mean, don't get me wrong… this is a nice chair," she says, gripping the back and jerking it back and forth like she's testing the wheels. "Sturdy. Encourages proper posture."

"Ergonomic is the word you're searching for, I believe."

"Mmm," she hums her agreement. She takes a step towards me, eyes playful. "But it's not the chair I want."

"No? You had another model in mind?" I ask, catching on to her game. I spin away from my desk.

She bites her lower lip, and her eyes drop to my lap. "Well, it's not the *seat* I want, I guess I should say."

"Ah." I lift a brow as she takes another slow step, letting the motion of her body rock all her gorgeous curves back and forth. "We have work to do, Madison," I say, playfully stern. "We can't get distracted."

"I'll be a good girl, Sir."

I grin, but I know it looks as dark as it feels when her eyes flash with excitement. "Then take your seat, my love."

With a thrilled little noise, she spins, grabs her new laptop, and slides it over to my desk. She sets it on the table and then turns and presents me with her ass.

"Wait," I instruct, and she pauses with her knee slightly bent. Her hair cascades down her back, and I want to grab a fistful of it and drag her down onto me, but I can't do that quite yet. I settle for grabbing a hip in each hand. "Panties off, first."

She laughs, a husky, pleased noise. Her hands go to the hem of her skirt. But instead of reaching under and tugging any material down her juicy, thick thighs, she flips up the back and shows me her stunning, bare ass. "You're assuming I'm wearing any, Sir," she says hoarsely.

"*Traviesita*," I hiss, reaching down to cup and then squeeze one of the tan globes. Giving in to the urge, I bend down and bite the thickest part—where it's roundest.

She squeals and drops in my lap, grinding her bare cunt into my trousers as she does so.

"We have work to do," I chide, grabbing her tightly to settle her.

With a hum of amusement, she begins working through the setup screen on her new laptop, and I open up the code I've been working on to create a back door we'll need to gain access to the system used in one of the cities that purchased the Safe-T Keeper package.

Clicking around with my right hand leaves my left free. I settle it against her lower stomach, taking a handful of her through her skirt and making her squirm.

"Eyes on your screen."

As she opens her mouth, there's a sharp knock at the door and Eleanor appears in the opening, hand over her eyes. "Everyone decent?"

Madison sighs, throwing me a look over her shoulder. "Unfortunately."

With a wide grin, Eleanor lowers her hand. "Hungry?"

"Starved!"

"Dinner's in the dining room in two minutes."

"The dining room?" I repeat, confused. As far as I know, the formal space that seats 12 has only ever collected dust on the polished mahogany and linen-covered chairs. "Why?"

Eleanor beams. "Family dinner! We're being extra. I even found candles in the drawer!"

"I love that." Madison lifts her arms, stretching out her back before she rises. "Do you need help setting the table?"

"It's all set up. Just bring yourselves."

Madison tugs me up, and we follow Eleanor down the hall. I almost can't contain my surprise to see a room that's stood empty for all this time with lit candles on the table and food arranged prettily in serving platters I wasn't aware we had.

"Eleanor, this is great!" Madison enthuses.

"Yeah, I thought it would be fun. Mac's grilling the steaks—he'll be in in a second," she says, popping into the kitchen and reappearing with a bowl of mashed potatoes. Nicole follows a second later with broccoli, and Dimitri has a stack of plates that he begins dutifully placing at each of the silverware settings.

I didn't even realize the long table condensed, because this shorter version is much more appropriately sized for the six of us. Much cozier.

Madison, Nicole, Dimitri and I choose spots at the table as Eleanor flits around with finishing touches and Mac strides in proudly, carrying a large platter of sizzling meat.

"Which one is the most done?" Madison asks, going up on her tiptoes and trying to see into the platter as he passes her to set it onto the table.

"The *most* done?" Mac repeats, like the very idea offends him. "I'm the grill master, Mads. There's nothing dry or burned on this plate. If you want *well-done meat*, you might as well eat one of Nicole's tofu steaks."

"I will take hers," Dimitri volunteers instantly.

Madison narrows her eyes at Dimitri and sticks a fork into one of the smaller steaks to lift it onto her plate like she's staking her claim, before turning back to Mac. "Rare meat is some *gringo* bullshit. *Mexicanos* like our *carne* marinated and sliced thin."

"Right. I guess I have to remember that you see the world from a different perspective." At Madison's curious frown, wisely not believing his contrition or easy defeat for a second, Mac grins. "That was a short joke. I'd ask if it went over your head, but," he levels his arm, sweeping it through the air above her, "everything does."

She raises a brow at him, wearing her bratty smile that gets my blood pumping. "Big words from someone who's lactose intolerant."

"What does that have to do with anything?" he snorts, piling broccoli onto his plate.

"I'm not gonna be spoken down to by a guy who can be taken out by cheese."

He turns to Eleanor, something akin to betrayal on his face. "You told her?!"

"I didn't know it was a secret?" Eleanor says skeptically, taking her seat at the head of the table.

Nicole and I laugh, and Dimitri shakes his head—something akin to amusement—and we all start digging into the lovely meal. Chatter is idle as we settle in, sticking to shallow, neutral topics like what show Eleanor and Mac are watching and a story about how George and Some Bills are getting along.

I watch Nicole decline a glass of wine and exchange a look with Madison. She gives me the smallest nod, and I grin. "When are you due?"

"August 11th," she replies, beaming at Dimitri, who offers a warm smile back.

"Wait, what? You're pregnant?" Mac asks, the words muffled by a mouth full of food. He looks around at all the smiling faces with accusation. "Am I the only one who didn't know?"

"Apparently," I reply loftily, refusing to admit that I just figured it out. At least I *did* figure it out.

"A Leo?" Madison repeats, grimacing. "Oof. That's gonna be rough for you."

"Why?" Nicole laughs, taking a big forkful of broccoli.

"Because you're a Virgo... Leos are super emotional and love the spotlight. Virgos are analytical and prefer subtlety. They show their love through fixing things and organizing."

"That's true," Nicole says thoughtfully. "I still can't believe you guessed it so accurately."

"It's my superpower," Madison announces proudly. When Dimitri scoffs loudly, she takes it as a challenge. "It is! I'll prove it. Okay, so, I know this guy is a Scorpio," she jerks her thumb at me, "and I've already confirmed Nicole's a Virgo. Mac said something about being born in April, but there's no way he's an Aries, so I'm going with Taurus."

"April 30th," Mac shrugs.

"Yup. Taurus. And Eleanor? Sweet, fair, charming, romantic, people-pleasing, hates confrontation... you're a Libra."

She grins and nods. "Yeah!"

"A lucky guess," Dimitri dismisses.

"And the big guy... hmm..." she strokes her chin thoughtfully. "I'm thinking he might be a Virgo too. Decisive, analytical, intense energy, honest and direct, has some trouble with expressing feelings?" she says, glancing at Nicole, who rolls her lips inward instead of answering. "Yeah. Virgo. Final answer."

"We don't actually know," Eleanor says with a laugh. "He won't tell us."

Madison's brows go up, but she chuckles. "Not surprised."

When she glances at me, I give her a subtle nod. Dimitri and I alone know, and he doesn't know that I know. But she's right. She grins proudly. "Well, that's four out of four, so I'd say that's better than lucky guesses."

There's some general chatter at that, on both sides—Dimitri resolutely maintaining the silliness of it all, and Eleanor convinced Madison is a witch. When it dies down, the silence settles in a way that's not uncomfortable, but heavy with a single, huge, unresolved question.

"So what's next? Fred's gone, and the program is hobbled, right?" Mac asks, breaking the ice. "But it's still out there?"

I nod. "Madison and I still have quite a bit of work to do to remove the rest of the copies of the program, but we should be able to manage without any more loss of life. I thought we'd continue to use this house as our center of operations. All our equipment is here—it doesn't really make much sense to go anywhere else."

"And what about you guys?" Eleanor asks, directing it at Nicole and Dimitri. "You'll... um... go off and start your family?"

They exchange a look. "Yes," Dimitri says. "Though not right away. I plan to pursue the names in the book that Felix gave to me. It will probably take some time to track them all down, and it is not safe for us to leave until I have killed them all."

At his words, there's a palpable snap in the tension across the table. I think everyone expected them to be the first to want to leave. And maybe it's just punting the problem, but it gives us some more time for... this.

For being together. For being a family.

"Sounds like you might need a hand with that," Mac says, grinning.

Dimitri's lips twitch. "I would not decline it if such an offer were made. I expect it will take a few months. Perhaps a year."

Mac nods, scrubbing the stubble on the edge of his jaw. He studies each of us, grin widening. "So... Eleanor and me? We're staying here," he announces.

Eleanor smacks him in the stomach, making him curl inwards with a soft *oof*. "Mac!" she hisses. "You said Wes owns the house. We were going to *ask*."

"Fuck that, he owes us this," he says, eyes flicking over to me. I understand what he means—he's giving me this as a way to make things right. "Plus, why are we pretending? We all know this is the best place for us. All of us. Like, we're 'retired,' but I think we all know we can't just retire like that," he snaps. "There's gonna be the odd hitman with a grudge, or *something*. Issues crop up all the time. And this property is already set up and can be monitored... Plus, we're better as a team than we are apart. Right?"

"Three adult couples cohabitating? This is not exactly a typical living arrangement," Dimitri observes.

"More common in some cultures," Madison says, shrugging one shoulder.

"It's worked pretty well so far. Everyone has their own spaces carved out," Eleanor contends.

"I don't want to leave either," Nicole confesses.

Dimitri's eyes cut to her, and his expression shifts and gentles. "No, my *med*?"

"No. It takes a village, right?" she says with a single laugh, hand going to her stomach. "This is a pretty good village."

"It was Wesley who brought us all together. I suppose, in a way, it is very fitting that it should be him that provides the means to keep us together. Very well. I approve."

"What do you think, Madison?" Eleanor asks.

The last addition to the house, the last word on the subject. She grins. "I mean, Wesley is stuck with me no matter what, but you think there's anywhere I'd rather be than in this giant house as Nicole and Dimitri fill it with their giant babies and giant dogs?" She winks at Nicole. "Aunt Madison. Has a nice ring to it. I'm *so* in."

"I will continue to train everyone so no one gets soft," Dimitri declares—or is it a threat? Either way, he seems chuffed at the prospect.

"Hey, guys," Madison interrupts, voice low. "In all seriousness, I just want to say... All I've ever wanted is to feel seen and understood and accepted." Her eyes cut to me, and her smile is so full of meaning that my heart aches with it.

"My *abuela* says that you need people in your life so you're not lonely. And she's right, but she's only half right—because I think I've come to realize that it's not just having people in your life that makes you feel less alone. It's having the *right* people in your life."

"The right people," I echo, glancing around the room at all the right people in mine. I reach for Madison and lay a heavy hand on her thigh. "Couldn't have said it better myself."

"To the right people," Eleanor declares, lifting her champagne.

"To the family we'll be," Nicole adds, lifting her water.

"To the one we are now," Mac counters, winking at her, lifting his beer.

"To... us. *Za zdoróvye!*" Dimitri finishes with a nod, considering the matter settled as he bangs his glass on the table and downs the entirety of his vodka without waiting to clink glasses with anyone.

"To us," Madison echoes, leaning forward and tilting her head up for a kiss.

I meet her halfway.

Epilogue

Madison

I wind my jacket over my arm, mostly out of habit, and knock on her door. "Hi Abuela," I greet her softly, crossing the room to join her at her puzzle table.

She turns to me with a slightly blank, but happy look. *"Ah, m'hijita! Ven, siéntate a mi lado."*

I sit, feeling an odd nostalgia at the kitten puzzle she's working on. I'm pretty sure I've seen it before. "I came to give you some good news, Abuela," I tell her, taking her hand in both of mine and giving it a gentle squeeze. "Wesley came with me. He's going to speak to the vice president about getting you into an experimental trial." The fact that he's still on the board here after all this time still amuses me.

"Wesley?" she repeats, confused. Her eyes dart behind me, and I know she's seeing him in the doorway. Her eyes brighten, and she gives me a coy look. "Wesley. Right. Your..." her eyes flick down and her brows shoot up. A smile cracks her face, deepening every wrinkle around her mouth and eyes. Excitement makes her voice thin and reedy. "Husband? Oh, *m'hijita*, you got married?"

She was there. She walked me down the aisle. "I did. It was beautiful," I tell her.

"He's so handsome," she says, leaning close and murmuring the words in a conspiratorial tone.

I giggle. "I know. Don't tell him that, though. *Ya es demasiado orgulloso.*"

She clucks her tongue and looks down at my ring, tilting her head a few times to watch how it catches the light.

"I'm pregnant, Abuela."

Like they have every time I've told her, her brows lift. Her eyes widen, then drop to my stomach. I get to experience her joy for me like it's new each time I tell her, and it fills me with so much sadness and gratitude for her in equal measure that I almost cry every time. "Rosemary," I tell her.

"Oh, *m'hijita*," she sighs, her smile radiant. "You're naming her after me?"

"Yeah, we are," I confirm.

She squeezes my hand and uses it to tug me forward into a hug. She's careful around my belly, and when she pulls back, she rubs it and whispers Spanish endearments at the baby inside.

We catch up and have a lovely visit. It's been a few weeks since I've seen her, and she just likes the company. When it's time to leave, Wesley holds up his arm for me, and I slot myself against him as we walk together out of Sunset Hills. We pass the vice president on our way out, who stops to shake Wesley's hand.

The days of motorcycles are temporarily over, so Wesley opens the door of the sensible sedan and helps me inside, even though I've told him a hundred times that I don't need his help into the car. I kind of need his help out of it sometimes, though...

"Let's go home," I tell him with a heavy sigh as he settles into the driver's seat. My feet hurt, and I just want to sleep in my own bed.

Wesley starts up the car, placing his hand on my thigh—where it *goes*—and begins the winding journey back to the mansion through the familiar streets of Ulysses. Our home.

"Milly is going to love the doll we got her in Chicago," I muse as I watch the scenery pass. "I sent Nicole a picture, and she showed it to her, so she knows it's coming. Do you think she'll even bother to say 'hi' to 'En Maas' and 'Unga Wuss' before ripping it out of my hands?" I ask, taking great delight in how Milly's two-year-old speech capability warps Wesley's name.

No one takes more pleasure out of it than Mac, though, who now *also* calls him Unga Wuss. As if Unga Muck has any leg to stand on...

"You spoil her," Wesley approves.

"Eleanor and I both do," I correct with a grin. "Hey, it's our job as official aunties. Eleanor's already talking about the baby shower she's throwing for me. She bought herself a t-shirt that says *Being an Aunt is Better* and has all these reasons written on the back."

"They are quite happy in their child-free life," Wesley agrees. "Mac nearly earned himself a black eye the other day when he cheerily pointed out that all of Dimitri's shirts have baby vomit on them."

I laugh. "That's going to be you, too, you know."

"A small price to pay."

As we leave the city line behind us, I heave another sigh, feeling sort of lost and hopeful. This was our last trip. Once we get home, we won't have to leave again until we *want* to. I've started planning our baby-moon to Vancouver, and Eleanor and Nicole want to do a girls' trip down the shore next month. But the shift from having a purpose to getting to truly do whatever we want is odd.

"So, we're really done—no more Gener-AI. We finally got the last copy. How does it feel?"

"To be done?" he repeats, considering the question as he rolls to a stop at a light. "It's... to call it a relief would be a bit of an understatement, I think. It's an inevitability. A longtime coming."

I hum my agreement. "It's all over. The end."

He lifts his hand from my leg and cups the bottom of my stomach that gets just a little bit bigger and a little bit rounder every day, tenderly sweeping his thumb across the stretched skin. The little *frijole* kicks at him.

"This isn't the end. This is just the beginning, my love."

Acknowledgements

Dear Reader,

Thank you for joining me on this journey. This is the first series I've ever completed, and I hope you enjoyed the ride!

I hope you enjoyed meeting the Hitmen of Ulysses, and reading these stories of fierce love, found family, and personal growth. I know what might have drawn you in was the promise of swoon-worthy heroes and action and spicy times (and hey, that's what makes it so much fun!)... I want to say that, for me, this series was not really about the men. Ultimately, this is a love letter I wrote to readers who find pieces of themselves in the books they read. To people in bigger bodies, who deserve to see themselves as an object of desire. To the messy, complicated women who deserve the right people in their life who *see* them.

You deserve someone who makes you feel like Eleanor, when Mac reflected back her insecurities and helped her see them as something other than flaws.

You deserve someone who makes you feel like Nicole, when Dimitri used actions to show his devotion because he never trusted words to do it for him.

You deserve someone who makes you feel like Madison, when Wesley spent the time and effort to learn how to give her what she needed.

Kindness is not too much to expect. Being treated well is not too much to ask for. Being seen is not too much to want. You don't just deserve it; it should be the blueprint.

Anywho...

With every book, the list of people to thank gets longer, and I love that for me! Thank you so much to my supportive (understanding) family and friends, especially Ben—always, forever.

To Dana, Lizzy, and Sarah—my early birds! Thank you so so much for taking the time and effort to give me your feedback and thoughts. To all the booktok girlies who've given me a home—especially Bri, for always keeping it 100. And to Sammie... girl, where would I even be without you? (A sadder version who uses the word blithe incorrectly...)

I will always maintain: every ARC reviewer is a rockstar. Love you all!
LM

Oh... Did you think I was done?

I mean, the hitmen are, maybe. But they're hardly the only tough guys in Ulysses who need a little softening up at the hands of a smart, curvy lady...

ABOUT THE AUTHOR

L.M. Whiteley writes dark, steamy romance with morally gray male main characters, relatable female main characters, obsessive love and hard-won happily-ever-afters.

When she's not writing, she can be found cooking, gardening, gaming, playing outside with her friends or letting book boyfriends written by other fantastic indie authors ruin her.

Loved the book?

The best way to support indie authors is by leaving a review!

Please consider rating and reviewing Caught in His Web on **Amazon** and **Goodreads**.

You can scan the codes below to be taken to Caught in His Web on Goodreads!

Stay Obsessed

Join the newsletter for exclusive content, sneak peeks, and bonus scenes:

http://lmwhiteley.com/contact-me/

Follow L.M. Whiteley on social media:

Instagram [@LMWhiteleyauthor]|
  TikTok [@LM.Whiteley]|
  Facebook: [@LMWhiteleyauthor]
  Website: [http://lmwhiteley.com]